I got up and headed toward the front of the shop, stopping for a moment to rearrange a display of money charms, when I heard the sound of glass shattering. I ran to the door just in time to see a shadowy figure dart away from my M3. My brand-new BMW M3! Leather seats, Harmon/Kardon stereo system. Not even paid off yet!

Adrenaline surged through me. It started with a ripple that passed up and down my body, like a warm wave under my skin. My back arched, and the blood pulsed in my veins; suddenly, the smell of the sycamore tree next door exploded into lush life, the humid night taking on a thousand new dimensions. I barely had time to get my jacket and blouse off before I was flicking my ears toward the footsteps receding into the distance. My skirt slid onto the front porch as I leaped down to the front walk, leaving my new Pradas adrift on the stoop. A moment later I was thundering down the pavement, trailing my panty hose behind me.

The guy who had smashed my window was about to learn a valuable life lesson: If you're going to break into a car, you'd better make sure it doesn't belong to a werewolf.

Howling at the Moon

Tales of an Urban Werewolf

Karen MacInerney

BALLANTINE BOOKS • NEW YORK

A Ballantine Books Mass Market Original

Copyright © 2008 by Karen MacInerney
Excerpt from *On the Prowl* copyright © 2008 by Karen MacInerney
All rights reserved.

Published in the United States by Ballantine Books, an imprint of The Random House Publishing Group, a division of Random House, Inc., New York.

BALLANTINE and colophon are registered trademarks of Random House, Inc.

This book contains an excerpt from the forthcoming mass market edition of *On the Prowl* by Karen MacInerney. This excerpt has been set for this edition only and may not reflect the final content of the forthcoming edition.

ISBN 978-0-345-49625-6

Cover illustration by David Stevenson based on photographs © iStock Photo

Printed in the United States of America

www.ballantinebooks.com

OPM   9   8   7   6   5   4   3   2   1

Dedicated to Carol and Dave Swartz,
with gratitude—and love

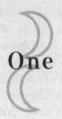One

I have a secret. A big, fat, hairy secret.

And I'm not talking minor-league stuff, like *I once let Joseph Applebaum feel me up behind the seventh-grade stairwell* or *I got a Brazilian wax after work last Friday* or *I'm hiding a neon blue vibrator called the Electric Slide in my night table.* Which I'm not, by the way. In case you were wondering.

No, this is completely different. And as far as I knew, only two—well, technically one, but we'll call it two—people in the entire world knew about it.

Until this morning.

Usually, I waltz into my office at Withers and Young with my skinny latte, extra foam, and find nothing but a neat stack of manila folders waiting for me. Today, however, next to the manila folders—labeled with the new apple green and pink stickers I'd bought last week—was a box.

Now, I should have been suspicious right off. I mean, it was too early for the mail, and the only thing on the front of the package was my name, in swirly letters. Not your normal business correspondence, for sure. And besides, I am an auditor. Who in the world would be sending me care packages?

But none of that percolated through my sluggish brain this morning. I had just picked up the box when my nosy assistant Sally walked in, wearing snug hip-huggers and a jarring floral blouse that barely contained her bosom. "Adele wants to talk to you about the Southeast Airlines account." She gave me a tight smile, accentuating the cupid's bow she'd drawn just outside the perimeter of her lips. Then her beady little eyes fastened on the box. "What's that? Something from that tennis-player boyfriend of yours?"

"I don't know." I shook the box, which had just the right heft for Godiva. "Probably chocolate." My boyfriend Heath had a penchant for surprising me with boxes of truffles. I loved them—especially those hazelnut cream ones—but it was starting to play hell with my waistline.

"Yum. Can I have one?"

"Sure." I tried to pry up the tape with my fingernail, but it wouldn't budge.

"Jeez, that's wrapped up tight."

Sally was right; it was the Fort Knox of chocolate boxes. I ran my tongue over my razor-sharp eyeteeth, tempted to use them on the tape. But with Sally hanging over my desk, it wouldn't be a good idea.

"I'll get scissors," she said, heaving herself off my desk and disappearing through the door. A moment later, she returned with a pair of shears, cutting the paper off with a flourish.

The box inside wasn't gold foil. It was plain brown cardboard. And my skinny latte must have finally kicked in, because my instincts were telling me I wasn't going to like what was inside. And since my instincts are on the strong side, I really should have listened to them.

But hindsight, as they say, is always twenty-twenty.

"Doesn't look like chocolate," said Sally, who was hovering over me like a flowery vulture, reeking of Aviance Night Musk.

"Not Godiva, anyway." A phone rang in the distance. "Isn't that your phone?"

Sally gave me a smile that told me I wasn't going to pry her out of my office with a crowbar. "No, it's Mindy's."

"Are you sure?"

"Positive."

She wasn't budging, so I went ahead and opened it.

Bad idea.

Instead of neat rows of chocolate nestled in gold foil, inside the box was a Ziploc bag of dried green leaves.

I slammed the lid down, hoping Sally wasn't an amateur botanist.

Sally's black-rimmed eyes grew huge. "Is that pot?"

"What?" I croaked. On second thought, maybe it *would* be better if she was an amateur botanist. Wolfsbane might be poisonous, but at least you couldn't be arrested for having it.

"The bag in there," she said, pointing at the box. "It looks like weed."

"Oh, it's just peppermint," I said, tossing off a light laugh that sounded like I was choking on a chicken bone. "Probably from my mother."

Sally narrowed her little eyes at me. "Why would your mother send you peppermint?"

"Peppermint tea," I said. "She knows I like it." Actually, it wasn't a total lie. My mother did send me tea regularly, only it wasn't peppermint.

I moved the box to my lap, resisting the urge to panic and trying to ignore the fact that Sally was still staring at me. A phone rang somewhere in the building. "Shouldn't you get the phone?" I suggested.

"No, it's Mindy's again." Sally wrinkled her nose. "That stuff doesn't smell like mint." She jabbed a finger at the corner of yellow legal paper that was sticking out from under the lid. "Is that a note?"

"You know, I'm kind of busy this morning."

"Aren't you going to read it?"

Just then, a ring that was unmistakably Sally's phone burbled from outside the door.

"Better go get that," I said brightly.

Sally pursed her lips. "It can wait."

I raised an eyebrow and tried to look official. "I don't think Adele would be happy to hear that." Adele was the head of the department and had an extremely low tolerance for anything short of professional. Which had always puzzled me, because it was Adele who had hired Sally.

Sally flashed me a nasty look and flounced from the office. When a few moments passed and she didn't reappear, I tugged the note out of the box and opened it.

> *Roses are red,*
> *Violets are blue,*
> *I know what you are*
> *And your boss soon will too.*

Well, crap.

I stared at the note. Despite what Sally thought, the stuff in the box wasn't pot. And it had a lot more punch than peppermint. Most people, in fact, would consider it poison.

But I wasn't most people.

I was a werewolf.

And somebody else knew it.

I took another sniff, inhaling the familiar bitter scent. Since I'm the daughter of a full-blooded werewolf and a psychic witch (lucky me), I've had to drink the stuff several times a day for years. Otherwise, I have a nasty tendency to transform every time something scares me.

Unfortunately, my mother didn't hit on the right recipe

until I was almost ten, which meant a lot of my child-hood was spent packing up my Barbie dolls (I learned pretty early on that there wasn't a Werewolf Barbie) and sitting beside my mother in a U-Haul truck. My were-wolf dad scarpered before my first birthday, so my mother raised me by herself, which meant I spent a lot of time in child care.

Which is hard enough if you're a regular kid, but an absolute nightmare when you happen to be a bouncing baby werewolf. Full moons were a problem, of course—although these days, with the help of my mother's brew, my involuntary changes were limited to four times a year—but what was worse was my propensity for sprouting teeth and fur every time something startled me or pissed me off. You can imagine what happened when I didn't get my bottle on time.

One of the more memorable episodes occurred in sec-ond grade, when a snotty little girl named Megan Soggs thought it would be fun to put a frog down my shirt at recess. I don't know who was scared more, me by the frog or Megan by the wolf cub in penny loafers. But a week later, we were back in the U-Haul again, off to an-other city.

Fortunately, by the end of third grade, my mother had figured out how to use wolfsbane tea to keep my issues under control without doing me mortal harm. So once we found a town that was werewolf free—which turned out to be Austin—my mother unpacked the U-Haul and bought a small house. Neither of us had moved since. I still drank gallons of wolfsbane tea, and it still didn't taste any better. As a kid, I'd taken it with chocolate syrup, strawberry syrup, and large quantities of honey, but these days I just used Splenda.

I gave myself a quick shake and reminded myself that all of that was behind me now. Since Sally was still on the phone, I gave the box a quick sniff. Coffee, cigarettes, the faint aroma of a woman, overlaid with the deeper notes of male sweat. An animal smell too—cat, maybe? I opened the Ziploc bag a crack. The wolfsbane was pure, probably grown in the Alps, if the woodsiness of the scent was any indication.

I fumbled the flaps closed and jammed the box into my bottom desk drawer, behind the Tension Tamer herbal tea box that I stocked with my own special tea bags. *Relax, Sophie, relax.* I pulled up the waistband of my panty hose and forced myself to take a few deep cleansing breaths, like my friend Lindsey had taught me. After the third breath, I gave up—otherwise, I was going to hyperventilate. Besides, I didn't want to explain what I was doing pulling my control-top panty hose up to my boobs if Sally waltzed back into my office. Instead I leaned back and stared at the bottom left drawer of my desk.

The box meant that somebody knew I was a were-wolf. And that was a big, big problem.

On the plus side—not that it was saying much—at least whoever it was didn't have all the facts. The New Age books all say that if someone like me gets within ten feet of the green stuff in the plastic bag, we wilt like pansies in August. Kind of a nonviolent version of a silver bullet. Or a stake.

But unless I ate an entire bag of the stuff, wolfsbane couldn't hurt me; in fact, I drank it three times daily. Religiously. As in I set a timer and plan my days around it. Because if I miss even one dose, things can get . . . well, let's just say . . . hairy.

I gave the drawer a moody kick, scuffing the toe of one of my new Prada pumps, and sank back in my leather chair.

A moment later, Sally walked back into the office on a fresh wave of musk. "Did you figure out what it was?"

I shrugged. "Like I said, just a box of tea. From my mom."

Sally narrowed her painted eyes at me. "Tea, huh?"

"Yeah," I said. It wasn't too far from the truth; since my mom *did* send me a box of special tea bags every month.

As Sally eyed me suspiciously, the phone rang. The call was from my mother's shop. Which just goes to show that you should never think about a psychic—particularly one you don't want to talk to.

After a pointed look from yours truly, Sally stalked out of my office. I couldn't help noticing that her too-tight pants had given her a major wedgie. Surprising, really; I would have pegged Sally as a thong girl.

I picked up the phone. "Sophie Garou."

"Sophie!"

It wasn't my mother. Nor, unfortunately, was it Heath, whose deep chocolate voice was even more delicious than the truffles he surprised me with. Instead it was my mother's assistant. I relaxed a little and gazed out the window at the Travis County courthouse, which was glowing in the morning sunlight as if everything in the world was hunky-dory and no nut job had left a nasty package on my nice clean desk. "Hi, Emily. What's up?"

"It's about your mom."

Of course.

I don't like to admit it—particularly not to my clients, and definitely not to my boss—but my mother is the owner of Sit A Spell, a magic shop she opened fifteen years ago smack dab in the middle of Austin.

"What about her?" I asked apprehensively. The last time Emily called, I had had to extricate my mother from a snafu with the IRS. My mother was many things—a fortune-teller, a spell-caster, and a medium, to name just a few—but she wasn't a stellar bookkeeper.

And the last thing I needed to deal with right now was my mother's crappy accounting practices.

"Oh . . . it's too horrible for words," Emily said.

"It can't be that horrible."

"Oh, but it is . . ."

"Did she forget to include the income from the mail-order spell business again?"

"It's worse . . ."

I groaned. "Don't tell me she forgot to file! After I filled out the forms and everything!"

"Your mother . . ." Emily sniffled, and I could hear her trumpeting into a tissue.

I sipped my latte and licked the foam from my upper lip. "Emily, just tell me."

"Well . . . you see . . . she's in jail for murder!"

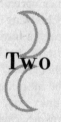

Two

I sat bolt upright, almost spilling my latte, and the waistband of my panty hose rolled down to my crotch. "What?"

"It was one of the city councilmen. You know, the 'Right makes right' guy? Ted Brewster?"

"What on God's green earth does my mom have to do with Brewster?" My mother was teetering out on the last few feathers of the left wing, and Brewster was about as Republican as it was possible to be without actually morphing into George W. Bush.

"Well, the thing is, he came into Sit A Spell, asked for a love charm. . . . Your mom said his wife died a few months ago, and he kind of had a thing for this young lady he met down at the library."

I tugged my waistband back into place. "What happened?"

"Your mother, she mixed him up a potion the other day. Told him when to drink it and all . . ."

I glanced out the window, trying to imagine Ted Brewster, who weighed in at around 250 pounds and whose head looked like a shiny egg festooned with wisps of brown Easter grass, ordering a love potion. "And?"

"Well, you see, he did everything she said . . . and instead of the library girl falling in love with him, he fell over dead as a doornail! And they came and took your sweet mother away, as if she would ever hurt a fly!"

My skinny extra-foam latte churned in my stomach. "You can't be serious. They charged her with murder?"

Emily sobbed into the phone. "Took her away this morning. She hadn't even had breakfast yet, poor thing."

I lay my head on the desk. *This day can't possibly get worse,* I thought.

I was wrong.

I called my best friend Lindsey on my way to the jail. Lindsey was the only other female associate on my floor at Withers and Young, and she had a tendency to make men forget I existed. Something about her long legs, short skirts, and Angelina Jolie lips did it to them. Still, it was a small price to pay for a great friendship.

"What's up, girlfriend?"

"Shut your door," I said.

"Uh-oh," she said. "Hang on."

A moment later, she was back on the line. "Please tell me you're not pregnant."

"No, I'm not pregnant," I said, veering to avoid a guy on a recumbent bike as I passed Whole Foods. He whipped his ponytail around and flipped me the bird. So much for world peace. "Why do you always think I'm pregnant?"

As I pulled up to the red light, a guy with long blond hair stepped out into the crosswalk. He looked up at me, and I just about dropped the phone.

His eyes were iridescent gold, just a shade darker than his hair. Under jeans and a tattered T-shirt, his body was tanned and muscular, gleaming in the morning light. And when he smiled, his teeth were pointed.

Our eyes locked. He stopped in the crosswalk, and it was all I could do not to hang my head out of the window and start panting.

I knew exactly what he was.

And I knew—don't ask me how, but I did—that the recognition was mutual.

As we stared at each other, the light changed. For a moment, nothing happened; then a car honked somewhere, and the long-haired werewolf sauntered the rest of the way across. He turned back to stare at me as I gunned the engine and drove blindly ahead, resisting the urge to pull over and pin him down. Who was he? Were there more of him? Were they just as gorgeous? Why was he in Austin? And while I had him pinned down . . .

I shook myself. Jeez. I was acting like a dog in heat.

Get yourself together, Sophie! I tore my eyes away from the rearview mirror—he still stood on the corner, watching my car with shimmering, predatory eyes, eyes that sent an involuntary shiver up my spine—and struggled to focus on the road.

I took a deep, shuddery breath and reviewed the two

werewolf sightings I remembered. Neither of them had been anything close to this one.

My mother had had a few run-ins with packs before we moved to Austin, but I had no recollection of those, probably because she shielded me from them. And even though I'd lived in Austin for more than twenty years, I'd encountered only two werewolves—one, a skinny, scraggly-haired guy I'd seen at a street corner asking for money, and the other, a Hispanic woman at the H-E-B grocery store on South Lamar. I'd been upwind of the guy, fortunately, even though he did reek of sour liquor and unwashed dog—it had been the shimmery eyes and his wolf-dog smell that tipped me off. The woman had been buying tamales from a stand in the store parking lot. She'd looked like a normal woman—except for her eyes, which flashed in the hot afternoon sun. And her scent. It was spicy and animal—and kind of scary, to be honest. I'd hurried back to the car and driven away, making a point to avoid the store in the future.

Neither one had spotted me—I'd gotten clear as quickly as possible, and both times the wind had been in my favor. And from what I knew of werewolves—the packs from my childhood hadn't been particularly welcoming, and despite my mother's assurances that it was for my own good, I still hadn't forgiven my father for deserting me—that was about as close as I wanted to get. (What I'd read on the subject hadn't exactly been flattering, either, since it mainly focused on tearing humans limb from limb and worshiping the devil at the full moon, neither of which I had any urge to include in my monthly regimen.)

My eyes were still glued to the rearview mirror, searching for the werewolf I'd spotted on the corner. When the road curved and he disappeared, I felt an unsettling, almost visceral stab of loss. Which annoyed me, to tell the truth. You see, I'd decided early on—and for very good reason—that the world of werewolves was not for me. But this morning's moment of connection—the being recognized—was disturbingly exciting. Titillating, almost. Was it just because he was gorgeous? I wondered. Or were my werewolf hormones messing with me?

"Sophie?"

The sound was coming from the seat beside me, and I realized I'd put the phone down. *Lindsey. My mother. Jail.* I grabbed the phone. "Sorry about that."

"Are you okay? You kind of zoned out there for a bit."

"I'm fine," I lied, hands trembling. "Just fine."

"So you're not pregnant."

No," I said, gripping the steering wheel. "It's worse than that, actually." I took a deep breath and attempted to force my mind back to my mother.

"Can't be," she said. "But tell me anyway."

As I turned left on 10th Street and approached the imposing white building that was the Travis County Jail, I struggled not to turn around and try to find the vanishing werewolf. Jeez, what was wrong with me? I'd worked hard to create my normal human life. As tempting as he was, I told myself, it was a very bad idea to get involved. Forget involved—it was bad enough that he'd seen me. There was just too much at stake.

In fact, if the little I'd gleaned about werewolves was true, going back and making my presence known might *result* in the use of some stakes.

Wooden ones.

So instead of turning the car around, I did my best to push Mr. Hot Werewolf out of my mind and filled Lindsey in on the phone call I'd gotten that morning.

When I finished, Lindsey sucked in her breath. "So your mom's in jail for murdering a Republican councilman. . . ."

"Congressman, actually. Well, future congressman. I think he just got elected to the House."

"Even better. So your mom's accused of murdering a *congressman* . . . and you just told your boss she's in ICU at the hospital."

"Pretty much," I said. "Adele wanted to send my mom flowers." Even as I talked to Lindsey, those gold eyes still haunted me. What was his name? Where was he from?

"Flowers?" Lindsey repeated.

"Uh-huh."

"What did you do? Give Adele the address of the Travis County Jail?"

"Of course not!"

"Well, what did you tell her, then?"

"I told her that Mom's allergic to anything that blooms."

Lindsey snorted. "You'd better hope Adele doesn't read the papers."

I turned the air conditioner up a notch. It was ninety-five degrees outside, and it was only ten in the morning. September in Austin. Austin. What was that werewolf doing in Austin? *Mother*, I reminded myself. *Jail*. We were talking about jail. And what would happen if Withers and Young found out about my mom. "I'm sure it's all a big mistake, and she'll be out by the end of the day. Besides, my mother's last name is different from mine."

"Well, that'll throw the reporters off for a day or two, anyway."

I winced. "You think they'll make the connection?"

"Honey, that's what reporters do. They find things out. And it's not like you're in the witness protection program or anything." She paused. "You're not, are you?"

"No, but maybe I should be." Withers and Young was

a Big Four firm, and if there was one thing Big Four firms didn't like, it was any taint of scandal.

Lindsey clucked her tongue. "Jeez. What a shitty day."

And Lindsey didn't even know about my surprise package. Or my werewolf sighting. Which still had my adrenaline pumping. And a few other hormones, too . . . "Thanks for the pep talk. To top it all off, I've got to finish the Termite Terminators account by Friday and I've got a presentation to get ready for by Monday. The Southeast Airlines thing." I groaned. "My mother always picks the best time to get in trouble."

"I've got a project due next Wednesday, but I bet I could give you a hand with the airline thing."

I perked up. "Will you?"

"If you'll tell me where the files are, I'll see what I can do."

A few minutes later, I fed six quarters into a parking meter and walked up the concrete walkway to the jail, feeling marginally better now that Lindsey had offered to take on at least one of my problems. I checked myself out in the plate glass window—had I looked okay a few minutes ago? Even though I wasn't interested—not even a smidgen—in having anything to do with a werewolf, I did want to be sure he hadn't been staring at me because there was a huge coffee stain on my blouse.

No coffee stain, as it turned out. Unfortunately, though, the heat had canceled out the heavy-duty hair gel I'd used that morning, returning my reddish brown hair to its natural state. Which was limp as wilted cabbage.

Oh, well. Other than that, I looked pretty good—silk shell, charcoal suit, gorgeous black pumps. If I didn't get out of the heat soon, though, my cream-colored shell would be stuck to my chest like Saran Wrap.

After surrendering my purse for security, I made my

way to the information desk and forced myself to focus on the business at hand. Which was getting my mom out of the pokey. "I'm here to see my mother," I announced to a cheerless Hispanic woman in brown polyester. The uniform's cut, I couldn't help noticing, was less than flattering. "Carmen Bianca," I added helpfully when the woman gave me a blank stare.

She grunted, and twenty minutes later, after I had been patted down again and metal-detected—they even checked my pumps for hidden blades—another dour woman escorted me to a cinder-block room with a Plexiglas partition. "You have fifteen minutes," she said gruffly before exiting through a metal door. With bars on it. Dear God, how had this happened? One moment you're auditing accounts for a termite control company; the next, you're visiting your mother in the slammer.

As I sat down on a hard plastic chair, a policewoman escorted my mother through the door on the other side. Both of them were laughing, and I shuddered to think what humorous tidbit my mom had just shared with her.

In the place of my mom's signature purple silk caftan was a pair of orange coveralls. You know, the kind the Unabomber wore for his publicity shots? And the color wasn't flattering; her normally luminous skin looked greenish. Then again, it could be the bank of fluorescent lights that lit the place up like the University of Texas football stadium at night. I struggled to keep my face bright as my mom said a few cheery words to the cop and hurried over to the Plexiglas window, easing her pillowy form onto the molded plastic chair. Except for the jailhouse duds and the absence of bangle bracelets, you'd never know she was in prison.

I, on the other hand, was about to have a heart attack.

"I'm so glad you're here," she said into the cheap plastic phone. Her brown eyes were lively. "Did Emily call you?"

"This morning. Did you get a lawyer?"

She waved me away. "Oh, honey, I don't need a lawyer. This will all be cleared up by tomorrow. Besides, this whole experience has been such an adventure. And would you believe I've got three new clients?" She leaned forward and whispered, "Gloria's having man troubles."

"Gloria?"

"That sweet, sweet woman who walked me in here. She just found out last week—her husband was having an affair with her niece!" She shook her head. "Anyway, I told her to swing by the shop." She grimaced. "It's too bad they took my purse. I could really use those business cards."

"So you don't have a lawyer." I leaned forward, pressing my forehead against the partition. "Mom, I don't think you understand. Being arrested for murder is serious business."

She blinked. "But darling, I didn't do anything wrong."

I tried another one of Lindsey's magic cleansing breaths, but it didn't do squat. "Did you talk to anyone about what happened?"

"Of course I did, sweetheart. When those nice police officers asked me questions, I told them the truth." Her brown eyes shone. "I'm innocent. So there's no harm in it, is there?"

"Mom, it doesn't matter that you're innocent. We need to get you a lawyer."

"Oh, fiddlesticks. Sophie, you worry too much. Always have. It's just my spirit guide, testing me," my mother said. "Another one of life's little trials. Besides, my roommate's husband brought her some stuff to read—back issues of *Better Homes and Gardens*, *Cooking Light*—and she's been sharing with me. I found a great recipe for bat cookies in one of the October issues.

I think I'll make a big batch of them for this year's Halloween party."

I gripped my plastic chair so hard it hurt. "Mom, let's get back to the lawyer thing. And Ted Brewster."

"Yes, I know. We need to find out who did that awful thing to him." She sighed. "Poor man . . ."

"Exactly what happened?"

She put her hands in her lap like a Catholic-school girl. Which she was anything but. "You want to hear what I told those nice policemen?"

"Yes," I said through clenched teeth. "Every word."

"Well, I don't know if you know, but Ted's been sweet on a librarian for just about forever."

"No, I didn't know, but that's what Emily said."

"Well, he snuck into the shop the other day—looked really nervous. He'd been in a few times before, but this time he was all done up. Hat, glasses, the works. Probably worried someone from church—or maybe one of those newspaper folks—would see him." She rolled her eyes. "You know how the fundamentalists are about charms and things. Anyway, he wanted a little something to light her fire, if you know what I mean." She winked at me. "Personally, I think if he got rid of that comb-over, it would be a big start, but I'm not a barber, so . . ."

I leaned forward. "What exactly did you give him?"

"A simple love potion. A little rose quartz, some tiger lily petals . . . Works every time."

I tried to imagine "Right makes right" Ted Brewster slipping a love potion into his morning coffee, but it wasn't working. "So he took it?"

"Gulped it down with his bacon and eggs." She sighed. "And then he dropped dead, poor soul."

"And the police think it was the love potion?"

"I guess they do," she said. "I just can't figure it out. I've mixed up that potion a thousand times. . . . Remem-

ber when Hector and Serena got married last summer?"
She nodded knowingly.

"Really? I always wondered how they got together."
Hector, who was short, chunky, and balding, had
worked at the Texas Railroad Commission for thirty
years. His wife Serena was a palmist with a penchant for
skydiving. "Whose idea was it?"

My mother winked at me. "Classified, my dear. Anyway, that potion is powerful stuff. Must be the rose
quartz. If you ever want any . . ."

"No," I said hurriedly, thinking of Heath, his chocolate brown eyes, his long, slow kisses . . . and all the
things I hadn't told him. And the way that werewolf's
muscles had moved under his faded blue jeans. *Ack!*

I glanced around to make sure no one was in earshot.
"Actually, I wanted to tell you something," I said in a
low voice.

Her right eyebrow twitched up. "What, sweetheart?"

"I saw another werewolf today."

"Oooh, Sophie. Really? How exciting!" It had been.
Exciting *and* terrifying, really. But I wasn't going to tell
her that. "Where?" she asked.

"On the way here, actually."

Her eyes got large. "Did he see you? Was it a he?"

A shiver passed through me. "Yes," I said, "it was.
And yes, I think he did."

"Was he cute?"

"Mom!"

She held up her strangely ringless hands. Usually, she
wore so much gold and silver that she set off metal detec-
tors as soon as she got within ten feet of them. It was disconcerting seeing my mother without her customary six
pounds of jewelry. "Just asking," she said. "It's just . . .
you're not getting any younger, dear. Don't you think it's
time to start thinking about starting a pack of your
own?"

I stared at her. A pack of my own? Had she been dipping into her own potions a little too much? "Mom," I said. "I have a boyfriend. A nice, successful, *human* boyfriend. Remember?"

"I know, sweetheart." She patted my hand. "And I know you're fond of him. But he's not . . ."—she shrugged—"well, you know."

I glanced at the guard, who was examining her blue-painted fingernails, and muttered, "A werewolf."

My mother nodded sagely. "Exactly, darling."

"You aren't either," I reminded her.

"And it was difficult," she said, her dark eyes looking misty in the fluorescent lights.

Uh-oh. *Here we go again.*

"We were in love . . . so in love. He was so strong, with those great biceps, and he had the cutest little butt. . . ."

I cringed. "Too much information, Mom." Although that werewolf today had had a pretty cute butt, too. . . .

"And his eyes," she continued. "They were gold, almost iridescent. Just like yours." She sighed, evidently far, far away from her molded plastic chair and the faint smell of disinfectant that hung in the room like a bad aura. "A woman could drown in those eyes. . . ."

"If he were around," I reminded her tartly.

"It wasn't his choice," she said, gripping my hands with hers. "We had to protect you. He left us because he loved us."

I resisted the urge to roll my eyes. Yeah, right. Twenty-eight years without even a "wish you were here" postcard, and my mom still thought my dad hung the moon. I'd heard the tragic saga of Carmen Bianca and Luc Garou a billion times, and I still wasn't buying it. How they'd met along the Seine when my mom was in Paris on a visit from the States, staying with one of her aunts. How she'd tripped stepping off one of those river boats along the Seine (they're called *bateaux* somethings—I forget what), how he'd bravely caught her just before she did a belly flop into the river. How their eyes had met, blah, blah, blah. Total cliché.

It was forbidden love, of course; my mom's gypsy family wasn't too keen on my mother consorting with anyone who wasn't a gypsy, much less a werewolf (not that they knew about *that*, of course), and the werewolves evidently felt likewise. So my parents pulled a Romeo-and-Juliet thing for a year—she decided to stay in Paris and ended up flipping burgers at an American café in Montmartre, while he did whatever it was werewolves did. Evidently they got together on their breaks. When it wasn't a full moon, I presume.

And everything went along just like a fairy tale—a warped fairy tale with the Big Bad Wolf as Prince Charming, but a fairy tale nevertheless—right up to the day I was born.

Once there was a squalling infant on the premises, suddenly my father felt that he couldn't stick around— the pack would smell me on him, was the story. In fact, he convinced my mother that it would be better if she left town altogether. Because if they discovered me, he said, the fact that I was half-blooded, and that their relationship hadn't been "sanctioned" by the big hoo-rah, meant my only value to the vaunted Paris pack would be as a light lunch. Maybe with some *frites* and braised escarole. Evidently the werewolf world felt rather strongly about the whole "pure blood" thing. Kind of like the French feel about polluting their language with words like *le hot dog*.

Elitists. Which is kind of weird, when you think about it. I mean, it's not like turning into a hairy beast once a month is a desirable characteristic or anything. There's no accounting for taste, I suppose.

Anyway, to make a long story short, my mother left

her werewolf lover and took me back to Upstate New York. Partly because that was where she was from. And partly because it was safer to go there than somewhere else in Europe, which according to my mother is stuffed with packs, all of them obsessed with their genetic heritage.

Charming folk, werewolves.

Of course, there was trouble on the gypsy side too, because my monthly transformations probably weren't going to go over too well with the family, who were already less than pleased that my mother wasn't forthcoming with the name of the daddy. My mother ended up moving home and staying with her parents for a few months, but when it got too tough to hide my hairy little secret from them, she moved away.

I suddenly realized my mom was still talking. "I know it was hard growing up without him," she was telling me. "But it was for your own good, Sophie. You know what would have happened if they had discovered you."

Like I said. Because I was a half-blood and the union hadn't been "pack-approved," if we were found, odds were good I wouldn't have made it to my first birthday.

But I still didn't understand why my father had let us go. If we could leave Paris, why couldn't he? I mean, it's tough enough being a single mother, but when you're afraid to put your kid in day care because there's a chance she might start sprouting teeth and fur in the middle of story time, it's got to be a total nightmare. My mother always told me my father cried when we left, promised to find us. But so far we'd heard neither hide nor hair of him, and he'd had twenty-eight years to track us down.

For some reason, my mother didn't find this a problem. But I did. Enough of one that I wanted nothing to do with werewolves. Including the one I'd seen today. As attractive as he might be . . .

"So, did you and this *lupin* talk at all?" my mother asked. As if she were reading my mind. Which might in fact be the case; after all, she came from a long line of psychic witches.

"The werewolf?" I said. "Not exactly." We'd panted after each other a bit—or at least I had panted after him—but it's kind of hard to carry on a conversation with someone when you're driving past him. "Why on earth would I?" Other than the fact that he was drop-dead gorgeous and did things to my hormones that had never been done before. *Ack! Don't go there.* This was *not* the time to lose sight of my no-werewolf policy.

"Haven't you ever thought about starting your own pack?" she asked. "I know the Paris pack was a bit . . . archaic . . . but this is the New World, dear. I'm sure things are different."

"Archaic?" I said. "Archaic? Personally, I think *fucked-up* is a little closer to the mark."

"But *your* pack wouldn't have to be that way."

"I don't want to start a pack, Mom." For *so* many reasons. Not least of which was that I had no desire to pass my little problem on to the next generation. "I'm more worried about being found out. If he's already in a pack and they find out about me, that could be bad news."

"Maybe," she said, nodding sagely. "But something tells me you don't have to worry about that."

"Oh?" I felt marginally better, actually; my mother's instincts were usually right.

"Besides, Austin doesn't belong to anyone, so what can they do?"

"We don't know that," I said.

"Sophie, you've seen how many werewolves since we moved here?"

"Two. Three, including the one today."

"Exactly. I've never known why—maybe because of

all the vampires—but there aren't a lot of them here." It was true. I'd never thought about it before, but there were a lot of vampires here. But not a lot of werewolves. "That was a good thing, particularly when you were young and vulnerable. But now . . . I'm afraid I've kept you from your kind for too long."

"I'm happy with humans, thank you."

"Sophie," my mother continued, "you're not a cub anymore. You're strong, beautiful; you'd make a fine alpha. And a fine alpha mate."

Enough with the wolf talk. Jeez. Next thing you know, we'd be baying at the moon. "I'll pass, thank you," I said, glancing at my watch and regretting I'd brought the topic up. "Let's move on from the whole werewolf thing. We don't have much time. And aren't we here to talk about *your* problems?"

She blinked at me. "What problems?"

"You don't view being locked up on murder charges as a problem?"

"You worry too much. Always have."

"Actually, I'm not sure I worry enough," I replied. "Now, let's talk about how we're going to get you out of here."

She rubbed her hands together. "I've already given it a lot of thought."

"Really?" I relaxed my grip on my chair. Maybe she *was* taking this seriously.

"Yes. And I know exactly what to do."

"What?"

"We have to get in touch with him."

"Get in touch with who? A lawyer?"

"Ted Brewster."

I stared at her. After all these years, I shouldn't have been surprised, but I was. "Ted Brewster?"

She nodded. "He'll be able to tell us what happened."

"But Mom, he's dead."

She shrugged. "So what? We'll call him—the equinox is coming soon, so the timing will be perfect. . . ."

I closed my eyes, wondering what exactly I had done in a previous life to deserve this. My mother, who was in jail for murder, did not feel the need to hire an attorney. Instead, her proposed defense consisted of calling the murder victim back from the dead to clear her name.

I spent an uncomfortable ten seconds envisioning the courtroom scene. My mother, dressed in purple silk with an armful of gold and silver, addressing the judge: *Well, your honor, we held a séance last night, and Ted Brewster said that I'm completely innocent.* What did she plan to do, cross-examine his ghost?

Besides, I couldn't do anything on an equinox. And my mother, of all people, should know that. "Not for me," I said.

"Oh, that's right!" she said, slapping her forehead. "Would you believe I forgot about that?" She chewed on a purple-painted fingernail. "That's okay, though. We can probably do it without you."

"But you're in jail," I pointed out.

She smiled at me brightly. "Well, then. You'll just have to get me out."

Three

"Sophie, I'm so glad you're here," Emily gushed at me when I opened the door to Sit A Spell at 6:00 that evening, feeling as if I'd been run over repeatedly by an eighteen-wheeler. After having my world turned upside down by my drive-by werewolf sighting and visiting my mother in jail, I'd spent the entire day on the phone with attorneys, trying to find a lawyer who didn't utter the words *insanity plea* the moment I explained my mother's situation. I'd finally found someone—maybe. He hadn't met my mother yet, though, so it wasn't a done deal.

"Glad I could help," I said, smiling at Emily. Emily Star was my mother's right-hand woman; despite her tight striped tank tops and heavy-duty nose jewelry, she kept my mom on the straight and narrow—well, as much as possible, anyway. She had dyed her hair white-blond since the last time I'd seen her, and I thought I detected a few new studs in her nose.

The crystals hanging in the windows sparkled in the waning light of sunset as Emily ushered me toward the back of the shop. Every available surface was crammed with books, charms, stone goddess statues, spell candles, and other "magical" items. My mother was as talented a witch as she was a psychic. Fortune-telling,

spell-casting, ghost-calling—it all ran in the family, and
my mother had inherited it in spades.

Fortunately, even though I had a propensity to change
into a werewolf every time the moon was full, I hadn't
inherited the mumbo-jumbo aspects of things. And there
were some benefits to having a mother well versed in
centuries of gypsy lore. Thanks to my mom's wolfsbane
tea, my involuntary transformations had been limited to
the full moons closest to the equinoxes and solstices.

And as for the voluntary transformations? As far as I
knew, there wasn't enough wolfsbane in the world to
prevent those from happening. But to be honest, there
were times when the ability to transform at a moment's
notice was actually convenient.

Still, wolfsbane was just the tip of the iceberg of my
mother's herbal and magical knowledge. And now she
was in trouble because of it. As we walked by a display
of rose quartz hearts labeled "For Extra Passion," I
wondered exactly what else was in the love potion the
councilman ordered.

Gregorian chants echoed through the rooms, and as I
followed Emily to the back, the mingled scents of
beeswax, herbs, and incense triggered a wave of child-
hood memories. Afternoons after school, doing my
homework to the sound of whale songs and Indian
pipes. The way my friend Annie's mom wouldn't let her
come over to the shop, afraid that my mother would
corrupt her daughter's Baptist upbringing. Never mind
the fact that Annie's father drank longnecks by the case
and had a nasty habit of goosing the waitresses down at
the Broken Spoke every Friday night.

I couldn't imagine what they would have thought if
they had known that their daughter's best friend was a
paranormal freak. (Actually, I could imagine. I'd seen it
before, when I'd sprouted fangs and bitten Miss Edna,
my day care teacher in Spokane, because she had given

me apple juice instead of orange juice. It hadn't quite come to tar and pitchforks, but thank God no one else had been around; the woman was convinced I was the devil incarnate. Fortunately, because there were no witnesses and it looked like a dog bite, my mother had managed—with just a bit of magical help—to convince the staff that the teacher was confused, perhaps a touch unstable, even. Still, for a while there, it had evidently been touch and go.)

Now, as we walked into the kitchen, where bundles of dried herbs hung from the ceiling, memories came flooding back. Those four days a year when I'd been confined to my room above the shop—there were still scratch marks from my claws on the door. The first batches of wolfsbane tea, which tasted like brewed bark and made me want to throw up. (The addition of cloves and sugar helped.) I even remembered my experiments with a home waxing kit, trying to find a hair-removal method that didn't lead to razor burn. (Bad idea, incidentally. Ouch.)

The place felt the same as it had ten years ago, right down to the scuffed wood floors and the antique pentacle collection hanging from the purple walls. Except for one thing: My mother wasn't there.

"Can I get you a cup of tea?" Emily asked as I pulled up a chair at the shop's kitchen table.

"Yes, please," I said as she put the kettle on the ancient gas stove. I crossed my legs and tugged my skirt down a few inches. "Just bring me a cup of hot water, though, if you don't mind—I have my own tea bags."

A few minutes later, I dunked a tea bag into my mug as Emily slid into the chair across from me.

•"How is she?" she asked.

I sighed. "Just like always. She wants to get in touch with Ted Brewster and find out what happened."

Emily's eyes lit up. "That's a great idea! Why didn't I

think of that?" Then her brow furrowed. "But if he was poisoned, he might not know who the killer was."

I resisted the urge to beat my head against the pentacle-studded wall. I knew Emily meant well, but a ghost-summoning was not what my mother needed right now. What she needed was a lawyer to corral her before she shot herself in the foot. Again. I sipped my tea, which was bitter, as always. The peppermint my mother added these days (I eventually got sick of cloves) didn't completely camouflage the taste.

"Do you need help with the shop?"

"Yeah, probably," she said, biting her lip. "I've got classes in the evenings, so I can't stay." She snuck a peek at her watch. "I hate to ask, but could you take over tonight? I've got to go in about fifteen minutes."

"Sure," I said wearily. Why not? I'd brought my laptop. Maybe, if I could get my mind off the facts that someone might be threatening to blackmail me, that there was a lust-inducing werewolf on the prowl, and that my mother was in jail for murder, I might be able to get something done.

Emily glanced at me, then looked away. "Did your mom mention anything about the shop?"

"The shop? No. Why? Is something wrong?" Other than the fact that its proprietor was in the clink for killing a city councilman?

"Well, not exactly," she said, fiddling with her tea.

"Spit it out, Emily."

She let out a long sigh, and her nose studs sparkled in the overhead lights. "Well, you see, we had a séance a while back. Marge Munson, one of our regular customers, was trying to get in touch with Jimmy Dean. To wish him a happy birthday." Emily gave me a knowing look. "She's always had a crush on him."

"Right. What does that have to do with the shop?"

"Well, you see, the thing is, we got something, but we

don't think it was Jimmy Dean." She looked at me side-long. "And whoever—or whatever—it was . . . well, he kind of moved in."

"Moved in?"

She leaned forward and whispered, "He likes wo-men."

"So what you're trying to tell me is that there's a ghost living here. And he likes women." Emily nodded vigor-ously, and I took a sip of my tea, thinking, *Why me, God? What have I done to deserve this?* I looked at Emily over the rim of my cup. "If you don't mind my asking, how can you tell?"

Emily's cheeks pinked slightly. "You'll see." Then she took a swig of tea, grabbed a backpack from a hook on the wall, and headed for the door. "Thanks for the help," she called over her shoulder. "I'll come and open tomorrow morning."

"Wait. What do I do about the ghost?"

"I don't know." She opened the door, then added, "Just be careful when you go to the bathroom."

Ghost or no ghost, the next two hours were unevent-ful. One woman came in, asking for an herbal remedy for a sick parakeet, but I told her I wasn't an animal spe-cialist, and she left with a packet of marshmallow root. "That's what Carmen always gives me," she said, and who was I to argue? The next customer hunched down in a jacket, even though it was still above eighty degrees outside. Obviously embarrassed to be in the store, she lingered around the charms table for a while before slinking out the door.

I waded through another ten pages of figures, but my mind kept returning to the werewolf I'd seen earlier today. That encounter, brief as it was, had shaken me to the core. My very private core, in fact, which was still feeling kind of warm just thinking about those shimmery eyes and the way his butt looked under those jeans . . .

God. I was beginning to sound like my mother. She'd gotten tangled with a werewolf, and look what happened to her. Abandoned to a life of traveling through the country alone with a half-breed werewolf baby, trying to find a day care center that wouldn't call animal control. No more lustful thoughts about werewolves, I vowed. None.

Instead, I tried to remember everything I knew about werewolves, which wasn't much. What my mother did know—that wolfsbane helped abate the need to change, that they were fiercely territorial and didn't like outsiders, that breeding was by permission (and only among werewolves), and that there was some mysterious code— she'd told me. It wasn't much, because obviously my father hadn't been around long enough to share a lot of salient information. And evidently he and my mother hadn't spent much of their free time together talking.

But between the little I knew from my mother and the terrifying accounts I'd read at the library (eating children, ravaging the countryside, and several similarly revolting pastimes), I wasn't sure I *wanted* to know more about werewolves. Of course, my mom always told me not to believe everything I read—after all, none of the books had been written from a werewolf's perspective. Then again, she'd fallen in love with one, so her opinion wasn't exactly unbiased either. But where there's smoke there's fire, right?

My little werewolf lust issue was the least of my problems right now, anyway. My mother seemed to think he was okay—even though she'd never even seen him—but I was still worried. What was I going to do if he spread the word about me? What if he wasn't alone, and a pack attacked me?

And then there was my mother, who was doubtless

clipping recipes from *Good Housekeeping* and building her clientele. Well, maybe *tearing* recipes—I didn't think they allowed scissors in the cell block.

What was I going to do if the attorney I had talked to decided he couldn't take the case?

And who had killed Ted Brewster?

I fought to concentrate on the numbers in front of me, but I was too distracted to do much other than mark time. Images of my mother in her orange coveralls kept plaguing me—and when I finally got my mind off of that subject, it started worrying away at the box I had found on my desk that morning. Or conjuring up disturbing images of the delicious-looking but scary man—correction, werewolf—I had seen that morning.

As I stared at the numbers on the laptop screen, I wondered where the handsome creature I'd locked eyes with had come from. I would have been willing to bet my canine teeth he was a born werewolf, but since I didn't have a lot of experience, it was hard to know. I knew from my mother there were three kinds of werewolves— the born ones were full-blooded, like my father, or illegal half-breeds, like me. The third kind weren't born werewolves but by some mysterious process were made, and evidently they didn't have quite the same wolfy oomph. I had no idea how the other two werewolves I'd seen would be classified, but I did know they didn't feel nearly as "oomphy" as the one I'd spotted this morning.

Whom I was sure was full-blooded.

I knew it the moment I saw him; he was like a triple shot of Starbucks espresso after a lifetime of drinking Folgers Crystals. I thought about his gold eyes, with that hint of iridescence in the morning sunlight. He had good arms too—nicely shaped, but not too pumped up. And those pecs . . .

I shook myself. *Enough, Sophie.* Maybe I should head over to visit Heath tonight; my hormones were obvi-

ously getting the better of me. I spent a few moments engaged in a fantasy involving Heath, a box of truffles,
and a can of whipped cream, but then Mr. Hot Werewolf showed up with a container of Hershey's Syrup and
I had to cut things short.

Stupid werewolf.

I took one last glance at the long rows of numbers and
decided it was time to call it a night. It *had* been a heck
of a day. My mom was in jail for murder. For the first
time, I'd seen and been identified by another werewolf—
a gorgeous one, to be sure, but still a werewolf. And let's
not forget the cute little poem on my desk, which meant
somebody was about to let the cat—or in this case, the
wolf—out of the bag.

I was about to close up the laptop and shut down the
store when the phone rang.

"Sit A Spell, can I help you?"

"Sophie?"

The blood rushed to my cheeks, and I almost dropped
my laptop. A brief recollection of my whipped-cream-
and-truffle fantasy made me cross my legs. Mmmm.
Then I realized that he was calling the store, not my cell
phone.

Crap.

"Heath. How did you know where to find me?"

"Lindsey told me."

"*Lindsey* told you?" I would have a few things to say
to *her* next time we talked. My mom's profession—and
the magic shop—was on the list of forbidden topics.

Heath's voice was warm and concerned, and I felt my
already-primed body respond as I wondered for the
thousandth time how I'd landed him. Not only was he
charming and successful—in its annual issue on attorneys, *Texas Monthly* had named him one of the rising
stars—but he had the physical attributes of Fabio.

Minus the fake blond streaks and puffy lips, anyway. Six feet two, tanned from weekends on the tennis court, shiny dark brown hair (again, shorter than Fabio's, but that was fine with me), and eyes as warm and brown as melted chocolate. I'd threatened my friend Lindsey with a baseball bat if she came within ten feet of him. So far, the threat of crushed kneecaps had worked.

Speaking of Lindsey, she was going to get a hot phone call from me as soon as I hung up with Heath. "When did you talk with Lindsey?" I asked.

"Just a few minutes ago. You weren't answering your home phone or your cell, so I called her."

I searched for my purse and realized I'd left it—and my cell phone—in the car. "Forgot to take it with me, I guess."

"She said there was some trouble with your mom."

"Yeah," I said noncommittally. "No big deal. I'm just helping out at her shop for a few days."

"A shop? I didn't know she ran a store. What's it called?"

"Sit A Spell," I muttered.

"Great name. What kind of stuff does she sell—rocking chairs?"

"Not exactly," I said. "Look, I've got some stuff to do. Can I call you back?"

"Is your mom okay?"

"She's going to be fine," I lied. "I'll call you later tonight, okay?"

"I love you, Sophie Garou."

My heart twitched in my chest. "I love you too," I murmured, banishing all thoughts of the werewolf on the street corner. "Call you later?"

"I'll wait up."

I hung up and replaced my laptop on the scarred wooden counter, heart still thumping. *Damn. Damn, damn, damn.* What had Lindsey been thinking?

Heath and I were great together. So great that I wouldn't be shocked to find an engagement ring hidden in one of the chocolate croissants he liked to pick up for me from Sweetish Hill Café and Bakery. The only hitch in our relationship, in fact, was that big fat hairy secret I was telling you about.

Unfortunately, it was a pretty big hitch. Well, that and the fact that he didn't know my mom was a psychic witch.

Or that she was in jail on murder charges.

I swore under my breath and dialed Lindsey's cell number. Of course, she didn't answer. *Chicken.*

I glanced at the clock; it was almost eight. Time to close for the night and go home to drown my worries in a bottle of Chardonnay and a bath. I got up and headed toward the front of the shop, stopping for a moment to rearrange a display of money charms, when I heard the sound of glass shattering. Outside in the darkness, a car alarm started wailing. I ran to the door just in time to see a shadowy figure dart away from my M3. My brand-new BMW M3! Leather seats, Harman/Kardon stereo system. Not even paid off yet!

Adrenaline surged through me. I flicked off the porch light and stepped outside, closing the door behind me.

It started with a ripple that passed up and down my body, like a warm wave under my skin. My back arched, and the blood pulsed in my veins; suddenly, the smell of the sycamore tree next door exploded into lush life, the humid night taking on a thousand new dimensions. I barely had time to get my jacket and blouse off before I was flicking my ears toward the footsteps receding into the distance. My skirt slid onto the front porch as I leaped down to the front walk, leaving my new Pradas adrift on the stoop. A moment later I was thundering down the pavement, trailing my panty hose behind me.

The guy who had smashed my window was about to

learn a valuable life lesson: If you're going to break into a car, you'd better make sure it doesn't belong to a werewolf.

Four

All of my worries—my mother, Heath, the wolfsbane on my desk, the rogue werewolf, my mother—slipped away as I pounded down the darkened street. My nostrils flared, picking up scents. A fire hydrant that was popular with the local dogs. Garlic frying somewhere, a late-blooming rose . . . and the jerk-off who had broken the window of my BMW.

A moment later, he sprinted through the bright halo of a street lamp. A guy in his twenties, with a black muscle shirt and tattoos of half-naked women covering almost every inch of his skin. Great. My car had been molested by a guy with breasts all over his arms.

He slowed as he turned the corner, taking a moment to wipe his forehead with his left hand. Why did he use his left hand? Because his right hand was clutching my Kate Spade purse.

My instincts were yammering at me to take him down and teach him a lesson. After all, he was a thief—what was he going to do, call Animal Control and complain?

But there were two problems with that plan. One, that

was my black kid Kate Spade purse he had in his right hand, and I didn't want to risk damaging it. Two, attacking people was one of those things I generally tried to avoid. I guess you could call it my personal werewolf code. Chasing squirrels—okay. Chasing people—not okay.

But did a dirty thief who had smashed my M3's window and snagged my brand-new purse really qualify as a person?

As I trotted along the grass after him, considering my options—sidewalks gave me terrible calluses, and I'd just dropped thirty bucks on a pedicure—the guy stopped and whirled around. I could see the whites of his eyes. But not his teeth. Because his teeth were brown—and quite a few were missing. Maybe he'd stolen my purse to pay for dentistry work.

A low growl erupted from my throat as I padded around a rosebush and prepared to spring. I wouldn't do too much damage, I decided—just enough to scare the bejesus out of him. And get my purse back, of course.

Unfortunately, the creep chose that moment to pull something out of his pocket. A second later, something twanged off the mailbox two feet away from me.

The little bugger had a gun!

Odds were in my favor that he wasn't packing silver bullets, but I still wasn't too jazzed about being shot at. Lead bullets couldn't kill me, but they could leave nasty scars. There would be hospital visits, plastic surgery . . . and I had enough to explain to Heath as it was.

Well, if Jerk-Off wanted to play hardball, I would too. A growl rose in my throat. I huddled down into a crouch . . . and sprang.

And hit the sidewalk snout-first.

My Sheer Nights panty hose were caught on the rosebush.

I scrabbled backward, grabbing the nylon with my teeth—what the hell did Nordstrom put into this stuff? As I tugged at it, Jerk-Off took another shot, and a rose exploded next to my left ear. This was ridiculous. A guy with *Playboy* bunnies tattooed all over his body was shooting at me, and I was stuck on a panty-hose leash.

I tugged harder, but it wasn't budging. Why was it that I couldn't wear panty hose for five seconds without getting a run, but yanking the crap out of it with my teeth couldn't break it? As he shot a second rose to smithereens, I switched tactics, trying to get it off instead of tearing it—and fell backward into a cactus with thorns the size of bear claws as another bullet whizzed past.

I barreled into him a split second later, and the gun clattered to the sidewalk—alongside my purse. I glanced over at the purse—so far, thank God, it still looked okay. Jerk-Off scrabbled to get up, but I had him pinned.

"What . . . what the hell . . ."

I growled menacingly.

I was gearing up for a second growl—a really deep and throaty one—when something scratched my stomach.

I looked down. A drop of blood fell from a shallow gash on my abdomen. He had a knife! The little fucker had a knife!

I grabbed his hand between my teeth and shook it like a rag doll. When that didn't work, I bit down a little bit harder, and that seemed to do the trick; within seconds, the blade clanged to the sidewalk.

Then the smell of urine flooded my nose. *Ew!* I dropped his hand like a rotten egg. And that was about how he tasted—a pungent cocktail of garlic, sweat, and old beer.

I never did understand all those myths about werewolves eating people. *Ick*. I mean, why go after a human when you can just sit down at a restaurant and order a nice, juicy steak? While I was recovering from the awful taste in my mouth, he scrambled to his feet and started running. But he wasn't nearly fast enough. He hadn't gotten farther than three steps before I was on him again, trying to avoid the peed-on places.

He hit the sidewalk like a ton of bricks. And this time, he didn't get up.

So much for my personal werewolf code.

I padded around him, listening. At least he was still breathing, and I could hear the regular thump-thump of his heartbeat. I decided to make an anonymous call to emergency services once I got back to Sit A Spell.

I gingerly retrieved my purse with my teeth—the panty hose was beyond redemption—and trotted back to my mom's store.

Ten minutes later, I closed the front door of Sit A Spell behind me and unlocked the BMW. Not that I needed to, since what had been the passenger window was now a gaping hole. Then I stuck the key into the ignition and headed home for some Band-Aids—and a jumbo glass of Chardonnay.

"Can you believe it? Another dog-mauling."

I looked up from my bagel at Lindsey, who had plopped down in my guest chair and was leafing through the newspaper. *No*, I thought. *It couldn't be.* Had the creep who'd broken into my BMW actually talked to reporters about it?

"What dog-mauling?" I asked.

"It happened last night," she said. "Right near your mom's shop." She peered at me. "What's that thing on your nose?"

I raised my hand to the scab—a little souvenir from

my panty-hose debacle the night before. "I tripped over something," I said.

"Looks nasty. Anyway, this guy says he was almost killed."

"Let me see," I said, grabbing at the paper. A piece of bagel stuck in my throat, and I gulped down some latte as she handed me the Metro and State section.

"Stupid dog owners," Lindsey said. "It's just crazy that people let their dogs run wild. This is the third incident this month." She leaned back and crossed her legs. "The guy says this massive German shepherd came after him. It was acting totally insane, like it was rabid or something."

Massive? Rabid? Totally insane? I glanced down at myself. I'd been hitting the hazelnut truffles a little too often lately, but I wasn't *that* big. And I had always been the sane one in the family. "Maybe he wasn't just going for a walk," I suggested. "Maybe the dog was protecting someone." Or something. Like a brand-new Kate Spade purse.

"True," she said. "The guy does look a little thuggy. But get this; the dog had no hair on its legs. And it was wearing panty hose. Panty hose! Can you believe it?"

I almost choked on my coffee. When I'd recovered, I said, "Weird," in my best nonchalant voice. Then I added, "Are you sure he wasn't on drugs?"

"Maybe. But they found the panty hose there, so maybe he wasn't making it all up."

I scanned the paper, wishing there was some way I could have shaved legs as a human and furry ones as a werewolf. It's hard enough trying to blend in with the other dogs when you're a wolf—harder still when your back legs look like plucked chickens.

Obviously, I was the dog in question. I mean, how many naked-legged wolves (or dogs) with panty hose could there possibly be in Austin? And sure enough, there was a picture of the guy, right there on the front page—complete with a pair of tattooed breasts sticking out of his sleeve. "Local man accosted by dog," the article read. A few lines later, I discovered that Jerk-Off's name was Greg Thompson.

I snorted with righteous indignation and pressed my hand to the row of bandages on my stomach. "Just out for a walk," he'd said. That asshole shot at me, knifed me, destroyed my BMW's window, and tried to make off with my brand-new purse. Maybe my personal werewolf code could stand a touch of revision.

I was imagining all the things I would like to do to Greg Thompson when Lindsey's voice pulled me back to more urgent matters.

"There's some stuff in here on your mom too," she said ominously.

I tore my eyes from the illustrated man. "How bad?"

She grimaced. "Could be better. The whole love potion thing is such a juicy tidbit that it's above the fold on the front page; and the only suspect they're talking about is your mom."

"Anything on me?"

"Nothing yet," she said, handing me the front page. "How's the lawyer search going?"

"It could be better," I said. Which was putting it mildly. Of the ten I'd called yesterday, nine had started babbling about plea bargains and "mental incompetence" the moment I uttered the phrases *magic shop* and *poisoned love potion*. But the tenth one sounded promising. "I've got an appointment with someone this afternoon."

"Looks like you'll need it," she said as I looked down at the front page.

My stomach turned over as I read. Splashed across the first page of the *Statesman* was "Magic Shop Owner Top Suspect in Councilman's Murder." I scanned the article—more background on Brewster, a mug shot of my mom looking like a Mediterranean Pollyanna, and no mention of any other suspects. According to the reporter, the coroner initially thought it was a heart attack, but either it was a slow week down at the morgue or something didn't look quite right, so they ran a toxicology report. The result? Death by nightshade poisoning. A search of Brewster's house and office turned up a nice little vial with a Sit A Spell label, filled with a heavy-duty dose of nightshade.

Lovely.

On the plus side, I thought—not that it was much of one—how could it be any worse?

Then I flipped to the second page of the article and just about lost my bagel. "It says here my mom threatened him on the news! That can't be right."

"On the news? What channel?"

"The local one, that runs all day. News 9."

"What was it about?"

"That big development—you know, the one they're trying to build right on top of Barton Springs." Barton Springs has long been considered one of Austin's crown jewels; it's a natural, spring-fed swimming hole less than a mile from downtown. When the plans for the new development hit the paper, half the city was up in arms.

"It can't be that bad," Lindsey said. "Everyone in town is protesting the development. They're probably just making a big deal out of it. Anything to sell papers, you know?"

I closed my eyes and lowered my head to my desk, thinking I'd have to ask the cleaning staff to change furniture polish—whatever they were using now smelled like cat piss.

Lindsey said, "You know it's up to us to get her out of there."

I raised my head enough to peer at Lindsey through

my limp bangs. "Yes, I'm aware of that. That's why I have a lunch appointment with a very expensive lawyer."

Lindsey crossed her legs and pursed her picture-perfect lips, and I thought for the eight hundredth time that if I didn't like her so much, I'd have to kill her. Fricking Angelina Jolie. "I don't know how much a lawyer will help. It looks like the cops are done investigating," she said. "They think they've got their murderer."

I wanted to tell her that she was wrong, but I knew she wasn't. "So what do we do?"

"We investigate."

" 'We investigate,' " I repeated. "I'm glad you said *we*. But when exactly are we going to find the time to do this?" I gestured at the stack of files growing on the corner of my desk. "I have to finish the termite account, the meeting with Southeast Airlines is coming up, I have to cover for my mom at the shop, and Heath has been complaining that we never see each other." Plus, it was nearing one of those magic times of year when I spent most of my time howling at the moon. "And last time I looked, you were an accountant, not a PI."

"It's your mom, Sophie."

"I know. That's why I'm spending all of my time and money looking for a lawyer. A professional, trained to handle difficult legal situations." I bit my comparatively anorexic lips. "Hey, is Johnny Cochran still practicing?"

"Not unless your mother can call him back from the dead. Let's face it, Sophie. If we don't find out who did it, your poor mom's going to be reading tarot cards in jail." She leaned forward. "Can you imagine your mother spending twenty years without her charging crystals? No full-moon meditations?"

I flinched at the mention of the full moon—my least favorite time of the month—and pushed back from the desk. My eyes drifted to the courthouse in the distance and the tall, white jail building behind it. My mother was in there someplace. And Lindsey was right; if we didn't manage to clear her name, it would be a long time before she was reunited with her charging crystals. And who would make my wolfsbane tea?

A scary thought niggled at the corner of my mind—a thought I'd been trying hard to avoid. Jail was a big problem, but it wasn't the only problem. Texas is a capital punishment state.

I looked back at Lindsey. "Where do we start?"

Lindsey sat up straight, and her gray eyes sparkled. "I knew you'd see the light. Just think; we'll be like Nancy Drew."

I appreciated the optimism, but my mom's being in jail wasn't exactly *The Clue in the Old Attic* material. "Nancy's mother was dead, not in the clink for poisoning a politician."

"Oh, don't be a spoilsport. It'll be fun!"

I grunted. If I had to figure out who'd left me that care package, it wouldn't hurt to poke around a little on the Brewster case while I was at it.

Lindsey chewed on a bee-stung lip and pulled out her Palm Pilot. Tapping the stylus on the screen a few times, she said, "Let's see. Somebody had a motive. The question is, who?"

"He was a politician, Lindsey. There must be millions of people who had it in for him."

"See? We're making progress already."

"I'll just pull out the phone book and start calling people, then."

She tapped the stylus against her cheek. "How about we start with the librarian?"

"The one he had a crush on?"

Lindsey rolled her eyes. "Oh, no, I thought we'd just pick one at random."

I ignored her. "You know, that's not a bad idea. My

mom probably has something of hers—you need that, to do a love spell."

Lindsey made a face. "I hope it's not a hair or fingernail clippings. *Ick.*"

Ick, indeed. I looked down at my own fingernails—they were growing like crazy because I hadn't been doing much to wear them down lately. Time for another appointment with Happy Hands. "I'll bet Mom wrote her name down. Or at least she remembers it."

"Well, then, we're off and running. Want to swing by Sit A Spell at lunch?"

"Can't do lunch today—I'm meeting with that attorney—and tonight I have to catch up on work."

Lindsey was about to answer when Sally and her cleavage barged in on a cloud of cheap perfume. Today's number was tight, purple, and frankly, not quite up to the task. We're talking imminent wardrobe malfunction.

"What is it, Sally?"

"It's your boyfriend. He's on line two."

"Thanks," I said, as she sashayed back out. Unfortunately, it would be at least twenty minutes before the rest of her perfume joined her, and as I usually did when Sally was around, I wished I could muzzle my sense of smell.

The door closed, and I turned to Lindsey. "Speaking of Heath," I said, "I thought I told you Sit A Spell was off-limits!"

She smiled sheepishly. "I just gave him the number, not the name. He was worried about you!" She returned the stylus to her Palm Pilot and stood up. "By the way, in all the excitement, I forgot to tell you. Somebody's spreading a rumor that you've got a big bag of pot in your desk."

Five

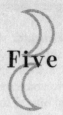

"What?"

Lindsey raised her hands. "Don't kill the messenger. I'm just telling you what I heard."

"Stupid assistant," I muttered, delivering a murderous glare at the door.

"Who, Sally?"

"I got a big box of . . . uh . . . tea yesterday. Sally was right here when I opened it."

"Why would she say it was pot?"

"It's a kind of herbal tea, with peppermint. My mom sends it to me." My stomach churned again as I remembered the note that came with it. Sally and her damned perfume; if she didn't spray it on by the gallon, I might have had a chance to trace the scent on the note.

Lindsey waved it off. "Oh, don't worry about it," she said. "As long as you don't have any actual weed, you're clear." She narrowed her eyes at me. "You don't, do you?"

"No!"

"Just checking. How about we get together tomorrow night?"

I sighed. "I guess you're on."

Lindsey pointed to the blinking light on my phone. "If I were you, I wouldn't keep that delicious man waiting."

Heath! I'd almost forgotten about him.

I glanced up at Lindsey, who was looking at me expectantly.

"Tomorrow night?" she said.

"Got it," I answered, and picked up the phone.

"How's my favorite girl?" Heath asked. Distracted as I was, his low voice made me quiver. Granted, it was that hormonal time of the month, so it didn't take much.

"Fine," I said. "How are you?"

"Is your mom any better?"

I thought of my mother, who was doubtless doing aura rehabilitation sessions with her cell mates at that very moment. "Nothing keeps her down for long," I said.

He laughed. "Sounds like someone else I know. Anyway, I'm glad she'd doing better. I'm dying to meet her."

"Ummm . . ." I groped around for another subject. "How's work?"

"I got a new case today. We're going after the city on it . . . it's quite interesting, really. I'll tell you all about it tonight."

"Tonight?"

"Over dinner, remember? I've got reservations at the Shoreline Grill."

Well, crap. No, I didn't remember. I had been counting on getting some work done—and maybe finding another attorney in case the one I was meeting at lunch started going mental on me. As in having my mother committed. I squinted at the Travis County Jail in the distance. "You know, I hate to ask, but could we postpone a bit?"

"You already postponed. Last Friday."

"I've got this big account coming up, and I'm trying to finish out the Termite Terminators audit . . ." *And get my mom out of jail and find out who had sent me that box of wolfsbane*, I added silently, thinking that this probably wasn't the moment to share those two particular tidbits. Instead I tried the workaholic angle. "Remember how hard you worked when you were up for partnership?"

He sighed. "I guess you're right. I just need to keep my animal impulses in check, I suppose."

I stifled a snort. Heath wouldn't know an animal impulse if it came up and bit him on the butt. I reached down to touch my legs, which were starting to feel like scrub brushes again; it was almost time for another shave. "As soon as this is done, I'll make it up to you."

"Good. Because I haven't had a decent filet in weeks."

"Poor deprived baby."

"Hurry up and get that partnership," he growled. "It's not just the filet I'm missing."

I laughed. "Go take a cold shower."

"I've already taken three this morning. My coworkers keep wondering why I feel the need to be so clean."

I thought of all of those lawyers in that gigantic office building Heath worked in. It was inconvenient, really; I couldn't call anyone who worked for Heath's firm, which had cut my legal options in half. Heath knew the Austin law scene pretty well—was there any way to get a read on the guy I was meeting this afternoon without tipping him off? Trying to sound casual, I said, "By the way, what do you know about Marvin Blechknapp?"

"Marvin Blechknapp? Why do you need to know about him? He's a criminal defense attorney." He was quiet for a moment. "Sophie, are you in some kind of trouble?"

"Oh, no," I said, forcing a chuckle. "It's just . . . a friend of mine had a little run-in with the law. I told her I'd ask your advice on the guy."

"He's sharp. Expensive as hell, but sharp. I'd want him defending me. And he likes a challenge."

He likes a challenge. Well, that explained a lot.

"Great," I said. "I'll tell her she made a good choice." And start tapping my retirement account.

"Let me know if there's anything I can do to help her out," he said.

"Thanks."

"And don't you dare schedule anything on our first-date anniversary." He lowered his voice to a sexy, throaty growl. "I've got plans for you, Miss Garou."

My hormones shot into overdrive again, and I crossed my legs tight. "Wouldn't miss it for the world."

It was only after I hung up the phone and looked at the calendar that I realized I had a problem.

Our anniversary was in six days.

And so was the full moon.

I arrived at the office of Blechknapp and Smythe at 12:00 on the dot. According to Heath, he was one of the best criminal defense attorneys in town. But what I liked most about him was that he didn't immediately start grilling me about the family's psychiatric history when I told him the situation.

Marvin Blechknapp, as it turned out, was a short, heavyset man in his forties. I was a little disappointed, really—from his voice on the phone, I was expecting someone taller. And blonder. Sort of a sun-streaked Clark Gable. Unfortunately, he was closer to Danny De-Vito.

"Thanks for coming, Miss Garou," he said, adjusting his power tie and waddling toward his office with me in his wake. My stomach rumbled as I followed the gleam of his bald head. I hadn't had time to eat, but he'd had steak for lunch—it was on his breath—and I kept having to swallow drool. When he glanced back at me, I got another whiff of steak-breath. Mushrooms on the side, and a touch of garlic. Yum.

"This is going to be a challenging case," he said, wedging himself into his plush leather chair.

I tore myself away from thoughts of red-rare steak and struggled to focus.

He folded his plump hands on the mahogany desk. "As I'm sure you've read, the . . . concoction . . . your mother sold Brewster was poisoned. And her occult background will be an issue."

"But we're in Austin," I protested. "I mean, we've got transvestites running for mayor. It's just a little love potion, for Christ's sake! Besides, it's not like she was caught sacrificing people by the full moon or anything." Not that I would know; I wasn't usually around at the full moon.

"We may be in Austin, but Texas is still firmly in the Bible Belt," he said. "Now, the first hurdle we have to clear is bail. Fortunately, I have a few friends down at the courthouse, so I think we can probably get the bail hearing set for tomorrow."

"Tomorrow? So she could be out that soon?"

"As long as we can convince the judge your mom isn't a risk."

I pooh-poohed him with a wave of my hand. "She's a middle-aged woman. How hard can that be?"

"She's a middle-aged witch, accused of poisoning a Republican councilman."

Put that way, it didn't sound so good. "Do you think you might come up with a little better way to phrase that?"

He gave me a strained smile. "Of course that's not how I'm going to present it. But that's what the prosecution will be saying, so you'd better prepare yourself. Do you know anything about your mother's relationship with the deceased?"

"I didn't even know she knew him until I found out she was in jail for killing him."

"Nothing at all, then?"

"I read something in the paper about her threatening him—something about that development. The *Statesman* made a big deal about it, but I'm sure it was really nothing."

His pudgy lips formed a grim line. "Have you watched the news lately?"

"No."

He pulled a videotape out of his desk drawer, opened the cabinet behind him, and thrust the tape into the VCR. How nice, I thought—an office where you could watch movies on your lunch break!

A moment later, my mother appeared on screen, dressed in her signature velvet witch hat and green silk robes. Beside her was a Katie Couric wannabe wearing way too much pink lipstick.

I suddenly had the distinct feeling that I would have preferred *Pirates of the Caribbean*.

"What do you think of the proposed development on Barton Springs?" said the anchorwoman, a perky faux blonde in a red suit. She thrust the microphone in front of my mother.

My mother shook her head, smiling a Buddha smile, her bracelets jingling like wind chimes. "If it goes through, the development will destroy a pristine spring and kill countless trees and animals," she said.

"So you think the council should vote against it?"

"Absolutely. If they agree to the development, the members of the council can add 'murderer' to their résumés."

The anchorwoman's tweezed eyebrows shot toward her artificially blond hairline. "*Murderer.* That's a strong word."

My mom shrugged. "Trees are people too. But the council should think long and hard about this decision." She narrowed her eyes, giving the camera the same look

I'd gotten when I'd flushed half a pound of saffron down the toilet in third grade. "Because what you put out into the world comes back to you," she said ominously. "Sometimes threefold."

The Couric wannabe pasted on a fake smile. "Thank you very much. This is Melanie Waters reporting from the protest at the Barton Springs site. Back to you, Fred."

Marvin hit the Stop button, and I sank back into my chair. I was right; a few minutes of Johnny Depp in eyeliner would have been much nicer.

I closed my eyes and massaged my temples. Had all the incense finally gone to my mom's brain? She'd leveled a veiled murder threat at the entire city council. On camera, for Christ's sake. And then one of them had to go and get killed.

Talk about bad karma.

I opened my eyes to Marvin, who was staring at me with a slightly smug look on his face. "Well, that answers my question about motive," I said.

"Perhaps she could have chosen her words more wisely," he agreed.

Well, duh.

"It doesn't look good," he continued. "But I think we can work with it. Does your mother have any kind of history I should know about? Anything unusual that might come up in a trial?"

Other than the fact that her daughter was a werewolf? I decided that it was best not to share that morsel of information. Unless I wanted a room down the hall from my mother in the loony bin. "Not that I know of," I said, thinking of the wolfsbane I'd found on my desk. I was going to have to find out who had put it there—and fast.

"Good," he said, fixing me with sharp, dark eyes. "If anything comes up, you will tell me, right?"

Like a full-moon transformation? Yeah, right. "Of course," I lied, crossing my legs and tugging down my skirt. The scrape of bristles rubbing against nylon made me cringe. He'd better hurry up—it was almost time for me to shave again.

By the time he was done outlining his plans and giving me pointers for dealing with reporters, I was sure I had started sprouting sideburns. I raced out of his office and into the bathroom. My face, thankfully, was clear, but my legs needed emergency attention. After a quick shave, I slunk back to Withers and Young—making a quick stop at Jason's Deli for a French dip sandwich— even more depressed than I had been when I'd left.

Later that afternoon, I was sitting in my office, staring at a column of numbers and trying very hard not to think about my mother, when there was a knock at my door.

"Come in!" I called, preparing myself for another wave of Sally's cheap perfume.

But it wasn't Sally.

"Heath!" I said, abandoning my computer and pushing my chair back.

"I had to see you," he said a tad huskily as I ran an appreciative eye over him and congratulated myself on my excellent taste in boyfriends. He was dressed in a Brooks Brothers suit that was wide across the shoulders and tapered nicely to his trim waist. The fabric was rich chocolate brown, just like his eyes.

"How did you get by Sally without having your clothes ripped off? And what made you stop by?" I suspected Sally's crush on Heath was a large part of the reason she couldn't stand me.

"I was thinking about our anniversary date," he said, closing the door behind him. "And then I was thinking about you, and then I couldn't stop thinking about you. So I came to see you." He paused and peered at me. "What happened to your nose?"

My hand flew to the scab on my nose. "Tripped on a rock," I mumbled, and thankfully he didn't press for details.

As he folded me into his arms, surrounding me with his spicy, masculine scent, I thought back to the night I met him. Had it already been a year? Lindsey and I had been at Chuy's for a young urban single professionals (unfortunately abbreviated *YUSP*) happy hour. Over a plate of chicken enchiladas, she was bemoaning the lack of available men when the bartender appeared with a frozen swirl. For me. From the gentleman at the bar, who was also a member of the YUSP club.

Heath.

He'd stopped by to introduce himself, and within the first thirty seconds, I was smitten. Heath was everything you look for in a singles ad: an up-and-coming attorney with plenty of self-assurance, a mischievous smile—and yes, those broad shoulders and trim waist. And that fabulous smell, of course, which I inhaled happily—CK One and hot human male. Very, very hot.

And without a whiff of werewolf.

That first night, he'd asked for my card and left us to our enchiladas. The next day a dozen red roses had arrived at my office with an invitation to the ballet. The ballet had been magical—something romantic and Tchaikovskyesque that I can't remember the name of—but it was what happened afterward that I could still recall the most vividly.

Mmmm.

All in all, I reflected, as Heath's Brooks Brothers suit pressed against me now, it was a date worth celebrating. I just wished it didn't coincide with the full moon. An image of that golden-eyed werewolf flitted into my head quickly, and I had time to wonder what he looked like as a wolf before banishing that whole train of thought. But I did need to find a way to postpone our anniversary. "About our date," I began, but then Heath's mouth was on mine, and all thought dissolved. Except for regret that my office didn't have a functioning lock.

"We can't," I murmured, forcing myself to detach from Heath.

"Why not?" His voice was thick with barely restrained lust.

As was mine. "The door," I said. "It doesn't lock."

"Can't we wedge a chair under it?"

"You think that will stop Sally?"

He sighed. "Damn," he said, releasing me. "Why is she always bothering us? And why does she wear so much perfume?"

As if on cue, there was a light tap and the door swung open. It was Sally, and it was all I could do not to cover my mouth and nose. Evidently she had given herself an extra spray of perfume now that Heath was here.

I stepped back and straightened my jacket. "Yes?"

"Adele wants to see you," she said, looking at Heath.

"Why? What did I do?" Heath said.

"Not you, silly." She tittered unappealingly. "She wants to see Sophie. But I've got a few new pictures you might be interested in." She ran a finger across the top of her spandex dress, over her bulging bosom, and it was all I could do not to roll my eyes.

"Stop by on your way out," she said in her best cabaret-singer voice.

"I'd love to," Heath said, straightening his jacket and then glancing at his watch, "but I'm running late. I just stopped by to say hi to my sweetheart."

Sally shot me a malevolent glance.

Then Heath swept me into his arms again and kissed me—hard. Sally was still glaring at me when he released me. I gasped for air, and as I sucked in a lungful of Sally's musk, I immediately wished I hadn't.

"Gotta run," he said. "Don't forget our date!" Then he winked at me and disappeared through the doorway.

Our date, I thought miserably, still trying to catch my breath. The date we needed to reschedule. Unless, that is, I wanted him to find out that his girlfriend was really a werewolf.

"Adele's waiting for you," Sally reminded me, still looking sour, then trotted down the hall after Heath. I watched her go. Then I checked my lipstick—a bit smeary, which wasn't surprising—fixed myself up, and dutifully headed toward my boss's office.

Of course, she wasn't there.

"I thought Adele wanted to see me," I told Sally when I stopped by her desk a few minutes later.

"Oh, didn't I tell you? She won't be back for an hour."

I scowled at her and stalked back to my office to attack those numbers again. Whoever said assistants were supposed to make work easier hadn't met Sally.

"So, are you going to the hearing?" Lindsey asked me the next morning. It was a good thing I'd burned the midnight oil the night before, because Marvin had been true to his word. The hearing was set for 10 AM.

"Of course. Why wouldn't I?"

"Reporters," she said ominously, raising a shapely eyebrow. "There will be tons of them."

"But they'll be there to cover my mom. I'll just be in the audience. Are they called audiences?"

"They always look for family. Haven't you seen those shots of distraught family leaving the courthouse?"

I shrugged. "They don't know who I am. Besides, I could go incognito. You know, wear a hat and glasses?"

Lindsey rolled her eyes. "Like that wouldn't be obvious. Plus, you've got a scab the size of a strawberry on your nose."

"Thanks for reminding me."

She peered at my face. "How did you do that, anyway? Not that it looks bad or anything . . ."

"I told you. I tripped."

Lindsey clucked her tongue. "Sounds to me like someone needs to cut back on the margaritas."

"Very funny. For your information, I only had one glass of Chardonnay." It was an iced tea glass, but that was beside the point. "And that was *after* I fell down and scraped my nose."

"Strictly medicinal, then," she said, grinning. "So you're going to this hearing?"

"How can I not? It's my mom."

"I could go for you."

"No, Lindsey, it's got to be me. And I'm sure it will be fine."

She gave me a dubious look and opened her purse. After a few minutes of fishing, she pulled out an eyeglass case. "Wear these, at least."

I opened the case and removed a pair of cat-eyed glasses. "What are these?"

"My glasses. For when my contacts are giving me trouble. Put them on," she urged. "They'll make you look different."

I slid them on, and the room immediately turned into an impressionist painting. Actually, to be honest, it was more like a big blur. I snatched them off my face and rubbed my eyes. "Jeez, Lindsey. I had no idea you were legally blind."

"Do you want them or not?" she said tartly.

"I'll take them," I said.

"Just don't lose them," she said, standing up to leave. "Call me when you get back. And watch out for reporters," she added on her way out the door.

A few minutes later, I left my office and headed for the parking garage. Once I'd reapplied my lipstick, that is; I was driving the same route this morning, and it didn't hurt to be prepared. After all, you never knew who you might run in to. Or over, if I was still wearing Lindsey's glasses.

I wasn't thrilled about leaving the office—it wasn't good policy to be out of the office half the time when you were up for partnership—but I'd done my best to cover myself. Earlier that morning, I'd ducked into Adele's office and told her my mom was having a procedure done. And strictly speaking, I hadn't been lying. After all, a bail hearing *is* a procedure, right? And Lord knew I could have used a shot of morphine right about then.

As I stepped out of the elevator into the parking garage, I stowed the glasses in my bag and wiped off my Plum Passion lip shimmer. Hot werewolf or no hot werewolf, I decided, I wasn't going to make any special effort. I already had a boyfriend—and the way things were going lately, the last thing my life needed right now was another werewolf in it. Besides, from my admittedly limited experience with the supernatural world, I'd gotten the impression male werewolves were not exactly long-term mate material.

If my mother had cast a spell to bring werewolves sniffing around, I decided, we were going to have to have a serious discussion. My life was chaotic enough right now without having to deal with what my mom called my "true nature." And personally, because the only time I really had to be in wolf form was when the full moon was in the sky (despite the horror movies, it really doesn't matter if it's night or not), I felt my "true nature" was more human than wolf, anyway. After all, I was half human. And thanks to the wolfsbane, I had to spend only about forty-eight hours a year with a tail.

Which was weird, when you really thought about it—and which I tried not to do too much. The moon ruled my life. But why? And what was it about the solstice and equinox that knocked out even the wolfsbane's effects? Thank God my mother had discovered how to brew up werewolf-preventive medicine, or I'd be missing work once a month. And I drank it every day, even when it wasn't a full moon; the closer to the full moon it came, the more my hair grew, and the wolfsbane helped cut my shaving time. Besides, no matter what the moon was doing, if you startled me or scared me, there was always the risk I would involuntarily transform. Which is not what you want to happen at, say, an office luncheon, when your boss accidentally dumps her Diet Coke on your lap. Or on a double date at *Pirates of the Caribbean*. (Remember that part where the zombie things pop up on the screen? Well, the audience—and Heath—almost got more than they bargained for that Friday night.)

I hadn't thought about any of this for a long time; I'd been too busy creating a nice, steady, normal, *human* life. But I still had to deal with it. And there was still a lot I didn't know—and that my mother couldn't help me with. Would the werewolf I'd seen yesterday have the answers to any of my questions? Or would he just want to tear me limb from limb? Or maybe even tear off my clothes? I felt a shiver of lust at the thought, which I damped down promptly. Stupid werewolf nature. Maybe my mother was at least a little bit right. Sure, I could repress my inner werewolf, but that didn't make her go away. I mean, since when did I find men in tatty T-shirts attractive? I generally liked my men in Brooks Brothers or maybe Armani. Definitely not Goodwill glad rags.

I climbed into the car with only one teensy-tiny look in the rearview mirror and headed toward the courthouse, practicing a composed, cool-as-a-cucumber expression in case I did run into Mr. Hot Werewolf again. As it turned out, it didn't matter anyway—whatever the werewolf had been doing yesterday, he was doing it somewhere else today.

I couldn't help feeling just a hair disappointed.

At 9:45, I walked into the courtroom, hoping that Marvin was as good as Heath said he was, and pushing all nonhuman thoughts out of my head. I hadn't worn a hat, but I had put on Lindsey's glasses. Which made me look different but also made navigating the courtroom a bit challenging.

The superlawyer was shuffling papers at a table in the front of the courtroom—I had to peer over the glasses to know for sure, because the lenses made him look like a charcoal blob. He didn't see me, and that was fine—my goal was to slip in and out unobserved. Sleek and stealthy—just like a wolf.

I took another stealthy step, feeling like a lupine James Bond. And did a spectacular face-plant right into a trio of blue-haired women.

Everyone in the courtroom turned to watch as two young men worked to disentangle me from the octogenarians. No broken hips, thank God, but one of their purses had upended its cache of Geritol and heart medications all over the floor. It took a full five minutes to corral all the little tablets, several of which had rolled halfway to the jury box.

"Sorry," I mumbled to the nearest blue-haired blob, who smelled rather strongly of mothballs.

"No problem, dearie," she said. "But you might want to get your prescription checked."

"Pardon?" I said, fumbling on the ground for another Geritol tablet.

"Your glasses."

"Oh. Right," I said, feeling around for another tablet.

When I was convinced it was an actual pill, I dropped it back into one of the containers. I hoped she could tell which pill was which; the last thing we needed was another poisoning in the family.

When the last tablet was back in its bottle, the entire courtroom watched as I bumbled into a seat near the back. I got the sense they were disappointed when I didn't do a repeat performance.

As the courtroom slowly recovered from the excitement, I sat with my hands in my lap, looking as boring as possible, and occupying myself by sorting through the mixed smells. Deodorant, sweat, baby powder, pancake makeup. And Pine-Sol—my least favorite floor cleaner.

The crowd's attention had finally drifted off, and I was trying to identify a perfume I didn't recognize but kind of liked when a modern-day chain gang shuffled in, all dressed in orange jumpsuits. Three of the inmates stared at the floor, listless. The fourth was looking around cheerily, as if she was wondering where they had hidden the birthday cake.

I was reeling from the sight of her—my mother, in shackles—when her brown eyes fell on me. Her face lit up even more as she yelled, "Yoo-hoo! Hi, Sophie!"

Six

The entire row of reporters wheeled around to stare at me as my mom raised a hand to blow me a kiss. The chains on her wrists wouldn't let her raise her hands high enough, but it didn't matter—the damage was done.

I gave her a quick smile and a nod of the head, trying to look cool and disinterested, but it was too late. A few of the reporters in the front row conferred; then one of them grabbed her notebook and got up, eyeing me speculatively.

It was time to leave.

I got up and whipped off the glasses, keeping my head down and trotting toward the door. Just my luck to get a reporter who spent her free time doing sprints; I'd barely made it through the door when she fell in behind me, smelling like Right Guard and breath mints. "Are you related to Carmen Bianca?" she asked.

"No comment," I said.

"Your name is Sophie. Sophie . . ."

"Don't you have a hearing to cover?" I snapped back, and broke into a run.

She might be good at sprints, but she wasn't a werewolf. I was around the corner and heading down the hall before she knew what hit her.

The clip-clop of her high heels was nearing the corner

as I paused at the ladies' room . . . and then took three more steps and barged into the men's room.

"Excuse me," I said to a man in a pinstriped suit. He was standing at one of the urinals looking stunned. "Emergency," I added as he popped Mr. Friendly back in and hurriedly zipped up, flushing red. He hustled to the door as I ducked into a stall and took a deep breath. And regretted it immediately; the restroom was screaming for a bleach bath.

I focused on breathing through my mouth and considered my situation.

It would only be a minute before Little Miss Reporter figured out where I'd gone. And the rest of the pack would probably be right there with her. If they followed me to my car, they could track me down through the license plate—and the M3 itself wasn't exactly incognito, since I hadn't gotten a chance to fix the broken window yet.

What now?

I could run fast, but my car was parked less than half a block from the courthouse, and I was sure they would spot me.

Then it occurred to me.

They were looking for a woman.

But they weren't looking for a wolf.

I don't like to change in public—clothes are a problem, to say the least—but desperate times call for desperate measures. I peeled off my jacket and unbuttoned my blouse, then wriggled out of my skirt, eyeing my purse and wishing I had gotten the next size up.

I slipped off my shoes, trying not to think about the range of bacteria on the floor, and took everything inessential—tampons, a wad of receipts, and a blush I wasn't crazy about—out of my purse. I spent a full minute looking for the sanitary napkin disposal box before I remembered I was in the men's room.

I didn't want to leave my stash of tampons, receipts, and old makeup on the floor—it was a good bet Ms. Reporter would come looking for clues to my identity, and even though I doubted a tampon would be enough to go on, the receipts would make it pretty obvious. So I opened the stall and padded over to the trash can, wearing only a bra and panties.

And that was when the door swung open.

Mr. Pinstripes and I stared at each other for a brief moment, during which he gave me the full up and down and turned an even brighter shade of red than before. I wasn't looking, but I was guessing Mr. Friendly had gotten a wake-up call. After a long and awkward moment, the door swung mercifully closed. I hurriedly disposed of my excess baggage and ran back to my stall, where I stuffed my clothes into my purse. The shoes, unfortunately, wouldn't fit, so I stowed them behind the toilet— maybe I'd get a chance to come back for them later. At least they weren't the Pradas.

Then I stripped off my underwear, jammed it into the top of my purse, and let the impulse that had been plaguing me for days have free rein.

A few minutes later, a wolf with a strawberry on its nose and snazzy Kate Spade bag in its jaws galloped past a middle-aged lawyer with a woody and a gaggle of surprised reporters.

All I can say is, thank God they don't allow cameras in courthouses.

"So how did it go?" Lindsey asked when I returned her glasses.

"Don't ask," I said gruffly. I had hidden behind a bush for a half hour before I'd felt it was safe to transform, and I was pretty sure I'd picked up a couple of fleas. My suit wasn't looking too fabulous either.

"Did your mom get out?"

I reached down to scratch behind my right knee. "I don't know."

"What do you mean, you don't know? You've been gone for two hours now. I thought you said you went to the hearing."

"I had to make a quick exit."

Lindsey slapped a Donna Karan–clad leg. "I *told* you they'd figure out who you were. How did you manage to get past them?"

"You wouldn't believe me if I told you," I said.

"What happened to your shoes?"

"I left them in the men's restroom. Do you have a spare pair? I didn't have time to go home."

"The men's restroom? What did you do, climb out the window?"

Why hadn't I thought of that? "It's a long story. Shoes, please?"

She rummaged in her desk and pulled out a pair of four-inch stilettos with red sequins glued all over them.

I picked them up gingerly. "Jesus, Lindsey. Sequins?"

"I had a dinner date a few weeks ago that canceled at the last minute."

I let them dangle from my fingers. "What kind of date? Or do I want to know?"

She stuck her tongue out at me. "It was tango night at Manuel's. But Todd got food poisoning, so we had to reschedule."

"You can walk in these?"

"It's a challenge," she admitted. "But they look so fabulous, it's worth it. Besides, when you're dancing, it gives you an excuse to lean on your partner." She eyed my green suit and bit her lip. "Not the best with green, though. I hope you don't have any client meetings."

I dropped the shoes and slid into them. "Thanks."

She winked at me. "Any time, Twinkle Toes."

*   *   *

"Where did you run off to so fast? And since when did you start wearing those awful glasses? Your eyesight is perfect . . . just like your father's."

I gripped the phone and stifled a sigh of irritation. I hadn't seen my father since I was born, but my mom still talked about him as if he were out of town on a short business trip. So he'd given me perfect eyesight. Excuse me if I didn't get too jazzed about that. Especially considering he also gave me the genes that turned me into a hairy, baying wolf from time to time—and made me go through so many razors I was considering buying stock in Gillette.

On the plus side, my mom was no longer in the county jail. The bail hearing had gone on without me—and Marvin had come through. "Sorry about that. I was trying to keep a low profile," I said. "After you waved, a reporter came after me, so I decided to clear out." I crossed my legs, squinting as the sequins of Lindsey's shoes caught a sunbeam, and tried to smooth out the wrinkles in my skirt. Maybe I needed to treat myself to a little retail therapy this afternoon. Lord knew I wasn't up to heading back to the courthouse men's room. And there was no way I was going to my Termite Terminators meeting looking like Dorothy in an adult-film version of the *Wizard of Oz*.

"Well, it's too bad you missed it. It was so exciting!" my mom was saying. "Just like *Matlock*. And that attorney you found me is so *clever*. . . . I'm going to do a good fortune spell on him." Her voice suddenly got dreamy. "He looked so manly up there. . . ."

Oh my God. My mother had the hots for Danny DeVito. "No love spells, Mom," I said firmly.

"Oh, Sophie. You're no fun."

"Mom."

"Okay, okay." She paused for a moment. "What about after the trial?"

How could she possibly be interested in Danny De-Vito? He was as about as appealing as a baked potato. Maybe less. "Once the trial's over, you can do whatever the heck you want," I told her. *Assuming she's found innocent*, a little voice inside me said. "Just keep the nightshade out of it, okay?"

"Sophie! I've worked with herbs for more than forty years. Do you think I'd make a mistake like that?"

"I know," I said, massaging my temples. "I'm just saying . . . be careful, okay?"

"I'm sorry, sweetheart. I know you didn't mean it," she said. "I just don't understand it. Why would I want to hurt him? After all, he was going to change his vote."

My ears pricked up. "Brewster? How do you know that?"

"We witches have our ways . . ." she said coyly. Before I could ask her what she meant, she said, "But I wonder who *did* poison that nice man?"

"You mean the nice man you threatened to kill on the five-o'clock news?"

"What are you talking about?"

"Mom, I saw the News 9 footage. The one from the demonstration."

"Oh, that? That wasn't a threat. It was all about karma, dear."

"It sounded to me as if you were about to throw the spell book at him."

"Not at all, my dear. Just the cycle of life. Any Wiccan would realize that."

I gripped the phone hard. "Well, since most of the rest of Austin isn't familiar with Wiccan philosophy, you might want to couch it a little bit differently next time you're in front of a camera. In the meantime, unless we find out who *did* poison Brewster, you're still on the hook."

"That's why I'm doing the séance tonight."

I bit my lip. "The séance."

"Remember? We talked about it when you came to visit."

"The one where you're going to ask Ted Brewster who killed him."

"Exactly!"

I once again resisted the urge to bang my head against the nearest hard surface. The strawberry on my nose was bad enough; I didn't need a giant bruise on my forehead to go with it. Instead, I took a long swig of tea and said, "I thought you were saving that for the equinox."

"Well, since you won't be around then, I figured we'd do it a little earlier. Of course, the timing's not optimal, but I don't think a few days will make a huge difference. Anyway, I've scheduled it for seven o'clock. Emily will be there, and you can bring your friend Lindsey if you want; the more, the merrier. Oh, and have you seen any more of that werewolf?"

"No," I said shortly.

"Really?" She sounded disappointed. "Well, I'm sure you'll run into each other again. Quite soon, probably."

"No spells, Mom. None at all."

"Oh, Sophie, don't be silly. Now, I'll see you at seven."

"But Mom . . ."

"Oops! A customer just came in. Love you, sweetheart . . . see you tonight!"

And then she hung up on me.

I was settling down to crunch some numbers for the Southeast Airlines meeting when Adele swept into the room.

I looked up and smiled. "Hi, Adele."

"Are you ready for the meeting?"

"Meeting?" I glanced at my watch and started; we were due at Termite Terminators in twenty minutes. "Shoot! I thought it was earlier." Even though we were running late, I downed the rest of my tea; it was bad enough having to wear Lindsey's sequined stilettos to a client meeting with Adele. I could only imagine how she'd react if I started sprouting fangs in the Termite Terminators' front lobby.

"I was just getting ready for the Southeast Airlines meeting," I said, slipping into my borrowed shoes and wobbling around the desk. "I kind of lost track of time. But I'm ready if you are."

Adele looked at my wrinkled suit, then down at my feet. "Interesting choice of footwear."

"My other shoes . . ." I hesitated for a moment. How was I going to explain that I left them in the men's restroom at the courthouse while transforming into a werewolf? "Broke," I finished with a feeble attempt at a perky smile.

"Broke?"

"The heel, I mean. One of them fell right off. So I borrowed a pair," I said, wishing fervently that I'd found time to hit the mall. On the plus side, I *had* found a minute to shave. I might look like an X-rated Dorothy, but at least I wasn't sprouting fur.

"Well, if they're looking for an auditor who can do a pole dance, we'll be prepared," she muttered.

I blushed and tried to look professional. Which is challenging when you're wobbling around in a green business suit and red sequined fuck-me shoes.

Well, if nothing else, I thought as I struggled to match Adele's pace—the shoes were a little big, and I was afraid I was going to sprain my ankle—I still had my smart little Kate Spade purse.

The ride to Termite Terminators was a little bit frosty, and not just because of the icy air blasting from the air vents in Adele's Mercedes. Usually we took my car— Adele doesn't like other people getting her seats dirty, I guess. Today, though, since my passenger seat was still covered in safety glass, I suggested the Mercedes might be a better option.

As Adele pulled the car out of the parking garage, I shifted uncomfortably in my leather seat, trying surreptitiously to stretch some of the wrinkles out of my lapels.

"How did your mom's procedure go?" she asked.

"It went great," I said. "She's back on her feet already." And probably brewing up another potion as we spoke.

Adele gave me a tight smile. "I'm glad to hear that. My assistant tried to find her at the hospital, but there weren't any Garous."

I swallowed hard. "She has a different last name," I said quickly.

"Ah," said Adele, inclining her highlighted head. "Well, I'm glad to hear she's better now." After a brief pause, she said, "We'll be seeing more of you at the office now, I presume."

Seeing more of me? I'd worked a lot of long hours lately, but I decided to let it ride. Adele was right; I had been out a lot during the day lately. And unfortunately, although this morning's "procedure" had gone well, my mom wasn't exactly out of the woods yet. "Absolutely," I said, with more authority than I felt.

"Good," she said. "I'm glad to hear that." As we turned onto 6th Street, she said, "I don't mind telling you that I've been a bit concerned lately."

"What do you mean?"

Her thin lips tightened. "I've been hearing some rumors."

"Rumors," I repeated, darting a glance at her beaky profile and shifting in an attempt to make my shoes as unobtrusive as possible. *Sally*, I thought. "What kind of rumors?"

Adele glanced over at my wrinkled suit and gripped the leather-bound steering wheel with a manicured hand. "Until now, your work—and deportment—have been nothing short of professional."

"Thank you," I said, ignoring the "until now" part.

But she wasn't done yet. "Sophie, I don't need to tell you that Withers and Young has a very strict policy regarding controlled substances."

I bit my lip and started making a mental list of tasks for Sally: scrubbing down the inside of the office fridge, realphabetizing all the file cabinets, cleaning the grout around the toilets with her toothbrush . . . "Oh, I get it," I said, tossing off what I hoped was a light laugh. "This is about the box of herbal tea my mom sent me, isn't it?"

"I don't know about herbal tea," Adele said. "But your behavior has been . . . peculiar lately." She darted a glance at my feet. "And I had HR pull your files; there seems to be a regular pattern of absences."

Uh-oh. "I like to take a few days off now and then, to keep myself fresh," I said. *And avoid scaring the bejesus out of my clients.*

Adele pulled into a parking space under a giant neon termite—the company's trademark—and turned to me. "I'm sure it's nothing. But I wanted to let you know that we're starting drug testing next week."

My mouth turned dry. I was almost sure wolfsbane didn't qualify as a restricted substance, but it still wasn't something I wanted turning up on my drug test. Still, I couldn't cut back now; it was close to the time when I needed it most.

When I realized Adele was waiting for a response, I nodded shortly. "Sounds like a good policy."

"I'm glad you think so," she said, and opened her car door. I grabbed my purse and files and stepped out into the parking lot after her, struggling to stay upright. How Lindsey managed to tango in four-inch stiletto heels, I'll never know.

Adele might not have been fond of my footwear, but

the audience at Termite Terminators was nothing if not appreciative. As the company president, a mildly obese man named Herb, ogled my legs, I went through the numbers as quickly as possible—the smell of chemicals from the warehouse next door was making my nose hairs curl.

Between the fleabites and the reek of insecticides, I wasn't sure I was going to survive, but finally, a long hour later, we were back in Adele's Mercedes. As I reached down to scratch my ankle—stupid fleas—Adele popped in a CD, and Barry Manilow's "Copacabana" oozed from the speakers. I glanced at the top-of-the-line sound system and cringed, then gritted my teeth as my boss sang tunelessly along.

Would this day ever end?

Seven

"I've never been to a séance before," Lindsey said, as we pulled up outside of my mom's shop that evening. After my little road trip with Adele, the rest of the day had been relatively uneventful, but I wasn't holding my breath about tonight.

"I'm sure it will be a barrel of laughs," I said.

"Tell me again what your mom's trying to accomplish by bringing Brewster back?" Lindsey asked, unfolding her long legs from the passenger seat of my BMW. I'd stopped off at Cash 'n' Splash after work to vacuum out the passenger seat; I still hadn't gotten the glass replaced, but at least you could sit down without perforating yourself. Or my leather seats.

"For some reason, my mom thinks Brewster will know who murdered him," I said. "And that by calling him back, we'll solve the case."

Lindsey snorted. "How would he know? I mean, obviously he didn't even know the stuff was poisoned."

"And he's dead," I reminded her. For some reason, nobody but me seemed to find that relevant.

"I keep forgetting about that," she said. "Still, if anyone can bring him back, it's your mom."

I'd taken my mom's suggestion and invited Lindsey to come along—we were planning on doing some sleuthing tonight anyway, so she was a natural. When I mentioned it to her, she lit up as if I'd offered her a gift certificate for a weekend at Lake Austin Spa Resort.

"Well, if nothing else, it'll be fun," Lindsey said, smoothing down her long hair and picking her way up the stone walkway. Since I was still wearing her four-inch heels, I followed behind her cautiously.

The bells above the door jingled as we entered, and the familiar aroma of a hundred mixed herbs, incense, and candles wafted over us. My mother swept into the front room as we shut the door. "Sophie, sweetheart! Hello!"

"Hi, Mom," I said as she enveloped me in a huge, aromatic hug. No shackles this evening, thank God—just her customary forty bangle bracelets. For tonight's ceremony she had draped herself in long black robes with little silver moons and stars sprinkled across them. It was a relief to see her in something other than a pumpkin-orange jumpsuit—but I did wish she'd cut back on the patchouli.

"Oooh, Sophie . . . love the shoes," she said, admiring my feet.

"I borrowed them from Lindsey."

"I should have guessed," she said, giving Lindsey a hug. "I swear, you look more gorgeous every time I see you."

"Thanks," Lindsey said, smiling big. No wonder she liked my mom so much. "What are these?" my friend asked, picking up a locket on a silver chain from a nearby table.

"They're attraction amulets," my mother said. "Just got them in last week, and they're selling like gangbusters. Go ahead, help yourself. Not that you need one, with your looks."

"Thanks," Lindsey said, fiddling with the clasp. "How do they work?"

"All you have to do is put it on," my mother said. "The men will be all over you."

I rolled my eyes. An attraction charm was the last thing Lindsey needed. If it actually worked, I'd be packing a crowbar and pepper spray the next time we did happy hour on 6th Street. I'd also have to forbid her to come within twenty yards of Heath.

As Lindsey fastened the chain around her slender neck, I asked, "Who else is coming?"

"Emily's here," my mom said. "And Tania."

My antennae pricked up. "Tania?" Tania was my mom's newest part-time helper. When I'd met her a few weeks ago, she'd been all round cheeks and smiles— kind of a brunette version of Mrs. Claus from one of those old animated Christmas specials. You know, the ones with Rudolph and the Abominable Snowman?

But something about her bothered me—and it wasn't just her JLO perfume. (Which was a little jarring, coming from Mrs. Claus.) "Couldn't we get someone else?" I said.

My mom pursed her lips. "We're already short one as it is."

"But she's so new," I said.

"She'll do fine," she said, patting my arm. "I just wish we had a sixth. I called Rosemary and Whitehawk, but they couldn't make it on such short notice."

Thank God, I thought. I'd met Whitehawk once. She wore feathers in her hair and punctuated every other sentence with a kind of strangled squawk. Not exactly the kind of person you wanted around when you were calling up dead people.

My mother turned to me. "You don't have another friend you could call, do you? What about that young man you've been seeing?" She tapped her chin with a finger. "What was his name? Heap? Heat?"

"Heath," I said. "And I don't think he's quite what you're looking for."

"Maybe not," she said. "He's a lawyer, after all, and lawyers aren't usually . . . well, *open* to the other side. But we must have him over to dinner soon."

"Mmm," I said. "So, is everything set up?" I asked, anxious to change the subject. It would be hard enough introducing country-club Heath to Carmen the psychic witch. But something told me that getting together to summon a dead councilman wasn't the ideal circumstance for a first meeting. Particularly since my mother was accused of murdering the councilman.

"Emily's in the back, getting the table ready, and Tania is just going to pick up a few more things. Come on back," she said, her robes fluttering behind her as she headed toward the kitchen. "And Sophie—is it time for tea?" she asked, her eyes surveying me.

"Yes," I said. "And I need to slip into the bathroom for a minute, if that's okay."

"I'll put the kettle on," she said.

Before I headed for the bathroom, I murmured to my mother, "I need some more pennyroyal, if you've got it."

"Fleas?"

I nodded. I'd been a big fan of pennyroyal baths for years—almost every time I went out as a wolf, it seemed, I came back with fleas. And pennyroyal sure smelled better than flea shampoo.

My mother took my arm, then glanced around to make sure we were alone. We were; Emily and Lindsey were chatting in the next room. "Have you seen the *lupin* again?" she murmured.

"No," I said, feeling a rush of heat just thinking about him. I did my best to quench it.

"I know you're dead set against it," she said in a low voice. "And I know you've never forgiven your father for what he had to do."

"You mean deserting us?"

"It was to save your life, darling." Her normally bright eyes darkened a bit. "And I know if he could have come with us, he would have. I often wonder what kept him . . ."

I snorted.

She squeezed my arm. "Sophie, I know it's been . . . well, painful for you. But you need to view this as a blessing, not a curse. Something to be embraced."

Oh, please. I'll bet that's what they said to people who found out they had cancer. I loved my mother, but sometimes her contact with reality was . . . shall we say, tenuous? I mean, the woman did IRS charms instead of filing her taxes. So far she hadn't been audited, but it was only a matter of time. "Somehow I don't think I'd be embraced too often if I stopped drinking my tea," I said.

"Humans don't understand, darling. We both know that. But even though I'm not like you, I can tell you that being with a werewolf is . . ." She stopped for a moment. "Well, it's just incredible."

So my father had been great in bed. Again, more information than I needed.

"And you can't deny your nature forever," she continued.

"Mom . . ."

"It's your destiny, sweetheart."

I looked at her sternly. "Please tell me you didn't cast a spell."

She glanced up at the clock. "Sophie, dear, we need to get started. Let me get you that pennyroyal, though."

"Mom . . ."

"I'll go get you some tea," she said. "And a packet of pennyroyal." Before I could stop her, she was bustling into the next room, leaving me with the deep suspicion that she had in fact done something I wouldn't approve of.

I vowed not to leave before I found out what it was.

When I emerged from the bathroom a few minutes later—minus a few leg whiskers—my mom handed me a mug full of wolfsbane tea. She must have gotten a fresh shipment in—it tasted stronger than usual, and I tried not to wince at the first sip.

"Is that the stuff Sally thought was pot?" Lindsey asked, peering at the green liquid.

"Uh-huh," I said, forcing myself to take another sip. What I really wanted was an extra-foam caramel macchiato—or maybe an extra-large glass of Merlot. But the whole séance thing was going to be weird enough without me sprouting tufts of fur.

"Smells interesting," she said, sniffing my cup. "Can I try some?"

Mom and I exchanged glances; the last thing we needed was Lindsey keeling over from wolfsbane poisoning. "It's kind of an acquired taste," I said.

"But I have some nice peach chamomile that would be

perfect," my mother said. "Relax you a bit before the séance."

Lindsey wasn't buying it. "What's so special about that tea?" she asked.

My mom put a hand on Lindsey's arm. "Sophie's got . . . well, a special medical condition," she murmured into her ear. "The tea helps it—but if you don't have the condition, it's not good to drink it."

Lindsey flashed me a concerned look. "A medical condition? Sophie, you never told me."

"It's congenital," my mother said soothingly. "And Sophie's fine. Thanks to her special tea, the condition is completely under control."

Well, that was stretching things a tad, I thought.

My mother smiled at Lindsey like a plus-sized version of the Good Witch Glinda. Without the Tinkerbell dress, that is. And the blond hair. "Now, how about some peach chamomile tea?"

"Okay, I guess," Lindsey said, letting my mother guide her toward the kitchen. "But I still want to know about this 'condition' of yours," she said.

"I get a little hairy sometimes," I confided as we followed my mother.

Her gray eyes widened. "And the tea helps?"

I nodded.

"Wow," she said, following my mother. "Do you have anything for cellulite?"

We'd been sitting around the séance table—which was the kitchen table draped in heavy purple velvet and covered with so many candles that it looked like an octogenarian's birthday cake—for almost a half hour before Tania burst in, carrying a big white bag. She was short and pear-shaped, and her red cheeks gave her a jolly look—like I said, a dead ringer for a young Mrs. Claus. But my hackles still rose a little as I caught a whiff of her scent—roses, baby powder, and something I couldn't quite put my finger on.

And barbecue.

Barbecue?

"Did you get everything?" my mom asked as Tania plunked the bag down on the counter.

"The brisket plate, extra-moist, right?" she asked.

"With new potatoes and coleslaw?"

Tania nodded.

"I didn't know it was a dinner séance," Lindsey said.

My mom laughed. "Oh, no. It's for Ted."

For what felt like the hundredth time, I reminded my mother that Ted Brewster was dead.

She ignored me. "Great," she said approvingly as Tania pulled a little plastic tub out of the bag. "You remembered the cobbler."

"I didn't get ice cream," Tania said. "I thought it might melt—I hope it's okay."

"It's perfect, darling," my mom said, unwrapping the brisket plate and setting it in the middle of the table, surrounded by the forest of candles.

Saliva flooded my mouth as Tania poured barbecue sauce over the sliced beef. I'd been missing a lot of meals lately; maybe I'd have to start carrying a snack bag of beef jerky.

"Is that from the Salt Lick?" Lindsey asked. "It smells heavenly . . . but what's it for?"

"It's Ted's favorite plate," my mom said, lighting a swathe of white candles. "It should help bring him back."

I wasn't sure I wanted to know how my mom was so familiar with Ted Brewster's dining habits. And because what I didn't know couldn't be wrung out of me during cross-examination, I decided not to ask.

Lindsey licked her full lips. "When he's done with it, can we have the leftovers?"

"I brought a little extra," Tania said. I swallowed more drool and looked at my mother's new assistant with new respect. Perhaps I had misjudged her.

"Is there any sausage in there?" Lindsey asked.

"Sorry," Tania said. "I only got brisket and chicken."

"We'll eat when we're through," my mom said as she lit the last few candles. "It shouldn't take long. He hasn't been away from this plane for more than a few days." The candles flared as the air conditioning kicked on, flooding the room with a mix of spices and floral scents. Mom must have anointed the candles with some kind of oil—whatever it was was almost strong enough to overpower the smell of brisket.

Almost. Maybe I could sneak a chicken leg before we started . . .

"We need to get going while it's still warm," my mom said as I eyed the grease-stained white bag. "The heat will draw the spirit."

"What do we do?" Lindsey asked.

My mom blew out the last match and turned off the lights. With the shades drawn and the lights out, the dark purple room transformed into a shadowy, candle-lit cave.

"Ready?" she said softly.

"I guess so," I said, as everyone settled in around the round table.

"Then join hands and relax," my mother said. I took a deep breath of meat- and candle-scented air, thinking it would be a lot easier to relax with a bellyful of chicken and brisket, and reached for my companions' hands. Lindsey's skin was cool and soft to the touch, thanks to years of weekly manicures. But I got an unpleasant little frisson as my fingers touched Tania's—and it wasn't just because of her bitten-to-the-quick nails. I darted a glance at her round face, but she was focused on my mother.

"Everybody relax," my mother said. "Once we're all attuned and the energy is right, I'll call him."

My stomach rumbled audibly.

"Empty your minds," my mother intoned. Easy for her to say; she'd probably had dinner. "And no matter what happens," she added in a low voice, "do not let go of each other's hands."

Well, that sounded ominous.

So I emptied my mind. Or tried to, anyway. Between the scent of barbecue and the disturbing way my thoughts kept returning to the werewolf on the corner, it wasn't working very well. Was my mother right about my true nature? I wondered. I was a werewolf.

But I was also a human.

Couldn't I choose which path I wanted to take?

Then the air conditioner kicked on again, sending a waft of meat-scented air my way, and my fantasies turned abruptly back to barbecue. For a moment, anyway; hot, full-blooded werewolves are hard to compete with, even for the Salt Lick. After a few minutes of us sitting there and staring at the brisket plate—which would probably be cold by the time we were done, I thought with a twinge of regret—Mom evidently judged the moment to be right.

"Everybody ready?"

I nodded slightly. I was ready, all right. Ready to get this show on the road.

"We call the beloved spirit of our recently departed Ted Brewster to be among us," my mother said firmly.

And that was when my cell phone rang.

I tried to ignore it, hoping that whoever it was would give up. And they did. But just as my mother opened her mouth to speak, the stupid phone rang a second time.

"Sorry. Just a moment," I said, breaking the little circle and scurrying to my purse. "Hello!" I hissed into the phone.

"Sexy voice, Sophie. What's going on?"

It was Heath.

"I'm . . . uh"—I glanced at the table, where everyone was staring at me expectantly—"busy."

"Too bad. I was thinking of coming over," he said. "I thought we might be able to finish what we started earlier on." Despite the fact that three people, including my mother, were staring at me and waiting for my assistance in contacting a dead councilman, I felt a little tingle thinking about this afternoon. "Where are you?" His voice was husky.

"Um . . . my mom's shop."

"Oh, the chair store. What's it called again? Sit A Spill?"

I chose not to correct him. All I needed was for him to check the phone book and show up halfway through the séance.

"You know, you really have to introduce me to her," he said. "It's been almost a year now, Sophie; what are you waiting for?"

"I . . . uh . . ."

"Besides, if she's anything like you, she must be a pistol."

I glanced over at my mother, who was draped in several yards of violet silk and about forty bangle bracelets. As much as I loved my mother, the similarities between us were less than striking. At least I hoped so.

"The food's getting cold, sweetheart!" my mother called out.

I hunched over the phone. "Look—can I call you later? I'm kind of busy."

"What's going on?"

"Can't talk—gotta run," I sang into the phone. "Love you!"

I didn't wait for him to answer before I hung up, turned my ringer to vibrate, and hurried back to the table. A moment later the phone started buzzing, but I ignored it and grabbed Lindsey's and Tania's warm hands. My mother nodded at me and repeated her request for Ted Brewster to stop by for some brisket. How, I wondered, did a ghost eat? As my mother intoned some strange words and I tried not to drool on myself, we all waited for Ted to make his appearance. I don't know what I was expecting—the lights to flicker maybe, or the table to start rocking.

But nothing did.

It may surprise you to hear this, but this was my first séance. Because my mother usually held them on a full moon near an equinox or solstice—what she called the "power" times of the year—I had never been in quite the proper state, if you know what I mean, to attend.

We sat for another few minutes in the darkened room, waiting for something to happen. I was about to suggest we split the new potatoes—maybe a little sustenance would help—when the candles flickered and an icy breeze swept through the room.

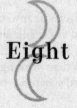

Eight

My first thought was the air-conditioning vents, but the breeze was coming from the other side of the room.

"Ted," my mother said in a low, rough voice.

Something bumped the table.

Holy shit.

"If this is Ted Brewster, rap once."

The table bumped again, and I was glad I'd emptied my bladder before we began. Goose bumps rose on my arms, and it wasn't just because of the chill in the room—even though the temperature had dropped a good fifteen degrees. I glanced at Lindsey, who was saucer-eyed, and then at my mother, whose eyes were closed and who looked so relaxed she could be asleep. "How do we know it's Ted?" I hissed.

My mother's serene look disappeared for a moment as she squinched her forehead. Then her features smoothed out again. "Ted," she intoned. "How many yards did Vince Young run for the final touchdown in the Rose Bowl?"

After a moment of silence—I guess Ted was thinking back to the game—the table knocked nine times.

My mom grinned. "We've got him."

The candles flickered in the middle of the table, and the smell of brisket intensified. Ted must be checking out the barbecue plate. "How the heck do you know how many yards he ran?" I murmured to my mom.

"I went to Burt Bunsen's Rose Bowl party, remember?" she whispered. Then she cleared her throat. "Ted. We called you to help us. We know your life on this earth was cut short; can you help us discover who hastened your departure?"

After a moment of silence, she added, "Just rap once for yes and twice for no."

The table thumped once.

"Great," she said, beaming. I stared at the middle of the table, where something was apparently poking at the brisket. Could it be—was Ted actually trying to eat it?

"Is it someone we know?"

He paused for a moment, then rapped. Three times.

"Once for yes, twice for no," Mom reminded him.

Again, three raps. And the brisket was definitely deteriorating.

After a long moment, my mother sighed. "I don't often do this," she said, "but if it would help you, you can use my body to tell us what you need us to know."

Whatever it was stopped poking at the brisket. My mom jerked once, and a moment later, she shook off the hands gripping hers and reached out for the plate. "Anyone have a fork?" she asked in a low, husky voice with a Texas drawl so thick you'd need a steak knife to cut it.

"Mom?" I said a little shakily.

"That's not your mom anymore," Emily hissed at me. Then, in a louder, voice, she said, "Forks are in the bag. On the counter."

My mom lumbered—I think that's the word—over to the counter and pulled out a pack of plastic silverware. "Mmm," she said a moment later, her mouth full of brisket. "I've missed this."

"Mr. Brewster?" Emily said as my mother shoved a forkful of coleslaw in after the brisket.

Through a mouthful of cabbage, my mom said, "Got any Shiner Bock?" Only it wasn't my mom; it was Ted Brewster. Jesus. This was just too, too weird.

Emily, however, took it in stride. "I'm sorry, Mr. Brewster. We're out of beer. Now, about your recent . . . demise. Do you have any idea who might have been responsible?"

Ted looked up. "For poisoning me?"

"For poisoning you," Emily repeated.

"Bluebonnets," he said, shoveling in another mouthful of brisket. A drop of barbecue sauce dribbled down his—my mother's—chin.

"Pardon me?" Emily said.

"Bluebonnets," he repeated in a gravelly voice. "The

360 Bridge. That's where you'll find what you're looking for."

The 360 Bridge? What did a picturesque spansion
bridge on the northwest side of town have to do with
anything? Unless Brewster's murderer had taken up res-
idence underneath it, which seemed unlikely. Ditto the
bluebonnets.

Maybe it was a good thing we didn't have any Shiner.
Ted was having a hard enough time staying on topic
while sober. "Um, Mr. Brewster?" I said to my mother.
To Ted, I reminded myself. "Can I call you Ted?"

"Sure, honey." He paused, looking annoyed. "Can't
you wait your turn?"

"Excuse me?" I said.

My mother's face went slack. A moment later, Lindsey
yelped.

"What is it?"

"Somebody goosed me!"

At first I thought it was my mother—well, Ted, really—
but both of her—his—hands were engaged with a fork
and knife. Then something pinched my left breast.

I gurgled, then let go of Lindsey and swiped at the in-
visible hand. But whatever it was disappeared. A moment later, a high-pitched giggle echoed through the
room.

"Join hands!" ordered my mother, who had dropped
the silverware and was back in the saddle again, so to
speak. Except for the barbecue sauce dribbling down
her chin, she looked completely in command.

I grabbed for Lindsey and Tania. When we had
formed a linked circle again, my mother's voice rang
out. "Thank you for visiting us, spirits, but now we ask
you to depart."

The candles flickered again, and the coldness dissipated.

After a long moment, my mother said a few more

words, then told us to release hands. "Well, since I don't remember anything," she said cheerily as she got up to hit the lights, "I'm assuming he came through. Did you get anything good out of him?"

"Something goosed me!" Lindsey said in an affronted voice.

Mom nodded. "The ghostly groper. I'm going to have to do something about him. Ever since Marge's séance, he's been a terrible nuisance. But what about Brewster? What did he say?"

"He sure liked the barbecue," I said. "By the way, you've got a bit of sauce on your chin."

She grabbed a paper napkin from the counter and dabbed at her face. "I knew the brisket platter would hook him. So, what little tidbits did you get?"

"Bluebonnets," I said.

My mother looked pensive. "Bluebonnets?"

"Don't forget the 360 Bridge," Lindsey added.

She pursed her lips and sighed. "Sometimes, unfortunately, the spirits aren't as direct as I'd like."

"He sure was direct about the Shiner Bock," I said.

My mom's eyes glinted. "He wanted a beer?"

I nodded.

"Good old Ted," she said. "Did he say anything else?"

"He didn't have a chance. I think whatever it was that goosed Lindsey"—and pinched me—"scared him off."

My mom pursed her lips. "Should we try again, do you think?"

"No," Lindsey and I said quickly.

"Are you sure?" she asked.

"Positive," I said. "Besides, I'm starved."

"That's odd," my mom said. "For some reason, I'm not." We all looked at what was left of the barbecue plate.

Emily grinned. "I guess it's true what they say; you can't take it with you."

After my mom snuffed all the candles—evidently blowing them out is bad metaphysical form—we split what was left of the barbecue. Tania excused herself on moral principles—she was vegetarian. Which made me happy on two counts; not only was she gone, but her departure left more to go around.

"So who's this 'ghostly groper'?" Lindsey asked, spearing a new potato. The room had warmed up quickly—after all, it was an old house, and it was almost ninety degrees outside—but I still felt a little chilled from our supernatural experience. After all, it's not every day your mother is possessed by a dead councilman. As I remembered the thick Texas drawl that had come from my mom's lips, I found myself wishing for a Shiner of my own. Instead, I settled for another swig of wolfsbane tea.

"We're not sure," said my mother. "We call him Freddie."

"Freddie?"

"Freddie Fingers," said Emily.

"Ah."

"Anyway," my mom continued, "he came during a séance we had a few months ago. We've tried a few banishing spells, but we haven't been able to get him to leave."

"Just when you think he's gone, he pops back up again," said Emily. "We had one woman here the other day—he pulled her thong right up out of the back of her skirt."

"Ouch," I said.

"She didn't believe me when I told her it was a ghost," Emily said.

"That's what happens when you wear an attraction charm," my mother said sagely.

"She wasn't wearing one," Emily said.

Lindsey reached up to touch her locket nervously. "Do you think that's why . . ."

My mom smiled at her. "I think he'd like you no matter what you wore."

"Thanks, Carmen," Lindsey said, still fingering the locket. "By the way, Sophie and I were thinking. Since the séance didn't exactly work out, maybe we should start asking around. See if we can find out who spiked that potion."

My mother raised her eyebrows. "What do you mean, it didn't work out? We got two valuable clues out of that."

"Right. Bluebonnets and the 360 Bridge," I said.

"Exactly," Mom said. "I'm sure they're important."

Lindsey tried another tack. "I'm sure they are too. But while we're waiting for the spirit world to be . . . well, a little more clear, maybe we could try some more traditional methods."

My mom nibbled at a pickle. "Like what?"

"We were thinking of talking to the librarian Brewster liked," I said, glad to be thinking about something other than that stupid werewolf. Something that was a strictly human concern. Even if it was my mother's impending murder trial. "Do you happen to remember her name?"

"Hmmm. Interesting idea. I think it started with a *J*. *Jennifer*, maybe. Or *Julie*."

"Do you keep records of the potions you make?"

"Good thinking, Sophie!" She stood up and bustled out of the room with a jingle. "I know they're here somewhere," she muttered, and I could hear the sound of drawers being opened and closed. I was amazed they were actually in a filing cabinet. Maybe my mother's organizational system was improving.

She returned a few minutes later with a big cardboard box jammed with papers, and I stifled a sigh. "Are they filed by date?" I asked. Hope, after all, springs eternal.

My mom bit her lip. "Not really," she said. "I just kind of toss them in. But it's weird; I can't find my spell book anywhere."

"I can't think why," I said dryly. Her "office" looked as if it had been rifled by burglars with a paperwork fetish. It was a wonder she managed to keep Sit A Spell going.

"I always keep it on top of the filing cabinets, but tonight it's not there." She bit her lip. "Well, I guess we don't need it. I know most of the spells by heart anyway, and the librarian's name should be in here somewhere." She dug a crumpled mass of papers out of the cardboard box.

"Why don't we each take a stack?" suggested Emily.

"Good idea," said my mother. "Ted's name should be on it—it'll be a love potion. Watch for anything with rose quartz crystal in it."

"Got it," I said.

As I leafed through the pile, I found myself amazed at the sheer volume of spells and potions. Not to mention the variety. How could my mom remember all of these? I knew many of them had been passed down through the generations; my mom's side of the family had been well known among the Rom for their abilities in the psychic realm. There were spells for love, money . . . even penile enhancement. "He didn't have money for surgery," my mother explained when I asked her about it. "My grandma said she could have fed the whole family with the money she made on that one." I grinned. Who knew the male obsession with penis size had such history?

"What's buckwheat for?" Lindsey asked, peering at a crumpled page covered with my mother's loopy scrawl.

"It's supposed to attract wealth." My mother looked a little dreamy. "It's also really good with pork."

"You just ate," I reminded her.

Mom shrugged. "I could always eat. Besides, that was Ted, not me."

"Then how come you still smell like onions?"

Lindsey interrupted us. "Some guy wanted 'Come to me, boy' oil. Weird."

"Usually it's the women who ask for it," my mother said. "But every once in a while a young man asks for some . . ."

I looked at her. "And you agreed to give it to him?"

She shrugged. "What's the harm?"

"Unless you're the boy in question," I muttered.

"Sophie!" Lindsey said. "I didn't know you had a spell done."

I lowered the papers I was looking at, remembering my mother's hesitation to answer me earlier. I had a bad feeling about the piece of paper Lindsey was holding up. "What are you talking about?" I asked, raising an eyebrow at my mother, who was reaching for the page in Lindsey's hands.

"Unless there's another Sophie Anne."

I glared at my mother. "You didn't . . ."

"It's right here," Lindsey said, peering at the page. "Sophie Anne. It was cast in August." She turned to my mother. "But what's Jezebel root?"

My mother turned bright red as I snatched the page from Lindsey's hands.

"What's Jezebel root for?" I demanded.

My mother cleared her throat. "Good fortune, darling." She tapped the paper. "Notice I took your advice, sweetheart, and started dating my work."

Like the fact that she wrote down the date made everything just hunky-dory. "Wait a minute," I said, scanning the page. "Tiger lily, rose quartz . . ." I looked up at my mother, who was suddenly focused on her fingernails. "This isn't for good fortune. You worked a love spell on me!"

She shrugged. "Oh, Sophie. What's the difference? Besides, it wasn't *exactly* a love spell . . ."

"Oh, no?" I had been embarrassed when my mother came to my ninth-grade career day dressed as Morticia Addams. I had been humiliated when she donated a basket of herbal marital aids to the school raffle. And I had been mortified when she'd insisted on checking out my prom date with a spirit pendulum.

But a love spell! I stared at my mother, but she wouldn't meet my eyes. "What exactly was it, then, Mom?"

She cleared her throat. "More of an attraction spell, really."

My breath hissed out from between my teeth. "An attraction spell. You worked an attraction spell on me." I studied the page again. Right beneath the rose quartz was the word *wolfsbane*. It wasn't just an ordinary attraction spell.

It was an attraction spell that involved werewolves.

I took a deep breath and was about to tell her what I thought of working spells on unsuspecting victims—not to mention *daughters*—when the front door jingled.

My mom leaped to her feet. "Better go get it!"

As she scurried to the front of the shop, I called after her, "I'm not done with you yet!"

Lindsey turned to me eagerly. "Well, did it work?"

I stared at her. "Did what work?"

She rolled her eyes. "The spell, dummy."

"God, no!" I said, reviewing the last few weeks mentally. Of course, Herb from Termite Terminators hadn't been able to keep his eyes off me. But you didn't need an attraction spell for that to happen; he tended to glom onto anything that walked. Besides, I'd been wearing Lindsey's cabaret-style tango shoes. And although he was hairy, Herb was definitely not a werewolf. "And it's a good thing too," I said. "I have enough on my plate as it is."

Just then, my mother walked back into the kitchen with a big grin. "Sophie," she sang out, "I believe there's someone to see you."

Nine

"That's impossible. Nobody knows I'm here."

"See for yourself," she said, her eyes glinting.

I heaved myself up with a sigh. "Fine. But we're still not done discussing that spell. In fact, I want you to reverse it. Immediately."

She ignored my last comment and started fussing with the table. "Can you girls help me get these candles taken care of?" she asked Emily and Lindsey.

As the three of them went to work clearing away the paraffin forest, I walked into the front room.

And came face-to-face—well, face-to-back, anyway—with a werewolf.

He was standing at a table across the room from me; I recognized his broad shoulders and his long blond hair immediately. But I didn't need to see him to know exactly what he was—I could tell he was a werewolf just from his smell.

Which was so intoxicating it just about brought me to my knees.

Maybe my mom was right about werewolves.

Don't go there, Sophie.

I whirled around, hoping to make it back into the kitchen, but it was too late. He'd picked up my scent.

His gold eyes caught the light as he turned to me. All of the questions I had in mind were gone; instead of asking for details on moon phases, I found myself staring at him with my mouth half open. After a flicker of surprise, he smiled—a long, lazy smile, studded with gleaming teeth. Before I could stop myself, I found myself wondering what it would be like, kissing someone with teeth like that. I smoothed my skirt and took a wobbly step forward. Of all the days to lose my shoes . . .

"Hi," he said.

It was just one little word. But something about the way he said it—husky, with a hint of a growl—made me want to melt into the floor right then and there. I lurched forward and grabbed the counter.

Get ahold of yourself, Sophie.

"Can I help you?" I said, just a teensy bit breathlessly.

His eyes roamed up and down me, coming to rest on my face. He was wearing the same faded jeans, and a black T-shirt that stretched across his broad chest. "How come I haven't seen you before?" he asked.

"You saw me just the other day," I said, hoping he remembered our encounter on Lamar Boulevard. Then I thought, *How embarrassing if he doesn't!*

"In the car. I know."

Whew.

"But I thought I knew everyone in Texas." Everyone in Texas? How many were there? I wondered. He walked forward and leaned on the counter across from me, his gold eyes locking on me. His accent was strange, almost clipped—definitely not from Texas—and he smelled spicy, with a strong undertone of something intoxicating. *Yum.* I took a deep breath. I'd never smelled anything quite like it before—it was wild and foresty, somehow. Almost savage. And whatever it was made my body respond in the most primal way. A disturbingly primal way.

Stupid werewolf genes.

I took a step back from the counter, hoping I didn't look like I felt—a dog in heat.

"Are you new here?" he asked.

I crossed my arms and attempted to look cool and collected. What was I thinking, to ask him questions? I had no idea who he was or who he was affiliated with. Or what he might do to me if he found out I wasn't full-blooded. A shiver crept down my spine; this time tinged slightly with fear. "I don't know what you're talking about," I said, sneaking another glance at him. Where was he from? Was he part of a pack? I almost asked him before I remembered I wasn't going to ask anything. Instead I said, "Can I help you with something?"

He held my eyes for a long moment, studying me, then pushed back from the counter. "No, I definitely would have noticed you. So you must be new."

"I'm not," I said, almost involuntarily. "New, I mean."

His eyes roamed me. "What pack are you with?"

Pack? "I don't know what you're talking about," I said primly, trying my best to sound like Julie Andrews in *Mary Poppins*. Which is hard to do if you're not British. And if you're having a conversation with a werewolf for the first time in your entire life and are dying to know more but terrified to ask and thinking about how he would look without his T-shirt. Which you shouldn't be, because you have a perfectly good human boyfriend who is gorgeous and loves you.

"No?" he said, staring at me. "No, I guess you don't," he said slowly. "How unusual. No one's approached you?"

I shook my head.

"Incredible." His eyes . . . well, they glittered. There was no other word for it. "So they really don't know you're here."

"No," I said, before I realized what I was saying. I had never told anyone—*anyone*—what I was, and here I was having a discussion about it—a cryptic one, certainly, but a discussion nevertheless—with a strange werewolf. "Who're *they*?" I asked. *And how do they feel about half-blooded werewolves?*

"The Texas packs, of course."

I straightened my back. If they had the same opinion of half-blooded werewolves as my father's pack had, then denial was the best course. Even though it was probably fruitless; we both knew he knew what I was. But I hadn't admitted it, so that was something. Maybe. "I really don't know what you're talking about," I said briskly. Yeah, right. But what was I supposed to say? I found myself staring at his gold eyes again. My mom was right—they were thoroughly drown-in-able, those werewolf eyes. I shook myself slightly and looked down at his hands. Large, with little golden hairs on them. Strong. What would it be like to feel them . . . ?

Don't go there. I looked up, focusing on a curly pentagram on the wall behind his left ear, and said, "If you need something, I'll get my . . . the store owner." I'd almost said *my mother*.

"You know what I need," he said quietly, and there was such suggestion in his tone that I blushed. I allowed myself another quick glance—after all, how often do you encounter a full-blooded werewolf? (Thankfully, not very.) And even though it was abbreviated, it was a good glance. His body was wiry and muscular, as if he worked out regularly—or took long lopes around the countryside, which was more likely. Longish blond hair, a strong, chiseled chin, and of course, those wide-set gold eyes. If his eyes had been blue, he would have been a shoo-in for the lead in a Wagner opera. Provided he could sing, of course.

He was, in other words, total eye candy. And, I reasoned, as long as he remained eye candy and nothing else, what was the harm in looking? And there was no denying that he had a Scandinavian vibe going. He smiled—a slow, seductive smile—and I saw that his teeth were sharp and white. The kind of teeth you can imagine grazing your earlobe. Or other things . . .

I shook myself. There was no way I was going to ride—or lope—off into the sunset with a werewolf. And the longer I stood here, the more tempted I would be to ask revealing questions. So there was no sense prolonging things. "I'll go get the shop owner," I said, pushing through the door into the kitchen . . . where my mom stood looking as if a Publishers Clearing House crew had just come to her door. "So?" she said.

"Mom . . ."

"How did it go?" she asked brightly.

Awfully. Terrifyingly. Lustfully. I took a deep breath and said, as calmly as possible, "You were mistaken. It's you he needs, not me."

Her eyes twinkled as she said, "I wouldn't be so sure of that." But she headed to the front anyway.

"What was that all about?" Lindsey asked when she'd left.

"Nothing," I said breezily. Sort of breezily, anyway.

"Well, if 'nothing' leaves you looking like that," she said, "I'd better go find out who nothing is." She adjusted the attraction charm so that it nestled in her cleavage, and I found myself wanting to grab her and hold her back. I had a very bad feeling about this. "Do I look okay?"

"Really, it's nothing," I said as she walked past me toward the front of the store. "My mom's got it under control."

"I won't be long," she said.

And then she was gone.

To seduce a werewolf.

Which was more than a little bit worrying, particularly because she was my best friend. What if he was one of those woman-eating werewolves I'd read about in *Werewolves in Lore and Legend*? What if he carried her away to maul her? Or, I thought, with an unpleasant twinge of jealousy . . . to molest her? Lindsey was, after all, gorgeous by any definition. And she was wearing an attraction charm, to boot.

I sank down into the nearest chair and picked up a stack of papers. As I blindly leafed through the rest of my mother's spells and strained my ears to make out the conversation in the front of the store, I kept going over the same disturbing thoughts.

Such as *What if he likes Lindsey?* (Of course, I knew *she'd* like *him*. I mean, what's not to like? As long as you don't know he's a werewolf, that is.)

Followed, naturally, by *What if my best friend starts dating a werewolf?*

And the most disturbing thought of all: *How long will I be able to keep my hairy little secret under wraps?*

"So I gave him my number," Lindsey said as I drove her to her apartment a half hour later. My mother refused, of course, to tell me what spell she'd cast and gave me a halfhearted assurance that she'd lift it as soon as she had the time. Lindsey had spent at least twenty minutes conversing with the werewolf in the front of the store, and I was just now getting the juicy details.

I almost veered into the median. "You *what*?"

"I gave him my number. And he gave me his."

I took a deep breath.

"Is something wrong? I thought you weren't interested."

I struggled to focus on the road. "Are you sure he's . . . well, your type?"

"What do you mean? You know I love those tall, Viking men. And with that hair . . . he can pillage me anytime." She nudged me. "Maybe we should get *you* one of those attraction charms."

"I have a boyfriend," I said primly. "Besides, my mom already did an attraction spell on me, remember?" Although I was guessing it was the wolfsbane, not the woo-woo spell, that had drawn Mr. Werewolf into the store.

"Yeah," Lindsey said as we headed up South Congress toward downtown. "She does seem to want you to hook up with someone other than Heath." What she didn't know was that my mom's criteria for a suitable boyfriend involved full-moon transformations and a taste for rare meat.

Criteria that fit the guy Lindsey had just traded numbers with.

As we approached Lady Bird Lake, the wind buffeted Lindsey through the gaping window, bringing with it a swirl of night smells—exhaust, rotting vegetation, and the faint aroma of honeysuckle. I sniffed; the werewolf—I suddenly realized I didn't know his name—was long gone.

"Did you catch his name?" I asked.

"Whose name? The guy in the store?"

"Yeah."

"Tom," she breathed.

Tom. Hmmm.

"Tempting Tom," she said. "Those arms . . . and did you see him when he turned around?"

"I guess he wasn't too bad," I admitted.

Lindsey turned to me in disbelief. "He wasn't too bad? Jesus, Sophie. That guy was *hot*. Maybe you *do* need glasses."

I shrugged.

Lindsey gazed out the missing window at the lights of downtown. "You know, I can't put my finger on it, but something about him seemed . . . different, somehow."

"Different?" That was one word for it.

"I can't quite pin it down, but yes. Something . . . dangerous, almost. And did you see his teeth?"

Yes, I'd seen his teeth. The bigger ones topped out at half an inch long, so they were kind of hard to miss. My own teeth were a bit on the long and sharp side, particularly my canines (of course), but maybe because I was half human, they weren't big enough to draw anyone's attention. Except my dentist's, who always teased me and called me his vampire client.

If he only knew.

"They were all pointy," Lindsey continued. "Almost like little fangs." She thought about it for a moment. "Do you think he files them?"

God, couldn't we talk about something else? *Anything* else? "How's the Southeast Airlines account stuff going?" I said as we turned onto 7th Street.

"Oh, fine," she said. Then she was back to her favorite subject. "You know, normally, I'd think the teeth were weird, but on him . . . it was kind of sexy. It just seemed to fit him, somehow."

Maybe it's because he's a fricking werewolf. "Mmm," I said noncommittally, and then attempted to change the subject again. Out loud, anyway; my mind was racing with werewolfy thoughts. I had been pretty good about avoiding questions. And I hadn't jumped him, even though the thought had more than crossed my mind. But I was still dying of curiosity. I was sure he knew all kinds of things about werewolves and packs—and maybe even better ways of avoiding transformation. Ways I wanted to know about.

And I was also suffering from a level of lust I'd never before experienced. Which meant I was doing a lot of wondering about what lay beneath that tattered black T-shirt. And those jeans . . .

I shook myself. Time for a cold shower. And, I reminded myself, a subject change. Particularly since Lindsey had staked Tom for her own, so to speak. Not, of course, that I wanted him. "Tonight was weird, wasn't it?" I said. "The whole Brewster thing. Honestly, I'm not sure the séance did anything, but at least we found the librarian's name. What do you say we go visit her during lunch tomorrow?"

"Do you think we should go to Uchi?" she asked. "I love sushi, but not everyone does."

"I was thinking we'd just grab a sandwich," I said.

"Not for you and me," she said. "I was talking about Tom."

Crap. There was no prying her away from her Viking werewolf. "For a first date? I think Sullivan's or Fleming's would be a better bet," I said with just a tiny stab of jealousy. And a big stab of misgiving. Still, why shouldn't Lindsey date Tom? *But he's a werewolf*, my conscience interjected. *What's she going to do when she finds out what happens during a full moon?*

I reminded my conscience that I too was a werewolf—and that I was dating a human. A human who was starting to talk engagement rings, in fact, and still didn't know that my "time of the month" required something a lot stronger than Midol.

Besides, whatever my reservations, I couldn't prevent Lindsey and Tom from going out on a date. And if they did, sushi just wasn't going to cut it. "He looks like the kind of guy who would go for a nice, juicy steak," I said helpfully.

"You think?"

I attempted to smile, but I'm afraid it came out more like a grimace. "Trust me," I said. "I just have a feeling."

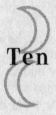

Ten

I don't know if it was Lindsey's plan to tango with Siegfried the Viking Werewolf, the prospect of visiting my mother in jail for the next twenty years, or the fact that after more than twenty years of keeping it under wraps, the whole werewolf thing seemed to be blowing up in my face, but after thirty minutes of prowling around my apartment, I realized there was no way I was going to sleep anytime soon.

I was brewing up another cup of wolfsbane tea and about to tackle some of the case histories for the Southeast Airlines account—if I was going to be awake, I figured, I might as well be productive—when the phone rang. It was Heath. Which was a welcome distraction.

"What are you up to?" he asked.

I sighed. "Working, unfortunately."

"That busy?"

"I've got that big pitch meeting coming up for Southeast Airlines. But the truth is, I'm having a hard time sleeping," I said, leaning back in my chair and closing my eyes.

"Want some company?" he asked, his voice slightly husky. "I've been thinking about you all day."

I felt a little tingle pass through me. "Your place or mine?"

"I'll be right over," he said.

I closed up my laptop with relief, and when Heath knocked on the door twenty minutes later, holding a single red rose—God, he was romantic—I jumped him.

The smell of him was an instant aphrodisiac. The rose tumbled to the floor as Heath kicked the door shut with his foot. "I've been thinking about you all day," he murmured, tugging at my blouse.

I moaned in anticipation, running my hands over his flat abdomen.

"God, I've missed you," he breathed into my ear.

I would have answered, but my mouth was otherwise occupied. He fumbled with the buttons on my blouse, and a moment later, the fabric slid away, revealing the ivory lace demi-bra I'd slipped into for the occasion. A moment later, his hands traced down my back, unzipping my skirt and letting it fall to the floor.

"Very impressive," he murmured.

"Thanks," I said, nibbling on his earlobe. "I've been doing lots of crunches."

"Well, that too," he said. "But I was talking about the matching underwear."

"Laundry day yesterday," I whispered.

"Ah." He reached around to fumble for the clasp of my bra. "That explains it. But I prefer you au naturel," he said, and proceeded to tear my coordinated underwear off and toss it into the nearest corner.

So much for laundry.

Now that I was no longer encased in Victoria's Secret stretch lace, he dipped his head from my mouth to my naked breasts, his slightly bristly chin brushing against my sensitive skin. I gasped and closed my eyes as his mouth covered first one nipple, then the other, before tracing a line down my abdomen.

When I thought I couldn't stand it anymore, he lifted me and carried me to the bed, laying me down across the sheets and plunging his hot tongue deep inside me. Wave after wave of heat shuddered through me, and I was on the brink of melting into one heck of an orgasm.

And then he stopped.

My eyes snapped open. "I was so close! Why did you stop? What are you doing?"

"Adjusting the clothing imbalance," he said, unbuckling his belt.

"Now?"

He smiled, a lazy smile that made me want to grab him and climb on top of him. But a moment later, his long, tan body now unencumbered by his Brooks Brothers suit, he grabbed my legs with his warm hands and resumed what he had started.

I was on the brink for the second time when he pulled away.

"No!" I cried.

"Yes," he said, and then he thrust into me.

"Yes," I whimpered. "Yes, yes, yes." And for one blissful moment, all of my worries dissolved into the heat between us.

We were sprawled across the bed, with Heath stroking my hair, when he said, "I'm really looking forward to our anniversary."

Oh, yeah. Our anniversary. The one that took place during a full moon. On the equinox, no less. "I wanted to talk to you about that," I said. "Is there any way we can postpone it a few days? Maybe until the weekend? It's a big day, and I want to be able to really enjoy it." *And be human for it*, I thought but didn't add.

"I've already got it all planned out," he said, smoothing my hair back. "You're not wriggling out of it."

"It's not that I'm not excited," I said as his fingers worried at a slight tangle. "It's just that on a weekend, I wouldn't have to worry about . . ." *About turning into a werewolf?* "About work the next day," I finished.

"I promise I'll get you to the office on time," he said. "It's our anniversary. It's an important day," he said, brushing my cheek with his lips. "I've been planning it for months. You know, I need to get you up to Connecticut to meet my parents sometime soon," he said as I shifted uncomfortably beneath him. "They'll love you. I just know it."

Yeah, I thought. *Right up until they find out I'm a werewolf, anyway.* "Sure," I said halfheartedly, thinking, *Thank God they live in Connecticut.*

"But your mother's right here in town," Heath continued. "When are you going to introduce me?"

I felt my body stiffen. "My mom?"

"Yes," he said, leaning over me and tracing my lips with his finger. "We're getting pretty serious here. At least I think we are."

"Oh, yes," I blurted in response to the question in his voice. "Of course. I think so too. I mean, that we're getting serious."

"Then what's the problem? Are you worried she won't like me?" His lips grazed my earlobe, and he growled, "I promise I'll be on my best behavior. At least until bedtime."

I swallowed. "Oh, no. It's not that. It's just . . . she . . . well, she travels a lot." I didn't mention it was to and from the courthouse. And the jail. "You know, I'd better go put that rose in some water," I said, leaping up from the bed.

Heath propped himself up on one elbow, watching me with those chocolate eyes. "Surely she's in town some of the time," he said. "After all, she's got a store here, doesn't she?"

"She's got an assistant who helps with that," I said as I filled a vase with water.

"Are you sure there's not some other reason you haven't introduced us yet?" he asked.

Was I that transparent? I swallowed. "To be honest, my mother's . . ." I trailed off. How exactly to put it? A psychic witch who had recently been arrested for homicide?

"Your mother's what?" Heath prompted me.

"Well, she's kind of . . . an acquired taste," I said. "She's a little unusual."

"What's so unusual about her? Outside of the fact that she has a gorgeous, smart, accomplished daughter I can't help but want to ravish?" He looked at me with more than a little bit of lust in his eyes.

Instead of answering, I slid the vase onto the kitchen table and hurried back to the bed, where for the next half hour, our communication was—thankfully—of the nonverbal variety.

Later that night, though, as I snuggled into the crook of Heath's arm, I found myself lying awake and worrying about my mother meeting him. How long would I be able to put off the inevitable?

And would the inevitable be taking place in a state penitentiary, with my mother dressed in inmate orange?

I could feel myself getting all tense again, so I tried thinking of something else. The problem was, the first thing that came to mind was Tom the werewolf. I thought of his long blond hair, his chiseled face. The way he had looked in his jeans the other day as he'd crossed Lamar.

I was still feeling unsettled by the visceral reaction I'd had to him. Okay, the lustful reaction. As sexy as Heath was, there was something about Tom that really stirred me up. I guess it was because he appealed to my animal nature, so to speak.

Until now, I'd never even considered that I could find a werewolf attractive, much less drop-dead sexy. I mean, the drawings of werewolves in books weren't exactly Harlequin cover material—unless you had a thing for hairy men with tails, some of whom had body parts dangling from their mouths. And the only other male werewolf I'd seen—the drunk one who'd smelled like unwashed dog—had been less than toothsome, if you know what I mean.

But Tom was unlike anything—or anyone—I'd ever encountered.

Which meant the books were wrong.

In fact, I was finally realizing that books were wrong about a lot of things. I'd just never thought about it. In everything I'd read, people lost all sense of themselves when they transformed into their furry alter egos. But when I was a wolf, I was still me—it wasn't as if all of my rational thought had been flushed down the toilet. My senses were heightened, of course, and it became tough to tango (which, come to think of it, wasn't much different from the way it was when I was in human form), but I was still very much *me*.

As I lay in Heath's arms, the whole world seemed to rearrange itself around me. I'd spent most of my life be-lieving everything I'd read about werewolves. That they were bloodthirsty, thoughtless, and somewhat repulsive. Somehow I'd managed to overlook the fact that I too was a werewolf. And I liked to think that none of those adjectives applied to me.

Could it be that I was wrong about werewolves in general? I mean, I knew what my mother had said about them, and I knew my father had abandoned me, pre-sumably so the Paris pack wouldn't be dining on Sophie tartare.

But the truth was, I really didn't know anything about werewolves. And the one I had met today was anything but repulsive.

I inched even closer to Heath, trying not to think about Tom. Whether I found him attractive was irrelevant, I told myself. I was here with Heath.

But ill-advised lust wasn't my only problem.

My days of anonymity were gone; not only was someone leaving little packages of wolfsbane at my office but also a full-blooded werewolf was now aware of me. And I had no idea how he felt about a half-blood werewolf living incognito in Austin. As I lay there on my 300-thread-count sateen sheets, I wondered what I would do if a group of werewolves carrying stakes showed up outside the door of my loft. Maybe I could convince them to give me some kind of homestead exemption or something. Or maybe offer free tax work in exchange for immunity?

And in the meantime, Lindsey was taking Tom out to tango. I knew he wasn't repulsive—in fact, he was anything but—but I had no idea whether he was bloodthirsty. He hadn't looked it—or acted it—but what did I know? It was enough to give me nightmares.

At what point, I wondered, was it my responsibility to warn my friend that her dance partner was actually a supernatural creature?

And would she believe me? Never mind the fact that I was her best friend and that I hadn't broken it to her that I was a werewolf too.

I rolled over, trying to banish all disturbing thoughts, and finally drifted off into a restless sleep involving Tom the werewolf, a Nordstrom dressing room, and—inexplicably—the University of Texas marching band.

Really. You don't want to know.

* * *

I swung by Lindsey's office at 11:30 the next morning, feeling like I hadn't slept more than two hours the night before—which could be because I hadn't. Lindsey was bent over her computer, staring intently at the monitor. I hoped that meant she was out of vixen mode and back into CPA mode. The last thing I needed right now was more mooning about Siegfried the Viking Werewolf.

"Ready?" I said brightly, thanks to the four cups of coffee I'd had that morning. It was time for our trip to visit Jennifer the librarian.

"Shoot. Is it that late already?" She glanced at her watch. "Do you want to eat first or go to the library? Whatever we do, I need to get back by one."

"I'm not that hungry; let's hit the library first and grab a sandwich on the way back to the office."

As we stepped into the elevator, my cell phone rang.

"Hey, Sophie sweets." It was Heath.

A pleasurable little tingle coursed through me. *Take that, Mr. Werewolf!* "Hi, Heath," I said in my sexiest voice.

"I called your office, but I must have just missed you."

"Well, I'm here now. What's up?"

"I was calling to tell you to be ready at six-thirty tonight."

"What's at six-thirty?"

"Our reservations at Fleming's."

"Sounds great. But shouldn't we save it for our anniversary?" I said, and immediately wished I hadn't. You know, the whole full-moon-equinox thing.

"I just can't wait that long," he said in a low, gravelly voice that sent another tingle shooting through me. "So six-thirty it is. Actually, the reservations are for seven, but I thought we'd get a drink first."

"How about I meet you there?" I asked. Fleming's was within walking distance of my office—and that way I could work a little longer. I wouldn't have a chance to change, but I was wearing a black suit that would be just fine.

"Are you sure you don't want me to pick you up?" he asked.

"No, that's fine. I'll meet you there. I need the exercise, anyway."

"You'll get plenty of that later on," he rumbled, and I laughed.

"What's the occasion?" Lindsey asked as I tucked the phone into my purse and we stepped into the building's lobby.

"Dinner date at Fleming's," I told her.

"Oooh. Maybe we'll have to all do that together sometime."

"Who?"

"You, Heath, Tom, and me."

I stumbled, and Lindsey caught my elbow.

"Are you okay?" Lindsey asked.

"Fine," I said, clutching my Kate Spade purse. "Just fine."

Eleven

Brewster's librarian turned out to be a tall, willowy redhead in a clingy skirt and low-cut top that made it easy to see why Brewster had been interested. It was also easy to see why he'd sprung for a love potion; Brewster had been old enough to be her grandfather.

"Can I help you?" she asked, looking perplexed at having been called to the front desk to meet with us.

"Do you have a few minutes?" I asked. When she nodded, Lindsey and I guided her to a secluded table in the corner. She smelled nice, like lilies of the valley, talcum powder, and . . . rabbits? Yes. Definitely rabbits. My nose twitched.

"I was hoping we could ask you a few questions about Ted Brewster," I said as we settled into ancient brown vinyl chairs. *Don't think about rabbits, Sophie.* Tom's gold eyes floated into my mind. *Or that, either. Hello! Your mom's been charged with murder, remember?*

As I marshaled my thoughts—or did the best I could, under the circumstances—Jennifer tapped her pink-painted nails on the chipped laminate table. "Ted Brewster?" she asked, a little wrinkle appearing in her lightly freckled brow. She looked like a *Seventeen* cover model—all fresh and springy. I couldn't help wondering if Ted Brewster had some repressed pedophile tendencies.

"He was a big guy," I said, holding my arms out to demonstrate girth.

"Balding," Lindsey added. "Kind of looked like a big, fat gnome?"

"Oh yeah," she said, her hazel eyes lighting up. "I know who you're talking about. The councilman, right? The one with the alligator boots. He's in here all the time."

"Was, actually," Lindsey said.

Jennifer scrunched up her lips like she was puckering for a lipstick ad. "Was?"

"He's dead," I told her. *Definitely rabbits*, I thought, inhaling again. *Two of them.*

Jennifer raised a pale hand to her throat. Her fingernails were perfectly shaped—I wondered where she had her manicures done. And her skirt was gorgeous too—from the new DKNY collection, if I wasn't mistaken. For a librarian, she seemed to be doing pretty well for herself. "Dead?" she breathed. "Oh, my God. I had no idea . . . I'm so sorry."

"It's okay," Lindsey said. "It wasn't like he was my uncle or anything. We just wondered if we could ask you a few questions. We're investigating his death."

My eyebrows shot up, and I gave Lindsey a warning glance. What if Jennifer asked who we were? We weren't exactly the police—or even licensed investigators.

Of course, Lindsey ignored me.

And fortunately, Jennifer wasn't the type to ask for credentials. "Sure," she said. "Although I don't know how much help I'll be."

"So I take it you didn't know him very well," Lindsey said.

"Not really," she said. "But he did like to ask me questions a lot."

"Questions?" I prompted.

"Research stuff. You know, how to find things on LexisNexis, and all that." She shrugged her slender shoulders and tugged at the hem of her skirt, which clung to her curvy hips like glue. "Weird stuff, really. Like about frogs and salamanders. All this endangered species stuff."

Strange. What would a pro-development politician be doing checking out endangered species? Unless he was trying to find the most efficient way to get rid of them.

"He always asked for me, for some reason," Jennifer added.

Gee, I couldn't think why.

"He was pretty cute, I guess," she continued. "In a teddy-bear kind of way."

Lindsey and I exchanged glances. Ted Brewster? Cute?

I guess if you had a thing for teddy bears with no hair and a gigantic spare tire, I could see it. Still. Maybe he *had* given her the love potion.

"Did he ever bring you anything?" Lindsey asked.

Jennifer tapped her nails again. "Bring me anything? Like what?"

"I don't know," I said. "Coffee or something? A drink?" I knew that for a love potion to work, both people have to take it. I'd heard my mother counsel many of her besotted clients over the years. Generally, she told them to give the potion to the object of their affection first, then to follow up with several self-administered doses—up to ten or so, which always seemed excessive to me—until the potion seemed to take effect. If it didn't work, she said, usually it was because the intended didn't get the full dose.

Now, I'll be the first to admit that my mother is gifted in the magic department, but the whole love spell thing had always seemed kind of suspect to me. On the other hand, I couldn't deny the fact that a werewolf had shown up at Sit A Spell not long after my mother cast a spell involving rose quartz and wolfsbane . . .

"No, he didn't buy me a coffee," Jennifer said, shaking her head. Then she stopped. "Wait. He brought me one of those Green Tea Frappuccinos last week—said he had a buy one, get one free card." She wrinkled her nose. "Must be a new flavor—it tasted kind of flowery. I drank some of it, but . . ."

"How much did you drink?" I asked.

"I don't know. Maybe half?"

"And you felt okay afterward?" Lindsey asked, leaning forward in her chair.

"Yeah . . ." Jennifer's eyes narrowed suspiciously. "Why do you want to know?"

"We think . . . well, we could be wrong, but we think Ted Brewster really liked you," Lindsey said.

"So?"

"We think he liked you so much that he tried to give you something to make you like him back," I said.

"You think? Gosh. Really?" Then she realized the full implications of what we had just told her. "Wait a second. You mean . . . he tried to drug me?"

Lindsey patted her hand. "We don't know for sure . . . but we do know he bought a love potion with you in mind."

She raised her hand to her throat. "Oh, my God. A love potion? Freaky!"

"Evidently it didn't work," I mumbled to Lindsey.

"It certainly didn't have the effect it did on Brewster," she replied.

"Good thing too."

Jennifer perked up a little bit at this exchange. "What do you mean? How *did* he die?"

"Should we tell her?" I said to Lindsey.

"I can't think why not."

I bit my lip. "Well, according to the papers . . . he was poisoned."

Jennifer gasped. "Poisoned? Oh my God . . ." Her hazel eyes widened. "You don't think . . . the Frappuccino . . ."

"Probably not," I said. "Because whatever he drank dropped him on the spot. You didn't feel sick or anything, did you?"

Jennifer shook her head.

"And he was a good bit bigger than you," Lindsey added. "By an order of magnitude, really."

"Is there a Starbucks near here?" I asked Jennifer.

"Why?" Lindsey and Jennifer asked simultaneously.

"I just want to do an experiment. See if the drink was doctored."

"There's one a block away," she said.

"Can you get away for a few minutes? I'll spot you another free Frappuccino."

"Let me check," she said. When she came back with the go-ahead, the three of us trooped over to coffee mecca. A blast of coffee-flavored air hit me as we opened the swinging door, knocking out just about every other scent—including Jennifer's distracting rabbity odor.

Five minutes later, as I sipped my skinny extra-foam latte and Lindsey munched on a piece of lemon pound cake, Jennifer took a tentative sip of a Blackberry Green Tea Frappuccino. She'd ordered the largest size, of course.

"How does it taste?" I asked eagerly.

She swished it around in her mouth and nodded.

"What does that mean?" Lindsey asked.

"Is it the same drink?"

Jennifer swallowed and squinted at the cup. "How many calories do you think are in this?"

Who knew? Who cared? "Same drink?" I prompted.

She took another sip, then shook her head. "Nope."

I looked at Lindsey. "See?"

"See what?" she asked through a mouthful of crumbs.

"The potion. It wasn't poisoned when it left my mom's shop. If it had been, she'd have been affected too."

"Your mom's shop?" Jennifer said. "Cool. Your mom owns a Starbucks?"

Lindsey ignored her. "We're assuming he put the potion in her drink. But there's no way to know."

"She said it tasted different today than it did the day he bought her one," I reminded her. "I'm guessing it's because he doctored it."

Lindsey turned to Jennifer. "How do you feel about Ted Brewster?"

Jennifer took another long sip and blinked. "I thought you said he was dead."

"Okay, okay," Lindsey said. "How *did* you feel about him?"

She shrugged her narrow shoulders. "He wasn't too bad, I guess. It wasn't like I wanted to marry him or anything. But he was kind of cute. It's a shame he died."

I raised an eyebrow at Lindsey. "Kind of cute. See?"

"Not exactly conclusive," she said.

"We're talking about Ted Brewster here. Remember? Bald, obese? It's not like he was Hugh Grant."

"True."

I turned to Jennifer. "When did he bring you the Frappuccino?"

"I think it was last Monday. Wait, no . . . last Tuesday."

"And according to my mother, he bought the potion Monday," I said. "So the timing lines up. And if Jennifer here didn't get sick after drinking it, then it must not have been poisoned when it came from the shop."

"It's something, I suppose," Lindsey said, licking the last of the lemon frosting off her fingers. "You didn't save the drink, did you?" she asked, looking at Jennifer.

Jennifer looked at her as if she were nuts and took another sip of her gigantic green drink.

Oh, well.

After dropping Jennifer and her venti Frappuccino back at the library, we headed to Subway in Lindsey's Miata. Since the M3 still had a gaping hole instead of a window, we'd decided to take her car. As we cruised through the city with the top down, a cocktail of late-summer smells swirled through the car: sycamore trees, the ducks on Lady Bird Lake, the exhaust of a diesel truck. And the vagrants on 6th Street.

Ick.

"Can we put the top up?" I asked.

"Why?"

"It reeks."

"You and your nose," she said, pushing the button to raise the top. "Sometimes I think you're part bloodhound."

Not exactly—but she wasn't far off either. "So we know the potion wasn't poisoned when it left my mom's shop," I said as we headed toward the sandwich shop.

"We still don't know he put it in her drink."

"Come on," I said. "She said Brewster was cute. What more proof do you need?"

"Saying someone's cute isn't quite the same as falling passionately in love with him," she said. "But she did say the Frappuccino tasted different."

"So the next thing we have to find out is who *did* put the poison in it."

"You know, I think you might just give Sherlock Holmes a run for his money."

I stuck my tongue out at her. "Okay, Nancy Drew. Any suggestions?"

Lindsey turned to me, her gray eyes glinting. "What do you say we pay a visit to Brewster's campaign manager? To find out who to write checks to now that the late councilman's no longer an option."

"You know, that's not a bad idea," I said. "Maybe we can find out some more about his personal life too."

"Maybe even nose around his office."

I shifted in my seat and checked my legs. What was with all the dog metaphors? Had I forgotten to shave or something? I peered at Lindsey. Was it possible . . . had *Lindsey* sent me the wolfsbane?

I dismissed the thought immediately. Lindsey didn't know. How could she? Besides, even if she did, she wouldn't try to blackmail me.

Right?

I shook off my suspicions and said, "Let's hope Brewster's campaign manager is a guy. That way you can distract him, and I'll snoop around."

"Sounds good to me."

"When we get back to the office, I'll call and set up an appointment. How about lunch tomorrow?"

"I'll pull out my best Junior League suit," she said.

I laughed. "Let me find out if it's a man or a woman first. We'll adjust your hemline to fit."

"I don't remember Nancy Drew seducing any of her suspects."

"Think of yourself as Nancy all grown up."

"Gosh," Lindsey said, examining her dark hair in the rearview mirror. "Do you think I should go strawberry blond?"

"Maybe you should ask Tom," I said. And immediately wished I hadn't. Partially because it had been nice not thinking about werewolves for a few hours—even if instead, we were thinking about my mother's impending murder trial. And partially because now I was going to hear all about Lindsey's infatuation with a sexy but potentially dangerous supernatural creature. On whom I unfortunately seemed to have a little crush.

"Mmm. He is something, isn't he?"

He was something, all right. Lindsey just didn't know exactly what that something was. "Have you talked with him since you met at the store?" I asked.

She glanced over at me. "Why?'

"Just curious," I said, trying to sound nonchalant.

"He called me last night, and we set up a date. Oh, and he asked about you," she said.

I could feel my ears prick up. "Oh?"

"Wanted to know how long you'd lived in Austin. I told him you'd grown up here."

I swallowed hard. "Really."

"For some reason, he seemed surprised he hadn't run into you before."

"I can't think why that is," I said, trying to slow my heart rate, which felt like it was approaching the high 200s. "So when are you going out?" I asked, trying to change the subject.

"Tonight, actually," she said.

My stomach tightened. "He doesn't waste any time, does he?"

"I just can't decide what to wear," she said. "Maybe I'll slip out early and head to Nordstrom."

I stifled a sigh. A pre-date Nordstrom trip meant that she was more than a little bit interested. Not that I could blame her. "Well, let me know how it goes," I said, even though I wasn't sure I wanted to know. "And be careful," I said. "You don't know anything about him. For all we know, he could be dangerous," I warned. "You might want to bring your pepper spray, just in case."

"Don't worry," she said, looking like a cat with a saucerful of cream. "You know me. *Careful* is my middle name."

That was *not* a comfort.

Twelve

By the time I turned my computer off at quarter after six, I was feeling a bit better about things. I'm not saying things were rosy—I still had a drug test coming up, my mother was still on the hook for murder charges, and my best friend was about to start dating a werewolf—but at least I had the Southeast Airlines account under control and I had a dinner date at Fleming's.

The sun was a hot orange ball dipping toward the horizon as I stepped onto the sidewalk a few minutes later, and the residual chill from Withers and Young dissipated quickly as I turned left and headed down 6th Street toward Fleming's. My mouth was already watering at the thought of steak. Okay, not just the steak. I loved a good cut of rare beef, but I'll admit that tonight I was more interested in the postprandial activities Heath had planned—and I don't mean coffee and crème brûlée. I did a quick mental review, hoping I hadn't put on my granny briefs that morning.

After a surreptitious check—bikinis, not briefs—I breathed in deeply, inhaling the mixed odors of downtown, which had already undergone its evening transformation from men in slacks to women in spandex. The reek of a few unwashed bodies still punctuated the humid air, along with the occasional bouquet of baked Dumpster, but I loved the mixed smells of a crowd of people. Especially the crowd on 6th Street at night, which was spiced with a good dash of sexual heat.

I took a deep sniff, trying to sort out the odors, and picked up a few vampires by their coppery, cold scent—which was only to be expected, since I was less than a block from the Drain, Austin's only vampire bar. Of course, most of Austin didn't know that. Like me, the vampire population liked to fly below the radar. Which must be hard when you have to bite people for a living. I took another sniff, doing another olfactory reconnaissance. No werewolves.

No Tom.

As I crossed 6th Street to avoid the vampire hangout—I knew about them, but as far as I knew, they didn't know about me—my mind drifted back to the werewolf I'd met at Sit A Spell, and that maddening scent of his. Were he and Lindsey really going to start dating? Or did he view her as an attractive midnight snack? Tom had made a reference to packs, but I didn't know whether he belonged to one. And how did American packs feel about werewolves dating humans? Had the past twenty-odd years brought civil rights to the werewolf world? After all, this was America, the big melting pot. Did the whole interracial acceptance thing extend to were-wolves?

As I passed the Chuggin' Monkey, which was already filling up with college students carrying fake IDs and swigging shots of 100-proof Kool-Aid, I ran through what little I knew about werewolf activity in Texas. I was pretty sure there were packs in the big cities—I'd caught whiffs of werewolf groups from time to time on business trips to Dallas and Houston. Despite my curiosity, though, I'd kept my distance. I doubted a were-wolf confrontation would do much to impress my clients. And besides, as far as the world of werewolves was concerned, I firmly believed that the longer they stayed ignorant of me, the higher the odds that I would remain blissful. Or at least alive. But somehow—I'm not sure exactly how—I'd always managed to stay out of range. And since no one had shown up on my doorstep asking if I wanted a pack membership card—or a wooden stake through the heart—I figured my secret was safe.

Now, however, someone was sending me wolfsbane care packages, which meant at least one person—well, presumably a person, but you never knew—had figured it out. One thing I was clear about, though. Whoever it was didn't have my best interests at heart.

I thought about Tom's gold eyes, the way they ate me

up, as if he was seeing deep inside my soul—either that or stripping me down mentally. I suppressed a little shiver. Tom knew about me too. Would he let the cat— or in this case, the wolf—out of the bag?

I let the air hiss out from between my teeth. After twenty-eight years of keeping my big hairy secret under wraps, suddenly my double life was at risk of being exposed. For the first time I could remember, I was wishing my father had stuck around long enough to give me some pointers on werewolf etiquette. Not that I had any desire to join the werewolf world. I mean, who wanted to be with a bunch of freaks who liked to chase people around for sport? At least I think they hunted people— like I said, I wasn't exactly up to speed on werewolf sports and hobbies.

No, I wasn't interested in becoming part of the fang-and-fur freak show. I just wanted to know how to stay under the radar. And if that wasn't possible, how to keep people from chasing me around town with a truck-load of wooden stakes.

I took a deep breath, trying to clear my head—and stopped short when I caught a new scent on the breeze.

Werewolves.

Jeez. What, was there a werewolf convention in town or something?

I had almost gotten a fix on it when a guy with 100-proof breath and less-than-fastidious hygiene habits plowed into me.

"Watch out, lady," he said gruffly, and proceeded to walk into a light pole.

I took a few steps away, resisting the urge to plant my pointy-toed shoe in his ample buttocks. No sense risking a leather scuff. As he grappled with the pole, I sniffed again, trying to get a read on the scent I'd picked up before Mr. Beer and Body Odor almost mowed me down.

It was weak—nothing like Tom—but it was definitely there.

But where?

A big part of me wanted to just keep walking. I was hungry, Heath was waiting for me, and I was dying for a nice big glass of Cabernet Sauvignon. And after all, if I couldn't see them, I reasoned, they couldn't see me.

But someone was threatening me. And if a werewolf was responsible, I wanted to know what I was up against.

I trotted away from my alcohol-steeped acquaintance, who was now locked in what looked to be mortal combat with a trash can, and slipped down the nearest side street. The beer breath was gone, but it had been replaced by the overpowering odor of rotting vegetables and rancid grease. I focused on the werewolf scent, trying to block out competing odors; I almost lost it for a moment, but a light breeze brought it back to me. A few minutes later, I turned a corner just in time to hear a snarl and a bitten-off scream.

I peered into a dark alley filled with three werewolves—and a well-endowed coed in a pink Tri-Delta T-shirt.

It looked like scene from a low-budget horror flick. But since there weren't any cameras around, it was a good bet that I was looking at the real thing.

As I watched, the biggest of the three—which isn't saying much, because they were all pretty puny—approached the girl, fangs bared. He had a funny tuft of hair over each eye—kind of like overgrown eyebrows. And the rest of him looked fluffy too, kind of like an overgrown Angora rabbit.

"Stop it," I said.

Fluffy whirled around, his poofy wolf eyebrows jerking up in surprise. The other two eyed me guardedly. One of them was so emaciated I had a sudden urge to throw him a couple sticks of beef jerky. The other one's fur was so matted it looked as if he was wearing wolf dreadlocks—and when a stiff breeze brought me a whiff of his pelt, I just about gagged. *Sweet Jesus.* I covered my nose with one hand and took an involuntary step backward. What, was he half skunk?

As I reeled from Stinky's personal bouquet, Fluffy recovered from his surprise. Poofing up his fur even more, he gave me another view of his yellowed fangs and took two steps toward me.

And that was when a low growl ripped out of my throat.

The biggest one froze, and the three of them—Fluffy, Scrawny, and Stinky—stared at me, ears pricked forward.

I gave Fluffy a big toothy smile of my own, fighting the urge to change—I could feel it seething under my skin. But the sorority girl was staring right at me as if I was the Wolf Whisperer, and I wasn't too keen on sprouting a fur coat in front of a human witness. It was almost too bad they hadn't managed to knock her out, really. I knew instinctively that these three mutts were no match for me—although I'm pretty sure I'd never encountered one before, it was obvious these were made, not born, wolves. Because their smell was far more human than wolf—and nothing at all like Tom, whose scent was just . . .

Stop thinking about Tom, Sophie. I mean, jeez. Here I was in a face-off with three werewolves, thinking about another guy . . .

Fortunately, another whiff of Stinky brought me back to the issue at hand.

"I want you to leave," I said, using the voice I like to use when Sally pisses me off. I was hoping it would have more of an effect on Fluffy, Stinky, and Scrawny than it did on her. "And if I ever see you again, I'll make sure you never hurt another person—ever." I looked at the cowering blonde. She *was* a Tri-Delta . . . but still.

Fluffy hesitated for another moment—I'd like to say he was thinking about it, but that might be overestimating him—and then took another step forward.

So much for the nontransformation strategy.

I was about to throw all caution to the wind—and risk ruining my Tahari suit—when a familiar scent washed over me.

When I turned around, a gigantic blond wolf stood there, smelling like the world's best cologne.

Fluffy's, Stinky's, and Scrawny's tails hit the ground faster than you could say *uncle*. Then, tails firmly between their legs—from what I could see, there wasn't much else there anyway—they slunk out of the alley in a flash.

"I had it under control, thank you very much," I muttered.

The giant wolf just stared at me a moment before ambling off after the packette.

I watched him go—even as a wolf he looked good, and no, I wasn't paying special attention to what was beneath his tail—until someone said, "Excuse me."

It was the Tri-Delta, who was climbing to her feet and brushing a stray morsel of dirt off of her pert derriere. "Am I dreaming," she said, "or did you just talk to those dogs?"

"I've just got a way with animals," I said. "Are you okay?"

"I guess," she said. "That was just so weird. What are they, like coyotes or something?"

"I don't know," I lied. "Look, why don't I walk you back to 6th Street?" I glanced at my watch—it was already past seven. "But we've got to hurry—I'm late."

"I'll be just a sec," she said, swinging her bottle blond

hair around and whipping out a compact to check her lipstick.

Jesus. What part of *late* couldn't she understand? "I'm late," I repeated.

"All right," she said grudgingly, adjusting the pads in her push-up bra.

I breathed through my mouth, then steeled myself to take a quick sniff of the air. The smell of rotten cabbage and old French fry grease was overwhelming, but I forced myself to do a quick olfactory check anyway.

Fortunately, the packette was gone—not that I couldn't have handled them, but I'd rather meet them when I didn't have a Tri-Delta in tow. I sniffed again—either I was imagining things or there was a tantalizing hint of Tom in the air.

Tom. Who looked just as good in wolf form as he did in his faded blue jeans. Suddenly all my tortured emotions about werewolves and misplaced lust and whether someone would hunt me down went out the window.

Where the hell had he come from? And did he think I couldn't handle a bunch of wolf wannabes?

I was starting to get worked up when the girl finished adjusting herself and trotted after me. "Gross," she said, brushing at the leg of her short shorts. "I got something disgusting on me."

"Better than it could have been," I said. Since I had just saved her from being mauled by a pack of scrawny werewolves who now knew of my existence—and had taken off before I could find out why they were in Austin—I wasn't feeling too concerned about her cut-offs. "So what happened?"

"I was just like, walking to the Monkey," she said in a voice so bouncy you could almost see the hearts dotting the *I*'s. "It's free Jell-O shot night, and the bartender is so-o-o-o cute. He's got, like, this tattoo of an eagle on his chest—"

"The pack," I reminded her.

"Oh, yeah. Right. Well, anyway, I was almost to Sixth Street when these coyote-looking things started following me. It was totally weird. One of them tried to bite me—can you believe it?"

Okay, maybe the books weren't entirely wrong after all. Why *had* Fluffy, Stinky, and Scrawny cornered her? Were they trying to make her a werewolf too? I'd read somewhere that a werewolf bite could turn a person into a werewolf. Which was something *I* would do well to keep in mind, I thought. Particularly during some of my late-night sessions with Heath. Maybe they just wanted to make a hot sorority werewolf to hang out with. "What did you do?"

"I just ran, you know? I mean, who wants to get bitten by a dog?" She bit her pink lip. "Do you think they had, like, rabies or something?"

"You never know," I said mildly. "Did they manage to bite you?"

"I don't think so. I mean, I would have like, felt it, right?"

I liked to think *I'd* notice if a set of fangs sank into my butt. "Probably," I said. "So what did you do when they started following you?"

"I just started running. I like, did a lot of jogging in high school. So I could eat without having to barf all the time, you know?"

As fascinating as her weight-control strategies might have been, I wanted to get back to the issue at hand. "So you ran," I prompted her.

"Yeah. I'm pretty fast—but I kept tripping on my shoes." She pointed to her platform flip-flops, which appeared to be constructed of two strips of sparkly dental floss and a couple of pounds of cork. It was amazing she'd actually remained upright. "I tripped . . ."

I could see why.

"And then they caught me in that alley." She shivered a little. "Hey, by the way, I want to say thanks. For doing, like, whatever it is you did back there. The whole growling and talking to the coyote thing. If it weren't for you, I'd be, like, dog meat or something."

"Glad I could help," I said, glancing at my watch as we stepped back into the throng on 6th Street. "Look, are you okay? I've got to go . . . I'm running late."

"Sure. The Monkey's right there."

"Do you have any friends who could walk you to your car?"

Her brown eyes got big. "Do you think they might, like, come after me again?"

"I doubt it," I said. From what I could smell, they were long gone. I sniffed again—was that Tom? And if so, where was he? "But you might want to have someone with you—just in case."

"Okay. Thanks," she said.

"No problem," I said. I followed her all the way to the Chuggin' Monkey—just to be sure—before hurrying over to Fleming's for a relaxing, romantic evening. It had to be more relaxing than a face-off with a trio of semi-werewolves. And Tom.

Where, I wondered as I hurried toward the Warehouse District, had he come from? And was he following me around?

On the plus side, I reasoned as I jaywalked across Congress Avenue, the rest of the evening would be strictly human. A nice steak, good conversation, and then . . . well, you know.

It was a good plan, anyway.

Thirteen

The smell of Fleming's—browned butter, steak, and a hint of garlic—was a delightful respite from the overripe smells of downtown in September. I was still shaken up by the encounter in the alley—I mean, after years of living a relatively werewolf-free life, suddenly I couldn't seem to walk ten feet without running into one of them. And I had no idea why they were here. Still, my mouth started watering as the door swung shut behind me, and I tried to focus on the evening ahead, leaving the werewolves, wolfsbane, and the rest of my problems far behind me.

Or not.

My hackles rose as I sniffed and scanned the room. Unless I was dreaming, Tom was still somewhere nearby. Was he lurking outside? Was he still following me?

As my eyes swept over the room a second time, I spotted Heath leaning up against the bar, looking like a *GQ* model posing as an executive businessman. Charcoal suit, tennis-tanned skin, crisp white shirt, and bleached teeth to match.

I brushed my hair back, straightened my suit jacket, and headed for the bar, already feeling a tingle of anticipation. Forget Tom; he could skulk in the alley all he wanted. Tonight was for Heath and me. I slunk up behind him, about to touch his shoulder, when I realized he was deep in conversation with a woman—a curvaceous vixen with long, dark hair and a barely there red dress. *Sheesh*. I'm fifteen minutes late and he starts chatting up women at the bar?

I put a proprietary hand on his arm—take that, vixen!—and he turned around and smiled. "Sophie! You finally made it! I was wondering if I needed to file a missing persons report."

Then the scantily clad woman beside him looked up. It was Lindsey. And beside her . . .

No. It couldn't be.

But it was. He gave me a big, knowing grin, flashing just a bit of his long, pointy canines.

I swore under my breath and contemplated an exit strategy. Like tackling him on the spot (that was my werewolf talking). Or alternately, and perhaps more wisely, running screaming from the building.

But before I could sprint for the door, Heath stood up and folded me in his arms. He smelled, as always, like laundry starch and CK One, but the aroma of Mr. Alpha trumped every other scent in the room. Even as I hugged Heath, I kept one eye on Lindsey's Viking werewolf.

Whatever else Tom was capable of, I had to give him points for pulling himself together fast. I didn't know where he'd stashed his clothes, but you'd never know that fifteen minutes earlier he'd been in full wolf regalia, menacing a bunch of straggly werewolves in an alley. And I had to admit he looked pretty good. Still in jeans, still in a T-shirt. But you couldn't help staring at him.

Or at least I couldn't.

Heath gave me a last squeeze, then released me. "I was sitting here waiting for you, and then Lindsey showed up," he said, his lips grazing my cheek. His familiar smell was strong, but not strong enough to dispel Tom's alpha-werewolf bouquet. I glanced at him apprehensively. And, yes, just a little bit lustfully.

What was he doing here? Was he following me? Was his constant presence a threat? And how did he always know where to find me?

It was worrying that I hadn't been able to pinpoint him when I walked in. Then again, I hadn't been able to trace whoever had left me the wolfsbane the other day either. Maybe it was time to revisit my antihistamine prescription.

"Sorry I'm late. I had a little difficulty getting here." I narrowed my eyes at Tom, but his grin just got bigger.

"Late meeting?" Tom asked innocently, his gold eyes glowing.

"You could call it that," I said, as coolly as possible. "I had things completely under control . . . until someone came in and tried to take over."

"Don't you hate that?" Lindsey said. "That happened the other day when I was meeting with Harvey. Every time I tried to say something, he kept cutting me off."

Tom's eyes glinted. "You never know. Maybe he was just trying to help out."

Help out? Had that been why he was there? "Or else he had his own agenda," I said, lifting my chin. "Besides, I can hold my own."

Heath looked from me to Tom. "Have you two met?"

Tom nodded. "We've run into each other before."

"Just a few minutes ago, in fact," I said.

Tom gave me another toothy smile. "I'm afraid you must be mistaken."

Mistaken?

I don't think so.

"What are you talking about?" Lindsey asked, peering at me. "I thought you said you were in a meeting."

Tom gave me a full-on view of his gleaming white teeth. *The better to eat you with, my dear . . .* "I don't think we've been properly introduced, though," he said. His voice was low and slightly rough.

I narrowed my eyes at Tom, feeling the strangest sensation—fear and a heat that pulsed through me—as he held out a giant paw.

"I'm Tom," he rumbled. "Tom Fenris."

Lindsey glanced at his hand, and then at me. I could almost hear what she was thinking. *Big hands* . . .

"Sophie Garou." I reached out to shake his hand, and almost jerked it back when our fingers touched. It was like touching a live wire. A little electric current seemed to shoot up my arm, and then down to the vicinity of my . . .

Stop it.

I grabbed Heath's arm. My boyfriend, Heath. My nice, normal, human boyfriend Heath. Who wasn't a werewolf and wasn't stalking me. *Get ahold of yourself, Sophie.*

"Shall we tell them we're all here?" Lindsey asked, touching Tom's shoulder. Staking her claim. Well, not exactly *staking* him . . . "I hope you don't mind us barging in," she said. "When you said you were going to Fleming's, I called Tom . . . and here we are!"

"I noticed," I said, glaring at Tom as Heath slipped an arm around my waist.

"I checked with the maitre d'," Heath said. "They're getting us a bigger table."

"How fun," Lindsey squealed.

"Yeah. A regular party," I said under my breath.

As I trailed after the three of them into the darkened dining room, I found myself wishing I'd joined the Tri-Delta for a few Jell-O shots. Or at least ordered a double martini at the bar. As soon as we sat down, I grabbed the wine list. Would it be bad form to order a bottle just for me?

"So," Tom said as I debated the merits of wine versus hard liquor. "Lindsey tells me you're an accountant." I glanced up at him; his eyes glowed in the candlelight. Those reflective eyes—along with a hyperactive nose and ears—were one of those werewolf features that never completely went away. (That much I knew from experience.) Even the made wolves of the packette had had them—but with nowhere near the intensity of Tom's.

I dropped my eyes to the wine list, then gave up and handed it to Heath.

Definitely hard liquor.

I looked for the waitress—I needed a martini, and I needed it now—but she had evidently fallen off the planet. "I'm an auditor," I said shortly.

Tom leaned back in his chair. "Interesting. I would have expected you to have a more . . . predatory profession."

Predatory? An image of those old werewolf woodcuts—animals with arms hanging from their toothy jaws—flitted through my mind, and I shivered.

"Oh, she's a predator all right," Lindsey said. "When she gets on the scent of someone who's hiding money . . . watch out."

"A regular bloodhound, then," said Tom.

I ignored him—which was difficult, to say the least, because every cell in my body was excruciatingly aware of his presence—and turned to Heath. "So, should we get a bottle of red or white? Or how about both?"

"Red," Tom said, leaning forward and staring at me. "Tell me, Sophie," he said, rolling my name around in his mouth as if it were a Godiva truffle. "How long have you been in Austin?"

I shivered a little, and said, with only a little tremor, "Why do you want to know?" Was he the one sending me wolfsbane? I wondered. But that didn't make sense. I mean, he seemed to have no problem confronting me.

Why hide behind cryptic notes? And why go to all the bother? It didn't seem to fit.

"I guess I'm surprised we haven't run into each other before," he said.

"I like to keep a low profile," I said.

"Yeah, right," Lindsey said. "Like that night at Fat Tuesday's?"

Oh, God. Not the Fat Tuesday's story.

"That bar on 6th Street?" Heath asked.

I stared daggers at Lindsey, but it was no use.

"It was a bachelorette party," Lindsey said. "Someone mixed the Hurricanes a little too strong, and Sophie here . . . well, you should have seen her."

Lindsey leaned forward and put her hand on Tom's knee. "Would you believe we actually had to drag her off one of the tables when it was time to leave?" I had no recollection of being dragged off a table. But since I woke up the next morning with a crescent moon tattooed on my right shoulder—which I also didn't recollect happening—I was in no position to argue.

"A regular party animal, eh?" Tom asked with a wicked, toothy grin.

"Where was I that night?" Heath asked. "The accountant lets her hair down, and I miss it?"

"Auditor," I corrected him, looking past him for the waitress. "I'm an auditor." God, I needed a drink.

Fortunately, Heath changed the subject for me. "So, Tom, where are you from?" Heath asked. "You don't sound like a Texan."

"Tom's from Norway, actually," Lindsey answered, gazing at her date with big, moony eyes.

Well, that explained the accent.

"Norway," Heath repeated. "What brings you to Austin?"

My ears pricked up.

"The . . . company I was with had a little shake-up," Tom said, glancing at me. "So I decided to try something different."

"What kind of business are you in?" Heath said, leaning forward.

"I do contract work," he said.

"Contract work?" Lindsey asked. "Like computers?"

"I specialize in getting rid of difficulties," he said, giving me a lopsided grin. "If an organization is having problems, they hire me to . . . well, to take care of them."

I didn't even want to *think* about what that meant. And whether I might be one of "them." I looked for the waitress—had she skipped to Mexico or something?— and then cut a quick glance at Tom. If he said he worked for organizations—other packs, I presumed—did that mean he belonged to one? Was he here to put pressure on me? If so, he was certainly succeeding. I surreptitiously wiped a bead of sweat from my forehead.

"And are you still with a company?" I asked.

Tom leaned back in his chair. "I'm more of a lone wolf, actually."

A lone wolf. I glanced at Lindsey and Heath, but they seemed oblivious to the fact that they were sitting next to a full-blooded werewolf. I studied Tom from the corner of my eye. With those gleaming teeth and those golden eyes, I couldn't see how anyone could mistake him for anything other than what he was. He gave me a quick, predatory smile, and I dropped my eyes to the menu. I half expected him to order steak tartare, with a side of raw rabbit.

At least he was solo, I told myself. Which hopefully meant I wouldn't have a pack breathing down my neck, telling me I was on its turf. Or whatever it was they called their little areas. But if he had been part of a pack once, why wasn't he now? And if he was from Norway, what was he doing here? Oh, yeah. Eliminating problems. I suppressed another shiver. "So you're not a big fan of, well, the pack mentality?" I ventured, still staring at my menu.

Tom's gold eyes bored into me. It was almost dizzying. My mother's words came back to me. *A woman could drown in those eyes* . . . "I've tried it," he said slowly. "But I decided I like a little more independence."

"Is most of your business here in Austin?" Heath asked, probing Tom for potential client leads. Sometimes I found that annoying, but at the moment, I was thankful to him for asking the questions that I wanted to know.

"I do have a job in Austin right now," Tom said, looking right at me.

The inside of my mouth turned to paper. He said his job was "taking care of problems." Was he talking about me? Or—I allowed myself a glimmer of hope— was he here because of the packette? And in either case, who had hired him—and what was the problem in question?

"Are you based in Texas?" Lindsey asked.

"Not really. I get calls from organizations all over the country, actually. Sometimes even abroad." His eyes flicked to me. "I'm becoming quite fond of Austin, though."

"Well, I hope you'll be here awhile," purred Lindsey, reaching out to touch his arm. I wanted to get up and yell, *He's a werewolf!*

But I didn't, of course. I just smiled and wished hard for the waitress to come back from Cancun or Mazatlán or wherever she was so I could order my martini.

Fourteen

Finally—*finally*—the waitress glided back to the table, and I ordered my double martini. Lindsey, like a true friend, joined me with a Cosmo, and Heath ordered a bottle of Cabernet Sauvignon for the table. Tom asked for an aquavit. Neat.

When the waitress left, Heath leaned over and gave me an affectionate peck on the cheek. "I almost forgot to ask about your mom. How's she doing?"

"Fine," I said quickly. *Jesus.* Didn't anyone talk about the weather anymore?

"Your mother?" Tom asked. I could almost see his ears pricking up, wondering if there was yet another werewolf in Austin he didn't know about.

"She had some medical problems," Lindsey said breezily.

"But she's doing much better now," I said, then leaned toward Heath, stroking his arm. As curious as I was about Tom, I really, really, really wanted to get off the subject of my mother. "But let's talk about something more interesting. Heath, didn't you have a case you wanted to tell me about?" I'd get back to questioning Tom later, I decided. After we'd managed to steer the conversation well away from my mother.

Heath smiled, exposing a row of straight, distinctly unfanglike teeth, and I relaxed. We were out of dangerous waters—for the time being, anyway. I looked at my young, dapper Matlock and squeezed his hand gratefully. Once Heath got rolling, no one would get a word in edgewise for at least the next half hour. "Well, it's not a case so much as a cause," he said, leaning back in his chair. "I don't know if any of you have been following the papers lately, but there have been some problems with packs of stray dogs in the area. Attacking people."

So much for finding safe harbor in the world of law. My eyes flicked to Tom's. He was studying Heath.

"Oh yeah," Lindsey said. "Like that big German shepherd. The one who mauled that guy."

I wasn't a German shepherd, and the innocent victim was a greasy, tattooed car burglar, but I let it pass. "That one wasn't in a pack," I reminded her.

Lindsey said, "I heard something on the news about another one. In the courthouse." She glanced at me. "In fact, that was about the time . . ." her eyes flicked to Heath, and she stopped just in time, remembering that my mother was supposed to be in the hospital—not jail. And not in the Travis County Courthouse, for that matter.

Fortunately, Heath hadn't caught the slip. "I read about it in the paper this week." He shook his head. "Just another example of how things have gotten out of hand."

"Yeah," said Lindsey. "The one the other night was wearing panty hose. And apparently this one was carrying a purse!"

Heath leaned forward, an intense look in his eyes. "The issue is that a stray dog made it into the courthouse."

"I don't know," said Lindsey. "Maybe the bigger moral issue is that there's been a rash of cross-dressing dogs."

I blushed slightly and inspected my fingernails, avoiding Tom's eyes. Could he possibly know?

"The issue," Heath repeated, hitting his stride on the subject, "is that there have been a number of attacks lately." He looked so earnest, dark eyes flashing, that if he'd been talking about anything other than rounding up stray dogs—or werewolves—I would have melted all over again. But he *was* talking about stray werewolves. I mean dogs. And personally, I thought a subject change was long overdue.

I glanced at Tom; his rugged face was impassive.

Heath continued. "And if we're not safe walking our own streets—even in our courthouses, for God's sake—isn't it time to ask the city to do something about it?" Heath looked around the table. For a moment, I wondered if he'd forgotten we were his dinner companions, not a jury.

"What did you have in mind?" Tom said smoothly.

"We need better enforcement of the leash laws, of course," Heath said.

"And what about the . . . strays?" I asked, my mouth dry.

"More dogcatchers," he said.

"But isn't that dangerous?" Lindsey said. "I mean, according to the papers, that dog the other day was just brutal. Even if it *was* wearing panty hose."

I shot a glance at Tom, whose eyes crinkled slightly. Could it be . . . did he suspect the German shepherd was me?

"Not if we equip them correctly," Heath said earnestly. "I've done some preliminary research. Sedative guns are an excellent option—they use them in Tulsa and Chicago."

"How would you get the dosage right?" I asked nervously, more glad than ever that I chose to leave town for my involuntary transformations. Years ago, my mother and I had found a small weekend house out in the middle of the Hill Country, right next to a big preserve, where I could go and indulge my animal nature free of human scrutiny. I had a standing reservation there, four times a year—and usually managed to have a good time chasing rabbits and scaring coyotes, believe it or not. There's something about being unfettered— totally ruled by instinct and not at all worried about my voice mail for a couple of days—that was almost a release. Even though I did need a good mani-pedi when I got back to Austin.

But now that Heath was sending out dogcatchers armed with poorly calibrated tranquilizer guns, I was doubly happy to have a refuge outside of Austin. Because the last thing I needed was to end up in a cage labeled "Frisky" at the Town Lake Animal Center adoption day.

"Well, you can't get it exactly right, but you can estimate. And if it's a vicious dog anyway . . ." he shrugged.

Vicious dog, my foot. I'd been protecting myself—and my Kate Spade purse! And at the courthouse, all I'd done was run down the hall. *Sheesh.*

"Just throw it to the wolves, right, Heath?" Lindsey said, grinning.

I swallowed hard and turned to Heath, hoping this was just a nightmare, and that I'd wake up soon. I closed my eyes and pinched myself, but when I opened my eyes again, they were all still there, staring at me— one of them with burning gold eyes that made my skin tingle. God, what a week. If my mom's karma theory was right, I must have really pissed someone off. "Why are you so interested in this all of a sudden?" I asked. Although I knew part of the answer. Heath had political aspirations, and championing causes was a great way to get press.

"I'm just interested in public safety, of course."

Yeah, right. That and a future in politics. I resisted the urge to roll my eyes.

At that moment—finally—the waitress arrived with a tray full of drinks. I took a few blissful swigs of my martini, watching Tom out of the corner of my eye as he downed his aquavit.

"So what's your plan?" I asked Heath, not sure I really wanted to know.

"I'm petitioning the city council," he said, puffing up his chest. "And I contacted the *Statesman* the other day; they'll be running a story in the next week or two. We may be circulating a petition soon too."

Lovely.

Lindsey raised her Cosmo in an impromptu toast. "To Heath's campaign to save us from cross-dressing dogs."

"Dangerous dogs," Heath amended.

I reluctantly raised what was left of my martini. Tom lifted his empty glass with a wry smile; as the glasses clinked, our eyes met—and locked. The noise in the bar, Lindsey, Heath—even the smell of browned steak—faded away, replaced by the heat of his gaze, and the answering pull from somewhere inside me.

"Sophie?" Heath asked, and I blinked, breaking the connection. "Are you okay?"

"Fine," I stuttered, shaking myself. In truth, I wasn't fine at all. I mean, here I was, sitting at the dinner table with a full-blooded werewolf who was able to reduce me to jelly with a glance. A werewolf who, moreover, was in Austin to take care of a "problem" and who appeared to be stalking me. Not to mention dating my best friend.

I glanced at Lindsey, who was leaning into Tom, obviously enraptured. *Oh, Lindsey*, I thought, with a mixed stab of jealousy and fear. How do you tell your best friend she's dating a supernatural creature? A potentially homicidal one at that?

My eyes drifted back to Tom, whose golden-haired arm was slung around Lindsey's bare shoulders. His gold eyes caught mine for an instant, but I looked away. Part of me was longing to corner him and assuage my burning curiosity. Despite my issues with the werewolf world, I had a feeling he could tell me just about anything I could want to know about the wide world of werewolves.

But what was I going to do, grab his arm and pull him out into the street to interrogate him?

I sighed. So many things I wanted to do, and so few actual options.

So instead of dragging Tom outside to play twenty questions or telling Lindsey she was dating a man with more than the usual amount of animal attraction, I did what any normal upset twenty-eight-year-old woman would do.

I drained the rest of my drink.

And ordered another one.

By the time we all staggered out of Fleming's, it was past nine. Over the course of the evening, I had polished off three martinis (strictly medicinal), two glasses of Cabernet, and a filet with a side of sweet-potato casserole. (And a crème brûlée, which I swear bypassed my stomach entirely and went directly to my thighs.)

Normally—thigh inflation aside—that would have made for a pretty good evening. Particularly since I'd shared it with Heath. But having Tom on the scene, pawing at Lindsey, shooting iridescent gazes my way, and sucking down aquavit like water—water that seemed to have absolutely no effect on him—had put something of a damper on the proceedings for me. And that was putting it mildly.

"That was fun," Lindsey said, leaning into Tom's broad chest, and I almost choked. He stroked her hair, and I forced myself to stare at something else. Unfortunately, the first thing that caught my eye was Leslie, a forty-year-old bearded man who spends a good portion of his time standing on street corners in falsies and a thong. My eyes swerved back to the happy couple just as Lindsey said, "We should do it again sometime."

Fun? Personally, I'd rather have cactus spikes pushed under my toenails—or stand on a street corner wearing falsies and a thong—but I smiled and said, rather slurrily, "We'll see."

"I need to get this young woman home," Heath said, pulling me into him. His laundry starch–CK One smell mingled with Tom's alpha aroma and sparked something deep inside me. Despite the nightmarish evening, I felt my body respond, and I pressed closer to him. "We have some unfinished business to attend to," he murmured into my ear, and I could feel the heat pulsing in me. If it hadn't been for Lindsey and Tom—and Leslie, come to think of it—I might have torn his clothes off right there on the street corner.

"It was nice to meet you," Tom said, extending a big paw to Heath. As the two shook hands, those golden eyes slid to me, holding me like an ant under a magnifying glass. "It's good to see you again, Sophie. I hope our paths cross again soon."

Heath's free arm tightened reflexively around me, and Lindsey's right eyebrow arched just a little bit.

"Austin's a small town," I said in a jolly tone, as if I didn't think he'd been stalking me. "You never know!"

"You never know," he repeated, eyes resting on me.

Lindsey brushed a strand of light hair from Tom's cheek. "Walk me home?" she purred.

"I'd be delighted to," he said in a low throaty voice,

exposing a line of pointed teeth. Oh, God. What did he have in mind for my friend?

"Be careful," I said to Lindsey, staring hard at her.

"Oh, I'll be fine, as long as Tom's with me," she said.

I glared at the tall werewolf, wishing I shared her assessment of his protective capabilities. "Be careful," I repeated, putting just a little bit of growl in my voice. Unfortunately, I suspected it was less than daunting.

His mouth twitched into a little grin, which kind of confirmed my suspicion. "I am always careful."

"Good," I said, as he draped an arm around Lindsey and steered her away from me. It was like sending Little Red Riding Hood off with the Big Bad Wolf, I thought as she leaned into him. All she needed was a little cloak to match her dress.

"What was that all about?"

"What?" I turned to Heath.

He was giving me that cross-examination look. "The whole 'be careful' thing."

I shrugged. "She's my friend," I said. "I worry about her."

"From what you've told me, he's the one who should be careful," Heath said. He was quiet for a moment. "Are you sure you and that guy—Tom—don't know each other?"

"We met when he met Lindsey," I said. Then I added in a low voice, "Your place or mine?"

"Mine," he growled back. "It's closer, and I don't think I can wait that long."

Leslie was checking his legs for stubble as we hurried past him, and I was thankful I'd excused myself to the bathroom for a few minutes during dinner. We barely made it up to Heath's loft before he pushed my jacket back and fumbled with the zipper of my skirt. "I was thinking about you all afternoon," he whispered as my skirt puddled on the floor.

"Me too," I whispered back as my bra sprang free. A moment later his mouth was on my breasts and my bikini panties had floated down to where my skirt was.

"What, no matching underwear today?" he asked, looking down at the tan bra and green panties.

"I've been a bit busy," I said, peeling off his jacket, unbuttoning his shirt, and running my tongue down his chest to one of his nipples. He tasted salty and soapy and delicious. "I hope you don't mind," I murmured.

"I think I can let it slide this time, Miss Garou," he said, his warm hands on my naked breasts. "Although there may be consequences," he said.

"Oh?" I asked, fumbling with his belt. "Such as?"

But before he could come up with a response, I freed him from the confines of his boxer shorts and took him into my mouth. When he was just about to come, I released him.

"Don't stop!" he panted.

"No?" I asked, grinning. Paybacks are hell, I suppose. I pushed him down on the couch and straddled him, hovering over him for just a moment before lowering myself onto him. He grabbed my hips and pulled me down onto him, his mouth rough against my nipples. I gasped, and then he thrust again, and again, deeper inside me, until I felt I would burst. For a moment, just before I exploded into a wave of orgasm, an image of Tom flashed through my head.

My eyes snapped open. *Heath*, I thought.

And then all thought dissolved as we both came.

When the last little ripples were gone, I lay my head on Heath's shoulder, feeling better than I had in days. "Worth the wait?" I asked.

"Always," he whispered. "I'd do anything for you, Sophie."

Anything? I wondered.

Even if you knew what I really am?

I banished the thought and forced myself to enjoy the moment. Carpe diem and all that.

And then, a half an hour later, we did it again.

As I lay in Heath's bed later that night, feeling warm and cozy and sated, I tried not to think about Lindsey and Tom and what they might or might not be doing. After all, there really was nothing I could do about it. And at least I knew they'd gone home with full stomachs—he'd put away quite a lot of rare sirloin.

So instead, I distracted myself with one of my favorite fantasies: constructing the life Heath and I would some-day share. We couldn't stay downtown, of course, not with kids; we'd probably get a nice house in Tarrytown, something with a two-car garage. I'd probably keep working, but other than that we'd be just like the Cleavers. A traditional two-parent household, maybe with a little girl and a little boy, and with no need to move from town to town to avoid being eaten by were-wolves. We could bake cookies together and go for walks in the park and do all kinds of wholesome family things that I'd never gotten to do. (Sure, I'd had some kitchen time with my mom, but we'd been making po-tions, not hot chocolate.)

And maybe, I thought with a wrench in my stomach, if we were lucky, the kids wouldn't be werewolves.

I snuggled into the crook of Heath's shoulder. How was I going to tell him about my little problem? As wor-ried as I was that someone else would blow my secret, the truth was, a time would come when I'd have to tell him myself. I could hide it now, when we weren't living together. He knew I drank herbal tea. And he knew I went away about four times a year, even though I was hoping he hadn't noticed the regularity of my little trips. Although since he'd scheduled a big date on the night of the full moon, it looked as if he was still clueless about my quarterly transformation issues.

If I told him what I was, would I lose him?

Or could I somehow keep my secret safe?

Fifteen

"Last night went pretty well. Don't you think?"

I choked on my coffee.

"Sophie?"

After Lindsey finished whacking me on the back, I said, "Well, the steak was good, I guess." I fought the urge to lay my head on the desk. I really wasn't up for this discussion before I'd finished my first cup of coffee—and before the Tylenol had had a chance to counteract the aftereffects of three martinis. But Lindsey had wedged herself into one of my office chairs, so it didn't look as if I had a choice. And I'll admit I was relieved to see her in one piece, without any signs of having been mauled.

"Steak, shmeak," she said. "They got along great, didn't they?"

"Who? Heath and Tom?"

"Of course, dummy. And Tom is such a gentleman. Would you believe he didn't even kiss me good night?"

"Really?" I said, feeling perkier all of a sudden. *Down, girl.*

"He said we should get to know each other better first."

"Oh," I said, feeling slightly deflated. For no good reason, really, because I should have been relieved that nothing had happened between them. Which I was, actually. Besides, I had a perfectly wonderful boyfriend with no excess-hair problems and absolutely no urge to howl at the moon. And last night—once we'd escaped Fleming's, anyway—had been pretty amazing. Despite my headache, I felt a little rush of heat at the memory.

I glanced at the drawer that held my box of tea. My stomach roiled at the thought of it, but I'd have to brew another cup soon.

"So we're going out again this Friday," Lindsey continued, reaching up to adjust her hair. Today it was pulled up into a French twist that accentuated the delicate oval of her face. With her pink lipstick and pink and proper suit, she almost looked demure. Then a wicked smile crossed her lips and the illusion vanished. "I'm going to give him his first tango lesson," she said.

Wonderful.

"By the way," she added, "did you remember our date with Brewster's campaign manager?"

"Shoot. That's today, isn't it?"

"Yeah. In about three hours, actually. I went total Junior League today," she said, indicating her pale rose-colored suit. "I even wore pearls." She touched the ivory strand around her neck.

"What time?"

"Noon." She stood up and straightened her knee-length skirt. "I'd better get some work done first. See you at eleven-thirty?"

"Can't wait," I said halfheartedly. As Lindsey closed the door behind her, I fumbled in my drawer for another couple of Tylenol and some Tums, wondering if antacids would show up on a drug test. I shook two Tylenol out of a bottle and was tossing them back when Sally opened the door.

I washed the pills down with a swig of coffee and looked up at my assistant. Today she wore a skintight pair of capri pants with a purple top that didn't quite cover her ripply midriff. A quick sniff told me she'd traded in the Aviance Night Musk for something more flowery but still capable of stripping paint on contact. Not to mention the membranes inside my nose.

Unfortunately, her eyes were fixed on the bottle of pills. Probably wondering if I was taking amphetamines in addition to smoking pot. "Sinus headache," I explained, trying to breathe through my mouth to avoid smelling her perfume. My stomach was upset enough already. I jiggled the bottle at her. "I was just taking some Tylenol. Can I help you with something?"

"You got another package," she said.

"The one from Southeast Airlines?"

"No," she said, with a nasty little smirk.

My heart rate picked up a few notches. "Where is it?"

"Oh, I'll get it," she said, and reappeared a moment later with a wrapped package, which she laid on the desk with a smug smile.

Shit.

Sally's eyes slid to the package, then to me. Same brown paper, same swirly script.

"Thank you," I said with a dismissive tone of voice. When she showed no sign of budging from my office, I said, "Don't you have some work to do?"

"I'm on break," she said. "Why don't you open it? I can't wait to see what your mother sent this time."

"Probably nothing important," I said, pushing the

package to the edge of the desk. "How was it delivered?" I asked, trying to sound nonchalant.

"I don't know." She shrugged. "I went for a cup of coffee, and when I got back, it was on my desk."

I snuck a glance at the box, then pasted on a smile for Sally. "Well, I'm on deadline for this Southeast Airlines account, so I really need to work. The meeting's next Wednesday."

"No, it's not," she said gleefully.

"What do you mean?"

Her penciled eyebrows rose in mock surprise. "Didn't Adele tell you?"

"Tell me what?"

"The meeting's been moved to Monday."

"What?" I barked.

"Monday. You know, the day after Sunday?"

Monday. The equinox.

"But . . ."

She sighed. "The client was adamant. That's the only day they can meet. So I guess you'll just have to postpone your other plans."

"I thought I told Adele . . . there's no way I can make it," I stammered.

"Good luck," Sally said, heading for the door. "And I can't wait to hear what your *mom* sent."

When the door closed behind her, I got up and locked it. Was there any way to get Sally reassigned? To somewhere like, say, Nigeria?

Pushing aside thoughts of what I'd like to do to my wardrobe-challenged assistant, I turned my attention to the package on my desk. Who had sent it?

I picked it up and sniffed it. Cats again, and body odor, but nothing strong enough to get a read on. Although it could just be Sally's perfume obliterating any and all competing scents. The box had been hand-delivered— like the last one, there was no postage mark.

I grabbed a letter opener and slit the packing tape open, then bent down for another sniff. No wolfsbane this time—something with a tang, instead. Metallic.

Inside was a small wooden box, with a piece of paper taped to it. I flipped the paper open to read yet another perky little poem.

> *Flowers are fine,*
> *To give them no crime,*
> *But this Cupid's dart*
> *Will go straight to your heart.*

After reading it a second time, I tossed it aside. What was up with the poetry? Was I getting hate mail from a demented English major? I lifted the lid of the wooden box, wondering what kind of dart it was. Did the whole Cupid thing mean someone had a crush on me?

I stared at the box's contents and swallowed hard. If someone did have a crush, it was of the fatal-attraction variety.

My heart hammered in my chest as my finger grazed the object's shiny casing, and I drew back quickly. It burned a little—kind of the way the juice of chili peppers feels if you touch it with your bare hands. Not enough to really hurt you, but enough to make you wear gloves when you're making salsa.

I shoved the note inside the box and flipped it closed, then jammed it into my bottom drawer, wedging it in between the Tension Tamer and the box of wolfsbane. Pushing the drawer closed with a toe, I sank back into my chair, gripping the armrests until my knuckles turned white.

Whoever sent this was no Robert Frost. But they didn't need to be. The message behind the silver bullet came through loud and clear.

Sixteen

"So who's got your panties in a twist?"
Lindsey asked as she gunned the Miata past a line of
parked cars. We were on our way to question Brewster's
campaign manager. Lindsey was right; ever since Sally
had delivered my little care package, I'd been having a
hard time focusing. The fact that Lindsey still smelled
faintly of Tom wasn't helping.

"Is it that obvious?" I asked as we pulled out of the
garage into the blinding sunshine.

"Duh," she said.

I sighed. "Adele moved the meeting to a day when I
can't do it."

"She scheduled it on your day off?"

"Yeah."

"You'd better reschedule your date, then," she said,
checking her lipstick in the rearview mirror. I had to
hand it to her; when she wanted to, she could look exactly like a Stepford wife.

"Not possible," I said.

"What do you mean, 'not possible'? Everything's possible," she said, replacing the cap of her lipstick.

Not exactly, I thought, but because her experience
with full-moon transformations was limited at best, I let
it pass. "The problem is the tickets," I lied. "They're
nonrefundable."

"Still cheaper than being unemployed," she said, peering at me. "And I'm sure Heath will understand."

Which reminded me that I still hadn't told Heath we had to postpone our little anniversary get-together. I could always tell him I had to work extra-late—as a partner in a law firm that virtually required a seventy-hour workweek, he shouldn't find it too hard to relate. The problem was, I *did* have to work. And the bigger problem was, unless I could come up with a reasonable excuse—such as being shot in the spleen by terrorists or coming down with the Ebola virus—I'd be attending the meeting in a natural fur coat.

I pushed the looming weekend into the mental "things to be dealt with later" drawer—which was already crammed to the gills—and focused on the issue at hand. "So what's the plan for this afternoon?" I asked as Lindsey headed west toward what I liked to call "the lawyer district."

"We go and chat with her about donations and political positions."

"That's it?"

"Well, I'd like to get into Brewster's office," she said. "But only if we have the opportunity."

"Maybe a well-timed trip to the ladies' room?"

"Might work," she said. "We'll play it by ear."

As I considered possible exit strategies for the upcoming weekend—maybe I could manufacture a skydiving accident or a distant relative's funeral, perhaps the result of an unfortunate sledding incident in Iceland—the Miata wound through the leafy streets of West Austin. Gorgeous mansions from the early 1900s lined the narrow avenues—only now, instead of well-to-do families, for the most part they now housed well-to-do lawyers' offices. I could smell the printer toner from the car.

Lindsey pulled up outside of a massive stone-and-wood bungalow with a deep front porch that would be perfect for a couple of rocking chairs or even a hammock. Instead, its only décor was a line of brass plaques indicating the names of the house's corporate inhabitants.

After a last quick check in the rearview mirror, Lindsey turned to me. "Ready?"

"Do I have a choice?"

"Lighten up, Sophie. It will be fun!"

"Easy for you to say. Your mom's not the one with a court date."

The smell of toner inside Brewster's office building was strong, but not enough to cancel out the smell of a lived-in building—seasoned wood, musk, soap, and copy paper. And microwave popcorn.

We climbed the creaky wood staircase to Ted Brewster's office, which occupied the entire top floor of the old building. Thick Oriental rugs were scattered around the dark wood floor, and expensive paintings adorned the cream-colored walls. Everything, including the heavy antique desk in the reception area, was top drawer—except for the woman behind the desk. Her bosom threatened to escape the confines of a tight green spandex top as she stood up to greet us with a toothy smile—Brewster's secretary, I presumed. She looked barely out of high school and reminded me of Sally, although unlike Sally, she was (thankfully) a bit more judicious in her perfume application. The microwave popcorn was hers—a half-eaten bag lay on the antique wood surface, and a popcorn hull clung to one of her front teeth. "Can I help you?" she said.

"We're here to see Maria," said Lindsey.

"Your name?"

"Lola Davenport," Lindsey said.

"I'll let her know you're here," the Sally look-alike said, sauntering down a short hallway. Her skirt—green leopard print, and no, I'm not kidding—was as brief as her top. Somehow I doubted Brewster had hired her for her filing abilities.

"Lola?" I whispered to Lindsey.

"You're Gertrude," she said.

"Gertrude?" I sputtered.

Before I could protest further, Miss Junior Prom jiggled back into the reception area with a tall, competent-looking woman in her wake. No spandex here—her suit was blue and conservative and looked to be the product of a first-class tailor.

"You must be Lola," she said, holding a manicured hand out to Lindsey. "I'm Maria Jiménez."

"Thanks for taking the time to meet with us," said Lindsey. "This is my friend Gertrude."

As Maria extended a hand, I felt a flash of something, but I wasn't sure what. Recognition, maybe? But I was sure I'd never met her before. "Pleased to meet you," I said, shaking her hand—cool and dry. I took a surreptitious sniff—even with the reek of popcorn, I could still make out her scent. Expensive soap, herbs . . . and something else, something exotic.

"Pleased to meet you," she said, studying me with narrowed eyes. "Have we met before?"

So she felt it too. "Not that I know of," I said.

"I'm sure it will come to me," she said, pushing a lock of raven-black hair behind one ear. "Why don't you come into my office? Can I get you a cup of coffee or something? A Diet Coke?"

Lindsey smiled politely. "No, thank you."

When I demurred as well, Maria turned and led us down a short hallway to a heavy wooden door. As we walked, I did a quick scan. In addition to Maria's office, there were two other doors. One was closed—the bathroom, maybe? I thought I could smell Lysol—but the other was ajar and smelled faintly of cigar smoke. I craned my neck as we passed. Inside was a massive desk with a big leather chair and a wall lined with photographs.

"Is that the councilman's office?" I asked as we passed.

Her lips tightened. "Congressman-elect, actually. And yes, it was."

"Oh, yeah," I said as we followed her down the hall and through a heavy wood door.

"What a beautiful office," Lindsey said—and she was right. Maria's office was large and airy, with elegant, sleek furniture and huge antique windows that let in the afternoon sunshine. A faint floral scent permeated the room. I thought of my office on the fifteenth floor of my downtown building, with the stale smells of recirculated air and Sally's perfume, and felt a stab of jealousy.

"Please sit down," Maria said, indicating two delicate antique chairs across from her desk. "What can I do for you ladies?"

Lindsey crossed her legs and leaned forward. "As I mentioned on the phone, we were both big supporters of Ted Brewster." She sighed dramatically. "Such a tragedy, don't you think?"

"Yes, a tragedy," Maria said, her face expressionless.

"I understand he had family in the area?" Lindsey said.

"Yes. He has—had—a son."

"It must be just awful for him."

"I can't say. I haven't spoken with him," Maria said stiffly, crossing her legs and sitting up straight.

"Will he be stepping into his father's shoes, do you know?" Lindsey asked.

Maria shook her head decisively. "I don't think he is called in the same way his father was."

"I can't think of his name," Lindsey said, biting a plump, lipsticked lip. "What was it again?"

"Tad," Maria said shortly, then steepled her fingers on

the desk. "Now," she said, steering the conversation back to the purported reason for our visit, "you called regarding continued contributions to the Brewster cause—or to his successor. But I'm a little embarrassed to admit that after we talked, I checked the files—and I couldn't find any record of your donations."

"We prefer to make them anonymously," Lindsey said, and launched into a political conversation that eluded me entirely. As they talked, I found myself sniffing. There were some interesting smells in the room—definitely incense, and some other herbs too. Which didn't seem at all in keeping with Maria's Ann Taylor–Laura Ashley dress-and-decorating scheme.

Suddenly I realized that Lindsey was kicking me. I looked up at her; she waggled an eyebrow and smiled.

I smiled back, and Lindsey jerked an eyebrow a few more times. It was on the tip of my tongue to ask what was wrong with her when I realized it was my cue. "May I use your restroom?" I asked.

Lindsey rolled her eyes.

"Certainly. It's right down the hall," Maria said.

"Now, who do you think we should support in Councilman Brewster's stead?" Lindsey asked as I slipped out the door and into the hallway. Only instead of heading for the bathroom, I headed for Brewster's office.

As I padded down the hall, I glanced toward the reception area. Brewster's secretary wasn't visible, but I could hear her talking on the phone to a friend. I heard her say "ladies' night"—evidently the discussion was about proposed Friday activities. She was probably a fan of the Chuggin' Monkey too. I hoped the debate would be a long one.

A moment later, I eased through Brewster's office door and scanned my surroundings. Huge mahogany desk, a bookcase filled with leather-bound antique books, big red leather chairs, and about a million framed photographs of Ted Brewster with important people. I only had a few minutes; where should I start?

The desk, of course.

As I hurried around the massive slab of mahogany, I glanced at the photos on the wall. Every one of them featured Ted, who looked like a mildly obese cut-out doll wearing different suits. The same shiny head, the same goofy smile—the only thing that changed was the suit and the arm accessory. Sandra Bullock, George Bush, Michael Dell, and a bunch of people I didn't recognize but was sure were regulars on the society pages.

I slid open the desk drawers, starting with the top ones. The police had been here, which wasn't surprising—I could smell (and see) traces of fingerprint powder. I just hoped they'd left something for me to find.

The first drawer contained a brush, a bottle of Aveda Volumizing Hair Gel—hope springs eternal, I guess—and a vial of Polo. I rifled through the rest of the drawers and discovered an appointment book with an amazing number of appointments and contacts, but nothing that looked suspicious, and a bunch of files with names I didn't recognize. If I had the time to go through them all, I might find something interesting, but because I was supposed to be in the ladies' room, I didn't have more than a few minutes.

At the very back of the bottom drawer, I found a well-worn manila envelope. My nose twitched as I undid the flap—was there something here? A moment later, I slid the contents out—three dog-eared copies of a *Barely Legal* magazine. I eyed the cover photo, which featured a young lady in a uniform that would have been right at home on a sixth-grade Catholic-school girl—except, that is, for the garter belt and the total and obvious absence of undergarments. I returned the magazines to the envelope and resisted the urge to run to the bathroom and sanitize my hands. Evidently Brewster *did* like them young.

With the envelope safely tucked back into its drawer, I gave the desk one more quick go-through. Unfortunately, either the cops had gotten everything of interest or there was nothing there to find. I leaned back in Brewster's leather wing chair, breathing in the strong scent of Cuban cigars, and glanced at the framed panoramic view of Austin on the wall across from his desk. A springtime view—the pictures always are, as if Austin was cloaked in bluebonnets and Indian paintbrush year-round—with a geographically impossible mix of Austin landmarks. The University of Texas Tower, the capitol, the 360 Bridge, and the skyline, set off prettily by rolling hills and a blue wash of Texas's state flower.

I jolted upright, and the hairs on my arms stood straight up. *Bluebonnets. The 360 Bridge.*

I was looking right at them.

Seventeen

The candlelit evening at Sit A Spell, the smell of barbecue, and Ted Brewster's rumbly voice came back to me as I rounded the desk and placed my hands on the picture frame. "You'll find what you're looking for," he'd said. Sucking in my breath, I eased the painting away from the wall and prayed Brewster wasn't wrong.

Either it was a big coincidence or Brewster really had come back from the dead for a plate of Salt Lick barbecue. Because tucked neatly behind the framed canvas was a flat metal safe, set into the plaster.

As I did a quick inspection, I listened for voices—if anyone caught me, it was going to be hard to explain how I missed the bathroom yet somehow managed to run across a hidden wall safe in Ted Brewster's office. It was about a foot and a half square, with a combination lock, which was good news. Given quiet and enough time, I would probably be able to get it open. Unfortunately, though, I had neither—the low hum of women's voices was getting louder, and I was already pushing the limits of what constituted a reasonable bathroom break.

As much as I was dying to know what was in there, there just wasn't time. I hurriedly replaced the picture—it wasn't quite straight, but it would have to do—just as Miss Junior Prom walked in.

She drew up short, jiggling like a bowl of Jell-O, and I had the sudden urge to take her to get fitted for a decent bra. If she didn't invest in some support soon, the girls would be down to her knees by the time she hit thirty.

I released the picture and stepped back, pretending to admire it.

"What are you doing in here?' she asked, blue eyes wide with surprise.

"I was looking for the bathroom," I said. "But when I walked by Mr. Brewster's office, I thought this picture was so beautiful, I had to see who did it."

A line appeared between her eyebrows. "But you can't see it from the doorway."

Excellent point. Now what? I glanced around, searching for inspiration, and my eyes fell on the wall of Brewster cut-out doll pictures. "I saw the picture of Mr. Brewster with Lance Armstrong, and I just had to get a better look," I said, hoping that there was indeed a picture of Brewster getting chummy with Lance somewhere on the walls. "I just *love* Lance," I babbled. "He's just got the best legs."

"What were you looking for again?"

"The bathroom," I said. "But now that you mention it, I think I'll wait." If I didn't get back to Maria's office soon, it would look suspicious. Although I was guessing things would be suspicious enough when Miss Junior Prom spilled the beans about my supposed Lance fixation.

I smiled benevolently and squeezed past her double-Ds, trying to look as if I hadn't just been sniffing around Brewster's office. Did she know Brewster had a couple of *Barely Legal*s tucked away in a drawer? Although, with the real thing just down the hall, displayed like cantaloupes on a platter, I couldn't see why he needed the magazines. I wasn't sure she'd bought my story about Lance Armstrong, but it was the best I could do. "I'll just get back to my meeting now," I said.

"Okeydoke," she said doubtfully, and stood watching me until I was at the end of the hallway.

Brewster's campaign manager shot me a dark look as I slid through the door. "Glad you made it back," she said, with a noticeable chill in her voice. "We were starting to worry about you."

"Oh, I'm fine, thanks. Just got turned around a little, that's all." I sat down and crossed my legs, realizing that I really did need to pee. Why hadn't I just taken a moment to visit the womens' room?

"That's Gertie," chortled Lindsey. "Always getting lost. You should have drawn her a map."

Gertie? Next time, I decided, *I* would be in charge of aliases. Squeezing my legs together tightly and wishing

I'd had a little less coffee that morning, I gave Maria a bright smile, folded my hands demurely in my lap and said, "What did I miss?"

"So, did you find anything?" Lindsey asked as we headed down the front walk to her Miata twenty minutes later.

"Remember that thing about bluebonnets and the 360 Bridge?"

"Yeah. What about it?"

"I figured out what Brewster meant."

Lindsey glanced over at me. "What do you mean?"

"There's a picture in his office—you know, one of those Austin montage things? Well, I looked behind it, and there's a safe."

"Oh my God. I can't believe it worked." Lindsey's huge eyes got even bigger. "How creepy—he came back from the dead and told us where his safe was . . ." She looked at me. "So, did you get into it?"

"What do *you* think?"

"Well, you were gone for forever. I was beginning to wonder if maybe you'd run out for a sandwich or something."

"I went through his drawers but didn't find anything. A few magazines, but nothing too incriminating."

"Magazines?"

I made a face. "*Barely Legal.*"

"Isn't that . . ."

"Yup," I said.

"Yuck."

"Yeah. And they looked . . . well, like he'd had them a while."

"Double yuck," she said, unlocking the car.

"I just wish I'd had time to go after that safe." And pee, but that was beside the point. "Even though the police probably beat us to it. It's a combination lock, so I bet I can crack it."

Lindsey eyed me speculatively. "What, are you suddenly Supergirl or something? Or did you minor in lock-picking?"

Shoot. I forgot Lindsey didn't know about my super-werewolf hearing. "I just have a knack, is all," I lied. Well, not really lied—I did have a knack—but it had more to do with my hairy little problem than any special lock-picking classes.

I slid into my seat and busied myself with the seat belt. When I looked up, Lindsey was still staring at me. "What?"

"Nothing," she said, sliding the key into the ignition. "For a moment there, I thought you were going to tell me you were a cat burglar or something."

Or something. Like a wolf burglar? I glanced at her quickly; *did* she know about me? But how? I'd been so careful . . . I squeezed my legs together and ignored the SOS from my bladder. "Did you find out anything while I was gone?" I asked, anxious to change the subject.

"Not really. But I did get the names of the top contenders for his spot on the council."

"I'll bet Maria's one of them."

"She didn't mention it, but I kind of got that impression too," Lindsey said. "And we did find out the name of his son. Tad, right?"

"Right. And whatever he is, he's not exactly in line to inherit the throne."

"Yeah. She didn't want to talk about him at all, did she? I wonder why not."

"We should track him down. See if he knows anything."

"Heck," Lindsey said. "He might be a prime candidate. From what I hear, Ted Brewster was sitting on a big chunk of change."

"Too bad we can't get our hands on the will."

"I'll see what I can find out about it," Lindsey said as we turned onto 15th Street, leaving the leafy lawyer district behind. I knew she meant that she'd be calling one of her legion of ex-boyfriends, who would all still happily bend over backward to help her.

I glanced up as we neared the intersection where I'd first seen Tom, sniffing the air. Where was he staying? I'd been sniffing everywhere I went, but I hadn't caught a whiff of him. Maybe I was wrong—maybe he wasn't stalking me after all. Which would be a relief but also a disappointment.

I couldn't see Tom, but the jail building was visible above the tops of the trees, a tangible reminder of what lay in store for my mother if I didn't manage to figure out who had killed Brewster.

"It gives me chills to know the séance worked," Lindsey said. "It's creepy."

"It could be a coincidence," I said.

Lindsey shook her head, and a tendril of dark hair clung to her cheek. She looked like she had stepped off the cover of a magazine; it was no wonder Tom had asked her out. And they had a tango date coming up Friday night.

Should I tell her he was a werewolf? But then I'd have to tell her I was a werewolf too. Which—for obvious reasons—wasn't too high on my list of priorities.

Just then, Lindsey's phone chimed.

"Hello?"

She cupped the phone to her ear, and her voice turned sultry. "Tonight? That would be great."

Tom. Had to be.

"Sophie? She's right here. Hold on a moment."

She handed me the phone. "It's for you."

"Hello?" I said.

"I'm not going to eat your friend," Tom growled,

sending a little thrill through me. Which I chose to read as apprehension.

"Glad to hear that," I said, glancing at Lindsey, who was looking at me with a raised eyebrow. "I'm rather fond of her."

"I wanted to warn you. Watch out for the made ones."

"Pardon me?"

"The made ones. Now that they know about you, they may try to find you."

"Why?" Could the three werewolves from the alley somehow be responsible for the wolfsbane care packages?

"They want what you have," he said.

"A job at a Big Four firm?" I looked at Lindsey again—her full lips were a thin line—and I decided it was time to get off the phone.

"No. They want your blood."

My blood? I glanced at Lindsey, whose lips were pressed together in impatience. "Ummm . . . how exactly does that work?" I asked.

"We need to meet and talk," he said in a low, urgent voice. "I'll tell you what you want to know, which I'm guessing is quite a lot. I've got a few questions for you too."

I was curious what questions he had for me, but not as curious as I was to find out everything Tom could tell me about the werewolf world—not to mention what he was doing in Austin. I was dying to set up a time and place. But how could I explain to Lindsey why I was planning a private tête-à-tête with her date?

"How does what work?" Lindsey asked suspiciously.

"That might be good," I said to Tom, ignoring Lindsey's question. What I really wanted to say was "When and where?" but I couldn't. Not with Lindsey sitting right next to me. I loved her, but at that moment, I wished more than anything that she were somewhere else. I was burning with frustration; I had no way to get in touch with Tom, except through Lindsey. And we couldn't exactly trade phone numbers.

"Call me," he said, and reeled off a phone number.

"Once more?" I asked, and he said it again. When I had repeated it to myself (silently of course), I handed the phone to Lindsey, who almost grabbed it out of my hand.

A moment later, she asked, "What time?" Her voice was noticeably cooler. "I'll see you then." She flipped the phone shut and gave me a chilly glance. "You and Tom seem awfully friendly. What were you talking about?"

"He wanted to assure me that his intentions are strictly honorable."

"I was kind of hoping they weren't," she said, relaxing a little. Good. The last thing I needed right now was a rift with my best friend. "You did give him kind of a stern look last night."

"I don't trust him," I said, mentally repeating the number he had given me a few minutes earlier.

"Why not?"

"He seems . . ." What? Werewolfy? "Predatory," I said.

"I know. That's one of the things I like about him. But what was he asking you about Withers and Young for?"

"I think he's looking for new clients," I lied, mentally reviewing the number like a mantra.

"Why didn't he ask me, then?" she asked.

"I don't know." Time for a subject change. I searched in my purse for a pen and paper so I could write down the number surreptitiously. Of course, I had neither. "What did you think of Maria?"

Lindsey glanced into the rearview mirror and changed lanes. "I think Maria's got some major ambitions."

"Me too," I said. And suddenly realized I had a PDA. Duh! I whipped it out and typed in the number, aiming the screen away from Lindsey. Whew. Now I could concentrate on the conversation at hand. I was planning on calling Tom the moment I got back to the office. I turned my PDA off and refocused on Lindsey, who was shaking her head and saying, "I still can't believe it."

"Believe what?"

"Ted Brewster coming back from the dead to tell us about his wall safe."

"He didn't exactly tell us to look for a wall safe," I pointed out, crossing my legs and looking longingly at a passing fire hydrant. And thinking about Tom and all the things he might be able to help me with.

"Oh, come on, Sophie. He told us where to find it, didn't he?"

Well, yes—if you counted stuffing your face with barbecue and rambling on about bluebonnets and Austin landmarks.

"We've got to figure out how to get into it," she said.

I wasn't so worried about getting into the safe. It was getting back into the office without Maria or Miss Junior Prom hanging over my shoulder that was the problem. "What do you think is in there?"

"I'm hoping for eight-by-ten glossies," said Lindsey.

I shuddered. "Not of Brewster, I hope."

"God, no. Any sane person would burn those."

"Excellent point."

"Well, once we get into that safe, maybe we'll know."

"Easier said than done," I said. "I might be able to crack the safe, but how are we going to keep Maria and the receptionist occupied?"

"That girl really needs a decent bra, doesn't she?" Lindsey said thoughtfully. So I wasn't the only one to notice the sag factor. "But I don't think we need to worry about distracting anyone. The front window isn't locked."

I sat upright, ignoring the sloshing from my midsection. "What?"

"The one next to the door. I unlocked it before we left. No alarms, either, as far as I can tell."

"You're brilliant," I said with admiration.

Lindsey shot me a sidelong glance. "So if you're as handy with a safe as you say you are . . ."

I leaned back in my seat and grinned, letting the wind blow through my hair. "Maybe you should think about going strawberry blond after all."

"Nah," she said, eyeing me speculatively. "Although you would make a good sidekick. Next time, instead of Gertrude, maybe I'll call you Bess. You know, like Nancy Drew's chunky friend?"

I sat up straight, knees clenched together. "Chunky?"

"Well, not exactly *chunky* . . ."

I would have kicked her, but she was driving.

Eighteen

Once I got back to the office, I sent a quick e-mail to Adele asking if we could reschedule the Southeast Airlines meeting for a more convenient day. Like a day when I wouldn't be howling at the moon.

And then I closed my door, pulled out my PDA, and called Tom.

Adrenaline pulsed through me as the phone rang on the other end. I was finally going to get some answers to the questions that had been plaguing me for years. It rang three times before someone answered. Or something, actually; it was a recorded message, informing me that the number I had dialed was not in service.

Shit.

I rechecked the number and dialed again.

With exactly the same result.

I tried a few variations of the number, but none of them led to Tom. I stared at my PDA, so frustrated I wanted to fling the thing across the room.

Instead, I forced myself to turn on the computer and try to get something done.

Unfortunately, either Adele was out of the office or she couldn't be bothered, because I didn't hear back. The rest of the afternoon I spent checking my e-mail for missives from Adele and trying to bury myself and my worries in work.

It was a good plan, but not a particularly effective one. As I sorted through endless columns of numbers, I couldn't help being distracted by occasional thoughts of Tom, of my mother—and the contents of my drawer, which I smelled faintly. A couple of times I closed the door and pulled out the most recent box, sniffing it all over, trying yet again to get a read on who had sent it. Except for that maddening hint of cat, though, I kept coming up blank.

Finally, when I couldn't stare at the computer anymore, I picked up the phone and called Heath. He wasn't at home, so I tried his office; he answered on the second ring. At least someone picked up when I called, I thought.

"Busy?" I asked in my most alluring voice.

"What did you have in mind?" he asked.

"Oh, I don't know . . . maybe a little coffee break?"

"I was hoping for something more than coffee . . . but can I take a rain check? This case goes to trial next week, and I've got to finish my brief."

So much for distracting myself with a visit to Heath.

"I'll let you get to it, then," I said.

"Damn. I really want to see you before I leave town . . ."

Oh, yeah. He would be leaving Friday night for the Valley and wouldn't be back until late Sunday night. So much for a nine-to-five job.

"There's always Monday," he said.

But Monday was a problem for me. A big, fat, hairy problem. "About Monday . . ." I began.

"I've got the reservations, so you're not wriggling out of it," he said, and my stomach sank. Maybe I could come down with bird flu or something hypercontagious between now and Monday. I'd have to think of something. For now, though, I said, "I'm sure we'll find a few minutes somewhere. Get to work. And then get some sleep."

"I could probably take a fifteen-minute break . . ."

I laughed. "No, counselor. Get your brief done. No distractions."

"I love you," he said, his voice doing that sexy husky thing again. He might be a tad overambitious in the work department, but he made up for it in other ways. Other, very interesting ways.

"I love you too," I said, and before I could be tempted, I hung up.

I sat and stared at my computer for the next twenty minutes, but it was useless; my brain kept veering back to thoughts of Tom, of my mother's impending jail sentence—and the mystery care packages in my bottom drawer. I finally gave up, grabbed both boxes, and headed downstairs to my car.

Twenty minutes later I pulled up outside Sit A Spell. When I opened the door, the familiar aromas of incense and beeswax mingled with the sharper aroma of fresh-cut herbs—and the smell of burned coffee. Something crunched underfoot; I reached down and picked up a dried pinto bean; a few more were scattered around the room.

"I'm in here, sweetheart," Mom called as the door jingled shut behind me. I followed her voice to the kitchen, where she stood at the table surrounded by bunches of herbs she'd plucked from the garden behind the shop. Beside her lay a white-handled knife—her *bolline,* which she used to prepare things for rituals and potions.

"How did you know it was me?" I asked, even though I knew the answer. After all, she *was* psychic. "And what's with the beans?"

"The beans? They're for Freddy."

"Freddy?"

"Freddy Fingers," she said.

Ah. The ghostly groper.

"It's a 'Get Away, Ghost' spell," she continued.

"Feeding the ghost beans will make him go away?"

My mom shrugged, and her hoop earrings flashed in the light. "I'm not sure how it works. Maybe it gives them indigestion or something. Still, it's worth trying."

"If that doesn't work, the burned coffee should," I said, walking over to the pot. "Can I throw this out?"

My mother laughed. "It's not the stuff in the pot, dear; I just made that a few minutes ago. I'm doing a double spell today: beans and burned coffee grounds." She gestured to a metal cauldron on the stove, which was filled with a foul-smelling black sludge. "So far I've used boneset and tiger lilies, and I even wiped the whole place down with Juno's Brew." She ticked them off on her fingers. "And every time, Freddy's come back."

"Juno's Brew?"

"It's complicated," she said. "But if the beans and coffee don't work, I'll have to get creative." Personally, I thought burned coffee grounds and pinto beans were pretty creative, but maybe that was just me. My mother sighed. "I wish I could find that spell book; I know I've got a good one that you can work on Samhain."

Samhain, I knew, was what Wiccans called Halloween. "Well, you've still got at least a month," I said. "I'm sure it will turn up."

"But enough about me. What brings you here? I can tell you've been upset," my mother said, coming around the table. Her wardrobe was remarkably subdued: jeans and an oversized man's shirt. Which I hoped she hadn't snagged from her lawyer's house. Best not to think about it, really.

I set the boxes down on the edge of the table and allowed her to envelope me in a hug. Her familiar patchouli scent was lighter than usual, masked by the smell of fresh herbs. I usually found it cloying—growing up, I used to scrub my face and hands as soon as I got to school, hoping that no one else would smell it. I couldn't do much about the incense scent on my clothes, so if anyone asked, I just told them it was perfume.

It was bad enough that I had to escape to the girls' room to shave every two hours as a kid. I still had nightmares about the time I left my razor home; it was early summer, and I was wearing a tank top, so you can imagine that things got a bit hairy. But try surviving high school with a mom who donates palm readings and free potions to the school raffle. Particularly when you live in Texas.

Tonight, however, the earthy smell was comforting, and I found myself relaxing in the familiar surroundings.

"I hope you're not worried about this whole court case thing," she said, releasing me. "You know I'll be just fine."

"It's not that," I said, even though just mentioning it sent my blood pressure shooting up a couple of points. "Well, not completely."

"Is it about that handsome werewolf?" She studied me. I wasn't sure I'd told her he was a werewolf, but with those eyes, anyone who was familiar with the species would know in a heartbeat. Hence her excitement; as much as I wanted to be human, she wanted to see me lope off into the sunset with another werewolf.

"No . . . well, maybe a little," I admitted, involuntarily thinking of Tom's gorgeous golden eyes and how much time he was spending with Lindsey and the phone number that didn't work. And about the pack that had attacked the Tri-Delta. The pack that now, thanks to my Good Samaritan instincts, knew I was a werewolf. "But right now, I'm worried about this," I said, pointing to the boxes on the table.

My mom's smile dimmed a few watts as her eyes found the cardboard boxes. "What's in them?"

"Wolfsbane."

"Wolfsbane?" my mother repeated, her eyebrows arching over her dark eyes.

"And a bullet."

She sucked in her breath. "It's silver, isn't it?"

I nodded. "I was hoping you might be able to help me find out who sent it."

My mother turned her attention to the boxes, closing her eyes as she touched first one, then the other. Picking up vibrations, or something. "Whoever sent these wishes you ill," she murmured.

Like I needed a psychic to tell me that.

"Where did they come from?" she asked.

"The first one was on my desk," I said. "The second one someone left with Sally. My assistant. There was a note with each of them," I said, digging out the slips of paper and unfolding them on the table.

As she read them, my mom wrinkled her nose. "Not quite Pablo Neruda, is she?"

"She?"

"I think it's a woman. Whoever wrote these is very closed—see the backward slant? And she has a secret of her own to hide. I can tell by the tightness of the hand—very cramped." She glanced up at me. "I think maybe we should do a reading."

"Cards?" For once I was okay with the idea. After all, she *had* managed to call Brewster back from the dead—and I was more than a bit anxious to find out who was sending me packages. Not to mention writing such awful poetry.

She nodded. "Let me just clear this away, and we'll get going."

I waved at the herbs. "What is all this for, anyway?"

"Let's see. I was working on a surgery amulet, a breast-augmentation potion, an immigration-authority spell, and a road-opener spell."

"A road-opener spell?"

"Yeah. They've been working on Barton Springs Road for ages—one of the restaurant owners wanted to know if I could hurry things along. Oh—and I almost forgot—a winged-foot spell. One of those suburban moms—she's looking to improve her time in the Danskin triathlon next year."

I stared at the mass of green on the table. "You're kidding me, right?"

"Nope," she said, pointing at something I hadn't noticed—a dirty shoelace. *Ick*.

"She doesn't really want wings on her feet, does she?"

"Only figuratively," my mother said, moving the herbs and the shoelace to the counter and spreading a blue silk tablecloth on the worn table.

"Where are Tania and Emily?" I asked. If we were doing a reading, I would prefer it be private—particularly from Tania, who for some reason I just didn't trust.

"They're gone for the night," she said. "Relax—it's just us."

As she finished arranging the piles of herbs on the counter, I wondered where the road-opening spell had come from. Despite her Romany roots—and her magical training, which had been passed down through the generations of her mother's family—I suspected my mother had branched out a bit to meet more modern needs. I eyed the dirty shoelace; I doubted Grandma Masitus had much call for spells involving race times back in Lithuania.

After dimming the lights, Mom lit a candle and some incense, took a few deep breaths, and laid her hands on the cardboard boxes while I sat across from her, watching. After a few minutes, she reached for the cards, an ancient deck as soft and pliable as fabric.

She handed them to me to shuffle. I smushed them together a few times—they were big and floppy, and I wasn't a particularly good shuffler even with a normal deck—and handed them back.

As I watched, she laid a series of cards out on the blue silk cloth. Unfortunately, I had little to no idea what they meant. When I was very small, I thought the pictures were interesting, but Mom said the cards were too delicate and old to play with. And later, when she wanted to teach me, I told her I was learning everything I needed to know in school. Now, fortunately, Emily was carrying on the family tradition of casting spells and telling fortunes. Which was a big relief; I wasn't about to change career tracks anytime soon. Besides, I figured

I made a sizable contribution just by keeping my mom out of the weeds with the IRS.

My mother laid down a card and glanced up at me sharply. I swallowed hard. Despite my lack of training, I was pretty sure the Death card she had just put down wasn't good news.

"That doesn't look good," I said, jabbing a finger at the skeleton.

"Sshh," she said, still laying out cards.

"What does it mean?" I had a pretty good idea, but I was hoping I was wrong.

"Hold your horses, dear."

"I'd love to, Mom. The problem is, there's already a horse—and it's got a skeleton on it," I said, pointing at the bony form, which was sitting on top of a pale horse. "I'm just hoping it's not me."

Her dark eyes flicked up to me. "It could be Brewster, dear."

"Oh." Excellent point. And one I was happy to get on board with.

Then she laid down another card and sucked in her breath.

"What?" I demanded.

She stared at the card. It was the Wheel of Fortune— and I don't mean like on the TV show. "We've got trouble."

Nineteen

I looked at the card—it looked like an old-fashioned version of the game-show wheel, only with people on it instead of dollar signs—and then back at my mother. "What do you mean, 'trouble'?"

Her rings flashed in the soft light as she laid down the rest of the tarot cards, then sat back and looked at the spread. "The problem is, it's reversed. Normally, it wouldn't be that bad, but with all of the swords in a reading . . ."

"What's wrong with swords?"

"A couple aren't so bad, but when there are a lot of them . . ." She sighed. "You're at a crossroads, my dear. And there are a lot of negative influences." Her hand glanced over the Death card, and she laid a finger on the High Priestess. "This is the card that 'crosses' you. Someone—someone powerful—is working against you."

"Great," I said, feeling a chill run down my spine. "I'll keep a lookout for a woman in blue and white robes, then."

"Sophie, this is not a laughing matter. You need to be careful. She's powerful—and for some reason, she's set herself against you."

I reached up to massage my temples, questioning my wisdom in asking my mom for help. So far, I wasn't getting too much value out of this reading—just a series of hints and veiled threats that were scaring me even more. Why couldn't there be a kind of divination that involved names and faces? Was there some reason the spirit world had to be so darned vague? A wisp of incense washed over me as I surveyed the spread on the table. My mom was right—it was positively prickly with swords.

Finally, my mother sat back and sighed. "She may be the one who's sending you these boxes, but it's just not clear."

Once again, not exactly helpful information. I stared at the woman's enigmatic smile. Did the card really represent the person who was threatening me with nasty notes? Or was the whole thing just chance?

"There are two men in your life, too," my mother said. My eyebrows shot up at that one. Two men? I was only dating one. "This one"—she tapped the Knight of Pentacles—"and this one." Her finger came to rest on the Knight of Wands.

I hoped their defining characteristics were not that they walked around in armor. Not that I had any problem with the whole knight-in-shining-armor thing—I would just prefer it to be figurative. And that there be only one of them.

"The Knight of Pentacles usually means a dependable young man. Not a lot of imagination, but a hard worker. Loyal."

Heath, I thought.

"The Knight of Wands, on the other hand, is very different. Individualistic, strong, often a traveler." She cocked an eyebrow. "Usually a pretty good lover too."

Well, unless he was a master of disguise, that sure didn't describe Herb from Termite Terminators, and other than him, my contact with members of the opposite sex had been rather limited lately. Limited to Heath and Tom, in fact.

Despite my best efforts, my mind kept circling back in

on the tall, long-haired werewolf. The werewolf who smelled like the most intoxicating cologne in the world. The werewolf who was dating my best friend.

"Sophie?"

"Sorry," I said, sitting up in my chair and trying to concentrate on the spread in front of me. "So what about these two men?"

"I think you may have a decision to make," she said, eyes glinting.

"But I'm only seeing one man."

"Maybe," my mother said skeptically, her smooth skin glowing in the candlelight. "But it won't stay that way."

I forced myself to think of Heath's chocolate-brown eyes, his masculine smell, the way his lips felt when he kissed me. . . . I would never give him up. And there was no way I was going to get involved with a werewolf. But to get my mother off the topic, I said, "All right. So my dating life may experience a shake-up soon. Unlikely, but possible." I pushed my hair behind my ears and leaned forward. "For now, though, can we get back to the whole weird package thing?"

"Unfortunately, we can guide the cards, but we can't dictate them. And all of these elements are intertwined." Her gold bangles jingled as she reached out to squeeze my hand. "Sophie, my dear, stay alert—there are at least two people out there gunning for you."

"Too bad I have no idea who they are."

"Whoever they are, at least one of them is a force to be reckoned with. And the second person is not what he or she appears to be," she said, releasing my hand and running a finger over the cards. "There's something hidden."

Lindsey? my mind whispered.

"As for the Death card . . ." My mother shrugged. "Sometimes it means death. In this case, it could mean

Brewster. Other times it means change." Her dark eyes flicked to me. "As in leaving an old way of doing things behind."

If she thought that meant I was going to ditch auditing and embrace my inner werewolf, she was barking up the wrong tree. "Gosh," I said. "That's encouraging." Maybe this whole card-reading thing wasn't such a swell idea after all.

"And then there's this card," she said, pointing to the picture I'd been trying to ignore. Two dogs, howling at the full moon. The hairs prickled on my neck, and I looked away. "You can't deny your nature," she said softly.

"It's worked for the last twenty-eight years," I said tartly.

"This man. The lawyer you've been seeing," she said quietly. "What is he going to say when you tell him what you really are?"

"Who says I have to?"

"I think he'd probably like to know before you have kids." She eyed me meaningfully. "Or should I say . . . pups?"

I wrapped my arms around myself. I'd thought about it before, of course. But I didn't want to discuss this right now. "You don't know that they'd be like me," I said.

The bangles slid down my mother's arms as she raised her hands. "I'm just saying . . ."

"Can we get back to the matter at hand?" I asked, giving the cardboard boxes a pointed look. "Because right now, someone's threatening me with silver bullets. And if I'm dead, the question of children will kind of be a moot point, won't it?"

She sighed. "I was hoping the reading would be a little more clear. Obviously there are a lot of influences right now—it's hard to separate them. They all seem to be connected. On the plus side, the outcome isn't decided yet."

"That's a plus?" I asked.

She tapped the last card, depicting a tower split in two by a bolt of lightning. "At least it doesn't spell disaster," she said. The people jumping off the top of the tower with their clothes on fire didn't look too happy to me, but I'm not the fortune-teller in the family, so I just nodded.

"But things will definitely change," she said. "Soon."

Great. My life was a wreck, with nothing but more problems on the horizon, and we were no closer to finding out who was sending me nasty care packages. I stared at the moon card and tried to stifle my disappointment as my mother recorded the spread in a big, leather-bound book.

"Doesn't that have another meaning?" I said.

"What, dear?"

"The moon card," I said. "I mean, not everyone's a werewolf, so it's got to have some other connotation, right?"

She sighed and fixed me with her dark eyes. "It also means deceit," she said quietly. "A dishonest person."

I squirmed a little on my wooden chair. Kind of like a werewolf who was dating a human and not coming clean about her supernatural tendencies?

"Are you sure that's all?" I asked. "No other possible meanings?"

"Well, sometimes it can represent an artist or a veterinarian," she said, her dark eyes twinkling. "But somehow I don't think those apply."

Oh, well.

A minute later, she swept the cards together and rewrapped the deck in a silk scarf. "Have you done a reading on yourself lately?" I asked.

Her mouth twitched into a grin. "Of course."

"And?" I prompted.

The grin grew bigger.

"No Death card?"

"No Death card," she said. "But I did pull the Lovers."

I put up a hand, thinking of Mom's pool ball–shaped defense attorney. "Don't tell me."

"I wasn't going to."

"Thanks. I just want to remind you that your relationship with your attorney should be strictly professional."

"I believe you've mentioned that once or twice," my mother said.

As she put the cards up, I said, "How is it that you ended up selling Ted Brewster a love potion, anyway?"

She smiled. "He came in here a while back. I was afraid he was going to bolt, he was so nervous."

"You mentioned he'd been in here a few times before, too."

"Yes. Obviously something here called to him. For a while there, I thought he might be a little sweet on me."

"But he really had the hots for the librarian."

She nodded. "Such a shame, isn't it?"

"So what did you two talk about?"

"Well, when I found out who he was, I started talking about the development."

"The one by Barton Springs?"

She nodded. "I figured maybe I could persuade him to change his vote."

"Well, you must have had some impact on him—apparently he was asking the librarian all about endangered species. What exactly did you tell him?"

"He was curious about Wicca, I think. I explained about the power in the earth—and how the whole earth is sacred, and some places in particular."

"How'd that go over?"

"Surprisingly well, actually. Of course, I might have helped things out a bit . . ."

Uh-oh. "What do you mean, 'helped things out a bit'?"

"Well, I might have . . . you know . . . made him a bit more receptive to new ideas."

I held up a hand. "Don't tell me, please." Once again, what I didn't know, I couldn't be forced to admit in court.

"Anyway, dear, it doesn't matter now. He's dead."

"Thanks for reminding me."

She looked at me with her warm brown eyes. "There was something else you wanted to ask about, wasn't there, dear?"

She always knew. Which had been highly inconvenient in high school—it's hard to sneak out when your mother can read your mind—but had its benefits now that I was an adult. Well, maybe not *benefits*—it still freaked me out when she called me three seconds before I dialed her number—but at least she didn't stop me from sneaking out anymore.

"There's a pack in town," I said.

Her head jerked up. "*Lupins?*"

I nodded. "They're the made kind. Did my father ever tell you about how that happens, by the way?"

She sighed. "I'm afraid not."

Shoot. If only I'd gotten Tom's number right . . . "I caught them attacking a sorority girl the other day," I said.

"Do you think they're connected with the werewolf that was here the other day?" she asked. "Although he looks like the real McCoy to me."

"He is," I said quickly.

She nodded. "That's right—you'd be able to tell, wouldn't you? I didn't think he was made. He's an old one. Probably from the north. Reminds me of your father, in a way—although without that fabulous French accent . . ."

"Did Luc ever tell you much about territories?" I asked. *Luc* just somehow seemed more appropriate than *Dad* when describing the big, furry ne'er-do-well who had donated half my genes.

"He didn't tell me much—I don't think they're supposed to talk about it—but from what he told me, I gather they can be pretty big. I think his pack controlled all of Paris, and several miles beyond. And the packs defend their turf fiercely; I'm surprised they've tolerated your friend. What's the born one's name, by the way?"

"Tom," I said. "He says he's not part of a pack, but I think he's working for one."

"Unusual. From what I was told, they don't usually like solitaries."

"I wouldn't know," I said. And it was true. As a child, I had gotten my hands on one of my mother's books about werewolves, and what I'd read had horrified me so much I vowed never to have anything to do with them again. Besides, when you're a kid, you don't want to be different. And at Travis Heights Elementary School, sprouting a full fur coat and a mouthful of canines every twenty-eight days wasn't exactly in the realm of "normal."

It's true that over the years, my mother had tried to fill me in on what she knew of what she called my "kind." But she didn't know a whole lot. And for a long time, unless it involved ways for me to avoid sprouting fur and fangs, I was almost afraid to know. Until now, that is.

"You've finally come around," she said. "I'm so glad, dear." She reached over and squeezed my hand; her skin was soft and warm. "Sophie, not all werewolves are bad. Your dad was a wonderful man, in his own way."

"I wouldn't know," I said frostily. "Our acquaintance was rather brief."

"Darling," she said, reaching out with a sympathetic hand. "I'm so sorry you were hurt."

I steered away from the topic of my father. The last thing I was in the mood for right now was a chat about my father's pack responsibilities and his need to follow his animal nature. I mean, come on. Can you say cop-out? "The three I saw the other night didn't look particularly friendly," I said. "But I can't tell about Tom."

"How do you know this lone werewolf isn't part of a pack?" my mother asked.

Uh-oh. "What do you mean?"

Her brown eyes glinted. "What I mean is, did you talk about it in the front of the store the other day? Or are you seeing him?"

"No," I said quickly.

"No, you didn't discuss this the other day?" I'll say one thing for my mother: She is certainly persistent. "Or no, you're not seeing him?"

"*I'm* not seeing him, no." I swallowed.

My mom's eyes widened in comprehension. "Oh, my goodness. The attraction charm. It's Lindsey who's seeing him, isn't it?"

I nodded.

"Have you told her?"

"What do you think?"

She pursed her lips. "Well, someone's going to have to."

"Mom . . ."

"I didn't say it was going to be me," she said, staring at me from dark-chocolate eyes. "After all, *I'm* not her best friend."

I closed my eyes and massaged my temples.

Things were definitely not looking up.

Saturday morning I dropped the M3 off at the dealership and headed in to work. I'd tried to convince Heath to move our little anniversary surprise to tonight, while I was still human, but it was no use. He was out of town until Monday. Ah, Monday. Our anniversary, the Southeast Airlines meeting, the autumnal equinox . . . and the full moon.

Around five, I gave up on the account and drove my loaner car down to the dealership to pick up my rehabilitated M3. When I picked it up, the car had acquired a rather pungent base note of eau de BO—one of the mechanics must have an aversion to soap—but at least the window was fixed.

As I rolled down the windows and reached for the orange-oil spray, I steered the M3 homeward. With Heath out of town and Lindsey doing God knows what—I had avoided calling her today, for some reason—the evening was my own, and I planned to enjoy it.

I had just finished off a Lean Cuisine dinner and was settling down with a glass of Chardonnay and a medicinal dose of reality TV when the phone rang.

It was Lindsey.

"So, are you up for it?" Her voice was bubbly with excitement, and I felt a sense of foreboding. She'd been out with Tom last night—and although I usually got the postmortem immediately, this time I really didn't want to know how it had gone.

I took a sip of wine and turned down the TV. "Up for what?"

"Another trip to Brewster's office."

"Brewster's office?" I had no desire to go to Brewster's office. I had my wine, I had my fuzzy bunny slippers—and besides, *What Not to Wear* was on, and we were still ten minutes from finding out how Stacy and Clinton were going to transform a 250-pound housewife into a runway model. Add to that my mother's ominous pronouncements about the mysterious people trying to mess up my life, and you had one werewolf who wasn't too keen on sticking her nose out anytime soon.

"When did you have in mind?" I asked. It was already after eight.

"Tonight, silly."

I stifled a sigh and focused on Clinton, who was holding an animal-print tube top up to the camera while its owner blushed.

"I don't know how long that window will be unlocked," Lindsey said as Clinton tossed the tube top into a trash can. "For all we know, they may have caught it already," Lindsey continued as I watched him pick up the next item—something stringy and pink—with kind of a sick fascination. "I would have called you so we could do it last night, but I was busy."

"Oh, yeah. Your date." I took a swig of wine. "How did that go?"

"It was fabulous," she breathed.

"Glad to hear it," I said shortly, stifling the urge to groan. Why couldn't it have been a washout? I forced myself to focus on something other than Tom and Lindsey—and the wardrobe of horrors unfolding on the screen in front of me. "So what's the plan for tonight?"

"We go, we break in, you get the safe open."

"Gosh. You make it sound so easy."

"Make sure you wear dark clothes, though."

"All right," I said, draining my wine. So much for *What Not to Wear*. "Are you coming by to pick me up or are we meeting there?"

"I'll meet you there, okay?"

"See you in twenty."

Twenty

I hung around just long enough to see the reveal. Stacy and Clinton were good, but they weren't quite fairy godmother material. I guess there's only so much you can do with fabric.

After fixing myself a quick cup of tea, I kicked off my fluffy bunny slippers and slipped into a pair of dark jeans. It was only when I arrived at Brewster's building that I realized I'd never figured out a good explanation for how I could open combination locks by ear.

"What took you so long?" Lindsey hissed as I closed the car door behind me.

"I got held up," I said, a little embarrassed to tell her I'd wanted to watch the end of a reality show.

"Hot date?"

I snorted. "Hardly. Heath's out of town on a deposition."

As I crept up the front walk behind my voluptuous friend, she said, "I checked the window, and I think it's still unlocked."

I half hoped it wasn't. Brewster's office had a menacing air tonight; the dark windows looked like bottomless holes. The idea of returning home to my bunny slippers and another rerun of *What Not to Wear* was sounding better and better. "Which one was it?"

"That one," she said, pointing at the big window to the right of the door.

"Well, then, let's give it a try." I glanced around warily. I had the uncomfortable sense of having eyes on my back, and I didn't like it one bit. After a quick sniff and another glance over my shoulder, I bent down and tugged at the window. It didn't budge. "Are you sure it's unlocked?"

"It was fifteen minutes ago," she said, flicking on a flashlight. My feeling of being watched intensified as she focused it on the lock. "Still is. Maybe they painted it shut."

"Let's try together," I said.

I was beginning to think I would have a second session with my bunny slippers when the window shot up with a thud.

Lindsey reeled backward across the porch. "Shit."

"What's wrong? Did you hurt yourself?"

"I think I broke a nail."

"A nail?" I said. "*Sheesh*. I thought you lost a finger."

"Easy for you to say. You didn't just drop fifty bucks on a manicure."

As Lindsey examined her nail, I glanced around, looking for the source of my uneasiness. Who was watching me? Or was it just my imagination? "Lindsey. We're about to commit an illegal act. Can we talk about your nail later?"

She said, looking up from her damaged nail. "Do you have any nail repair?"

"I didn't think I'd need it. Now, let's go." A moment later, we clambered through the window into the front hall. I had hoped being inside would make me feel better, but if anything, the feeling of foreboding increased. I took a deep breath, and my hackles rose.

"There's something different," I said. "It smells funny in here."

"Smells like dust to me," she said, brushing off her skirt. Only Lindsey would wear a skirt to a break-in, I thought. At least it was black.

"These are for you, by the way," she said, handing me a pair of orange rubber gloves.

"Are we going to be washing dishes later?"

"Fingerprints," she said. "Let's get going—I need to get this nail fixed before it totally rips off. How come this always happens the day after I get a manicure?"

"Can we discuss this later?" I whispered.

I headed up the stairs after her, cringing as a step creaked. The smell grew stronger as we climbed; by the time we reached the door to Brewster's offices, it was enough to fell an ox. Not to mention a werewolf.

"You don't smell that?" I hissed, covering my nose with one hand and trying not to lose the contents of my stomach.

"No, I don't," she said, stopping before the heavy wood door. "But I totally forgot that there was another door. Shoot."

"Maybe it's unlocked," I said, knowing that it wasn't. Somebody didn't want us here; I could feel it in the air. It was heavy, almost cloying—and there was more to it than the awful smell. Who didn't want us here? Maria? Brewster's perky assistant? Or was it someone else?

I tested the doorknob. Sure enough, it was locked.

"Now what?" Lindsey said.

"Maybe we should just go home," I said, taking a step back from the door to get away from the smell.

"We need to find out what's in that safe," Lindsey reminded me as she followed me down the stairs to the front window. The smell was making me sick; I couldn't wait to get outside.

"We can't leave without at least trying to get in," she continued. "It may be the only way to clear your mom's name." Lindsey thought a moment. "What about the upstairs windows?"

"What about them?" I asked, with what can only be termed serious misgivings.

"We can climb up," she suggested brightly.

"Climb up?"

"Well, actually, I was thinking you could climb up. You see, I've got this fear of heights . . ."

Lovely.

"It'll be easy," she said. "This place is surrounded by huge oak trees."

I was about to throw in the towel and head back to my bunny slippers—and the rest of my bottle of wine—when it occurred to me that there was an advantage to Lindsey's plan. If I could actually get in through the window, I would have a chance to tackle the wall safe without Lindsey watching me. "I guess it's worth a shot," I said, as I climbed through the window to the front porch. As Lindsey followed me, I searched the darkness with wary eyes, trying to find the watcher I could sense, but couldn't see.

The scent of dead leaves and mold wafted up to me as we rounded the building. I glanced up at the second-story windows, then squinted up at the branches.

"That one looks pretty close," Lindsey said, pointing to a curved branch that angled in about five feet away from one of Maria's office windows. I wouldn't call it close—more like in the general vicinity—but it was really our only option.

I sighed. "I guess I'd better get this over with. Help me up, will you?"

With Lindsey pushing and grunting (unnecessarily, in my opinion) from behind, I managed to lever myself up onto the lowest branch. Just as I found my footing, something exploded from the top of the tree with a squawk. I was a hairbreadth away from toppling onto my best friend when my left hand made contact with a branch. I grabbed it just in time.

"What was that?" Lindsey hissed as I pulled myself upright and tried not to go into cardiac arrest. I knew this was a bad idea. So why was I still doing it?

"I don't know," I whispered back, heart pounding in my chest. "Some kind of bird, I guess." The bark was rough under my hands as I grabbed the next branch and propelled myself upward. Before long, I was on the same level as Maria's window. A breeze swept by, and for a moment, I caught that awful smell again—even with the window closed, it was strong. A second breeze swirled by as I prepared to lean out from the branch, and I jerked back immediately.

Somewhere nearby was a werewolf.

My hackles rose as I sniffed again, straining to pick up the scent, but it was so faint I couldn't get a fix on it. The next moment, it was gone.

I grabbed the rough bark of the branch, steadying myself. Was it Tom? It wasn't the packette, but I hadn't gotten enough of a read to tell much else.

"What's wrong?" Lindsey called up from below.

I jumped at the sound of her voice. "Nothing," I said. "Thought I heard something."

"How are you going to get in?" she asked.

"Shhh. I'm thinking."

And trying to get a read on a werewolf. Another breeze eddied by, but the whiff I'd gotten was gone. I sniffed a few more times, and when the scent didn't come back, I edged closer to the window, trying to get a good look at the locks on the other side of the glass panes. In the light of the almost-full moon, I could see that two of the latches were snugly locked. I squinted at the third window; the latches were free.

The problem was, how was I going to get close enough to open it?

Of course it had to be the window farthest from the branch. I looked around for a way to get a foothold, but there was nothing but empty air filling the two yards between the branch and the side of the building.

I was going to have to get creative.

I edged along the oak limb until I was as close as possible to the window. Then I held my breath and took a giant step with my left foot, hoping the office had kept the woodwork in good condition.

"What are you doing?" Lindsey hissed as I straddled several feet of dead air and prayed that I wasn't depending on a termite colony to hold me up.

"The last one's unlocked," I said.

"This isn't a good idea, Sophie."

I didn't remind her that this whole escapade had, in fact, been her idea. Instead, I focused on finding a better footing on the wood windowsill, which was not quite as solid-feeling as I would have liked. In fact, it creaked rather ominously as I shifted my weight.

"Jesus, Sophie. Maybe I should just call 911 now."

I reached out with my right hand and pushed upward at the window. It didn't move even a millimeter. I put the pressure on again, a little harder this time. Too hard, and I'd risk breaking the woodwork, but I pushed my luck a little more and gave it a big shove. Again, it didn't budge. Had it been painted shut?

"What are you doing up there?" Lindsey hissed as I braced myself against the window and gave a mighty shove.

A split second later, the woodwork gave way, the window shot up, and I did a belly flop onto Maria's windowsill. Unfortunately, I also landed on an African violet in a quaint orange pot.

And then—as if chunks of terra-cotta embedded in my midriff weren't bad enough—I began to slide.

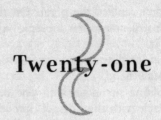

Twenty-one

"Sophie!" Lindsey screeched from below as I scrabbled for the sill. I caught it just in time. If it weren't for that little extra something being a werewolf gave me—and the benefits of semiregular trips to the gym—I would have been toast. I hauled myself into Maria's office and landed on the floor with a thud.

"Are you okay?" Lindsey called up as I lifted my shirt and picked shards of terra-cotta out of my stomach. I'd broken open the gash Jerk-Off had given me the other night, and now I had an exciting set of new puncture wounds to go with it. At least I hadn't worn my new DKNY T-shirt. I took a deep, shaky breath, and gagged. The putrid smell was worse inside than out.

"Fine," I called down, trying not to think about the stench around me. It sure wasn't the light and airy mix of flowers and antiques from earlier today. Trying not to throw up on my shoes, I surveyed the dirt and flowerpot shards scattered on the floor. So much for a stealthy entry.

"Sophie!"

I leaned out the window, thankful for a breath of fresh air. "What?"

"I'll come around; can you let me in?"

"Give me a minute," I said, surveying the mess on the floor. I could clean up the dirt and pottery shards, but I couldn't replace the plant. On the other hand, Maria didn't strike me as the domestic type. Maybe she wouldn't miss it.

The dangling trim on the outside of the building, on the other hand . . .

Holding my nose with one hand and my bleeding stomach with the other, I tiptoed around the smushed plant and headed into the hallway, pausing by Brewster's office. Should I give the safe a shot now, before Lindsey got there?

As I nudged the door open and stepped inside, a wave of foul air swept over me. I slammed the door shut and gasped for breath. The office staff evidently needed to reassess their choice of cleaning products—either that, or stop hosting skunk conventions. Was I going to be able to concentrate enough to get the safe open? And what the hell *was* that smell?

I had just staggered out Brewster's door when Lindsey started knocking. I hurried toward the front door, thankful to be away from the source—whatever it was—of the reek. The whole place felt oppressive, and not just because of the smell. Somebody didn't want us here. I was sure of it.

I slid the dead bolt and opened the door, and Lindsey scurried through.

"I was afraid you were toast there for a minute," she said.

"Yeah, me too."

Lindsey flashed her light at my exposed stomach. "Jeez. You really did yourself in. Are you all right?"

"I'll be fine," I said. I wasn't sure I'd be wearing a bikini anytime soon—the hit-by-shrapnel look isn't exactly sexy—but I could tell it wasn't major damage.

"What did you do to yourself?"

I grimaced. "I landed on a flowerpot."

"Ouch." Lindsey flicked on the flashlight and peered

at my midriff. "Sophie, that looks pretty bad. Maybe we should bag it and go to the emergency room."

"No way," I said. "I just about killed myself getting up here. I'm not going to do it again." So what if my stomach looked like a mosaic? At least I had a chance of finding a get-out-of-jail-free card for my mother. The only problem was what I was going to do with Lindsey while I used my wolfie powers to open the safe.

"What are we going to do about the flowerpot?" she asked, heading toward Maria's office.

Ask and you shall receive, I thought, trying to ignore the feeling of foreboding. And the stench of rotten eggs. "We need to get rid of the dirt and the broken pot. Tell you what. I'll get to work on the safe if you'll find some way to clean up the mess."

"Where do you think the cleaning supplies are?"

"Check the bathroom. I think it's down the hall," I said. As Lindsey scurried down the hall, I pressed a clean section of my T-shirt to my face—the faint floral scent of fabric softener wasn't exactly an air purifier, but it was better than nothing—and hustled to Brewster's office.

The smell hadn't dissipated in my brief absence, unfortunately. Bracing myself, I opened the door and darted in, anxious to get it over with before I puked. I lifted the heavy painting from the wall and propped it up against Brewster's desk, then took a deep breath and regretted it instantly. Total eau de skunk—only about 100 times worse.

Concentrate, Sophie.

I grabbed the dial of the combination lock and blocked out everything—the awful reek, the feeling of being watched, the bits of terra-cotta in my stomach, the fact that my bladder felt like an overfilled balloon—and pressed my ear up against the safe, rotating the dial to the right. The police had probably already gone through the safe, but I was hoping they'd left something for me to find.

I had gotten it three ticks when a bang sounded from down the hall.

"Lindsey!"

"Sorry," she mumbled, and I tried again.

I could hear the tumblers, or whatever they were, spinning around in there—and then I heard a click. I glanced at the number—thirty-four.

Holding my breath, I turned it to the left again, waiting for another click. As I listened, I realized I had no idea how many clicks I'd need to open it. I was assuming it worked like the lock on my high school locker—I mean, how fancy can you get with a combination lock?—but I didn't really know.

Which, frankly, was making me a little nervous. I should have researched the lock before coming. I mean, what if I couldn't get it open? I didn't want to break in a second time. The first time had just about killed me. I was about to turn it again when a car door slammed outside. I hurried to the window; someone was coming up the front walk.

"Lindsey!" I hissed.

"What?"

"Switch off your flashlight! Someone's coming!"

I slipped out of Brewster's office so I wouldn't throw up, and took refuge under Maria's desk. Would whoever it was notice the open window? As I crouched on the hardwood floor, I heard the jingle of keys, and the front door swung open. I held my breath. Partly from fear and partly because the place smelled awful.

The door slammed shut below, and I waited for the sound of footsteps on the stairs.

But my luck must have changed, because they didn't come. There were a few creaks from downstairs, and the sound of a drawer or cabinet slamming shut. Then the front door opened and thunked closed again. After another jingle of keys, whoever it was hurried down the front walk and left.

I know because I hurried to Brewster's window in time to see a dark car pull away.

"Do you think they noticed the window?" Lindsey asked from the doorway to the former councilman's office.

"I don't know, but if they called the cops, we'd better hurry up and get out of here."

Lindsey glanced at the safe, which was illuminated by the faint glow of the streetlamp outside. "Looks like you still have some work to do," she observed.

I bit my tongue as she headed back to Maria's office.

My palms sweating and my nose hairs curling, I tackled the safe again, spinning the dial to the left. *Please, please, please, let it work,* I prayed silently, listening for the sound of approaching sirens. Although would the cops use sirens if they were trying to sneak up on a burglar?

Then I heard it. Seventy-two.

I turned the knob to the right one last time, hoping, hoping that it was just like my old lock . . . and apparently three was the magic number, because—thanks be to God—it opened.

"I got it!"

I heard the clatter of broken pottery, then Lindsey calling out, "You're kidding me!" As I swung the safe open, she came in to join me.

"What's in it?" she asked, training her flashlight on the safe's interior. The police had already been here—I could see traces of fingerprint powder—but they'd put back what they found, apparently.

"Don't know yet," I said. "There's some kind of a box in here."

"Oooh," she said. "What do you think it is?"

"I don't know," I said, picking up the box—it was light and about half the size of a shoe box—and handing it to Lindsey. "I'll grab the papers—we've got to move fast. If whoever just left saw the open window, they might have called the police. Let's take it to Maria's office."

"Got it," she said.

As I grabbed the stack and followed Lindsey down the hall to Maria's office, a book slid from my hands onto the hardwood floor.

Lindsey bent down to pick it up, and trained the flashlight on it. "Bizarre."

"What?"

"It's that Al Gore book. You know, the one about global warming?"

"He kept that in a safe? I wonder what else is in here?"

"I don't know. A Greenpeace membership card?" Lindsey said as I deposited the stack on Maria's desk and glanced at the contents of the short pile, which included a few hardback books, some papers, and the box.

"You might not be too far off. He's got a couple of environmentalist books here," I said. "*Silent Spring* and *Earth in the Balance*."

"So he keeps the dirty magazines in his desk and the environmental books in the safe," Lindsey said, picking up *Silent Spring* and shaking it. "Just in case he hid something in the pages," she explained.

"If he did," I said glumly, "I'm sure the cops already found it."

When nothing fell out, she glanced at the back of the cover. "Hey, isn't this price tag from your mom's shop?"

I grabbed the book. Lindsey was right—I recognized my mother's handwriting on the little white sticker. "I always thought he was super pro-development. Do you think maybe he was having a late-life change of heart?"

"Either that or your mom put a spell on him."

From what I'd gleaned from my mom, I'd say the odds of that were pretty good, but I preferred denial. "I'm going to go with the change-of-heart theory," I said as I grabbed the box. "Let's see what's in this one."

We lifted the lid, revealing a plastic tube attached to one of those pumplike things they use to tighten the armband when you're getting your blood pressure taken.

"Is this some kind of medical equipment?" I asked, straining my ears for the sound of sirens. Or cars. All I could hear was crickets, though, and the distant hum of traffic. I still had that uncomfortable feeling of being watched.

"What do you think this is for?" Lindsey said, picking up the tube. The little pink cushion-shaped ball dangled in the air.

"I don't know. Are there instructions?"

She peered into the box and pulled out a pamphlet. "How to use your . . . oh, my God."

"What is it?"

"It's a penis pump."

"A *what*?" I grabbed for the instruction manual; sure enough, the cover read "The Engorger."

"It's supposed to make you . . . well, *bigger*. You know . . . pump it up?"

"Gross." I quickly banished an image of Ted Brewster and the Engorger. Where did he use it, anyway? The desk chair? I'd sat on that desk chair. . . .

Ick.

"Why keep it in the wall safe?" I asked.

"Would you want someone finding that in your drawers?"

"You mean desk drawers, right?"

She whacked me with the pump.

"Ew," I said, brushing off my sleeve. "That thing's been used, you know. Besides, we need to hurry up. The cops could be here at any moment."

"Good point," she said, shoving the tube into the box and wiping her hands on her skirt. "Do you think he washed it?"

"I don't want to think about it."

"I always wondered who bought these things," Lindsey said.

"Now we know," I said.

Lindsey pursed her lips as I pulled the stack of papers toward me. "Do you think Brewster remembered what was in there when he told us to look behind the picture?"

"Assuming it *was* Ted Brewster at the séance."

"Come on, Sophie. Who else would it be? Besides, it's not like finding this stuff could harm his political career. I mean, that kind of died when he did."

"True," I said, squinting at the top page of the papers. "But this looks kind of interesting."

"What is it?" Lindsey asked.

"A copy of his will, I think."

"Who's the beneficiary?"

I flipped through it. "Tad Brewster."

"Let me see." Lindsey moved around next to me and peered over my shoulder. "Pretty nasty will," she said, training her index finger on a dense paragraph halfway down the page. "He inherits . . . but only on the condition that he's already pulling down at least fiftyK a year."

"So he has to be making money to get money," I said. "Interesting motivational strategy."

"You think?"

"I get the impression that Brewster Jr. wasn't exactly following in his father's footsteps."

"Maria sure didn't want to talk about him, did she?"

asked Lindsey, handing me the will and squinting at the papers beneath it. "But the cops obviously saw the will," she said. "So why are they targeting your mother, instead of hauling Brewster Jr. in for questioning?"

"I guess with the poisoned potion from Sit A Spell, they figured they didn't need to look any further."

"Unfortunately, you're probably right. I was kind of hoping we'd find the potion bottle here, but I haven't seen it."

"Which makes me think it may not be the only thing the cops took," I said glumly. I was hoping that the police hadn't also taken whatever Brewster had wanted us to find.

Lindsey pulled out another sheaf of papers. "I wonder what this is. It looks like a deed of some kind."

"Let's see." I leaned over her shoulder and read the top page. "It's for the property next to Barton Springs. The one they're going to build the lofts on. Apparently most of it is owned by a trust of some sort."

Lindsey pulled out a stapled stack from beneath it. "There's an environmental assessment in here too."

I looked up. "Huh. Why would he keep this in his safe?"

"I don't know," she said. "Maybe he secretly owns the property. He's not supposed to vote on a development if he has a vested interest in it, is he?"

"Good point."

"And didn't the librarian say he was doing research on endangered species?" Lindsey quickly flipped through the pages. "This makes no sense to me, but we don't have time to go through it. I'll go make copies of everything."

"Including the instructions for the Engorger?"

Lindsey shuddered. "Only if you want to." She grinned at me. "Although from the look of him, I wouldn't think Heath would need it."

I kicked her under the desk.

"All right, all right," she said, rubbing her shin. "The copier's by the receptionist's desk, isn't it?"

"If you'll do the copies, I'll take the books back to the safe."

"Better take the Engorger with you too."

"I was hoping you'd take care of that, actually."

"If I'm going to make copies," she said, "the least you can do is put the penis pump back in the safe."

She had a point.

I repackaged the contraption, touching as few surfaces as possible and trying not to imagine the extent of Ted Brewster's relationship with it. When it was all boxed up, I took a deep breath and carted the first stack to Brewster's office. As I slid the books into the safe, I accidentally nudged the painting, which I'd propped up against the wall, with my foot. It started to fall, but I caught it just in time.

As I leaned it back against the wall again, I noticed a corner of paper sticking out from behind the backing. I bent down to take a closer look; it was the corner of an envelope, actually. Someone had pried up the paper backing, tucked the envelope in, and resealed it. But not very well.

Excitement surged through me; could this be what Brewster had meant at the séance?

Still holding my breath, I eased the envelope out from the backing and hurried out into the hall, where the smell wasn't as strong. There was no powder on the envelope, and I was guessing the police hadn't discovered it. It was addressed to Brewster at a West Lake Hills address—his house, maybe?—and was postmarked just three weeks earlier. I pulled out the contents and almost lost my cookies for the third time that night.

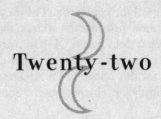

Twenty-two

It wasn't an eight-by-ten glossy, and for that I was thankful. Because even though it was four-by-six and blurry, there was already much, much more of Brewster than I had ever wanted to see.

"Lindsey!"

"I'm in here," she called. I followed her voice to the copy room.

She looked up at me from the whirring copier. "I'm not done yet. What's up?"

"Look at this," I said, turning the photo in her direction.

Her eyes grew wide. "Ew. That's disgusting." She looked closer. "Wow. I can see why he bought the pump."

I hadn't wanted to look that closely. "It was tucked behind the picture," I said.

Lindsey examined the photo again, her lip curled in distaste. I glanced at it again: It was a picture of Brewster giving his all (which, as it turned out, wasn't all that much) to a girl in knee socks and saddle shoes. And nothing else. "I understand why he kept it hidden. But who do you think the poor girl is?"

"I don't know, but she looks young enough to be his granddaughter."

"Was there anything with it?" she asked.

Good question. I shook the envelope, and a slip of

paper fell into my palm. The message on it was printer-generated, just like the address on the envelope.

"What does it say?" Lindsey prompted me.

" 'If you don't make the right decision on October 7, look for this image in the *American-Statesman*.' "

Lindsey's eyebrows rose. "Sounds like blackmail to me."

"But change his mind about what?"

"I don't know," she said. "Any return address?"

"Nope." I looked at the photo again, and this time I noticed a date stamp in the corner, right on top of Brewster's voluminous right buttock. "This was taken a while ago," I said.

"How can you tell?"

"It's dated two years ago."

"Then this might not be related to his death at all," she said.

"But the postmark is from two weeks ago," I reminded her.

Lindsey turned the photo to one side, squinting at the ripply white expanse of Brewster's buttock. "Well, whatever this is about, the photographer sure didn't get his good side."

As Lindsey finished making copies—including one of the photo—I retreated to Maria's office. The feeling of foreboding hadn't decreased—if anything, sitting and waiting for Lindsey only made it worse. I sat down in Maria's desk chair, straining my ears for the sound of sirens, and looked out the window at the almost-full moon. God, I hated the moon. As I stared at the white disk, which looked a little like a lopsided tortilla tonight—or maybe I was just hungry—a breeze stirred a little bit of dust on the windowsill and the foul odor got stronger.

I glanced down and noticed it was very thick dust.

Dust distributed in a straight line, in fact—except where I had smashed the flowerpot. I reached down to touch it and sniffed my fingers.

Which was a bad idea, because my hand now smelled like concentrated skunk.

I wiped my hand on the rug—I hated to do it to such a nice rug, but I couldn't stand to have the stuff on my fingers a moment longer. Then I stood up and walked around the room, examining the baseboards with the flashlight; sure enough, the stuff had been distributed all around the perimeter. But what was it? And why was it there?

As I wiped my fingers on the carpet a second time—they still smelled awful—it occurred to me that it might not be a bad idea to check Maria's office out while I was waiting. I sat down at the desk and prepared to do some more snooping.

The copy machine whirred down the hall as I rifled through the campaign manager's drawers. Nothing much of interest—she had a Crabtree & Evelyn habit, excellent choice in label colors, and very neat handwriting—but to my disappointment, everything looked to be on the up-and-up. I found a file with a list of recent donations, and flipped through it, looking for something that might ring a bell. Unfortunately, nothing did; I was surprised, however, to discover that many of Brewster's campaign donations came from San Antonio and Mexico. Was that why he had hired a Latino campaign manager? If so, her connections with our southern neighbors had certainly worked to his advantage.

I was about to quit when I found a weird thing shoved in next to her pencils.

It was a little wax doll, and the moment I picked it up, my skin crawled. Someone had carved crude features on it—a gash for a mouth and holes for eyes. A scrap of brown fabric and what looked like a couple of hairs had been worked into the wax near the doll's middle.

I was holding it with the tips of my fingers, looking at the crude face and the lumpy little limbs, when Lindsey hurried back in.

"Ready?" she said.

"What do you think this is?" I asked, training my flashlight on the ugly little doll.

"It looks like a voodoo doll or something. Where did you find it?"

"In Maria's desk," I said.

She shrugged. "Maybe it's a worry doll or something. Something you can knead with your hands when you're stressed or something."

"Maybe," I said. It sure wasn't comforting to me—in fact, it gave me the heebie-jeebies. I shoved the doll back into the drawer and closed it, relieved not to have it in view. "I figured out what the smell is, by the way. There's powder sprinkled all around the room," I said, gesturing at the windowsill behind me. "And I'll bet there's even more of it in Brewster's office, but I don't plan on going back to check." I pointed to the line of powder on the windowsill. "Can you smell it?"

She leaned down and sniffed. "Smells a little like sulfur, but it's not too bad."

I blinked. Not too bad? That stuff would fell an ox.

She straightened up. "Anyway, who knows what it is? I got the papers back into the safe and put the picture back up. Let's get out of here."

I glanced at the drawer with the doll one more time and then headed for the window. "Come on," I said to Lindsey. "Let's go. I can't wait to get out of here."

"Call me crazy, but I thought we'd go through the front door."

"But we don't have a key to lock it."

"You think they'd notice?"

"Wouldn't you?" I said. "How about you go through

the door, and I'll lock up after you and head out the window."

"Are you sure?"

I glanced at the empty windowsill. "At least there aren't any potted plants to deal with this time."

I let Lindsey out and did a quick sweep to make sure everything was in place—well, everything except for the African violet, but there wasn't much I could do about that. Then I climbed out onto what was left of the windowsill and stretched one leg toward the oak branch.

I had just managed to get both feet on the branch and had turned to close the window when a loud crack sounded beneath me. I had just enough time to think, *This really isn't my week.*

Then I plummeted a full story, landing flat on my back in a pile of dead leaves.

I lay there for a moment, half-dazed, looking up at the moon through the branches and moving my arms and legs experimentally. And praying that whatever werewolf I'd scented earlier didn't pick this moment to swing by. Stupid tree branch.

Lindsey trotted around the building as I was staggering to my feet.

"Oh my God," she said. "Are you okay?"

"I'm still alive, anyway," I said, massaging my ankle and peering up at the window, which gaped open above us. "So much for a stealthy entry."

"I just *knew* that branch wasn't safe. Can you walk?"

"I think so," I said. My ankle twanged as I put my weight on it, and I winced.

"We probably should have both gone through the door," Lindsey said.

Hindsight is always twenty-twenty. "Yeah, well, it's too late now."

Lindsey squinted up at the window. "You think she'll notice the open window?"

I gave my friend a look that she probably couldn't see and leaned on her as I hobbled back toward the car, still sniffing for werewolves. Fortunately, the coast seemed to be clear. My ankle wasn't feeling too hot, though—it wasn't broken, but I wasn't going to be doing any marathons in the near future.

We were a few yards from the M3 when something large flapped far above us, and for a moment, I caught another whiff of werewolf. What was up with that? I mean, these days I couldn't go more than ten feet without a werewolf popping up.

Or was someone stalking me?

"Hang on a moment," I said, and Lindsey paused.

"What?" she said.

I closed my eyes and let the night smells cascade over me. Leaf mold, lantana, two-day-old garbage from a nearby trash can.

No werewolf.

"Go ahead," I said, opening my eyes. "I thought I heard something, but I must have been wrong."

As I gingerly inserted myself into my BMW, I thought about the open window—and the broken branch—we had left behind. Not to mention the missing windowsill. I probably should have gone ahead and grabbed the wax doll so I could show it to my mom—after all, we'd been about as subtle as a herd of elephants.

I glanced back at the dark building, thinking of the gaping second-story window, the broken tree limb, and the dangling window trim. Whatever the future held for me, I decided, I probably wasn't going to make it as a private investigator.

"So what do we do now?" Lindsey asked as we reviewed copies of the files we'd found in Brewster's safe. She'd followed me to my loft after our late-night escapade. I'd popped some Motrin, washed my hands a zillion times to get rid of the smell, and wrapped and iced my ankle. Now we were sitting at my kitchen table, poring through Brewster's papers.

"We need to find out what that deed's all about," I said.

"Do you think it's connected to the poisoned potion?"

"Maybe. And we should probably talk to Tad. See if he was in town between Tuesday and Thursday last week."

Lindsey nodded. "Because it had to be after the librarian drank it . . ."

"But before Brewster died," I finished. "So whoever did it had to be around at the beginning of last week."

"*And* have access to the potion."

"Right."

"What do you think of Maria?" I asked. "She definitely had access to his office."

"It's possible—but there wasn't anything about her in the safe."

"True."

"Besides, what's her motive?" Lindsey asked.

I shrugged. "Moving up in the political world? Brewster just scored a seat in the House of Representatives . . . you know, to replace the guy who got shot a couple of months ago?"

"Oh, yeah—the emergency election. I'd almost forgotten about that."

I nodded. "Maybe Maria figured she could pick up his supporters and make a bid."

"It's possible," Lindsey said. "But we need to look at Brewster Jr. too. He's a millionaire now."

"Provided he's pulling down fifty$K$ a year."

"Good point," she said. "From what I hear, they don't pay that much at ThunderCloud Subs."

I blinked. "Ted Brewster's son makes sandwiches for a living?"

"Apparently he's worked down at the one on Lake Austin Boulevard for a year."

I let out a low whistle. "No wonder Maria wasn't too jazzed about him. Can I see that will again?" I asked.

"Sure." Lindsey pushed it across the kitchen table to me.

I glanced at the date on the first page. "This is a recent document."

"So?"

I flipped through to the last page. The signature line was blank. "I think we need to move Tad up on the list of suspects," I said.

"Why?"

"Because unless there's another copy of this, Brewster never signed it."

Twenty-three

By the next morning, my ankle felt much better; thanks to Motrin, ice, and my werewolf genes, I was almost good as new.

I tossed my robe on, wolfed down a bagel and some coffee, and was just gearing up to call ThunderCloud Subs when the phone rang.

It was Frank the doorman.

"You've got a visitor in the lobby, Miss Garou. Okay to send him up?"

Visitor? Had Heath made it back early? "Is it Heath?"

"Nope. A guy named Tom Fenris."

A thrill passed through me. *Tom*. All those questions I had . . . Tom would be able to answer them. I just knew it. And we'd be alone together. . . . I repressed a shiver.

But how did he know where I lived?

"Miss Garou? You still there?"

"Yeah. I mean yes. Yes, I'm here."

"What do you want me to do?" he asked.

"I guess you can send him up."

"Will do," he said, and hung up.

Shit. Shit, shit, shit. I ran into the bedroom and shucked off my robe. Why hadn't I asked Frank to give me a few minutes? I checked my hair in the mirror as I wriggled into a bra, then trotted to the closet and hesitated. What should I wear? Something casual but not frumpy. Not too sexy either.

As I stood there half naked, debating between a black tank top and a more modest, kind of romantic white lace blouse, the doorbell rang.

I grabbed the blouse, pulled on a pair of jeans, and ran to get the door.

When I pulled it open, Tom's intoxicating werewolf scent hit me like a freight train. He wore faded jeans and a faded green T-shirt that brought out the gold of his eyes, and every cell in my body started thrumming. I took a deep breath; he smelled—and looked—good enough to eat. I stood there staring at him for a second before he cleared his throat and pointed at my chest. "I think you forgot to button up."

"What?" I looked down; sure enough, my blouse gaped open, exposing my cream-colored Victoria's Secret bra to the world. Or at least to Tom. Blushing, I grabbed the two halves of my shirt and muttered, "Come in."

He followed me into my loft as I hastily buttoned my blouse. When I was decent, I turned back to Tom.

"What are you doing here?" I asked. "How did you know where I live?"

"I have my ways," he said, giving me a measuring look that made me quiver. "May I sit down?"

"Sure," I said, perching on the edge of my armchair and reminding myself that the lust-inducing, golden-haired man across from me was not in fact a man. Because he was a werewolf. Who was dating my best friend. I closed my eyes and prayed that Lindsey didn't decide to swing by with doughnuts or something this morning. Because if she did, how was I going to explain what her potential boyfriend was doing in my living room?

"I tried to call you earlier," I said. "I must have written the number down wrong."

"I was wondering why I hadn't heard from you."

I stared at him for a moment, mesmerized. There was something mysterious about him, about those eyes that seemed to look right through me. I wondered what those eyes had seen. How long had he been a werewolf? I wondered. Were there lots of werewolves in Norway? What would it feel like to touch him? I remembered the bolt of energy that passed through me when our hands had brushed. "Where are you from?" I blurted. "What are you doing here?"

"In your apartment?"

"Well, that too. But I mean here. In Austin. Did somebody send you to . . ." To what? To dismember me? To excommunicate me? To rip off my clothes and . . . *No, Sophie. Don't go there.* I took a deep breath. ". . . to *do* something to me?"

He shook his head slowly, a hint of a smile twitching his mouth. "No," he said. "I knew nothing about you. And neither did anyone else. Or if they did, they didn't tell me," he said, still gazing at me with those fiery eyes. "But how have you stayed hidden for so long?"

"I don't know," I said. "Maybe because I'm . . ."—I looked up at him, hoping I wasn't about to sentence myself to death—". . . half-human?"

"Maybe." He continued to stare at me. "But I don't think that's all of it."

I swallowed hard. "I understand that in France, they're not too keen on half-bloods."

"You would be correct. How did you come by that bit of information?"

"A relative," I said vaguely, and then pressed onward. "And in the States? Do they share that opinion?"

"Fortunately, they're a bit more lenient here," he said.

Well, thank God for small favors. I bit my lip. "But you're not from here."

He shrugged. "I'm not from anywhere anymore."

"I thought you were from Norway."

"Originally, yes." His eyes bored into me. "But now, I have no allegiance."

"So the half-blood thing doesn't bother you?"

He shook his head slowly. "No. It doesn't bother me. But I can't speak for the werewolves in whose territory you're living."

It felt like someone had dumped a bucket of ice water on me. I blinked at him. "What? But there are never any werewolves here. That's why I live here. It's kind of a neutral zone."

"Austin isn't neutral."

Crap. Another illusion shattered. What now? "Then whose is it? I haven't seen anyone here. And how many are there? Where the heck are they all living?"

"Houston," he said quietly. "Austin belongs to Houston."

"You're kidding me. That's like one hundred fifty miles away from here." I swallowed. "What will they do if they find out about me?"

He shrugged. "They haven't so far. Maybe they won't."

A shiver ran down my spine. Would Tom tell them about me? "You're working for Houston, right?"

He nodded.

"Does that mean you'll have to tell them about me?"

"I didn't see it in my contract," he said with a little grin.

I sagged in relief. I hadn't realized until now how much the fear of having to move was eating at me. I had a home here—a job, a life. I didn't want to leave. I looked at Tom, who was gazing at me mildly. Well, not really mildly—he was still smoldering a bit, but maybe that was just my lust talking. And my lust wasn't just talking, it was shouting at me. Shouting at me to throw myself at him.

Down, girl. I crossed my arms and smiled politely. "I've never really talked with a werewolf before, so I'm sorry if I have a lot of questions."

"What of your sire and your dam?"

"Sire?"

"Your parents," he said.

"Oh. Well, my mom's human, and my dad . . . well, he didn't stick around long. That's why I'm a bit behind the eight ball on the whole werewolf thing."

Tom raised an eyebrow, but I didn't elaborate. "Werewolves in general—sorry for all the questions, but you're the first person—er, werewolf—I've had a chance to talk to—well, about werewolves." God, Sophie, could you sound any dumber? "Well, anyway, I've done a lot of reading, and there's some pretty scary stuff out there."

He nodded.

"They don't . . . I mean *we* don't . . . hunt humans or anything, do we?" I asked, remembering the packette and the little episode with the Tri-Delta the other night.

"For the most part, no. There are a few, though . . ."

"Like the ones we saw the other night?"

"They are young," he said. "They do not know the code."

"Somebody made them," I said.

He nodded.

"How does that work?"

"It passes through the blood. The made ones will never be as strong, but they will be bound by the moon." He stared at me. "Just as you and I are."

I felt myself blushing. "So you can't get it from just a bite?"

"Not usually, no. And are you usually this inquisitive?"

"Always," I said. "I'm an auditor, remember?"

He chuckled, showing just a bit of his white teeth. Enough to make my heart pound in my chest. "I don't appear to be going anywhere anytime soon," he said, "so may I have a drink?"

"Oh, I'm so sorry. Of course. What can I get you? I don't have aquavit, but . . ."

"Coffee would be fine, if you have it."

"Cream and sugar?" I asked, sounding like Martha Stewart.

"Black," he said.

"I'll be right back." I hurried into the kitchen, where I checked the buttons on my blouse and took a deep breath as I poured a mug of coffee. Then I checked my reflection in the door of the microwave, fluffed up my hair a bit, and headed back to the werewolf in the living room. Whose very presence was a potent aphrodisiac.

As I handed him the mug, our fingers brushed again, and another jolt shot through me. I backed away from him, toward the safety of the couch—*he's a werewolf, he's Lindsey's, you're Heath's*—as he asked, "What else do you want to know?"

I took a swig of my own coffee and tried to compose myself. Tom was dizzyingly sexy in a way I couldn't even describe. It was almost disorienting. But he was strictly off-limits. My goal here was to get as much useful information out of him as I could. I took a deep breath and said, "Why aren't there any werewolves in Austin? Is it because of the vampires?"

"Partially," he answered. "But more because it's at the edge of the territory. Close to the neutral zone."

"The neutral zone." At least there *was* a neutral zone. Maybe I could move there and commute. "How far does the neutral zone extend?"

"It starts north of San Antonio and extends down to where the Mexican pack territories begin."

There were Mexican packs? How interesting. "But you're not part of the Houston pack," I said. "Or the Mexican packs."

"No," he said. "I work for them, but I do not belong to them."

"That's right," I said. "You take care of problems."

"Yes."

"So if it's not me you're here to deal with . . . what's the problem in Austin?"

"You met them the other night," he said.

"The packette."

His eyebrow twitched up a bit. "Interesting name. We call them the made ones. But yes. I am here because their presence is not sanctioned and because they are causing trouble."

I took a deep breath, and my pulse rate increased in response to his smell. God. What was it? Pheromones? If they could bottle Tom's scent, they'd make millions. "Can't the pack deal with it?" I asked, trying not to think about what was under his T-shirt. Or his jeans.

"It is easier for someone like me to handle it. I am an outsider."

"But you weren't always," I said slowly, and something like pain flickered through his eyes. I had the urge to go and comfort him. Only for a moment, though. Then I came to my senses.

"No. I wasn't."

"What happened? Why did you leave?"

He gave me a strained smile. "It's a long story. And now that I've briefed you on the world of werewolves, I have a few questions for you."

I wasn't done asking *my* questions yet—I still wanted to know about this werewolf code thing, where exactly in Norway Tom came from, how many werewolves were in the Houston pack, and if their favorite food was half-blood werewolf tartare—but apparently my time was up.

"I guess that's fair. What do you want to know?" I asked guardedly.

He shrugged. "It's not often I run across werewolves who are . . . well, unaffiliated. I want to know how you have stayed that way."

"No one knows about me," I said, trying not to stare at him.

"So I gathered. But why?"

"I don't know," I said. "I just figured it was because they didn't swing by Austin very often."

"They should know about you. They do reconnaissance." He shook his head, and the light from the window gleamed on his blond hair. God, he was gorgeous. "But I guess if they knew about you, you'd know it. How long have you been here?" he asked, in that growly, sexy voice.

"My whole life," I said, struggling against his magnetic pull. "Well, since I was ten, anyway. We moved around a lot before that."

"Pack troubles?" he asked.

I nodded, fighting off yet another urge to throw myself at him. I glanced at him, looking for some sign that he felt the same way about me—had he felt the electricity too? Unfortunately, though, he didn't seem to be having any trouble resisting the urge to get closer to me. I stole a glance down at myself. Was I that unappealing? Granted, I hadn't brushed my teeth yet, but I thought I looked okay in the mirror. Had I missed something? Was there some spinach from last night's dinner stuck between my teeth?

Or was he just interested in me professionally—and because I had a gorgeous best friend?

It doesn't matter, I told myself. Probably easier without having to deal with a mutual attraction, anyway. Too many complications . . .

"Are your parents here too?" he said as I surreptitiously ran my tongue over my front teeth, searching for stray spinach. Just in case.

"My mother is."

"So you've done all of this without any help from a pack. It's amazing that you've made it this long without attracting Wolfgang's notice."

"I guess. Who's Wolfgang?"

"The alpha male of the Houston pack."

"Do they really call them that? Alphas?"

"Yes," he said.

"So the alpha is Wolfgang," I said. What a goofy name for a werewolf.

"You mentioned your sire," Tom said slowly, his golden eyes on me. I was acutely aware of his body, the heat of it, under the T-shirt and faded jeans. His quadriceps were amazing, and I found myself wondering what they looked like without denim over them. *Stop it, Sophie.*

"I find it incredible that your sire let you develop with no guidance. None at all."

I stared down at the floor, my lust dimmed slightly by

the old sting of abandonment. "What is his name?" Tom asked gently.

"You probably wouldn't know him." I shrugged, feeling a wave of discomfort at the direction the conversation had taken. It was closer to embarrassment, almost; I was getting the impression that even in the werewolf world, it wasn't kosher to abandon your child. Which was kind of an unpleasant surprise, really. I always figured that was just the way things were done. "I'm not even sure if he's still alive," I admitted.

"Try me," he said. "I may have run across him."

I sighed. "Fine. It's Luc. Luc Garou. Last time I heard, he was in Paris."

Tom's eyebrows twitched in surprise.

"You know him?" I asked.

"I've heard of him." Something about Tom's tone made me wonder exactly what he'd heard. Whatever it was, I was under the impression that it wasn't exactly flattering.

My curiosity blazed even hotter. What did Tom know about my father? I almost asked; I was forming the question with my lips. But at the last second I stopped. It was probably best not to know. If my father had a penchant for running around the countryside eating people and abandoning kids, I reasoned, that was information I'd rather not have. Were there others like me? I wondered. Did I have a series of disenfranchised half-siblings roaming the globe?

It was something I'd never thought about before, but now wasn't the time. But I did realize there was an important question I hadn't asked. "I appreciate all the information you've given me—and your offer to keep my secret safe. But I have something I need to ask you."

"You may ask," he said.

"It's about Lindsey."

"Ah, yes. Lindsey." He smiled, giving me a nice view

of his gleaming canines. "Your friend is a beautiful woman."

I felt like doubling over as the words left his lips. Whether it was because he found her more attractive than me or because I feared for my friend, I couldn't say. Probably some of both. "Yes," I said. "She is beautiful. And kind. And human. Which brings me to another question; when exactly were you planning on telling her you're *not*?"

"I'm not beautiful and kind?" he asked mildly.

"You know what I mean," I muttered, blushing.

He smiled even bigger, which I wouldn't have thought possible, and my heart lurched. Well, maybe it wasn't my heart. It might have been something a little lower down, actually.

"And have you told your boyfriend about your little issue?" he asked in that low voice of his, eyes fixed firmly on mine. "What is his name again? Heat?"

"Heath," I said shortly. "And what I tell Heath is none of your business."

He shrugged a broad, well-muscled shoulder, and I found myself wondering how sex between werewolves might be different. Even from across the room, he felt hot—literally hot—as if his whole body ran at a higher temperature. What would that feel like against my skin? And those sharp white teeth . . .

Tom gave me a smile that exposed a good half inch of those teeth. His voice was a sexy growl. "Then why is it your business what happens between Lindsey and me?"

"Because she's my friend," I said, standing up. "And I'm worried about her."

"I appreciate your concern," he said, leaning farther back into the cushions. My loft was going to smell like werewolf for a week—which, to be honest, wasn't entirely a bad thing. His golden eyes bored into me. "But Lindsey is safe with me."

"I'm glad to hear it," I said, even though I wasn't sure I believed him. "Speaking of Lindsey, you really shouldn't be here." I could have kept him there for hours, just grilling him, but I suddenly felt like it wasn't such a good idea. "In fact, I think it's time for you to leave."

"But we were just getting acquainted," he said, patting the couch next to him and shooting me a seductive look that turned my insides to jelly. "Please, sit down. I still don't understand how you've managed to evade the Houston pack for almost two decades. Surely there's some insight you can give me . . ."

Although every cell in my body was yammering at me to jump him—it was like a werewolf biological imperative or something—the human in me stood her ground. I crossed my arms tight across my chest. "Maybe I just don't get out much."

"Ah. Then the incident at Fat Tuesday's was an anomaly."

I blushed even harder. Why had Lindsey needed to bring that up?

"Sophie." I looked up; Tom's voice had gone from teasing to serious. "Even if you never left your building, the pack would still know of your existence. So there must be another reason."

We were moving into territory I didn't want to visit. So to speak. "Look," I said. "I really have no idea why they don't know about me. And I'd love to chat, but I've got an appointment." The appointment wasn't for three hours, but he didn't need to know that.

"I guess we'll have to continue this conversation later, then." Tom stood up, and a whole new wave of alpha werewolf scent washed over me. Despite my apprehension, it was all I could not to throw myself at him right there in the middle of my living room. *Think of Heath,* I told myself. Sexy, handsome, *human* Heath.

I tried not to notice how well he filled his jeans as I followed him to the door. But when he was about to step into the hallway, I reached out impulsively and touched his arm, jerking my hand back at the jolt that passed through me. He turned to face me, so close I could feel the heat of his body. Had he felt it, too? I felt dizzy all of a sudden, and hot. Burning hot. Standing this close to him was like standing next to a sunlamp. A highly erotically charged sunlamp. And his scent . . .

"Did you change your mind?" he asked, his voice heavy with invitation.

"No," I stammered. "It's just . . . you're sure you won't tell the Houston pack about me?"

"No," he said, in a low, quiet voice, and the heat intensified so much I thought I might faint.

I was leaning forward, on the brink of kissing him, when he said again, quietly, "No, Sophie Garou."

I took a step back, confused. No, he didn't want to kiss me? Or no, he wouldn't tell anybody about me? I blinked, feeling the blood rush to my face.

Before I could say or do anything else, he leaned forward, and his mouth was on mine.

The world collapsed around me, then expanded in a million different directions. His teeth grazed my lower lip, and his taste—spice and that exotic werewolf scent—filled me, intoxicating me. I was no longer in control of myself; the human part of me was lost in sheer animal lust. I grabbed at Tom, feeling his heat under my hand, and when he wrapped his arms around me, everything dissolved but Tom and me. I had never felt anything like this before.

Anything at all.

He pulled away then, gently, leaving me stranded in the doorway, panting for more. As I stood there, reeling with lust and confusion, he reached out to smooth a strand of hair from my eyes.

"Your secret is safe with me," he said, but I could barely formulate a thought, much less respond. And which secret? The fact that I was a werewolf? Or the fact that I had just kissed the man—rather, werewolf—who was dating my best friend?

If you could call it a kiss. It was more like an out-of-body experience, to tell the truth—in fact, I wasn't sure I had fully returned. And if that was just a kiss, I could only imagine what it would feel like to . . .

No.

I shut down that line of thought as quickly as I could. But before I could gather my wits enough to ask what he meant about a secret, he smiled again, showing me just a bit of his gleaming white teeth. A moment later, he was gone.

Twenty-four

It was a half hour before I had regained my composure sufficiently to consider using the phone.

What had just happened was a complete anomaly, I told myself. It had been a necessary meeting—I now knew a lot more about werewolves in general—but the combination of the waxing moon and my hormones had gotten the best of me. I shuddered to think what I would have done if he hadn't broken off that kiss . . .

The kiss that never should have happened, I reprimanded myself sternly.

The kiss that had been unlike anything I'd ever experienced.

After giving myself a good shake, I checked myself in the mirror—no spinach between the teeth, thank goodness, and although my hair was a little flat on one side, at least my blouse was fully buttoned now. Even the scab on my nose was almost gone, which was a relief; after all, I didn't want to go into the Southeast Airlines meeting looking like I'd been mugged.

While the outside looked reasonably okay, inside I was a total jumble. What was wrong with me? I'd almost molested a werewolf in the hallway thirty minutes ago. A werewolf who was dating the woman I called my best friend.

After some hair fluffing and a few shots of hair spray, I brewed myself a cup of wolfsbane tea and plucked up the courage to call Lindsey. No need to tell her about Tom's little visit, I decided. It was bad enough that he'd come to my loft at all—speaking of which, how had he figured out where I lived? Besides, our relationship—if you could call it that—was strictly platonic. If by platonic you meant there had been no actual physical contact. Other than that kiss—that amazing, mind-blowing kiss. But I hadn't initiated it. Had I?

Stop thinking about it, Sophie. Which was easier said than done. Because I was in serious lust with a werewolf. And had just learned that I was living in another pack's territory.

After the fourth ring, Lindsey answered, sounding sleepy, and I felt a pang of guilt for lusting after Tom. Some friend I was. "What's up?" she asked, yawning. And to think I'd been worried she'd stop by with doughnuts!

"I thought we'd pay Tad Brewster a visit today," I

said, struggling to focus on the business at hand. "He's working until two."

"Good," she groaned. "Because there's no way I could face a sandwich right now. I haven't even had my coffee yet."

"Why don't we meet at around one? That way you'll have a few hours to caffeinate yourself."

"I called a friend of mine to ask about Brewster's will, by the way."

"Before coffee?" I asked.

"Are you kidding me? No, I called last night. Remember Jesse?"

"Jesse." I thought about it for a second. "Nope."

"I dated him last year. Remember? He was a tax attorney. Red hair, good biceps."

"Still not ringing any bells," I said. I needed a spreadsheet to keep up with Lindsey's boyfriends. Except Tom, I thought with a shiver. Tom was a little tough to forget.

"Anyway," Lindsey continued, "he told me Brewster's lawyer would file the will as soon as he or she knows Brewster's dead, so it's probably public record by now."

"So now we know what we're doing on Monday," I said.

"Then you decided to cancel your big anniversary date?"

Crap. Monday. *The equinox.* Another problem I hadn't dealt with. "On second thought, maybe *you* could go down and check it out."

"Oh, that's right. You'll be meeting with Southeast Airlines."

"I think I feel a case of Ebola coming on," I said.

"Well, wait until after we've talked with Tad, okay? I'll meet you there at 1:45."

I hung up and headed for the kitchen—and away from Tom's scent, which was still maddeningly strong. As I struggled to clear my head, I brewed up an extra-strength dose of wolfsbane tea; every cell in my body was aware of the waxing moon, and I could feel the change coming, a roiling feeling, just under my skin. I would have welcomed a Valium too, but unfortunately, that wasn't an option.

If I could just make it through the next few days, I thought, as I sipped my tea and sorted through my clean laundry, trying to banish thoughts of Tom's kiss from my mind.

Lindsey was sitting on a plastic chair outside the sandwich shop when I arrived, wearing a bright red sundress that left very little to the imagination. I was glad she'd thought to look fetching; I was still wearing the jeans I had on earlier, and despite the fact that I'd had three hours to prepare, I'd been so distracted I hadn't gotten around to putting on makeup. I looked at Lindsey and grinned; who could resist her?

I just hoped Tad Brewster wasn't gay.

"Ready?" Lindsey said, standing up and straightening her dress.

"Let's go."

If I had any worries about identifying Ted's son, they dissipated almost instantly. There were two people behind the counter. One was a woman with so much metal in her nose that she would probably improve TV reception just by driving through the neighborhood. The other was a clone of Ted Brewster—a little more hair, maybe, and a few pounds less in his spare tire—but other than that, almost frighteningly similar.

I ignored the woman and headed for Tad's side of the counter.

"Can I help you?" he asked.

"Yes," Lindsey purred, leaning over the high counter. His muddy eyes flicked toward her cleavage.

"We'd like to order a few sandwiches," Lindsey said,

pressing her breasts up against the counter, which made them look a little like Parker House rolls that had been left to rise too long. "But we'd also like to talk to you."

"Me?" Tad glanced behind him, a look of frank disbelief on his face. Evidently the self-esteem hadn't transferred along with Ted's physical attributes. When Brewster Jr. had ascertained that Brad Pitt was in fact *not* standing just behind his left shoulder, he swallowed hard and said, "Okay."

"Thanks," I said a few minutes later when he handed us two bags filled with turkey sandwiches. It had been touch and go—once, while sneaking a glance at Lindsey's Parker House rolls, he'd almost lopped off his finger instead of the end of a cucumber. "Why don't you join us outside when you're ready?"

He nodded, and his eyes followed us out to the porch. Well, followed Lindsey, mainly.

We'd made it only halfway through our sandwiches before Tad Brewster tripped out the door toward us, struggling to release the knot of his green apron.

Lindsey smiled a big, predatory smile. "Thanks for joining us," she said.

He sat down in a vacant plastic chair and pulled the apron over his head. "You said you wanted to talk to me?"

"Both of us did, actually," Lindsey said.

"You look familiar," I told him.

"Like somebody famous," Lindsey purred, leaning forward more than was strictly necessary. If she spread it on any thicker, I'd have to get her a trowel.

Tad's ears turned pink, but his voice was steady. "You must be thinking of my father. We look a lot alike, and he's been in the papers a lot lately."

"Who's your father?" I asked.

"My father is . . . was . . . a councilman. Just got elected to Congress, actually."

Lindsey's eyes grew round. "That's it! You're Ted Brewster's son! That poor man who died . . ." She put a hand on his freckled arm. "How awful for you."

"And to be working so soon after losing your father!" I chimed in.

He shrugged. "Gotta pay the bills."

"I wouldn't think that would be a problem for you," Lindsey said. "I thought your father was a very well-to-do man. Wouldn't that pass on to you?"

I gave Lindsey a warning look, but I needn't have worried. Tad looked so pleased with the attention that I didn't think it would have mattered if she'd asked for his wallet point-blank.

"The lawyers are working on that now," he said. Despite the fact that he lacked his father's charisma, he didn't seem like a bad guy. A little large and awkward, perhaps, but nice. "You know he was murdered?"

"Murdered?" Lindsey's slender hand leaped to her throat.

"Yeah," Tad said, and a flicker of pain crossed his doughy features. "The cops arrested some whacked-out woman who thinks she's a witch."

"A witch?" I said, as if this was the first I'd heard of it. I decided not to take offense at the description of my mother as whacked-out; to be honest, he kind of had a point. "How bizarre," I said mildly. "Do you really think that's who killed him?"

Tad shrugged. "I don't know. It does seem a bit far-fetched—if she sold him something, why would she poison it? She had to know the cops would be on to her."

"But from what I read," I said, "the cops don't seem to think anyone else had a motive."

Tad snorted. "Oh, come on. Dad was a politician. There were tons of people who had it in for him."

"Like who?" I asked.

"Well, Austin's a pretty liberal town. And my dad . . ."

"Wasn't," I said.

Tad Brewster's brown eyes twinkled just a little bit. "Exactly. But I'll tell you what," he said. "I think even some of his cronies weren't too happy with him."

"What do you mean?" I asked.

"Well, he got the house seat and was supposed to be a shoo-in to head up the immigration committee. But lately, he hadn't been toeing the conservative line quite as much."

"No?" Lindsey asked.

"It was causing problems. Usually he was pro-development, but he was dragging his heels a bit on a new development that was up for vote on the council."

"The one on Barton Springs?" I asked.

He nodded. "That's the one. I heard a few phone calls at the house."

I thought of the deed in Brewster's safe. I didn't know why it was there, but if what Tad just said was true, it was a good bet he wasn't part owner. Even so, if my mom had cast a spell on him to make him change his mind, it must have been a pretty good one.

"You live with your dad?" Lindsey asked, leaning forward so much I had to avert my eyes. *No wonder Tom is smitten.*

"Yeah," Tad said, transfixed by Lindsey's décolletage. "Ever since my mother died . . . he said the house was too big for just him."

"Oh, that's right," I said, forcing myself to concentrate on Tad. "You lost your mother a few years ago."

"Just last year," he said, glancing at me. "Heart attack."

I glanced at Lindsey, who looked to be thinking the same thing I was. The photo we'd found in Brewster's safe must have been taken while Brewster was still married. And unless she'd had some major plastic surgery, the woman with him hadn't been his wife. "And he didn't remarry?"

"No," he said abruptly.

Lindsey switched tacks. "So, any chance you'll be following in your father's footsteps?" she asked, widening her long-lashed gray eyes and pursing her bee-stung lips.

"You mean, will I have a spectacular law career and then go into politics?" He jerked his head back toward the shop and gave Lindsey a wry grin that tugged at my heart a little bit. "What does it look like?"

"Why not?" Lindsey said, shrugging. "I mean, you even *look* like your dad. It could be a family legacy. Like the Bush family. One of your grandfathers was governor, wasn't he?"

"Oh, yes. I grew up hearing all about Theodore Brewster." He sighed. "I ran for office once. It didn't work out." He gave a bitter laugh, cutting his eyes at Lindsey, then away. "Besides, I don't think the conservatives would be too fond of me."

I leaned forward. "What did you run for?"

"The Texas Senate." His mouth wrenched to the side. "As a libertarian."

I let out a long, slow whistle. "No wonder the conservatives didn't like you."

He rubbed at a stain on the plastic table, then looked up with a rueful grin. "Especially since my platform was the legalization of drugs."

Whoa. No wonder Maria wasn't exactly jumping up and down about Tad stepping into his father's shoes.

After sneaking another peek at Lindsey, Tad glanced at his watch. Either Lindsey had forgotten to wear her attraction charm, or the spell was wearing off. "Look. Was there something you wanted to talk to me about?"

Lindsey shrugged. "You just looked like a nice person to talk to," she said.

His lips were a thin line. "Yeah, right. What paper do you work for?" he asked.

"I don't."

"Uh-huh." He turned to me. "What about you?"

I shook my head. "I'm an auditor."

"An auditor?"

"Scout's honor," I said, pointing at Lindsey. "She is too."

"Then why are you so interested in my dad?"

"We're interested in the truth," Lindsey said.

"Why?"

Good question. Lindsey and I stared at each other. Should I tell him the whacked-out witch was my mother?

"Does it matter?" Lindsey said finally, leaning forward once again to give him the benefit of her low-cut dress. No attraction charm today, I confirmed—but she really didn't need it. "With any luck, Tad," she purred, blinking her long-lashed eyes, "what you just told us will get us a little closer."

"I guess you're not going to tell me what you're really after. Not that it matters." He snuck another glance at Lindsey's cleavage, then looked away. "Anyway, if you find out who did it, let me know. Because even though they've got that woman in jail, I think they're missing something." He ran a hand through his hair, suddenly agitated. "They even questioned *me*. Like I'd poison my own father," he said bitterly.

"I'm sorry about your father," I said gently. And I was. I knew what it meant to lose one.

He took a deep breath, and I could feel pain emanating from him in waves. "Thanks for the visit," he said, "but I've got to go." He got up and hurried back into the shop, eyes red-rimmed. I wasn't sure, but I think he wiped away a tear.

When the door slammed shut behind him, Lindsey

turned to me. "Well, I'm not sure how productive *that* was."

"Poor guy," I said.

"He did seem pretty torn up about it," Lindsey said, finishing off her turkey sandwich. "But he could be a good actor."

"I really don't think he did it," I said, wrapping up the remains of my sandwich and stuffing it into the bag. Somehow I'd lost my appetite. "But it was interesting what he said about his dad not toeing the line. Do you think someone might have gotten fed up with him?"

"I don't know," she said. "But it won't hurt to ask around. Tomorrow's Monday—I'll make some calls."

Monday. I winced. The moon was so close to full I could feel it, tingling on my skin, urging me to change. There was no way I was going to make it through that meeting tomorrow—much less my date with Heath—but I still hadn't gotten in touch with Adele. Nor had I managed to manufacture a viable reason to be elsewhere. Would a megadose of wolfsbane tea keep my animal nature under wraps? I'd never had to do it before—my mother had always warned me of the dangers of overdosing—and until now, I'd always managed to manufacture a reason to be out of town.

But not this time.

What exactly would a huge dose of wolfsbane do to me?

Unfortunately, it looked like I was going to have to find out.

And hope wolfsbane didn't show up on a drug test.

Twenty-five

I started the next day with my traditional skinny latte . . . and a quadruple dose of wolfsbane tea.

"There's no way you can get out of it?" my mother had asked when I called her to ask about upping the dosage.

"Nope."

"Sophie, I have a very bad feeling about this. I'm really worried. We both know you can handle more than most people, but wolfsbane is still toxic—and you're not a full werewolf. Besides, even if you drank gallons of the stuff, there's still no guarantee it will work. And have I mentioned the side effects? Profuse sweating, hallucinations, speech problems . . ."—she paused—". . . maybe even death."

"I don't have a choice," I said, suppressing a shiver. Surely the stuff I drank daily wouldn't kill me. "I'm counting on the human half to get me through the day."

"Even your father was careful with his dosage," she said. "And he was a full werewolf. We've calibrated it well, but we've kept the amounts pretty low. I have no idea what will happen if you take too much."

"Mom . . ."

"This is a very bad idea," she said.

"Maybe," I said. "But until I come up with something better, it's the only plan I've got."

I hung up a few minutes later, not feeling quite as optimistic as I had when I'd gotten on.

But what choice did I have?

Earlier that morning, I had finally gotten in touch with Adele, who had stayed on the phone long enough to make it clear that nothing short of a death certificate—with my name on it—would excuse me from the Southeast Airlines meeting. My phone call to Heath had gone no better.

"I won't take no for an answer," he said. "You've been working way too hard lately. You need a break; besides, I've been planning this evening for months."

"But Heath—"

"No buts. I'll pick you up at the office at six. Love you."

He hung up before I could answer.

I rolled into the office at 8:00, shouldering my briefcase and clutching a tumbler of tea.

"Good morning," Sally said coolly, adjusting her cleavage and sweeping her eyes over me. She wore strappy platform sandals and a spandex minidress in a lurid rainbow of colors that made her look like she was auditioning for a spot as one of those bikini women on the wrestling circuit.

I, on the other hand, had worn my best Donna Karan suit, with my new Prada pumps and a brand-new pair of sheer hose. Now, if I could only make it through the day without sprouting a fur coat, I'd be fine. "Good morning, Sally," I said coolly, striding past her desk with my chin tilted up.

"Oh, you're here," she said. "Don't forget your test."

I wheeled around. "My what?"

Sally shoved a plastic cup and a sheaf of papers across her desk toward me. "Your drug test," she said, with a gleam of triumph in her eyes.

"Oh," I said, grabbing the papers from her desk. *Shit,*

shit, shit. Of all the days to have a drug test, it had to be the day when I was drinking so much wolfsbane my skin was starting to turn green.

"And Adele wanted me to remind you that the meeting's at nine," she said, her voice edged with acid. "I hope you're ready."

"I am," I said. And barring a few minor issues—like the fact that already the hair on my legs was a quarter inch long, and I'd shaved a mere half hour ago—it was true. It was too bad waxing caused me so many skin problems; it would be great to have a longer-lasting alternative. But the last time I'd tried it, I'd ripped half the skin off my left leg, so I was more than a bit leery of the process.

I closed my office door behind me, took a big swig of tea, and grabbed a razor and some lotion from my top drawer. My panty hose were pooled around my ankles and I was just starting on the second leg when a knock sounded on my door.

"Just a minute," I called, shoving the razor into the drawer and yanking on my hose. I hadn't gotten it up to my knees when the door opened and Adele walked in.

"Glad to see you're here," she said.

"Wouldn't have missed it," I replied, pulling my chair up to the desk to hide my bare legs and surreptitiously tugging at my hose. My tongue felt a little weird, I noticed—kind of like it does when you get back from the dentist. I stopped tugging at my hose when I realized one leg was still covered with lotion and just shoved my legs deeper under the desk.

Adele nodded at the stack of papers and the cup on the corner of my desk. "I see you got the testing apparatus."

Apparatus? A plastic cup qualified as apparatus? "Sure did," I said lightly, tongue tingling. "Isn't that usually done at a lab?"

"Usually, but with the meeting going on, they agreed to let us drive the samples over. We just need to have witnesses for the samples."

"Witnesses? Like someone in the stall?"

"No," she said. "You just need to have someone in the bathroom with you."

Personally, I thought the whole protocol seemed a bit unorthodox, to say the least—but right now I had other things on my mind. Besides, it was an on-your-own-time kind of test, so maybe I could put it off until some of the wolfsbane was out of my system. "Let's talk about the meeting," I said. "What's the game plan?"

Adele perched on one of my office chairs. "We show them our track record of finding irregularities—and inefficiencies," she said.

"And demonstrate how much money we can save them," I finished.

"Exactly. Do you have the presentation ready?"

I patted my laptop. "It's all in here," I said. I'd stayed up until 2:00 putting the finishing touches on it.

Adele smiled, her thin lips exposing a line of slightly crooked teeth. "Wonderful."

"They're coming to the office, right?"

"They'll be here at nine-fifteen," Adele said. "We'll meet in the Bluebonnet Room, then take them to lunch at Sullivan's."

"Sounds good," I said thickly, thinking it sounded anything but. I could think of about a zillion things— skydiving in Antarctica, walking over hot coals, having my bikini line tweezed—I'd rather do than stand up and give a presentation today. Particularly if this numb-tongue trend continued.

Adele gave me a sharp glance. "Are you okay?"

"Fine, fine," I said reassuringly. I was on the verge of turning into a fairy-tale creature with stubbly legs, but other than that, everything was just peachy.

"Good. Glad to have you on the team," Adele said. "We all need to be in top form today—this is an important account." She leaned forward, fixing me with her icy blue eyes. "A corner office just opened up. If we land this account . . ."

Corner office. *Partnership*.

"Got it," I said, fighting my sluggish tongue.

"See you at nine-fifteen, then," she said, and gave me a quick wink before walking out of the office, leaving the door open, unfortunately.

I waddled to the door with my hose around my ankles and shut it quickly before scuttling back to my desk to finish shaving my legs. I wiped the blade with a tissue and jammed the razor into the drawer. Then I changed my mind and hid it in my purse—just in case the meeting started getting hairy. My tongue felt a little fuzzy, but so far, so good—particularly because under normal circumstances, with the full moon rising and the equinox at hand, I would be in full wolf mode by now. The tea—thank God—seemed to be working.

I took another swig of bitter wolfsbane and ran through my presentation one last time. I was just about to do a last shave and brew up another tumbler of tea when Lindsey called me.

"Hello?"

"What's wrong with your voice?"

"Ethcuse me?"

"Sophie. Are you drunk?"

"No," I said, fighting to control my rubbery tongue. "What do you mean? I'm fine."

"Good. I was just calling to wish you luck in your meeting," she said. "I heard a rumor that if it all goes well, you're a shoo-in for partnership."

"That's what Adele said—sort of, anyway," I said. "By the way, thanks for helping me get it all together. I couldn't have done it without you."

"Don't sweat it," she said. "And while you're wooing the big dogs, I'm going to see what else I can dig up on Ted Brewster."

"Thanks a million," I said.

"Are you still on with Heath tonight?"

"Don't know yet," I said.

Lindsey was quiet for a moment. Then she said, "Are you sure you're okay? You sound a little weird."

"No, I'm fine," I said.

"Probably just need more coffee."

I didn't know what to say. The truth was, I needed a lot more than coffee.

"Well, I've got to run. Go knock 'em dead, Sophie."

"I'll do my best."

After hanging up, I did a last touch-up with the razor, grabbed my laptop, and tossed four tea bags into my tumbler. Then I checked my reflection in my plate-glass window—not too bad, considering I'd had about two gallons of wolfsbane tea and would normally be walking around on all fours by now—and headed for the conference room, stopping along the way to fill up my tumbler with hot water.

Adele was already set up in the conference room, which, like every other room at Withers and Young, was decorated in business beige, with a pull-down screen for presentations. My boss was accompanied by a stoutish woman from the accounting department.

"Sophie, you've met Koshka?" Adele said as I walked in.

"I think I've seen you in the halls," I said, reaching out to shake her hand. She smiled and fixed her big green eyes on me, and my nose wrinkled. I could tell this was one of those women who had a houseful of like fifty cats or something. The smell of ammonia just about blew me over. Sure enough, the shoulder of her slightly wrinkled red suit, which bunched unflatteringly around her hips, was dusted with pale cat hair.

"Nice to meet you," she said, staring at me intently.

"Likewise," I said, though something told me she and I would never be best buddies.

She continued to stare, and I started to feel self-conscious. Had I started sprouting whiskers?

"Do I have something on my face?" I asked, struggling to make my tongue work correctly. It really did feel as if I'd just come from the dentist.

"No. Your eyes are just an unusual color, that's all."

Yeah. Werewolf gold. *Just like Tom's.* "Thanks," I said. "I think."

"Why don't you have a bite to eat before they get here?" Adele said, indicating the table with a sweep of her manicured hand. The big round table was laden with food—croissants, strawberries, a carafe of coffee, and a variety of muffins and scones.

"Don't mind if I do," I said. Maybe food would help counteract some of the side effects of the tea. I plucked a chocolate croissant from the nearest platter and plugged in my laptop.

I excused myself for one last trip to the bathroom—I figured I'd shave while I could—and after a quick session with my razor, headed back into the conference room.

"Ready, ladies?" Adele said, a predatory look on her narrow face.

"Never better," I lied, jamming half the croissant into my mouth and trying to chew it without mangling my tongue, which felt like a wad of rubber. I chased it with a big swig of scalding hot wolfsbane tea and closed my eyes, trying to quell the shivers that tore through my body, urging nature to take its course.

Could I make it another three hours?

Did I have a choice?

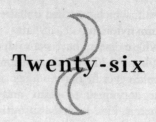

Twenty-six

Sally showed the Southeast Airlines crew in at 9:20, and they fell on the plate of goodies like a pack of starving wolves. Okay, bad analogy. But they did make quite a dent in the pile of pastries as Adele exchanged pleasantries with them and warmed them up for the pitch. I picked at the remains of my croissant, nodding vigorously as the woman next to me told me about the triathlon she'd finished the previous weekend. I'm here to tell you, when you're trying desperately not to sprout fur and teeth, it's kind of hard to lose yourself in a discussion of flat bicycle tires, algae growth in local lakes, and dehydration.

The cocktail of smells assaulted my nose, making it difficult for me to concentrate—the triathlete beside me was a big fan of Secret deodorant, and someone in the room—I couldn't tell who—hadn't showered after his workout. One of the women in the room was in love—I could pick up the acrid odor of infatuation—and yet another was wreathed in the soft scent of an infant. I took another swig of tea and struggled to look like nothing was more fascinating than the details of this woman's training schedule, even though I was convinced I was growing sideburns. As she launched into a description of her most recent knee injury, I crossed my legs and winced at the sound of bristles rubbing together through the thin nylon.

"Where do you have your nails done?"

"What?" I looked up at the triathlete, who was staring at my hands. *Uh-oh*. My nails were at least a quarter inch longer than they had been that morning. I reached for my tea and glugged some more down. Was I going to turn into a werewolf halfway through my pitch?

I set the tumbler down and said, "Happy Hands," in a strangled voice.

"Are they real?" the woman said, reaching for my hand, which—I then noticed—had started sprouting a few reddish hairs.

I jerked my hand back, and the triathlete gave me a funny look. Fortunately, at that moment, Adele said, "Ready, Sophie?"

I smiled at her in relief—lips closed, so my teeth, which I could feel growing longer, wouldn't show—and nodded woodenly. As I stood up, a ripple coursed through me. I grabbed at my tumbler for another swig of tea.

"That's quite a coffee habit you've got there," joked the CEO, looking sleek and predatory in a gray suit.

"Tea, actually." I smiled at him, wondering what it was about his smell that was different. Smoky, somehow, but not like cigarette smoke. More like a campfire. "Keeps me human," I said.

"Whatever works for you," he said, lifting his cup in a mock toast.

As I finished setting up the projector, Adele launched into the pitch. "Now, Sophie's put together a presentation that I think will show you why Withers and Young is the right firm for Southeast Airlines."

I was plugging in the projector when something snapped at my finger. "Ouch!"

Adele's head whipped around. "Is everything all right?"

"I swear this thing bit me," I said, pointing to the end of the cord. I looked up and realized that the entire room was staring at me. Was this what my mom meant by side effects? "Sorry," I mumbled, and picked up the cord again.

"That's quite all right," Adele said in a chilly voice. "Now, as I was saying . . ."

I bent down and inspected the end of the cord, but it looked normal—no teeth. I plugged it in and sat back, glancing down at my legs—little hairs were poking through the nylon again, but what was I going to do? Ask everybody to take a ten-minute break while I dashed off to shave my legs?

As Adele droned on, I took another sip of tea and glanced around the room. My eyes slid past Mr. Armani—the CEO—and then slid back.

Was it my imagination, or did he have horns?

I was staring at his head, trying to determine whether it was an unfortunate pair of cowlicks or whether he did in fact have horns, when Adele tapped me on the shoulder.

"Sophie."

I whipped around. "What?"

"You're up," she hissed, her blue eyes flashing.

"Oh. Of course," I slurred, standing and heading to the front of the room, my eyes still glued to the top of the CEO's head. They *were* horns—I was convinced of it. And his eyes were very blue. Striking, actually. Not as striking as the horns, though . . .

"Thank you all for coming," I said, forcing my eyes away from the CEO's head. Koshka stared at me, her green eyes unblinking. "What I'd like to talk about today is what Withers and Young can do to help

Thoutheast . . . I mean Southeast . . . Airlines operate at maximum efficiency."

I turned to the screen and wiggled my tongue a few times, trying to will it into submission. If I could just make it through this presentation . . .

The first slide popped up on the screen, and I started through the reel. "I'm going to run you through a few case histories now . . ." My tongue slipped from time to time, but I managed to keep things under control and was actually starting to feel pretty good. My mother's concerns appeared to be completely unfounded. Why hadn't I tried upping the dosage earlier? Then I wouldn't have to leave town four times a year—in fact, I wouldn't have to transform at all. I took another swig of tea and launched lispily on to the next slide.

And that's when the hot flashes started.

I stifled a groan. I had made my way through the first two case studies and had the entire room nodding along with me—even the CEO, whose horns were now at least an inch long—and why was I the only one who noticed?—but now, it felt as if my skin was burning.

I paused for a sip of tea, but that only made things worse. Soon, my back was drenched with sweat, and my silk shell was clinging to my body. I could feel a droplet bobbing on the end of my nose. Out of the corner of my eye, the laptop cord moved, and I could swear I saw the plug start to work its way out of the wall.

"Tho as you can thee," I said, pointing up at the screen and ignoring the power cord, which was now writhing around like a wounded earthworm.

"Sophie?" Adele was looking at me strangely.

"Yeth?"

"Are you okay?"

"Fine," I lied. "Just fine," I repeated, struggling to enunciate the s. I wiped my forehead and ran my rubbery tongue over my teeth. *Shit.* They were longer than they had been.

I reached down for the tumbler and gulped at the tea—the hair on my legs was longer too, and I could feel an itching under my skin. I glanced up at the screen. I wasn't going to make it through lunch, but if I could just get through this presentation . . .

As I fumbled through the last case study, trying as hard as I could not to stare at the CEO's horns or the wriggling power cord, something started meowing.

I stopped midsentence.

"Sophie?" Adele stared at me.

I started up again, but so did the meowing. It seemed to be coming from the corner. I craned my head to look—nothing.

"Is it just me," I said, "or is there a cat in here?"

They all stared at me blankly—including the horned CEO—and I concluded that I was the only one who'd heard it. But the smell of cats was definitely getting stronger. I glanced at Koshka. Were her eyes different?

God, what was happening to me? Maybe Mom was right after all, and the wolfsbane tea wasn't such a hot idea. Although it felt like 150 degrees in the conference room now, so perhaps *hot* wasn't the right adjective. Something tickled my chin, and I realized I was drooling.

Dear God. I was sprouting hair, growing teeth, lisping, hearing imaginary cats, and drooling on myself—all in front of the biggest potential client I'd ever had. I didn't dare look at Adele, but I could feel her eyes boring into me as I sweated through the end of the presentation.

Finally—finally—I got to the last slide, talking louder and louder to drown out the cat's insistent meowing. Koshka stared at me with unblinking green eyes, and the horns on the CEO's head gleamed in the fluorescent light. The power cord was still straining to release itself from the outlet—once or twice, I was sure I heard it grunt.

I ran through my final points as quickly as I could. "Any questionth?" I asked, praying fervently that there weren't. Or that if there were, they didn't involve my drooling or my sudden lisp.

"I think you just about covered it," said the CEO, and I could have kissed him, horns and all. Come to think of it, he was pretty sexy—even with the things sticking out of his head. Not as sexy as Tom, though . . .

I shook myself and gave the Armani devil a toothless, and hopefully drool-less, smile. "Thank you very much."

Avoiding Adele's eyes, I scuttled to my seat, surreptitiously mopping the sweat from my forehead. It was only 10:30. The meeting was scheduled to go on for another hour, then break for lunch.

I ran my tongue over my teeth and took another sip of tea, trying to ignore the sound of a cat yowling in the corner. There was no way I was going to make it that long.

"Isn't that what happened during the Prevco audit, Sophie?"

My head whipped around to Adele, who was staring at me expectantly. The power cord gave a quick jerk and popped out of the wall, then started wriggling toward my left foot.

"Ethcuthe me?"

"The Prevco audit. I was telling them about the tax compliance issues."

"Oh. Oh, yeth," I said, surreptitiously lifting my feet—that damned thing had bitten me, I was sure of it—and nodding like a bobble-headed doll.

Adele was silent, waiting for me to continue. I mopped my forehead with a paper napkin. Prevco. *Prevco.* What the heck was Prevco?

Then I remembered. Something about tax evasions . . . "Got them out of a nathty lawthuit, if I recall." The cord drew closer, and I raised my feet farther.

"I was hoping you could tell us a little more about it," Adele said icily.

"Actually, I'm not feeling too well right now—I'm going to have to excuse mythelf—myself—for a minute."

And as Adele and the horned CEO stared at me, I grabbed my Kate Spade bag and fled to the bathroom. I wouldn't swear to it, but the power cord seemed to droop in disappointment.

Twenty-seven

Sally's painted-on eyebrows rose almost to her hairline as I raced past her desk to the ladies' room. A moment later, the bathroom door swung shut behind me, and I glanced under the stall doors for feet. I was alone.

Then I faced the mirror.

If there had been any question regarding my ability to continue the meeting, it was answered the moment I caught a glimpse of myself in the glass. Rivulets of sweat poured down my face, and my soaked blouse clung to my chest. *Ick*. But more disturbing still were the fangs poking out from under my lips. And no razor in the world was going to be able to keep up with my bristly legs—or the sideburns that had started sprouting on my cheeks.

In short, the only way I could go back to that conference room was with a paper bag on my head. And from the feel of the fur curling under the sleeves of my suit, even that might not be enough.

I wiped the sweat from my face and fluffed out my blouse a bit more, preparing to face Sally. There was nothing I could do about Adele—I'd just have to have Sally share the news of my sudden illness. After my lispy, drooly performance, I was betting it wouldn't be a shock. But first, it was time to tackle those sideburns so I could get out of the building without terrifying my coworkers.

I dug through my purse and grabbed my razor, then soaped up my cheeks. I had finished the right side and was about to tackle the left when the bathroom door opened, and the smell of Aviance Night Musk filled the tiled room.

Sally.

I jammed the razor back into my purse and busied myself splashing water on my face as she sauntered into the bathroom. I glanced at her out of the corner of my eye; the rainbow colors on her dress appeared to be swirling. I was slightly surprised to discover she was horn-free.

"You don't look so hot," she said, a malicious little smile on her face.

"Actually, I'm burning up. I've got a really high fever," I said, zipping up my purse and trying to keep the furry side of my face turned away from her. "Could you tell Adele I had to leave early?"

"She told me that if anything went wrong with this account, heads would roll," Sally said in an ominous voice.

"I'm thick."

"Pardon?"

"Sick," I said with an effort, slinging my bag over my shoulder. "I'm headed to the doctor. Tell her I'm thorry . . . sorry . . . I had to leave early."

"There's just one thing I need you to do before you go," she said.

"What?"

She held up a plastic cup. "Adele said it had to be done today."

"Right now? I've got a fever of like a hundred and three. And isn't that the kind of thing you usually go to a lab to do?"

She folded her arms and leaned against the tiled wall, her dress swirling around her. "It's a new company."

"Sounds like a company that needs a procedures audit."

"You can take that up with Adele later. Right now, I need a sample. I promised I'd have all of them to the lab this afternoon."

"I'll do it tomorrow," I said. "At the lab."

"Like I said, you can talk to Adele about it. I'm just doing my job."

"But . . ."

"It'll only take a moment. I'll wait."

By the time I made it to the car, my skin was crawling and the parking-lot lines were slithering around the concrete like snakes. Stupid wolfsbane. But it *had* gotten me through the meeting at least partially human.

It took me three tries to get the keys into the ignition. I was in no state to drive, but with my fangs and sideburns sprouting, it was probably the only option; the odds of getting a taxi to stop for me right now were pretty low. I might have better luck hitching a ride with animal control.

I was still fuming over Sally—what gall, to sit outside the stall while I peed in a cup! Granted, the extra time *had* given me the opportunity to shave off my other sideburn.

Still.

I reminded myself that the humiliation of tinkling into a plastic receptacle with Sally standing outside the door was pretty low on the list of problems right now. I mean, my mom was up on murder charges, Lindsey was dating a werewolf, and I was standing my fiancé up on our anniversary. Plus, I had to drive home without wrecking the M3—and my hands were rapidly morphing into paws.

Not to mention the fact that a drug-testing company now had my urine sample.

I mopped at my face and swerved out of the parking garage, barely missing a man in a bikini. At least I think he was wearing a bikini; because I was convinced that the CEO of Southeast Airlines had horns, I wasn't sure of anything right then. I reached for my tea—hallucinations or no hallucinations, I needed to stave the transformation off for at least another ten minutes—and realized I'd left my tumbler in the conference room.

Shit.

I gripped the steering wheel. Not only had I left my tumbler behind but also my drawer was chock-full of wolfsbane tea bags. And I would bet my last nickel that Sally knew it.

Could I break back in tonight and get rid of the box? Too risky. I'd never make it past the security people—and even if I did, how would I operate the elevator?

Before I passed the point of no return, I grabbed the phone and dialed Heath.

"Hello?"

"Honey, I'm going to have to cancel." Only it came out more like "canthel."

"What?"

"I'm thick," I said. "I'm going to the doctor."

Heath's deep voice was urgent. "Sophie, what's wrong? You sound awful."

"I'll call you when I can," I said. "I'm tho thorry. I love you."

"Sophie . . ."

"I'll call you later . . . gotta go," I growled, and hung up while I still could. Poor Heath. He'd been planning this evening for months, and it tore my heart open to cancel on such short notice, but what could I do? Show up on all fours? It sure would give new meaning to the phrase *doggie style*. Stupid werewolf genes.

I had just tossed the phone back into my purse and driven into the parking garage when the phone rang again. Heath? No; the number was from Withers and Young. Adele? Better get it. I grabbed it with a hand that was starting to look more like a paw than a human appendage. A nicely manicured paw, but a paw nevertheless.

"Hello?" I growled.

"Sophie?"

"What?"

"It's Lindsey. What's wrong with your voice? Sally said you looked like you were going cold turkey or something."

Sally again. She'd have me drawn and quartered if she could. "I'm thick," I muttered. I had to get off the phone. Had to.

"You're what?"

I struggled to enunciate my words. "Sick. Fever. Frog in my throat."

"Sounds like it's bigger than a frog."

"I'm going to the doctor."

"Do you need a ride? Like, to the hospital?"

"No." *Wolfsbane*, I remembered suddenly. I'd left the

tumbler in the conference room. But worse, I'd left the box of tea bags in my desk. "Lindsey."

"What?"

"The tea. In my dethk."

"Tea? Sophie, what are you talking about?"

"The thtuff my mom thends me. Get rid of it."

"Why? Oh, right . . . you're worried about the drug test." She paused. "What *is* in that tea?"

"Doethn't matter," I rasped as I pulled the car into the parking garage. If I could only make it to the second level. I closed my eyes as a ripple passed through me. I couldn't hold off much longer. "Gotta go," I barked, and punched the End button with a painted claw.

Two minutes later I nudged the M3 door shut with my nose, poked at the Lock button of my key chain with a claw, and shoved the keys behind the tire with my paw.

I just hoped no one was paying any attention to the security cameras.

If I ever had the bad fortune to transform in Austin again, I decided as I crouched behind a Dumpster in the alley next to my building, I would have to find somewhere better to do it than a downtown parking garage.

It had been two hours since I'd heeded nature's call, and the sun was still high in the sky. Too high, really—I wasn't sure if it was the residual effects of the wolfsbane or the natural fur coat, but the alley felt more like Death Valley than an Austin city street. If only I'd managed to stave off the change until I'd gotten to my apartment, I thought. Unfortunately, in my current state, there was no way I was going to get past the doorman, much less punch the correct elevator button and unlock my loft. Never mind the fact that it would look weird; I couldn't even hold a key.

You never realize how useful opposable thumbs are until you don't have them anymore, I guess.

On the plus side, the other side effects of the tea seemed to be wearing off; none of the pedestrians I'd glimpsed were sporting horns, not a single inanimate object had bitten me, and the sweating had diminished from gallons to pints. I couldn't tell about the tongue yet—it felt okay, but it's hard to talk when you're a wolf.

But boy, could I smell.

And boy, did I wish I couldn't.

I shuffled to the far side of the alley, away from the Dumpster, and lay down in the cleanest spot I could find. Exactly what was *in* the Dumpster to make it smell so awful? I covered my nose with a paw. I know most dogs love rolling around in foul stuff, but I've never shared the canine fascination with disgusting organic substances. Then again, most dogs don't shell out for professional waxing jobs, either.

If there hadn't been so much frenzy in the papers lately, I might have chanced it and trotted down to the greenbelt, where I could at least walk around without scaring the locals. But with the packette on the loose and the animal-control trucks I'd seen trolling the streets, I was leery of showing my furry face around town until the sun went down. After the week I'd had—and it was only Monday—a trip to the pound would just be the icing on the cake.

I was scratching my hindquarters and checking myself for fleas when a door thunked open.

I scurried over behind an empty trash can and watched as a young Latino opened the Dumpster and heaved a fresh bag of garbage into it before disappearing back into the building.

Without closing the Dumpster.

If the smell was bad before, it was ten times worse now. I swallowed back my gorge and backed into the farthest corner from the Dumpster, but a breeze carried the rank odor in my direction, then swirled it around a bit in the dead end.

Yum.

There was no way I was going to be able to stay in this alley until nightfall.

I padded down the short alley to the street, giving the Dumpster as wide a berth as possible. I was only six blocks away from the Lady Bird Lake Hike and Bike Trail; there, if I stuck to the bushes, I might be able to cross the bridge and get to Zilker Park without attracting too much notice. Why Zilker Park? Well, it had a great Snow-Kone stand, of course, but that afternoon I was more interested in the greenbelt next to it. If I could make it there and stay off the trail, the only people I really risked seeing were the homeless folks who camped in the woods—and chances were, some of them probably thought they were werewolves themselves.

Unfortunately, those six blocks were chock-full of cars and pedestrians—not to mention dogcatchers and cop cars, both of which I had observed patrolling regularly.

I hesitated, watching a gaggle of businesswomen in strappy heels tripping down the sidewalk, and pulled my nose back in. There was no way I could get down the sidewalk without being seen.

But a fresh breeze reminded me there was no way I could spend the next two hours in the alley.

I waited until the group of women turned down a side street. After all, what did I have to lose? It just couldn't get much worse.

Could it?

After a quick mental pep talk—there had been some pretty friendly dogs in the shelter last time I'd visited—I broke cover.

Two minutes later, a man in loafers and Sansabelt pants stared as a naked-legged wolf galloped down Colorado Street, narrowly missing the front bumper of an animal-control truck.

I lurched out of the way just in time and ran as hard as I could. But a moment later, something sharp sank into my left buttock.

Twenty-eight

I glanced back at my butt and just about ran into a fire hydrant.

A tranquilizer dart was dangling from my right cheek. He'd shot me!

Stupid Heath. If it weren't for his get-rid-of-wild-dogs campaign, I could have made it to the greenbelt unmolested by overenthusiastic dogcatchers. Why couldn't he find a reasonable cause to support—such as Toys for Transvestites or Save the Children or something?

I skidded to a stop, frantically biting at my hindquarters, and got the dart out on the third try. As it clattered to the sidewalk, I paused for a split second to glare at the dogcatcher—a tall, spotty man with scrawny legs and an unfortunate pair of glasses. He raised the gun a second time, and I did my best fierce werewolf impression.

Like that was going to work.

A second dart ricocheted off the wall beside me as I raced down toward 3rd Street. What was with all the people trying to shoot me this week? Was I wearing a sign or something? The spot where he'd shot me burned, and I could smell the blood. *If I have a scar on my butt,* I thought, *I'm suing your ass.*

Of course it might be tough to find a lawyer to take the case, but I'd worry about that later.

By the time I reached 2nd Street, I was starting to feel a little woozy. Either it was a side effect of the wolfsbane or I hadn't gotten the dart out fast enough. Mr. Dog-catcher was still hot on my heels, looking like he was a regular in the Boston Marathon. Why, oh why couldn't I have gotten one of the tubby ones?

I crossed 1st Street at a dead run, bounded over a few bushes, and finally made it onto the trail. It was easier to go fast on the trail than in the bushes—and since Marathon Man was already after me, I galloped through the clots of exercisers, figuring it didn't matter who saw me. A big Airedale strained at his leash, his tongue hanging out, and I couldn't help feeling a touch smug. Shaved legs or no shaved legs, evidently I still had some sex appeal—even if it was to a dog that looked like an over-sized dust mop.

I slowed up a little, figuring that Marathon Man was far enough behind that I could take a little breather. Be-sides, I was kind of enjoying the surprised looks on peo-ple's faces as a half-shaved wolf trotted past them.

Too bad I forgot about the bicycle cops.

"There it is!" someone yelled behind me. I glanced over my shoulder to see two burly men in blue uniforms and short shorts bearing down on me. Normally, that wouldn't be such a bad thing—those bicycle cops have great legs. But in my current state, I didn't think they were hunting me down to ask me to dinner.

Crap.

I put on an extra burst of speed. If I could get across

the bridge, I could disappear into the bushes and sneak over to the park.

But with a couple of gallons of wolfsbane still pulsing through me—not to mention the effects of the stupid tranquilizer dart—I wasn't quite in top form, and the bridge was still a few hundred yards away when the faster one caught up with me.

We paced each other for a few moments, and I wondered exactly what he had in mind. He didn't seem to have a tranquilizer gun, and he wasn't reaching for his real gun. Were we just going to trot along together? Or was he going to try something heroic—like running over me?

I glanced to the side. He was fiddling with something in his belt; that probably wasn't good news. I took advantage of his distraction to put a little bit of distance between us—the fact that he had to dodge out of the way of a triple stroller didn't hurt either. A moment later, he caught up with me, and I narrowly missed being clubbed by a nightstick.

That was all I needed: a new contusion to go with the scab peeling off my nose. And the hole in my butt. On the other hand, at least it wasn't a gun—or a tranquilizer dart.

He swung again, and this time it grazed my left ear. Thank God we'd almost reached the bridge. I raced toward the staircase, dodging yet another wild swing, and took the steps three at a time. The cops had to take the ramp, which slowed them up a bit, and I was halfway across the bridge before the first bike appeared. I resisted the urge to stick out my tongue at them—I knew I was home free now—and sprinted the rest of the way.

By the time they made it across the bridge, I had dodged an enamored Doberman pinscher and two Labradoodles and was safely hidden in a stand of leafy bushes.

As the cops whizzed by me, I took a moment to inspect the dart wound. It hurt like hell, but it wasn't too bad—I'd snagged the skin a little pulling the dart out, but it should heal without too much of a scar. I don't know if it was the wolfsbane, the sudden sprint, or the tranquilizer dart, but I was feeling kind of lightheaded. When the men in polyester didn't reappear after a couple of minutes, I turned around three times and lay down with my head on my paws. My eyelids drooped, and the last thing I remember was the mixed bouquet of dead leaves, the lake, and the sharp scent of sweat from the nearby joggers.

The sun had long since dipped below the horizon when I opened my eyes. I was still in my little stand of bushes rather than a reinforced wire cage, so I figured my cop dodge had worked.

At least something was going right this week.

The moon filtered through the trees above as I stood up and shook off the dead leaves, stretching my stiff muscles. I took a deep sniff of the night air. Nutria, squirrel, a couple of unwashed drunks. And dog pee. Lots and lots of dog pee. The cops might not have found me, but the local dog population sure had—it smelled as if half the canine population of Austin had decorated the bushes around me.

I brushed off the last of the leaves and padded up to the deserted trail, taking care to step over the puddles of semidry urine.

I had several hours to kill as a werewolf, I thought as I trotted onto the trail. Since the brouhaha with my mother had started, I hadn't been hitting the gym quite as much, and my clothes had been getting just a touch snug. (Not that I was wearing any now, of course.) I figured my odds of getting mugged or raped on the trail were at an all-time low, so it might be just the night for a moonlit jog on the four-mile loop.

I stretched my legs and picked up the pace a bit, enjoying the night breeze through my fur. My butt still hurt a bit, but it wasn't too bad. What time was it, I wondered? Had I stood up Heath yet? Was Tom out doing the tango with Lindsey?

Did I still have a job?

I was also worried about a less important but more immediate consideration: In short, what was I going to do for clothes when I switched back to human form?

With an effort, I pushed those thoughts out of my head. I was a wolf whether I liked it or not, so checking in with my boss or my boyfriend wasn't exactly an option. And I'd have to deal with the clothing issue later; for now, I was stuck with a fur coat.

As I trotted along, I tried swallowing, and my swollen tongue stuck to the top of my mouth. God, I was thirsty. I'd sweated buckets because of the wolfsbane, and all the exertion in 100-degree weather hadn't helped, either.

The lake was only fifteen feet away, slapping lightly at the muddy shores, but I wasn't that desperate. In fact, I wasn't sure I'd ever be that desperate. Besides, wasn't there a water fountain somewhere nearby?

I loped up the trail, listening to the tree frogs and looking for somewhere to get a drink. I was starting to think I might have to lower my standards and reconsider the lake—ugh—when I caught a glint of chrome.

Thank God, I thought, picking up the pace. I could already taste the cool water as I stood up on my hind legs and put one paw on the button, my muzzle poised next to the fountain.

I pushed at the button with my paw.

Nothing happened.

No matter how hard I clawed at the button, my paw couldn't put enough pressure on it to get the water going. It was ridiculous—here I was, a werewolf, with supernatural speed, strength, and, if I say so myself, plenty going on in the looks department, too—unable to get a simple drink of water.

I paced around the fountain a couple times, looking for an alternate solution. Sure, there was a little doggie dish and a spigot below, but I wasn't sure I could turn that on either. Besides, that was almost as bad as the lake. Maybe worse, actually. I didn't know if werewolves could catch distemper, but I didn't want to test it and find out.

I reared up on my hind legs again, determined to make the fountain work. After several attempts, finally, a little driblet of water appeared—and I'm almost ashamed to admit that I licked it up. With a bit more experimentation, I found a position that created a steady drip, and was busy lapping it up when something growled behind me.

I knew who it was before I even turned around.

The packette had found me.

Twenty-nine

There are many ways of facing an adversary. Standing on top of a giant boulder and howling is one. Baring a mouthful of teeth and snarling menacingly is another.

Rearing up on your hind legs and licking water from a fountain doesn't quite make the top-ten list.

I dropped down into a crouch, water still dripping from my muzzle, and gave them a good view of my teeth. Better late than never, right?

Stinky looked a little nervous, but Fluffy just puffed up bigger and growled back at me. After a moment, Scrawny followed suit.

How had they snuck up on me? Usually I could smell just about anyone—not to mention a werewolf with major hygiene issues—long before they got anywhere near me. I took a deep sniff; I could certainly smell them now. If anything, Stinky's bouquet had gotten even fruitier since our little run-in on 6th Street.

Maybe the wolfsbane had screwed with my wolfie senses. Or maybe the tranquilizer dart was throwing me off.

It didn't really matter now, though. Fluffy took a menacing step toward me, with his minions right behind him.

I glanced behind me—they'd backed me into a corner, with nothing but a stone wall and the lake behind me— and growled again. Tom had said the made werewolves weren't as strong as those of us who were born, and I was pretty sure I could take them. I might be a touch woozy from the wolfsbane—not to mention ravenously hungry—but I could definitely handle these three.

Couldn't I?

The trio advanced a little farther, fanning out in front of me. Stinky seemed to have regained his courage, unfortunately, and was so close that I had to breathe through my mouth. As I looked for an opening to slip through, I found myself feeling a touch less confident all of a sudden. In fact, I decided, it might be best not to get into a scrap right then because I wasn't exactly in top form.

I bunched my muscles up, preparing to spring past them. Then something the size of a pterodactyl burst out of the trees beside me, flapping up toward the moon.

I jerked my head around to look. Which wasn't a good move on my part, because it was just then that Fluffy came at me, yellow teeth gleaming in the moonlight.

The first thing I noticed was that Fluffy could use some mouthwash; whatever he'd been snacking on recently wasn't exactly fresh.

The second thing I noticed was that his teeth were imbedded in my neck. And I do mean imbedded; it hurt like hell.

If he'd been a full werewolf, I would have been toast—he'd have crunched right through the bone. Fortunately, however, he wasn't that strong, and a good shake sent him reeling into the bushes, although it probably did some additional damage to my poor skin. I growled and backed up, smelling my own blood for the second time that day. From the feel of it trickling down my neck, I guessed I'd be wearing turtlenecks for some time to come.

Before Fluffy could get back on his feet, I lunged after him, but Scrawny took the opportunity to latch onto my butt. *Oh my God.* It hurt—man, did it hurt—but the indignity of it all was worse. Here I was, a half-blood werewolf, and a scrawny little made werewolf had sunk his dirty teeth into my right cheek.

Stinky still held back a little, but having one wannabe werewolf hanging on to your derriere is bad enough.

And then—would you believe it—he started licking me!

Ew!

I kicked out at him, landing a hind paw right in his midsection. It wasn't a perfect shot, but it was enough to get his slimy tongue off my butt.

I glanced around. Fluffy was crouching, ready to spring again, and Stinky looked as if he was thinking of getting in on the action.

Time to go.

I broke past them and galloped up the trail, ignoring the sore spots where I'd been bitten and trying to figure out what to do next. They weren't full werewolves, but they still had a powerful sense of smell, so it would be hard to throw them off my trail. And I was pretty badly hurt, which put me at a major disadvantage. I might be able to put a bit of distance between us, but they'd eventually close the gap.

And then what?

I glanced at the moonlight sparkling on the lake. I could always try the dog paddle. But they'd know I went in, and if they came in after me, I wasn't sure being in deep water would be an advantage.

More than ever, I was wishing I could have found a way to sneak up to my loft and settle in with a bag of beef jerky and a good movie. Maybe even a *Sex and the City* rerun.

Beef jerky. Despite the pain, I could feel my salivary glands kick in—kind of like Pavlov's dogs. I hadn't eaten anything since that chocolate croissant, and I was starving. And tired. And . . . dizzy. The moon started doing loop-the-loops off to the right somewhere, and the trees seemed to be closing in around me. *Focus on the trail, Sophie.* No matter how hard I tried, though, the trail kept wriggling around in front of me—it just wouldn't stay put. A few moments later I sideswiped a cypress tree, adding yet another scrape to my growing collection of flesh wounds.

I stumbled back onto the path, listening for the sound of paws behind me. There was a rather steep cliff about five feet to my right, so I decided it might be prudent to slow down a bit.

Which is not what I needed to be doing at that particular moment. What with the packette coming after me as if they were a bunch of jolly old English hunters and I was the poor little fox.

This can't be happening, I thought. I was a born werewolf, for God's sake. I sniffed the night air, hoping that maybe they'd given up the chase and I could crawl into a bush and rest. No such luck. Stinky's bouquet was not far off, trumping the smell of honeysuckle.

I needed to run.

I made it another fifty yards before I started reeling to the side. *Get off the trail, Sophie.* With my last ounce of energy, I stumbled into a nearby bush and collapsed into a pile of leaves. There was the swoop of dark wings overhead, a low growl, and then, suddenly, a wave of primeval scent. I opened my eyes; there, on the trail, stood a huge wolf, his fur silvery in the moonlight. Despite my compromised state, a shiver of lust passed through me. It was probably a good thing that I could barely move, because at that moment, I'm not sure I could have kept myself from throwing myself at him. Even as a wolf he was incredible—that solid barrel chest, those eyes, that smell . . .

As I stared at Tom's muscular body, reminding myself that it was Heath's and my anniversary, the packette skidded to a stop on the trail, whining and cringing. I blinked. Then the moon wobbled once more and went out.

Evidently a little bit of time went by there somewhere, because when I opened my eyes, the moon was gone and it was no longer night. In fact, the sun was high in the sky, and it was so damned bright it hurt.

I squinted and moved around a little, trying to assess the damage, and realized that more had changed than the time of day.

I wasn't a wolf anymore.

And I was stark naked.

I sniffed hard. What had happened to the packette? They had been out for blood last night, and I hadn't exactly been a moving target. Then I remembered the wings. And the wolf. I sniffed again, and the blood rushed to my face.

Tom had been here.

And I was naked.

Oh, God.

I looked around and realized that I wasn't where I had been when I had collapsed—I was deep in a bamboo thicket. How had I gotten here? I was sure that Tom had had something to do with it. It must have been him who had chased off the packette for me. Which was kind of embarrassing, considering I'd told him off about interfering in the alley the other night. Granted, there had been extenuating circumstances—after all, it's not every day that you take a quadruple dose of wolfsbane *and* get hit by a tranquilizer dart—but still. My face burned as I remembered our conversation—and wondered when exactly my little shift from wolf to human had occurred. With everything that had been going on, I hadn't had time to find out when moonset happened.

Had Tom seen me naked?

The crunch of shoes on gravel reached my ears, and I realized I still wasn't far from the trail. Which brought up another problem. How exactly was I going to get back to my loft without being arrested for indecent exposure?

I looked around, trying to come up with something I could use to cover myself. I could always transform back into a wolf, but after yesterday's little game of chase, that option wasn't tremendously appealing.

My butt throbbed as I staggered to my feet. I twisted around to examine the damage on my backside, only to discover that a sticky salve coated the tooth marks on my right cheek. When I reached up to touch my neck, my fingers encountered the same gooey substance.

Tom.

I had to admit that for a werewolf, he was a pretty stand-up guy. He'd run off the packette, moved me to a more hidden area, and even treated my bite wounds. I decided to operate under the assumption that he'd performed his ministrations while I was still in wolf form. If not, I was hoping it was too dark to really notice the little bit of cellulite on the backs of my thighs.

Too bad he hadn't taken a few extra minutes to find me something to wear.

I glanced around to assess my options. Bamboo leaves, which wouldn't leave a whole heck of a lot to the imagination. Tree bark, which aside from being fragile, looked incredibly scratchy. And a straggly grapevine, which I supposed I could wrap around me in some kind of weird Garden of Eden getup, if I had a bit more experience with centerpiece- and wreath-making.

In short, I was screwed.

I rooted around in the leaves for a bit, hoping that someone had dropped a shirt or something. Heck, I'd have been happy to find a dish towel—at least I'd have had something to work with. But after ten minutes of pawing through dead leaves, all I came up with was a sun-bleached Slurpee cup and half of a shredded Mrs. Baird's bread bag.

As I slumped against a tree, a flash of color through the bamboo caught my eye—a woman in pink spandex, jogging past a trash can.

A trash can.

Maybe I wasn't out of luck after all.

I crept forward toward the trail, hoping there might be a spare bag in the can—and that it wouldn't be clear plastic. I might not be inconspicuous in a Hefty bag, but at least I would be covered. And after all, this *was* Austin.

I waited for a lull in the traffic and darted to the trash can. Evidently it hadn't been emptied in a while; it was overflowing with goldfish baggies and empty Gatorade bottles. And—*ick, ick, ick*!—lots of dog doo in little plastic bags.

On the plus side—not that it's saying much—the trash can liner was black.

Pulling the edges of the bag aside, I reached down into the can, hoping to find a spare. But the thud of approaching footsteps sent me back into the bamboo, and I had to wait for what felt like three more hours before there was another break in the traffic. Until then, I hadn't realized what a fit city Austin was, and I found myself wishing people would take a little more interest in developing their inner couch potatoes.

Finally there was a break in the spandex-clad foot traffic, and I dashed back to the trash can and tugged at the bag again.

There were no spare bags beneath it.

I glanced around—the coast was still clear, thankfully—and dug through the bag's contents, looking for something—anything—I could wear. I'd settle for an old tube top or a ratty bandana—heck, I might even have worn a used thong just then. At least it would have covered *something*. But unless I could rig something up with Doritos bags and Gatorade bottles—or dog poop bags—I was out of luck.

Well, maybe not *completely* out of luck. I examined the trash bag, which was coated in a variety of organic substances. All of which had been marinating in the heat for a couple of days.

Ick.

Still. Unless I wanted to do a Lady Godiva impression—without any long, flowing hair to cover the important parts—it was my only option. So after a moment's hesitation, I pulled the bag out, dumped its contents into the trash can, and scurried back into the bamboo stand, trying to ignore the smell of fermented Gatorade and overripe turkey sandwich. And dog doo. Five minutes later, I emerged on the trail wearing an aromatic and slightly stretched garbage bag—and praying that none of my clients was an exercise fanatic.

Thirty

The answering machine was blinking when I let myself into my loft a half hour later. I locked the door, tore the bag off, and tossed it into the trash—the smell still oozed through the closed lid—before glancing at the clock. It was already half past nine.

A good little employee would call Adele—if nothing else, to find out if she still had a job—but partnership or no partnership, after I'd spent thirty minutes limping along the trail in a trash bag that smelled like a cross between a Dumpster and a men's restroom, it wasn't my top priority. I'm not sure how, but I'd managed to make it through the parking garage and up the back stairs without running into anyone I knew. Now I was ready for a drink, a steak, and a very, very hot bath. Not necessarily in that order.

As the tub filled, I wiped the worst of the stuff off with a towel and headed for the kitchen. I opened the fridge, hoping to rustle up some roast beef, and found a big tub of soup, with a sleeve of saltine crackers next to it.

Where had that come from?

I eased the lid off and sniffed; it was chicken soup. From Heath; his scent was all over it.

I put the soup back in the fridge and searched in vain for fresh cold cuts. Finally, I gave up and went for the beef jerky. My stomach clenched as I put the kettle on for tea—the regular kind, not wolfsbane. My mind kept going back to the chicken soup in the fridge. I'd told Heath I was going to the doctor. Did he think I was in the hospital? Why hadn't he left a note? And how long had he been here?

I had to call him and tell him I was okay. But since I couldn't stand to be in the same room with myself, I decided that the bath was the first priority. I'd call him as soon as I was done.

I had taken my mug of tea to the bathroom and climbed into my bubble bath—in case you were wondering, hot water on werewolf bites hurts like the dickens— when the phone rang.

I was tempted to let it go, but on the off-chance that it was good news—maybe they'd dropped the charges against my mom; maybe the Houston pack had been beamed to Saturn; maybe Lindsey had fallen in love with a nice, human attorney; or maybe I'd won Publishers Clearing House—I hauled myself out of the water and ran to grab it.

It was Lindsey.

"Hi," I said, wishing I'd stayed in the tub.

"Sophie! You're back! Are you okay?"

"I'm fine, but I'm taking a bath. Can I call you back?" A puddle was forming at my feet, and I was starting to shiver. As much as I liked Lindsey, I was wishing I'd let the machine pick up.

"Heath called me last night. He was frantic."

"I saw the chicken soup he left. When was he here?"

"He headed over right after you called. Then he called me in a panic. Your car was there, but you weren't."

"How did he get in?"

"The building manager let him in. He thought you might be . . . well, unconscious. You sounded awful on the phone."

"I know," I said.

"Then he called the hospitals—even thought about contacting the cops."

I swallowed a chunk of beef jerky and almost choked. "He called the cops?"

"I talked him out of it. I guess he finally gave up and went home."

My eyes slid to the fridge, and I thought of the tub of chicken soup.

"But where did you go?" she asked.

Why, I was out dodging dogcatchers and brawling with a bunch of werewolves. Including Tom. I thought of that steamy kiss, and guilt washed over me. I had betrayed my own friend. Not to mention my chicken soup–delivering boyfriend.

"I went to a clinic," I said. "To find out what was wrong with me."

"Without your car?"

Oops. How had I gotten there, if my car was still in the garage? "I took a cab," I improvised. "I wasn't sure I would be able to drive there."

"You took a cab," she said in a voice that didn't exactly sound convinced. "And you were at the clinic all night."

"There was a long wait," I said lamely.

She snorted.

"They had me wait a while. Under observation. I guess I was dehydrated or something."

"Uh-huh." Lindsey sounded a tad skeptical. "So, have you told all this to Heath?"

"Not yet," I admitted.

"Well, you probably should. I talked to him five minutes ago. He's called you six times this morning already—three times at work."

"Wonderful."

"If I were you, I'd call him ASAP," she said.

I took another bite of jerky and glanced back toward the bathroom. I had been hoping to put off the whole calling people and lying thing until I had at least washed all the trash out of my hair.

An itch started on the back of my thigh, and I reached back to scratch it. "Couldn't you call him for me?" I asked through a mouthful of dried beef.

"Nope. He won't believe it until he hears from you. Even then, I'm not so sure."

"Can you at least tell Adele I'm still sick?"

"Oh, yeah. I almost forgot about her."

"What about her? Did she freak out?"

"I told her you had a high fever. She kept going on about something you said—something about a plug biting you?"

I blushed. "Hallucinations. High fever."

"Sally . . ." Lindsey trailed off.

"Sally what?"

"Never mind," she said quickly. "I'll tell Adele you're still under the weather."

"Thanks," I said.

There was a buzzing sound, and Lindsey said, "Gotta go—client's here. Call me later. And don't keep Heath waiting!"

I hung up and headed back to the bathtub. I didn't care what Lindsey thought; the phone call to Heath would have to wait until I had washed all the garbage off.

An itch flared on my stomach. Had I picked up fleas again? With all the dogs that had been on the trail, it wouldn't surprise me. Another itch started on my lower back, and I reached back to rub it. Maybe I should add a few scoops of pennyroyal to the bath.

I wrenched another piece of jerky off with my teeth, dropped my towel, and turned to get into the tub. It wasn't until one foot was submerged in the hot water that I caught a glimpse of myself in the mirror and yelped.

My entire body was covered in red welts.

Crap.

I stared at the mirror, taking in the red marks all over my body and resisting the urge to claw at my skin. Between the bite marks and the welts, I looked as if I'd spent the last twelve hours frolicking with vampires and heavy-duty bondage freaks. If I went to work looking like this, I could only imagine the rumors that would be flying around by Friday.

Where could this rash have come from? Could it be a reaction to Fluffy's licking me? I shuddered just thinking of it, but the bite wounds didn't look inflamed at all. Maybe it was a side effect of the wolfsbane overdose? Kind of like seeing horns on the CEO of Southeast Airlines and hearing cats meow in the middle of the conference room. At least I was hoping that was a side effect of the wolfsbane.

A new itch started behind my left knee, and as I reached to scratch it, I noticed a series of little blisters. Suddenly it clicked.

I had poison ivy.

As if it had been waiting for me to figure out what it was before kicking in fully, the itching suddenly flared up all over my body. This had happened before—kind of an unfortunate side effect of my nocturnal romps through wooded areas—but usually my fur worked as a kind of low-tech barrier. But not this time. The welts were so bad that the leaves had to have made direct contact with my skin. And since I'd woken up in a bamboo grove, not a stand of poison ivy . . .

Despite the pink rash covering my body, I could feel myself blush. *Don't think about it, Sophie.* But there it was. You don't get poison ivy from bamboo leaves. Which meant I must have transformed before Tom moved me.

I tried to distract myself from thoughts of exactly how much of me Tom must have seen by digging through the medicine cabinet. I finally located the Benadryl and downed two capsules immediately. Then I grabbed a bottle of Ivarest and headed back to the bathtub.

The phone call to Heath would definitely have to wait.

By 10:30, I was covered in pink calamine lotion and a fluffy bathrobe. And I still hadn't called Heath.

I knew that putting it off was only making it worse, but I just couldn't bring myself to pick up the phone. What would I say? That I came down with the flu and was kidnapped by aliens? That I'd accidentally gone to the wrong building and only figured it out this morning? They say the truth is always the best policy, but somehow I didn't think telling Heath I'd stood him up because I had turned into a werewolf was the best plan right then.

I should probably just stick to the story I'd told Lindsey. You know, the one that involved hailing a cab to take me to an all-night clinic?

But Heath cross-examined people for a living, and it wouldn't take more than a few questions before my story had more holes in it than I did. And after my run-in with the packette and the dogcatcher, that was saying something.

I was trying to remember the name of an all-night clinic—if I was going to tell a whopper, details such as the name of the clinic I had supposedly visited would be good to have—when the phone rang. I glanced at the Caller ID: Of course it was Heath. After three rings, I hit Talk and crossed my fingers.

"Hello?" I said in my best weak and pathetic voice.

"Sophie! Where have you been? Are you all right?"

"I've been sick. Really sick." I paused to cough. "But I'm feeling better now, thanks."

His words came out in a rush. "What happened? Why didn't you call? I thought something awful had happened to you."

"It . . . it just came on suddenly." My involuntary transformation *had* been a little abrupt, so it wasn't exactly a lie.

"What did?"

"Um . . . the flu." Okay, so maybe that part was a lie. But come on. What was I *supposed* to say?

"I came by your place last night."

"I know," I said, feeling a rush of guilt. While Heath had been here with a tub of chicken soup, I'd been on the trail, lusting after another man. Well, maybe not a *man,* exactly, but still . . . "Thanks so much for the soup," I said. "And the crackers. It was so thoughtful."

His deep voice was strained. "Your car was in the garage. The building manager let me into the loft, but you weren't there." There was a short silence. "I was ready to call the cops, but Lindsey talked me out of it."

I swallowed hard.

"Sophie," he said. "Is there something I should know?"

For a moment, the urge to confess was overwhelming. I was about to tell him everything—that I was a werewolf, that four times a year I had no choice but to transform, that I'd spent the night being attacked by a pack of bad-smelling werewolves, and that I'd walked home this morning wearing nothing but a trash bag—but at the last moment, my common sense kicked in. Why on earth would he believe me? And even if he did believe me . . . what then?

I took a deep breath and conjured up an image of Heath—his dark, silky hair, the twinkle in his brown eyes, his firm, muscular abdomen, the way it felt when he took me in his arms. I couldn't bear to lose him. "It's my mother," I blurted out, feeling sweat bead on my forehead.

"Your *mother*?"

"She's . . . she's up for trial soon. I didn't want to tell you, didn't know what you'd think . . ."

"So the defense attorney you asked about the other day . . . that was why you needed to know."

I swallowed hard. "Uh-huh."

"What are the charges, Sophie?" he asked calmly.

"Homicide," I said in a small voice.

There was a long pause, and I cringed. Oh, God. What had I done? It was better than telling Heath I was a werewolf. But not by much. Finally, he said, "Homicide?"

The words tumbled out of my mouth. "They said she poisoned Ted Brewster, but she didn't. It was all a mistake. . . . We talked to the librarian, and she took the potion, and nothing happened to her—"

"Wait a moment," he said. "Your mother is the witch who's all over the papers? Carmen something?"

"Um . . . yeah."

"But sweetheart. Why didn't you tell me? I could have helped."

I held the phone for a moment. "But I thought . . . I thought you'd have trouble with it."

"With what?"

With what? Was he kidding me? "With the fact that my mother's a witch. And that she's been arrested for murder."

"Sophie," he said gently. "I love you. Your family is my family. God knows I've got enough weirdos on my side. Did I ever tell you about my Great-Uncle Geoffrey? He was a one-man band. Used to embarrass my mother at every family event—you know how she is. All stiff upper lip. To be honest, I'm almost relieved."

I couldn't believe it. Heath was okay with finding out about my mother—and evidently last night's transgression was forgiven as well. I felt like a huge weight had been lifted from my shoulders. "Relieved?" I asked.

"Yes. You've just been so distant lately, I thought you might be . . . well, seeing someone."

I felt a flash of guilt at the thought of Tom and that steamy kiss. And at the thought of the other secret I was keeping from him. Heath might be okay with my quirky mother, but the whole werewolf thing might be a bit tougher to swallow.

"It was Marvin Blechknapp, right? I'll get in touch with him tomorrow," Heath was saying. "Your mom's out on bail, isn't she?"

"Yes," I said. "Yes, she is. The trial is set for a few weeks from now, though."

"Well, then, I want to meet her." He was all business now, full of can-do energy, and it made my heart swell. "Let's plan a strategy meeting," he said. "Does Marvin have any other potential suspects lined up?"

"No," I said, feeling much more optimistic about the whole investigation now that Heath was involved. It was such a relief to have everything out in the open. Or if not everything, at least my mother. "But I've been doing some investigating of my own, and I think there are a few options the police haven't considered." Best not to mention the whole breaking and entering, though, I decided.

"Good girl, Sophie. Can we get together for lunch? Maybe tomorrow? I can't wait to meet your mom!"

"I'll call her and see what I can do," I said.

"I'm so glad you told me. But last night . . . was it just your mom? Or were you really sick?"

"Both, really. I had a fever," I said, which was totally true, "and now I've got this terrible rash."

"Are you feeling better this morning?"

"Somewhat," I said. "I'm just glad you didn't run the other way when I told you about my mom," I confessed.

"I love you, Sophie. All of you. It's nothing to be ashamed of."

"Thanks," I said, feeling all warm and cozy inside. "I love you too."

"No secrets," he said softly. "If you're in trouble, you let me know. I'm here for you, now and always. Okay?"

"Right," I said halfheartedly, no longer feeling quite so warm and cozy—I'd just lied, yet again. But in my defense, my options were rather limited.

"Don't worry about your mom; we'll take care of her. You just work on getting yourself better," he said. "And we'll all have lunch tomorrow."

I hung up the phone a moment later, feeling less than fabulous. No secrets, he'd said. And I'd agreed.

Could I ever confess the truth to him? It had never been an option in the past, but I'd just told him my mother was a psychic witch up on murder charges, and instead of turning tail, he'd raced to my rescue.

As I opened yet another bag of beef jerky, I thought about our conversation. I'd always assumed Heath would run at the first sign of anything . . . well, unorthodox.

But so far, he hadn't.

Was there some way I could make this work out after all?

Thirty-one

"You look awful," Lindsey said when I opened my front door that evening. She was in a tight "Keep Austin Weird" T-shirt and cutoffs, and in her arms was a grocery bag.

"Gee, thanks." I tugged at my turtleneck; even with the temperature cranked down to sixty-eight degrees, it was still warm.

"No, really. Your face is puffed up like a chipmunk." She hesitated. "You're not contagious or anything, are you?"

"No, I'm not contagious."

"Good," she said, stepping through the doorway and heading for the kitchen. "I stopped by Whole Foods to pick us up some dinner. No wonder they call it Whole Paycheck. A cup of fruit salad is like five bucks."

I followed her into the kitchen. "I thought you were going out with Tom tonight."

"I decided you needed me more than Tom does," she said, plunking the bag down on the counter. Then her lips twitched into a wicked little smile. "Besides, sometimes it's good to keep them guessing a little bit." She unloaded the bag. "I got some king ranch chicken casserole, fruit salad, some chocolate cookies, and . . ." She pulled a bottle out of the bag. "I splurged on a bottle of Conundrum."

Yum. My favorite white wine. "For that, I can almost forgive you the chipmunk comment."

She held the bottle away from me. "If you're okay to drink, that is."

I made a grab for it. "I'm not dead, am I?"

She eyed me speculatively. "Maybe not now, but you look like it might be imminent." She eyed my swollen face. "Did you ever call Heath?"

I rummaged for a corkscrew. "Actually, I didn't get a chance; he called me."

"How did it go?"

"He knows about my mother now."

"I figured as much. After all, he's not stupid; he did make it through law school."

"Actually, he found out because I told him." I located the corkscrew and popped the cork, pouring two glasses while Lindsey gaped at me.

"You're kidding me. What did he say?"

I downed a big slug of wine, then followed it with another one. For medicinal purposes, of course. I just hoped it wouldn't react with the six Benadryl I'd taken. "He offered to help, believe it or not. Wants to meet with my mother and me for lunch tomorrow."

"You stood him up on your big date, you've been avoiding his calls, and you spent last night somewhere other than your apartment . . . and he's fine with it?"

"Yup," I said, not really wanting to go into more detail about last night's escapade. Time to change subjects. Should I ask about Tom? No, not Tom. "How's Adele?" I asked lamely.

Lindsey cocked an eyebrow. "She wasn't happy about

you leaving in the middle of the meeting yesterday, I can tell you that."

"I figured as much. I called her a few times, but she didn't pick up. I left a message on her voice mail."

"At least you made the effort," she said. "Let's just hope Southeast Airlines doesn't take offense."

"I was sick," I said.

"If you go in tomorrow looking anything like you do today, nobody's going to think you were faking it."

"Thanks a lot," I said.

"Which is probably a good thing, because . . ." Lindsey hesitated.

"Because what?"

She sighed. "Because your assistant keeps spreading rumors about some weird drug deliveries you keep getting."

I choked, spewing a mouthful of wine onto my turtleneck. "She said what?"

"Something about these packages you keep getting. I've told everyone Sally's got a few screws loose, but still . . ."

I closed my eyes and took another medicinal swallow of wine. Then I opened them with a start. "Lindsey." I gripped the table. "Did you get the tea?"

Wolfsbane wasn't exactly a drug, but if someone nosy—say, someone like Sally—decided to go looking, how was I going to explain keeping a toxic substance in my desk? Particularly when my mom had recently been arrested for poisoning a politician. Not that anyone at the office knew about that little issue. Not yet, anyway.

"Tea?"

Not good. "The tea. Remember? I asked you to get the tea."

She bit her lip. "Shoot. I knew I was forgetting something."

My stomach did a little flip-flop, and I reached up to massage my temples. "Oh my God. I can't believe you forgot the tea."

"What's the big deal? I thought it was just some herbal remedy."

"You wouldn't believe me if I told you," I said.

"Your mom said it was for excess hair growth," she said, staring at me. "But it's for something else, isn't it?"

"No. Yes. Well, sort of. It's a complicated condition. Someday I'll tell you about it," I said. I wasn't sure it would ever be the right moment to explain my "medical condition," but I was pretty confident this wasn't it.

Lindsey took a sip of wine. "You're holding out on me," she said.

"Can we discuss something else?" I asked. *Such as politics or global warming or birth control?* Heck, I'd even be willing to hear about her tango date with Tom.

"Fine," she said. "Keep your little secret, then." She speared a blueberry with her fork. "But at least tell me why you're wearing a turtleneck. It's like ninety degrees outside."

"It's the only thing I've got clean," I lied, and took another big sip of Conundrum.

Lindsey leaned forward in her chair. "I did a little digging into Brewster's will today."

"And?"

"The new one was never filed."

It took a moment for this to sink in. "Wow. So because Brewster died before he changed it, Tad gets everything?"

"Yup." Lindsey nodded. "I also had a friend of mine at the *Statesman* see what he could find out about that deed we found in the safe."

"Gosh. You've been busy."

"Well, somebody's got to work," she said. "Guess who owns a third of the property?"

"Who?"

"Patti Pendergast's husband."

I let out a long, low whistle. "Patti Pendergast is the big environmentalist on the city council, isn't she?"

"Bingo."

"So even though she's gone on record as protesting the development, her husband is selling the land to the developers."

Lindsey speared a blueberry and popped it into her mouth. "Her constituency probably wouldn't be too jazzed about that, would they?"

"That certainly puts a new spin on things," I said, swirling the wine in my glass. "Heath will be all over that one, I'll bet, even though the police seem to be conveniently ignoring it. Do you think Brewster was threatening to let the cat out of the bag?"

Lindsey shrugged. "I don't know—but it is kind of strange that he'd have the deed locked away if it wasn't a sensitive document."

"On the other hand, he also had Al Gore's book behind lock and key."

"I'd say Gore's a sensitive guy," Lindsey said.

"You know what I mean." I scraped up the last bit of food on my plate. Despite Lindsey's Whole Foods haul—and two bags of beef jerky—my stomach was still rumbling. I grabbed a chocolate cookie and bit into it, resolving to restrict myself to salad for lunch tomorrow. If I didn't stop wolfing things down soon, I was going to start looking like one of Disney's dancing hippos.

"So, do you think his new environmentalism interest was kind of a midlife crisis?" Lindsey asked.

"A little late for a midlife crisis, don't you think?" I said through a mouthful of cookie. "I mean, he was pushing sixty-five, wasn't he?"

"From what I've read, these things can hit anytime."

"Still. Don't they usually go for flashy cars and young women?"

"Remember the librarian?"

I thought of Jennifer, who wouldn't look out of place in a high school cafeteria. And the *Barely Legal* magazines in Brewster's desk drawer. "Good point."

"So at least we've got two suspects," Lindsey said.

"It's a start," I said.

"There's only one problem."

"Only one?"

"We've got two suspects with motives. But what are the other two things they're supposed to have?"

"Means and opportunity?" I supplied.

"That's it," she said.

I reached for another cookie. "Well, as far as means goes, nightshade grows like a weed around here." I didn't know much about plants, but after I'd tried to make a nightshade-berry pie as a kid, my mother made sure I knew the poisonous ones. And in Austin, there were a lot of them.

"So everyone had the means," Lindsey said. "But who the heck knows what nightshade looks like? I wouldn't recognize it if it came up and bit me. For all I know, I'm growing it in my yard."

I touched my neck at the mention of bites—it still burned a little where Fluffy had sunk his teeth into me. Stupid werewolf. "It's that little purple flower with the silvery leaves," I said. "It's all over the place. Besides, even if you can't identify it off the top of your head, it's not too hard to look up poisonous plants on the Internet."

"True," she said, tapping her wineglass with a frosted pink fingernail. "But what about opportunity?"

"Well, whoever it was had to know about the potion—and be in a position to poison it."

"That's the tough part," Lindsey said. "I don't imag-

ine Brewster advertised the fact that he'd had a love potion made up. Even if he did, I doubt he'd be chitchat-
ting about it with a political rival."

"He might have told his son," I said.

"You're right." She sat up a little straighter. "See? I
told you we couldn't rule him out."

I thought of Tad Brewster's tired, doughy face. Was he
really torn up about his dad's death or was he just looking for sympathy from Lindsey? Or maybe a pity date?
"I don't know," I said. "I just keep thinking there's
something we're missing."

"Like what?"

"If I knew that, we wouldn't be missing it. It's just a
feeling."

"Well, until you can turn your 'feeling' into something
a little more concrete, we're going to have to focus on
what we've got."

I sighed. "Which means Patti Pendergast and Tad
Brewster."

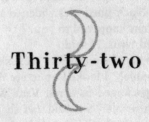

Thirty-two

I don't know if it was the Benadryl or the
calamine lotion, but when I woke up the next morning,
the reflection in the bathroom mirror looked more
human than it had in days. My cheeks still looked like I

might have tucked a couple of hazelnuts in there some-where, but at least they were no longer the size of grape-fruits. And my welts, though still itchy, no longer looked like I had a thing for being tied up and slapped with a riding crop.

Of course, my neck still looked like Swiss cheese, as did my right butt cheek. But my plans for the day didn't involve mooning anyone—not even Sally—so I just had to worry about the area above the collar.

After a half hour with my razor and some pancake makeup, I gave myself a once-over and declared myself ready to face Adele. And potentially a meeting between Heath and my mother.

I was still trying to figure out what restaurant would be the perfect place for introducing my mother to Heath as I stood in the elevator on my way up to Withers and Young, latte in hand. The moment the door opened, I knew it was another Aviance day for Sally.

I took a sip of my latte, checked to be sure the scarf I'd tied around my neck was covering my lacerations, and strode through the lobby toward my office. My assis-tant's black-lined eyes widened as I swept past her desk.

"What happened to you?"

"Bad virus," I said.

"Looks like mumps to me," she said.

"Sophie!" I looked up to see Adele striding down the hall, packaged in a red Vera Wang power suit. "You look horrible!" she said, her sharp eyes focusing on my swollen cheeks. *Gee, thanks.* I reached up to touch my puffy face. Maybe I had left the loft a bit prematurely after all.

"I'm actually doing a lot better today."

"We were worried about you," she said, shooting a glance at Sally, whose painted lips curved into a smile that told me worry hadn't been her primary emotion.

"Just a bad virus," I said. "I'm sorry I had to leave the

meeting early—the fever came on really fast, and I was afraid I was going to pass out. Did everything go okay after I left?"

"It went fine, Sophie, just fine," she said, beaming and slapping me on the back so hard that some of my latte sloshed onto Sally's desk. "I just got the call. We made it to the next round!"

I stood speechless, my latte dripping from my cup. Even with my hallucinations, drooling, excessive hair growth, and a rubber tongue, we'd made it to the second round of interviews.

Adele peered at me. "Sophie? Are you okay?"

"Fine . . . I'm just . . . that's great! I can't believe it!"

Adele clapped me on the back again, sending another jet of latte in Sally's direction. My assistant shot me a nasty look and dabbed at the spill with a tissue.

"The CEO thought you were really sharp," Adele said. Could that be because I was the only one who had noticed his horns, I wondered? "If we get the account," Adele continued, "he wants you to lead the team."

I blinked. "Me?"

"He asked for you specifically. You really impressed him," she said.

"Wow," I said. "I had no idea."

"You deserve it," Adele said, giving me another thump on the back and splattering a bit more foam onto Sally's desk. "You left your laptop and your drink behind, but I had Sally plug the computer in at your desk and wash your cup out for you."

My eyes shot to Sally, who was smirking at me. What else had she done while she was in my office? "Anyway," Adele continued, "I'm on my way to meet a client, but the next meeting's scheduled for two weeks out. You did such a good job preparing for Monday's meeting, it should be a snap."

"Of course," I said mechanically. I opened my mouth

to ask her about the fly-by-night company that was doing the drug testing, but before I could say a word, she was talking again.

"I'll catch up with you later," she said, flashing me a smile that was, weirdly, almost maternal. As maternal as a woman who looks like a kestrel in Vera Wang could look, anyway. "Good work. If you keep it up, I think things will go very, very well for you, Sophie."

"Thanks," I said, but she was already halfway down the hall, the smell of expensive leather and Dial soap lingering in her wake.

Sally cleaned up the last of the latte spill with an exaggerated swipe of a tissue, sending a fresh wave of musk in my direction. "By the way," she said, "I sent your sample in on Monday."

"Sample?"

"Remember? The drug test?"

I swallowed. Speak of the devil. I really would have to bring things up with Adele. On the plus side, because I hadn't actually been at the lab when I peed in the cup, if anything *did* turn up, I could always claim it had been contaminated or switched or something. Which made me wonder; why didn't we have to go to the lab?

"Results should be in by the end of the week," she said.

Gee, I could hardly wait. "Well, I've got to get to work," I said nonchalantly, taking another sip of coffee with a hand that shook so bad I looked like I had Parkinson's. Giving Sally a strained smile, I sauntered into my office and shut the door behind me.

Then I scrambled around my desk and yanked open the top drawer. The Tension Tamer box was still there. But unless I was hallucinating again, at least a few of the tea bags were missing.

*   *   *

Because there was nothing to be done about the missing wolfsbane—I mean, what was I going to do, go out and ask Sally if she'd swiped my Tension Tamer tea bags?—I decided to get a head start on the Southeast Airlines account. But first, I called my mom to see if we could get together for lunch, even though, to be frank, I wasn't exactly looking forward to it. Hearing about my mom was one thing; meeting her was something else entirely.

I'd decided El Sol y la Luna, a little Mexican restaurant on the south side of town, would be perfect. Not too funky but not too straightlaced either. And they served big, strong margaritas, which I suspected I'd be needing.

Fortunately—or unfortunately—my mother wasn't at the store when I called. I left a message with Emily and crossed my fingers; maybe we could put off this little tête-à-tête a bit longer.

After hanging up the phone, I pushed all thoughts of boyfriends and werewolves out of my head and stared at my desk, trying to decide what I could do that would be productive. I considered calling to set up an appointment to meet with Patti Pendergast, but after Adele's reaction to my cheeks, I decided it might be better to wait until the swelling died down a bit more. Besides, something told me Patti wasn't the reason for Brewster's death.

I just wished I knew who was.

I was at a dead end on the whole murder rap thing, so I decided to focus on work. I was halfway through a case study on a garbage-collection firm—and in danger of falling into a boredom-induced coma—when Lindsey popped in to rescue me, wearing a pearl-gray suit and silk camisole that exposed just a touch of her impressive décolletage. The silver attraction charm glinted against her pale skin, and I couldn't help but think that if Tom were here right now, he would probably be drooling. Tom. God, what was it about him that made me react like a lust-driven teenager?

Lindsey sat down across from me and crossed her long legs. "Wow."

I leaned back in my leather chair. "What?"

"I thought you said the swelling was down."

I narrowed my eyes at her. "Gosh, it's good to have supportive friends."

"Touchy, touchy."

"Wouldn't you be? Anyway, compared with yesterday, it *is* down," I said.

"Has Heath seen you yet?"

"No."

"Let me know how that works out for you."

"Thanks," I said, resisting the urge to stick my tongue out.

"Oh," she added, "and by the way, since you're out of commission, I scheduled a lunch date with Patti Pendergast."

Great minds think alike. "How'd you manage that?"

"Gave her the 'looking to make a substantial contribution' line."

I raised an eyebrow at her. "You know, there are going to be a lot of disappointed politicians around here when they all find out you're broke."

"Yeah, but at least we'll find out what we need. I did a little poking around on her, by the way."

"And?"

"Guess what she studied in school?"

"Political science?"

"Nope." She leaned forward and grinned at me. "Botany."

Thirty-three

After Lindsey left, I attempted once again to absorb myself in the financial details of the garbage-disposal company, but for some reason it just wasn't working. I kept thinking about Patti's botany degree and how it might be able to get my mother off the hook. What would Heath do with that bit of information, I wondered? If we had lunch today, maybe I'd find out.

Finally, I gave up on the garbage and picked up the phone again.

My mother answered on the third ring. "Sophie!"

"Sometimes I wish you had Caller ID," I said.

"But I don't need it!"

"Exactly. It's kind of creepy. Did you get my message?"

"Sorry, sweetheart. Emily told me, but I just didn't get a chance to call you back. In fact, I just got off the phone with that handsome lawyer," she said. For a moment I thought she was talking about Heath, and my blood ran cold. Then I realized she meant Danny DeVito.

"And?"

"We're meeting this afternoon," she purred.

Uh-oh. "Mom, it's not a date. This man is trying to help you beat a murder rap," I reminded her.

"I know," she said. "Isn't it romantic?"

I reached up to massage my temples, trying not to

imagine my mother out on a date with Danny DeVito. Or kissing Danny DeVito. Or . . . no. I just couldn't go there.

I forced myself to focus on something else. Anything else. Like my fingernails, which, after my little fracas on the trail, were in need of another trip to Happy Hands.

"Well, before you go gallivanting off with your attorney, are you free for lunch? I've got some new information you might want to bring up with your attorney."

"Lunch with my favorite daughter? Of course!"

I took a deep breath. "And Heath."

"That lawyer boyfriend of yours?"

"Yes," I said. "I told him about you, and he wants to meet you. He may be able to help out."

"I can't wait," she said. "How fun! When and where?"

"I've got to check with Heath, but how about noon at El Sol y la Luna?"

"I'll be there with bells on," she said, and I believed her. "I'm having a two-lawyer afternoon, it seems."

"No mention of werewolves," I warned her. "And no love potions!"

"Of course, darling." From the tone of her voice, I was guessing she already had one or two vials of the stuff on hand, ready to slip into Marvin Blechknapp's milk shake. "How did yesterday go, by the way, darling? I never heard back from you. Did the extra wolfsbane work?"

"Oh, it went just fine." If you discounted the whole hallucination-and-numb-tongue thing, that is. I hadn't broken out into a natural fur coat, though—and we had made the cut on the interview—so overall I guess it *was* fine.

"Thank goodness," she said. "I was worried about the side effects all day—the last thing we need is for you to end up in the hospital."

For a moment I fantasized about being propped up in bed with a remote control and a bevy of friendly nurses attending me. No stress, no Sally, no Tom . . .

"I almost stopped by your apartment," she continued, pulling me out of my fantasy, "but I had a feeling you weren't there."

"I wasn't." Sometime I'd tell her about the whole run-in with the packette—except for the bit about Tom, that is—but not just now. "I found something I wanted to ask you about, though. It was in the desk of Brewster's campaign manager."

"His campaign manager's desk? Sophie, how did you manage that?"

"Doesn't matter," I said. "Anyway, it was this little doll thing. Made out of wax."

My mother sucked in her breath. "Hmmm. Sounds like a voodoo doll."

"That's what I thought. Can you tell what it's for?"

"No, I don't do much with that branch of magic. Do you still have it?"

"No, I left it behind." I remembered the unpleasant feeling I'd had when I handled it, and I shivered.

She clucked her tongue. "That's a pity. You might want to swing by the Yerberia Verde, though—they may be able to help you figure out what it was for." She gave me an address on the east side. "I'll see what I can dig up here, but I think the Yerberia is probably your best bet."

"Thanks, Mom."

"Any time, honey. I wish I could be more help. By the way, did you ever find out who's been sending you those boxes?"

"Not yet," I said.

"Watch your step, sweetheart. This is a dangerous time for you."

I fingered the scabs on my neck. Once again, I didn't

need a psychic to figure that one out. "I'll be careful," I said.

"I just hope that's enough. See you at noon, then, sweetheart. Looking forward to it!"

I don't know how I'd envisioned the meeting between my mother and Heath—probably with him swearing off me (and my mom) forever or at least making the sign of the cross—but the two of them were bosom buddies before we were halfway through the first basket of chips.

As we sipped our margaritas—I had a strawberry, my mother was drinking something frozen and blue, and Heath had a classic Cuervo Gold on the rocks—my mom pointed to my face and said, "Sophie looks like she's gone six rounds with Muhammad Ali, doesn't she?"

"She says it was worse yesterday," Heath said, as I smiled thinly and sipped my margarita.

My mom readjusted her bangles and leaned in toward Heath. "Sophie, you never told me he was so good-looking! Look at those biceps," she said, reaching over to massage Heath's forearm.

"Mom," I growled, but she ignored me.

"So, how long have you known Marvin?" she asked Heath. "He seems like a marvelous attorney. So confident and knowledgeable!"

"He's been practicing for decades; you made an excellent choice. Sophie tells me you have a meeting with him this afternoon?"

"I do," she said. "Would you care to join us?"

"I wish I could," he said, "but I've got a deposition. I'll see if I can have lunch with him soon, though. Sophie mentioned she's got a couple of leads."

"Yes, I do." I filled both of them in on what I knew of Tad Brewster's upcoming inheritance and Patti Pendergast's botany degree; thankfully, the discussion of legal matters got us almost halfway through our enchilada plates.

At which point, unfortunately, Heath decided to change topics. He turned to my mother and said, "So, I'm sure you have some juicy stories to tell me about your lovely daughter. What was she like as a kid? She won't tell me anything . . . even though I told her all about losing my shorts at the seventh-grade diving competition."

"You didn't!" my mother squealed. "How embarrassing! What did you do?"

"I did," he said. "It took me five long minutes of swimming to find them and get them back on."

My mother laughed. "Sophie never told me you had such a sense of humor!"

"I suspect there's a lot of stuff Sophie's not telling," Heath said. I busied myself with my margarita, which was almost empty, and started looking for the waitress.

"So, Carmen," Heath drawled as he finished off his own drink. "Fill me in on all the juicy details."

My mother laughed coquettishly and said, "Oh, she was just an animal!"

I shot her a warning glance. If she even thought about trotting out that old chestnut about Megan Soggs and the frog, I would kill her myself.

"Still is," Heath said, giving me a very suggestive glance that made me wish I was just about anywhere else on the planet. But considering my mother was well into her second margarita, there was no way I was going to leave the two of them unsupervised. Before we knew it, she'd be telling Heath all about the time I almost chewed off Miss Edna's hand.

"I'm afraid Sophie's childhood wasn't ideal," she said. "I'm sure she told you I raised her by myself."

"Rough divorce?" he asked, and my whole body tensed. *Be careful, Mom.*

My mother smoothed down her tie-dyed silk tunic, her bangles jingling slightly. I had been concerned that Heath would run the other way when he saw her, but actually, he seemed enchanted. I suppose my mother was a refreshing change from the country-club set he grew up with. "Sophie's father had to leave when she was very young, and we never really reconnected," she said.

Heath reached out and gave her hand a sympathetic squeeze. "I'm sorry, Carmen. It must have been very difficult."

"Oh, we survived. I've got such a mobile profession—there's always a market for witches."

I glanced at Heath, but he seemed to be taking all this just fine, thank God. I, however, took another swig of my margarita.

"How did you decide that was your calling?" Heath asked.

"It's a family thing," my mother said. "Didn't Sophie tell you? She comes from a long line of Rom witches."

"Rom?" Heath looked at me inquisitively.

"It's another word for *gypsy*," I answered tersely, anxious to change the subject. Next thing I knew, she'd be regaling him with recipes for penile enhancement. "Speaking of business, Mom, have you gotten your tax stuff together yet? We need to make your estimated payment."

"Evidently the witch thing skips a generation," Heath said dryly. "Although Sophie does work magic with a ledger."

"Oh, I think she may have more than she knows," Carmen said with a wicked twinkle in her eye. "There's a lot more to Sophie than she's willing to admit."

I shot her another warning look, but she ignored me

and glanced at her cell phone. "Oh my goodness. I had no idea it was so late. I need to go!" She fumbled in her purse, but Heath shook his head.

"My treat," he said.

"Are you sure?"

"Absolutely, Carmen. It's been delightful to meet you."

"Likewise," she said, beaming. Several hugs and kisses later, she was jingling through the restaurant toward the door while Heath paid the bill.

"She's a lovely woman," Heath said as we left the restaurant together a few minutes later. "Why were you so worried about introducing us?"

"She is a bit . . . unusual," I said.

"She's charming." He reached out and pulled me to him, his voice husky. "Just like her daughter." His fingers traced my back, and his eyes were dark with desire. "Can I see you tonight?"

"What time?"

"Seven o'clock," he said. "My place."

"I'll see you there," I said, feeling a shiver of anticipation. Why had I ever even thought about Tom when I had a red-blooded human male like Heath around?

I drove back to the office with new resolve—and a good bit of anticipation about what tonight would hold.

By seven o'clock, I was at Heath's doorstep in a slinky black dress, my Prada heels, and precious little else. Despite the Benadryl, my cheeks were still on the puffy side, and the poison ivy welts crisscrossed my legs and back. I'd done the best I could with pancake makeup and had concocted a cover story that involved cross-country running, poison ivy, and barbed wire. There was nothing I could do about the teeth marks but hope for dim lighting.

I hit the doorbell of his loft and waited, trying to strike a seductive pose.

Unfortunately, he didn't answer.

I leaned on the bell again, then knocked on the door just in case it wasn't working. I was about to knock a second time when the door swung open.

"Hi," I purred, looking up at Heath through half-lidded eyes.

"Sorry about that," he said. "I was on the phone."

"Oh," I said, feeling a little put out.

"But I'm off now," he said, and drew me into his loft.

Heath's loft looked immaculate, as always. Lots of low-slung brown leather couches, a plush geometric rug on the concrete floor, smooth and uncluttered granite counters in the kitchen, and a neat stack of *GQ*s on the coffee table. You could have lifted the whole place right out of a Pottery Barn catalog.

Tonight, though, it was lit with candles, and a bottle of champagne lay chilling in a bucket on the coffee table. Heath installed me on one of the couches with a kiss, then popped the cork—Veuve Clicquot—and poured two glasses before sliding in beside me. I closed my eyes and inhaled the smell of leather, coffee, and Heath's spicy scent. His spicy, entirely *human* scent. I leaned into him, nuzzling against his starchy shirt, and his fingers traced my neck.

"What's up with this rash?"

"I went for a walk the other day and got into some poison ivy. I'm violently allergic to it."

"Evidently," he said, and before he could ask anything else, I kissed him.

His lips were hungry on mine. After days of suppressing my hormones, I felt almost dizzy with desire as he pulled me into his lap. I wrapped my arms around him, groaning as he nuzzled my ear; then his lips moved south, and his hands roamed up my back, feeling for my bra strap.

Of course, there wasn't one.

"Finally," he said in a husky voice. "My favorite underwear."

"Just for you," I whispered.

He nuzzled my neck and froze. "What happened?"

"Nothing major," I said, and reached down, hoping to distract him.

Evidently it worked.

A moment later his fingers closed on the zipper of my dress, pulling it down in one smooth motion. Then his lips were on my breasts, his tongue teasing my nipples. I reached down and caressed the growing bulge in his khaki chinos, fumbling with the zipper. He pushed my dress up around my waist as I tore off his boxer shorts.

"God, I've missed you," he murmured as I positioned myself over him and drew him into me. We found our rhythm quickly—that tennis sure paid off in the bedroom—and before long the poison ivy and the fang marks were forgotten, and I was moaning, begging for more.

But not for long.

Later, as we lay on the rug together, Heath's fingers stroking my damaged skin, a thought drifted through my mind. If anyone knew what the city council had on its docket, it would be Heath, who followed local politics with an interest bordering on obsession. "Heath, when is the hearing on the Barton Springs development?"

He stopped tracing the marks on my back and looked up at me, confused. "What?"

"The Barton Springs hearing. At the city council."

"I think it's the first week in October," he said, puzzled. "Why do you ask?"

"I read something about it in the paper," I said

vaguely, stretching out on the rug next to him again. And before he could ask me any more questions, I turned his attention to other, more immediate matters.

It was almost five in the morning when I pulled into my parking garage and gave myself a quick once-over in the rearview mirror. Nothing too incriminating; my face was a bit red from beard burn, but not obviously so. Particularly because I still looked as if I were recovering from the mumps. I checked the bandage on my neck to make sure it was still in place; Heath had had a few questions about the bite marks, but I'd mumbled something about barbed wire and attacked him before he could ask anything else.

I don't know if the lobby is usually busy at 4:45 in the morning—I try not to be awake then as a rule—but this morning it was swarming with people. And several of them were dressed in brown polyester.

"Sophie!" It was my neighbor, Mrs. Gerschwitz, dressed in a pink satin robe and matching marabou mules. She would have been an octogenarian sexpot if it weren't for the plastic curlers and the hairnet.

"What's going on?" I asked as she grabbed my hand with a bony, ring-laden hand.

"I'm so glad you're okay! We were terribly worried about you!"

"Worried?" I glanced over at the police officers, who were gathered around a prostrate form I recognized as Harry, one of the doormen. Two paramedics were taping a wad of gauze to his forehead.

"There was this bunch of hoodlums—they held up poor Harry and went up to your place. Broke down the door." She shuddered gleefully. Since her husband Floyd had died, Mrs. Gerschwitz hadn't had too much excitement in her life. "Thank God you weren't there."

Thirty-four

I took a step back. Hoodlums had broken down my door?

"I was sure they were going to . . . molest you, or worse." She shuddered dramatically, then peered at my face. "What happened to your cheeks, dear?"

"Allergic reaction," I said. "Poison ivy."

"Looks terrible," Mrs. Gerschwitz said. Her dark eyes looked me up and down, registering my short black dress and high heels, and one of her penciled-on eyebrows rose. "Where were you last night, anyway?"

I could feel my face burn and reached to tug down my skirt. "Late night at the office," I muttered.

"Hmmm," Mrs. Gerschwitz said, looking unconvinced. Then she reached up to adjust one of her curlers and continued. "Anyway, Harry says they demanded to know where your place was—held a gun on him, the poor man—then went up and broke down the door. When I heard all the fracas—I'm a light sleeper these days—I called the police."

"Did they catch them?" I asked, not sure if that would be a good thing or a bad thing.

The plastic curlers bounced as she shook her head. "The cops didn't get here fast enough. Probably too busy wolfing down doughnuts at Krispy Kreme. But they're dusting for fingerprints."

Which meant yucky powder everywhere, probably. And with the cops crawling all over the place, I hoped they hadn't totally knocked out the intruders' scent. "Thanks for watching out for me, Mrs. Gerschwitz." I glanced at the pack of cops and reached up to push my hair behind my ears. "I'm going to see if I can go up to the loft yet."

"Let me know if they find out anything."

"Of course," I said, tugging my skirt down again and walking over to the nearest cop, a burly man with an evident fondness for doughnuts. Mrs. Gerschwitz had been right about Krispy Kreme; he smelled like raspberry jelly and yeast, and a slight dusting of powdered sugar decorated his collar.

"Excuse me," I said.

"Ma'am?" He turned and looked me up and down, and my nose wrinkled. Jelly doughnuts and Drakkar Noir—not a good combination.

"I'm the owner of the loft," I said, trying to breathe through my mouth.

The cop's eyes drifted back to my chest, which the over-air-conditioned lobby had made noticeably perky. I crossed my arms, wishing I was wearing underwear. Or at least a bra.

"We'd like to ask you a few questions," he said, leading me over to the gaggle of polyester-clad cops surrounding Harry.

Great, I thought. Just my luck; the one night I spend at Heath's, I come home at 4:45 in the morning—sans underwear—to meet a dozen of Austin's finest. I was tempted to ask if I could go upstairs and change but figured that was probably a nonstarter. Besides, who wants to root through their underwear drawer with a bunch of strangers looking on? Next time I seduced Heath, I promised myself as another cop's eyes roamed over my unsupported chest, I would at least pack a bra and undies in my purse.

As it turned out, it was significantly more than twenty questions. Over the course of a couple of hours, the men in polyester and powdered sugar asked me where I'd been and who I thought might have broken in and advised me to get a locksmith to replace my lock. I'd smiled and nodded, but since the marauders had bypassed the whole lock thing in favor of breaking my door down, I wasn't sure how getting a new lock would help. Getting an actual door was a bit higher on the priority list.

On the plus side, despite what I told the cops, at least I knew who I was dealing with. The packette—and Stinky in particular—had left a trail so strong it was amazing the cops couldn't smell it.

It was almost 7:30 when I finally closed what was left of the door—the management had nailed a few pieces of plywood to it, but it wasn't exactly solid—behind the last brown uniform and opened every window I could. It was already in the eighties outside, but the fresh air was a necessity; my loft reeked. Plus, the forensics team had used about three pounds of fingerprint powder, which kept making me sneeze.

As a faintly Dumpster-scented breeze lifted my Crate & Barrel curtains, I turned to survey the damage.

The packette had torn things up a bit—my favorite Picasso print, which I'd just had framed, lay shattered on the wood floor—but aside from rifling through my drawers (embarrassingly, my bras and panties were strewn across the room) and overturning my couches, they hadn't done much permanent damage. In fact, as far as the cops and I could tell, they hadn't taken anything—even my sapphire jewelry was intact.

While the damage wasn't too extensive—thankfully, Fluffy and his minions hadn't slashed up my new couch

or anything—it was going to take a bit of work to repair. The cushions had been thrown everywhere, my
books lay open-faced on the floor, along with my
undies, and my CD collection had been upended in a
corner. I bent to pick up a stray disc, and a spray of broken glass sparkled in the light. It occurred to me that it
might not be a bad idea to run a broom over the floor. I
was punctured enough as it was without adding shards
of glass to the mix.

Where was Tom when I needed him? I wondered. If
only I'd gotten his number last time he visited. I desperately needed to talk with him. Why was the packette
after me? Why tear up my apartment? And if he was
here to hunt them, well then, in my opinion, he needed
to step things up a bit. I was half tempted to call Lindsey
and ask for Tom's number. The only problem was, I
couldn't think of a plausible excuse for wanting it.

As I pushed the broom under the couch to sweep up
the glass, something rolled across the stained concrete
floor, and I took an involuntary step back.

It was a syringe.

Ick! I put the broom down and hurried to the kitchen
for a roll of paper towels. Then I bent down and used
one of the paper towels to pick up the syringe, holding it
with the point facing away from me. It didn't look as if
it had been used, but you never knew—and the last
thing I needed was to pick up some weird disease from a
crack-addict werewolf. Come to think of it, did crack
addicts use syringes? Or was that more a heroin thing?

I remembered what Tom had said, that werewolf
blood could make you stronger. Ugh. Still, I found myself wondering how the police had spent three hours in
my loft and missed finding a syringe big enough to de-
liver a month's supply of insulin. Or heroin. I briefly
considered calling to let the cops know that they needed
to revamp their investigative training program—or at

least get the forensics people's eyes checked—but decided against it. With all the drug test stuff going on at work, maybe it was best that they hadn't found it.

But why was it here?

When in doubt, always follow your nose. Particularly if you're a werewolf. I lifted it to my nose for a quick sniff, then immediately wished I hadn't.

It was definitely Stinky who had last touched the needle-tipped piece of plastic.

I gingerly set the syringe on the counter and looked under the couch to see if the cops had missed any other disgusting goodies, but other than a few baby dust bunnies and a chunk of glass, the floor was bare. A few minutes later, after sweeping up the last of the glass and leaning the print up against the wall, I propped a chair up under the door and then slid a table across the floor to reinforce it. Front door or no front door, I wasn't going to work until I had a shower.

It wasn't until I was standing under a stream of hot water with a palmful of vanilla spice shower gel that it hit me.

If Stinky, Fluffy, and Scrawny had found my loft, that meant they knew my name.

It was almost 9:00 when I lurched into the office, feeling as if I hadn't slept in days. Which, come to think of it, I hadn't.

"Glad you could make it," Sally said as I dragged my poor wolf-bitten, poison-ivied derriere past her desk.

I gave her a tight smile and resisted the urge to flip her the bird. The truth was, it didn't matter what Sally thought. Even if Adele did give me a hard time about it, I could always get the cops—or Mrs. Gerschwitz—to back me up. Besides, with the Southeast Airlines account practically in the bag, my stock was pretty high right now.

The phone rang as soon as I sat down at my desk. I grabbed it and wheeled around in my chair, staring out the window at the Travis County Jail. Surely Lindsey and I—or maybe even my mom's $300-per-hour lawyer—would come up with some way to keep my mom out of the clink. "Hello?" I said.

It was Lindsey. "How'd it go with Heath?" she asked.

"Great," I said, feeling a rush of warmth at the thought of what had transpired on Heath's leather couches last night. And the Pottery Barn rug. And the kitchen counter, come to think of it. I hadn't actually fallen into the sink, but I'd come close.

"What'd you do?" she prompted.

I crossed my legs. I was still a bit sore, but it had been worth it. "Perhaps the better question is, what *didn't* we do?"

Lindsey laughed. "I take it the cheeks didn't get in the way. What did you do, have him over for dinner, with you as dessert?"

"Nope. I made a house call, and everything's fine now." I hoped things were fine, anyway. They'd seemed pretty good while I was on the kitchen counter last night. Or was that this morning?

"Well, that's good news. And at least someone had a little excitement last night."

"I could use a little less, actually."

"Oh, please. Enough bragging. Tom couldn't go out, so I ended up staying home and watching reruns of *Friends*."

"I'm serious," I said. "Someone broke into my loft while I was at Heath's."

I could hear the sharp intake of breath on the line. "What?"

"They broke down the door and trashed the place."

"Thank God you weren't there," she breathed. "Did they steal anything?"

"No, but the loft's a mess. I just got into the office; the police didn't leave my place until an hour ago." I didn't tell her about the syringe. The next thing I knew, she'd be doing some kind of drug intervention. And wolfsbane was one thing I absolutely refused to give up.

"Jesus, Sophie. You're like the Bermuda Triangle lately."

"No kidding."

"Do they have any idea who did it? Maybe it's the same guy who broke into your car the other night."

I'd forgotten about that. "I'm pretty sure it was someone else," I said.

"You never know," she said.

Actually, I did—I would have recognized the car burglar's rotten-egg smell anywhere, even alongside Stinky's distinctive bouquet—but I couldn't explain that to Lindsey, so I let it pass. "What happened with Tom?" I asked, grasping for a safe subject. Well, kind of safe, anyway.

"I don't know. Something came up last night," she said. "But he's swinging by the office later."

"Mmm."

"We'll be sure to stop by and say hi," she said.

"Great," I said, and to my credit, I sounded like I actually meant it.

"By the way, I went to talk with Tad, and he's quit his job."

I sat up straight. "When did this happen?"

"He called yesterday and told them he was giving notice, effective immediately."

"I guess with the inheritance, he doesn't need to slice cucumbers anymore."

"Guess not. And it's a good thing we still have one suspect."

"What happened to Patti Pendergast?" I asked.

"Didn't you read the paper this morning?" Lindsey asked.

"Yeah, in my copious free time."

"Well, then, you should know."

"Lindsey. What's up?"

"Apparently Patti was blackmailing politicians. She had a 'dirt' file on as many of them as she could and used to use it to influence votes."

I thought of the photo in Brewster's safe. "So the four-by-six glossy—"

"Was probably a little love note from Patti."

"How did it come out?" I asked, suddenly feeling a lot more optimistic about things.

"One of the council members she was trying to 'persuade' blew the whistle on her. Turned her in. I talked to my friend at the *Statesman*; apparently a few other politicians were involved, but the paper didn't name names."

I let out a long, low whistle. "So she was trying to convince Brewster and the other council members to vote *for* the development."

"Right. So she wouldn't have to."

"Lindsey, that's great! Talk about a prime suspect. She's got motive, she's got means . . ."

"There's just a teeny-tiny problem with the 'opportunity' part."

"What do you mean?"

Lindsey heaved a sigh. "She was in Alaska when Brewster died."

I squeezed my eyes shut. "No."

"I checked on it; she even gave a little talk up there. To a women's knitting group."

"Crap," I said. "So we're back to square one."

"There's always Tad," she reminded me.

I thought of Tad Brewster's doughy face. I didn't know why, but I was sure he wasn't a murderer. "Like I said, we're back at square one," I repeated, and glanced out the window at the Travis County Jail.

"Hey, can I call you back? I've got to finish getting ready for a meeting, and I've got a date with Tom tonight."

Tom. "Sure," I said.

"Talk to you later," she said, and as I hung up the phone, I wondered again what had driven Tom to become a loner.

And why he had such a strong effect on me.

I was just packing up to leave when the tantalizing smell of werewolf wafted through the doorway, and I looked up into Tom's gold eyes.

Thirty-five

I dropped my purse and crossed my arms over my chest, trying to quell the heat rushing through me. And trying not to think about what Tom might or might not have seen the other night.

On the plus side, he was finally here. Which meant I could get some answers to my rapidly growing list of questions.

Tom leaned against the door frame, sending another waft of his intoxicating foresty scent in my direction, and I couldn't help admiring the way his broad shoulders filled out his chambray shirt. He really did look like a Viking warrior; he was six foot five at least, with a body you couldn't help staring at. Or I couldn't, anyway. Which was kind of disturbing.

"So where's Lindsey?" I asked, trying to sound casual.

"She'll be here in a minute," he said, in a voice that made me shudder.

"Oh." I cleared my throat. What exactly *was* the protocol for talking with a werewolf who had recently seen you naked? Ignore it, I decided. "Would you mind closing the door?"

"Sure," he said, stepping into my office and pulling the door shut behind him.

Now the room was completely doused in über-werewolf pheromones, and it was all I could do to keep from panting. Tom pointed at one of my chairs. "Mind if I sit down?"

"Um . . . of course not," I said, flustered. He sprawled in the nearest chair, a bit of gold hair glinting at his collar, and I found myself gazing at his iridescent eyes. When I realized I was staring, I forced myself to focus on the diploma on the wall behind him. *Sophie Anne Garou, bachelor of arts, summa cum laude.* I might be a werewolf, but I was also a highly trained professional, cool, and collected. Right?

"Look," I said firmly. I could be professional all I wanted, but every cell in my body was annoyingly alive with the knowledge that another werewolf—a particularly good-looking werewolf, with a smell that I longed to bottle and carry with me—was four feet away from me, sprawled in my visitor's chair. "I, um, just wanted to say thank you for helping me out the other night."

He nodded. "Ah, yes. The little issue you were having with the made ones." His eyes sparkled in a very knowing way.

Oh, God. He *had* seen me naked. Clearing my throat, I said, "I, er, appreciate your assistance."

I looked away from the diploma and took a quick peek at him. God, he was hot. *Stop it, Sophie. Think professional.* Don't think about that kiss. That long kiss that made my insides turn to jelly . . .

I refocused on the diploma. Too bad it was in Latin— I could have used some reading material I could understand. "Usually I'm not out and about in Austin like that, but it was kind of a bad day."

"I see," he said.

"At any rate, I wanted to tell you . . . they're not gone yet."

"I know. But how do *you* know?"

"Because they broke into my loft last night," I said.

His gold eyes burned with intensity, and he said something under his breath. It could have been a swear word, but I don't speak Norwegian, so I couldn't say.

"How did they know how to find me?"

"I wish I knew. But I'm sorry I wasn't there to help you."

"It's not your responsibility," I said, even though some part of me was melting at Tom's rueful knight-in-shining-armor thing. Okay, wolf-in-shining-armor. Close enough.

"Did they harm you?" he asked, his eyes roaming my body. For new welts, I told myself.

I shook my head. "No . . . I wasn't there. By the time I showed up, they were gone, and the cops were all over the place." For some reason I didn't want to mention that I was at my boyfriend's house. "But they did leave a syringe behind."

He sucked in his breath. "It is because they want your strength."

I had been right about the syringe, it seemed. "So they

were going to draw my blood out of me and inject it into themselves? That's disgusting."

He shrugged. "And dangerous. But that is what they intended. I should have been there."

"How were you supposed to know?" I said. "Besides, it's not like you're my bodyguard. But the whole blood thing—if it's dangerous, aren't there rules against that? I mean, there's evidently some kind of a code out there; any way I could get a copy of it?"

"It is not widely circulated. And it is usually taught from birth."

"I'm afraid I missed the whole werewolf initiation ceremony."

"So I understand."

"So can you get me a copy?"

"I will see what I can do."

I gave up looking at the diploma and just stared at him. After all, I told myself, I'd been werewolf-free for most of my life. Now that I had one five feet away from me, it was okay to be curious. And, admittedly, a bit lustful. Okay, more than a bit lustful. But who could blame me? Other than Lindsey, of course. Who would probably come looking for Tom at any moment, come to think of it. "How long will you be here?" I asked. "How can I get in touch with you? There's a whole lot I want to know." Which made me think of one of the things I had been wondering about. "Like, how did you find me the other night?"

"I was stalking the made ones."

"But not me."

"No," he said. "Not you. Not yet, anyway."

"Not yet?"

"Because the Houston pack doesn't know about you, you are not the problem. Not now."

Goose bumps rose on my arms. "Does that mean if they ask you to, you'll hunt me down?"

Tom leaned forward in his chair, staring at me in a way that made my entire body want to melt on the spot, even though I was terrified of what he was going to say next. "I did not say that."

"So you wouldn't."

"No," he said. "I wouldn't."

Well, thank goodness for small favors. "How do you eliminate werewolves, by the way? The whole wooden stake thing?"

He shrugged. "I will unmake them," he said, as if he were going to pick up a can of Raid and take care of a few roaches.

"Unmake them?" I wasn't sure I wanted to know what that meant. Maybe there were worse things than wooden stakes. Was he talking vats of acid or something?

"It does not mean killing them."

"Ah. Okay." For a moment there, I was wondering if Lindsey was dating a murderer as well as a werewolf. "But how the heck do you 'unmake' a werewolf? I mean, is there a special drink for that or something?" And was there some way I could get some of it? I added silently. It would certainly solve a lot of problems.

Unfortunately, before Tom could answer, the door opened and Lindsey swept in, her tango shoes glittering in the overhead lights. Her smile turned to a frown when she registered Tom's wolfie presence in my visitor's chair. "What's going on in here?"

Tom glided to his feet in a movement that was every bit as predatory as he was. For a second, I had an urge to pull my friend away from him, but the feeling passed just as quickly as it came. Which is a good thing, because I wasn't sure Lindsey would be too keen on me yanking her boyfriend out of her arms. Well, her date, anyway. I hoped he wasn't her boyfriend.

"Sophie and I were just getting to know each other," Tom said smoothly, leaning down to kiss her forehead.

Lindsey shot me a questioning look, and I felt myself blush again. "He was telling me you're taking him out to tango," I added.

"You and Heath should join us sometime," Lindsey said, arching one brow meaningfully and wrapping a proprietary arm around Tom's waist.

I almost choked, thinking I'd rather have my fingernails removed with pliers than join Lindsey and Tom on a tango date. Well, maybe not pliers, but you know what I mean.

"Are you ready, darling?" she purred, looking up at him through lowered lashes. I noticed the attraction charm still nestled between her breasts, which I couldn't help but notice were prominently displayed in a tight-fitting red dress. For a second there, a pang of jealousy shot through me, but I shook it off.

"Of course." He squeezed her and turned to me. "I enjoyed our conversation, Sophie." His gold eyes bored into me. "Please be sure to take care of yourself."

"I will," I said. And a moment later they were gone, only a tantalizing hint of Tom's scent in their wake.

I sat at my desk for a long time, trying not to dwell on what Lindsey had planned for her evening with Tom. My mind kept circling back on what Tom had said. There was some way to unmake werewolves. Could I convince him to do it to me?

And did I really want to be human if he could?

I tapped my fingernails on the desk, frustrated. The packette had broken into my apartment, my mom was accused of murdering a politician, and someone was leaving threatening care packages on my desk. Plus, I was secretly lusting after a werewolf. With whom my friend was currently tangoing.

Don't go there, Sophie. I forced my thoughts away from what I couldn't control—Lindsey and Tom—and tried to think of things I might have some impact on.

Such as the outcome of my mom's impending murder trial. I knew she thought her spirit guides would see her through, but I wasn't so comfortable relying on the supernatural world's ability to beat the rap.

Still, as much as I wanted to find out who had killed Brewster, there was nothing I could do on that score right now either; we'd already questioned Brewster's son, and Lindsey had pretty much ruled out Patti Pendergast.

I was sure I was missing something. But what was it?

I glanced down at my desk, and my eyes fell on the slip of paper I'd scribbled on earlier, when I was asking my mom about the doll in Maria's office. I might as well go and check it out. If nothing else, it was better than sitting here at my desk—or going home and watching *What Not to Wear* in my bunny slippers again. Which was a likely scenario, because Heath had an evening meeting tonight. It was 5:00 now; if I hurried, I might be able to get to the store before it closed.

Besides, if nothing else, it would distract me from the fact that my best friend was seducing Tom the werewolf.

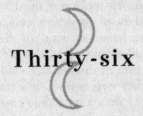

Thirty-six

The Yerberia Verde was a pink bungalow tucked in between a taco stand and a *frutería*. Outside, a big red hand proclaimed that palm readings were available, and the smudgy windows were cluttered with pillar candles, each dedicated to a different cause—money, sex, lawsuits—or saint. I was tempted to buy the lawsuit one for my mom, but I figured she'd already covered herself magically on that score—as much as was possible, anyway.

A heady mix of candles, incense, and herbs hit me when I walked in the door. It was a different smell from Sit A Spell—spicier, somehow, with a heavy undertone of musk that made me think of Sally. I glanced around at the offerings, looking for something that resembled the doll I'd found in Maria's desk.

The front counter was unstaffed, but I could hear someone rustling in the back. While I waited for the shopkeeper to appear, I did a quick survey of the store's contents.

Next to the candles was a table covered in little jars, all labeled in Spanish. Although my command of foreign languages is pretty much limited to the phrase "Where's the bathroom," the pictures—many of which featured voluptuous, scantily clad women or stacks of dollar bills—gave me a pretty good idea of what they were for.

To the left was a wall filled with jars of herbs that reminded me of my mom's shop, although I didn't recognize the names of many of them. There was a whole table full of vials, all labeled in Spanish, and in the back, a selection of candles that made me want to cross my legs. They were penises, in a startling array of colors—and they were huge. I didn't want to think about what they were used for—I'd have to ask my mom. Or maybe not, come to think of it—there are some things it's best not to know.

I had picked one up and was looking for a wick when I heard a noise behind me. I hastily replaced the candle, which was about the size of a Pringles can, and turned to face a wizened woman with flashing dark eyes.

"Can I help you?" she said, her English heavily accented. Her eyes darted to the candle I had just been holding. "You having problems in the bed?"

"No, no," I said. "Just fine in that department, thanks."

She nodded knowingly. "These candles . . . *mucho ayudo* . . ."

"Um . . . if I ever have trouble, I'll keep it in mind." I glanced over at the display; for the first time, I noticed there were vulva candles too.

Ew.

"You sure?" the woman persisted.

"Positive," I said, taking a few steps away from the whole Kama Sutra candle section. "I do hope you can help me, though."

"What is the problem?"

"I had a question about a doll I saw the other day." As I described what I saw, the woman's face became guarded. "What do you think it was?" I asked.

"Hoodoo." She went into the back room, returning a moment later with a wax doll that was the twin of the one in Maria's desk.

A shiver went down my spine. "Hoodoo," I repeated, reaching out a tentative finger to touch the doll. Unlike what had happened in Maria's office, though, when I touched the wax, I felt nothing. I looked up at the woman behind the counter. "What do they do?"

"It is to . . . *come se dice* . . . to control a person," she said slowly. "Make a person love you. Or to hurt a person." She shrugged. "Without seeing the doll, I cannot say."

I stared at the candles in the distance. "When I picked it up, it felt . . . bad," I said.

"*Malo*," she murmured.

And I knew she was right.

"There was something else," I said. "Some powder—

it smelled terrible. It was sprinkled all around the room."

She nodded. "*Polvo de retiro*, probably."

I nodded back, even though I had no idea what that meant.

As I stood there, wishing I had thought to bring a Spanish-English dictionary along, the old woman shuffled over to the wall of herbs. Then she pulled out a jar of powder, opened it, and held it up for me to smell.

I walked over to sniff it, then stifled a sneeze. "It was a little like that," I said, rubbing my nose. And it was true; I recognized elements of it. "But worse."

She bit her thin lower lip. "*Mas malo?*"

"*Si*," I said. "Like a skunk." I had no idea how to say *skunk* in Spanish, and I didn't even want to try.

Fortunately, she seemed to understand what I was getting at, because she nodded again, pulling a jar of yellow powder off the shelf. Her dark eyes were alive with curiosity as she loosened the lid; she was probably wondering who had it in for a *gringa* like me. I could smell the stuff even before she held it up to me—rotting eggs.

"Yes," I said, holding my nose and turning away. "That was it—mixed with the other stuff. What's it for?"

"For scaring away," she said. "*Donde?*" she asked, curious, no doubt, where I had encountered a voodoo doll and *polvo de* something-or-other.

"At a politician's office, strangely enough," I said, and the woman stiffened. I looked at her. "Did I say something wrong?"

"No, no," she said, screwing the lid back onto the jar. "You need something more?"

"I don't think so," I said. Then I started feeling bad; after all her help, I should buy something. My eyes fell on a rack of little leather pouches on strings. Each one was marked with a little animal symbol; they looked like necklaces the Indians would have worn. "What are those for?"

"*Protección*," she said.

"I'll take one," I said, reaching for one that had something that vaguely resembled a wolf on the front of it and handing it to her. It was only fitting, after all. Besides, the way things were going, I could use all the *protección* I could get. I handed the amulet to the dark-haired woman; she disappeared to the back of the shop for a moment, then returned.

"What did you do to it?" I asked.

"*Yerbas*," she said shortly. I assumed that meant "herbs."

As I fished in my wallet for ten dollars, the woman wrapped the little pouch up with deft hands and shoved it across the counter toward me, suddenly unfriendly. What had I said? Had I crossed some cultural boundary? The incense-laden air felt heavy and oppressive as I headed for the exit, glad to push through the front door into fresh air—and the smell of browning taco meat. I could feel the woman's eyes follow me out to the parking lot.

Back in the M3, I wondered what I had done to offend the woman. She had certainly been in a hurry to get me out of her shop. Had she somehow figured out I was a werewolf? I was pretty sure I had picked up a whiff of wolfsbane among all the other herbs in the shop—if you drink as much of it as I do, you can smell it from about a mile away. On the plus side, whatever had turned her off to me happened after I'd found out what I needed to know. Of course, the knowledge that Maria used a nasty voodoo doll and yucky powder to keep people out hadn't gotten me any closer to solving Brewster's murder, but I guess you have to track down every lead. Besides, *What Not to Wear* was a rerun tonight.

As I sat in my leather seat, swallowing back a bit of

drool—I love Mexican food, and the smell of browning meat was making me hungry—I unwrapped the pouch I had just bought, brushing my fingertips over the little wolf picture. If I got a bad read off the doll in Maria's office, the little leather bag gave me just the opposite feeling; its weight was comforting in my hand. On a whim, I lowered it over my head, tucking the little leather bag in so it was hidden beneath my blouse. Then I turned the key in the ignition and fastened my seat belt, feeling a bit more optimistic now that I had some good juju of my own.

It was only when I was pulling out of the driveway that I noticed the name on the bottom of the *yerberia* sign.

Yolanda Jiménez.

Thirty-Seven

Jiménez.

No wonder the woman had shut down when I mentioned finding the powder in a politician's office; she was probably the one who had provided it. And the voodoo doll too. *Jiménez* might be a fairly common Hispanic surname, but I would have bet my last nickel the woman I had just talked to was related to Brewster's campaign manager.

I backed into a parking space and hurried back up to the store's front door, but it was now locked. I peered through the clouded window; the little old woman was nowhere to be seen. She was probably on the phone calling Maria.

As I headed back to the car, I pulled out my own phone and dialed information. A few minutes later, thanks to 411 and my laptop, I pointed the M3 in the direction of Maria Jiménez's apartment.

Maria must not have been doing too badly for herself; her apartment was in a graceful old brick house in Tarrytown, the front walk lined with zinnias that were just past their summer glory. Hers was the door on the left, and as I walked up to it, my nose recognized a familiar odor. Sure enough, sprinkled across the doorstep was a line of the powder I had smelled in the *yerbería*.

I held my breath and knocked, not quite sure what I would say if Maria answered. Fortunately—or unfortunately—I didn't have to think about it, because either she wasn't home or she wasn't answering the door. Despite the stinky powder on the ground, I took an exploratory sniff—Maria's light floral scent was definitely present, but it didn't seem recent.

I knocked one more time, just to be sure. Then—just on the off chance she would sprinkle stinky powder all over the place and forget to turn the dead bolt—I tried the door.

Of course, it was locked.

I stepped back from the stinky powder and considered the situation. I don't know why—maybe I had more of my mother's psychic powers than I was willing to admit—but somehow I knew that I had to get into her apartment. I didn't know what I was looking for, but for some reason I was convinced that the answers to my questions—well, some of them, anyway—were behind that door.

But how to get in?

The front door was solid wood. I could do what the packette did and try to break it down, but cars were whizzing by ten yards behind me, so that probably wouldn't be the best course of action. Unless I wanted to spend some more quality time talking with the police, that is—and as far as I was concerned, the three hours I'd spent in their company that morning was more than sufficient.

As I walked around the building looking for an alternate entrance—something like a back door—a giant black bird squawked and burst out of the trees above me, scaring the socks off of me. Well, the panty hose, really. Man, was I jumpy. But what was up with the bird population in Austin? It seemed as if every time I turned around lately, one of them was exploding out of a bush or something.

When my heart resumed beating at a reasonable rate, I continued my investigation of the side of the building. Maria's apartment must have had a lot of natural light—six full-sized windows stretched across the side of the building. I tried to peek in, but the long white curtains were closed. But it wasn't too hard to figure out that they were hers, because each one of them had been liberally doused with the same rotten-smelling concoction. *Polvo de* whatever, with a side of sulfur.

Of course, they were all locked. I glanced at the busy street; I could break a window, but there was nothing protecting me from view of the street. Like, nothing—not even a shrub.

I crossed my arms and leaned against the side of the building, frustrated. I'd exhausted the easy options. If I wanted to get into Maria's apartment without going to jail, I'd have to get creative.

I padded back around to the front of the building and knocked on the door of the neighboring apartment. A young woman with bright blond hair answered; from the foam dividers separating her toes and the reek of acetone, I was guessing I'd interrupted her mid-pedicure.

"Hi," I said. "I'm one of Maria's friends . . . Susan."

"Hi, Susan. I'm Kelly."

"Oh, Kelly!" I said with a big smile. "Maria's mentioned you so many times."

"Really?" She looked surprised. "I just moved in a month ago."

"Yes," I said. "But you two must have really hit it off." Kelly gave me a dubious smile, but I plowed on. "Some of us are planning a surprise party for Maria, but we don't want to tip her off. I hate to ask . . ." I trailed off.

"Ask what?"

"Well, I don't know if you have a key to her place, but I was wondering if you could let me in so I could . . . measure it."

The young woman blinked at me. "Measure what?"

Excellent question. I only wish I knew. "Well, part of the surprise," I stammered, "was that we were going to get her a . . ."

Kelly stood there looking at me blankly.

"A . . . a couch she wanted. Yes. A couch."

She blinked at me, a furrow between her brows. "A couch."

"Yes," I said, nodding furiously. "A couch."

"But I thought she just bought a new couch."

I stifled a groan. "A matching chair, I mean. For the new couch. Well, more of a love seat, really."

"A love seat," Kelly repeated. To be honest, I was starting to find the whole repeat-after-me thing a tad annoying.

"So I have to get into her apartment and measure," I said, bringing Kelly back to my original premise. "To make sure it will fit."

"You have to measure," Kelly said, and I resisted the urge to strangle her. Finally, she seemed to come to a decision. "I'd love to help," she said brightly, and I could have kissed her. "The only problem is, I don't have a key."

Well, so much for that plan.

Then she added, "But I think the lady upstairs does," and all of a sudden I felt a lot more optimistic.

"Really?"

"I don't know if she's in, but we can go and check. Let me just get these foam things off my toes," she said. Then she closed the door, leaving me standing on the doorstep.

I glanced down at my watch while I waited, feeling a bit impatient. And more than a little bit nervous. I had no idea when Maria was coming home. If she did, it was going to be pretty darned obvious that she and I weren't bosom buddies. And if she walked in while I was in her apartment, ostensibly measuring the living room for an imaginary love seat . . .

Fortunately, Kelly opened the door before I could take that thought any further, and a few minutes later the nice neighbor from upstairs—a matronly woman with an unfortunate weakness for frosted coral lipstick—was unlocking Maria's door for me.

The lipstick lady disappeared up the stairs with a colorful smile, but Kelly lingered.

"Thanks," I said, flashing what I hoped was a dismissive smile.

"Anytime. Do you need some help?" Kelly asked.

"Help?" I said.

"Someone to hold the tape measure," she said.

"Oh, no," I said, patting my purse. "I'll be fine. Thanks again—I'll lock up when I leave." I started to close the door behind me.

"What did you say your name was again?" Kelly said.

"Susan," I said. "I'm sure I'll see you both at the party—

you should be getting invitations soon. I'll write down your apartment number before I leave."

That seemed to satisfy her, and a moment later I found myself alone in Maria's apartment.

I was right about the windows; even with floor-to-ceiling curtains, the evening sun flooded the room with soft light, making the hardwood floors gleam. I might not have liked Maria's choice of window dressing—the smelly stuff was making me gag and the bowls of lavender around the room didn't even begin to mask the smell—but her taste in furnishings was enviable. Particularly the new couch, which was a pale sage green with peach and white throw cushions. I fingered the fabric, wondering where she had bought it, before remembering I wasn't here to take notes on interior design.

I was here for evidence.

But what kind of evidence?

I started with the bookshelf in the corner. A shelf of political science books—no surprise there—and beneath it, several well-thumbed tomes on interior design. If I was looking for a guide to poisonous plants or *Five Hundred Ways to Kill Your Boss*, though, I was disappointed. There was a little booklet on making your own potpourri, but that could hardly be considered incriminating evidence.

I hurriedly worked my way through the rest of the room, listening for footsteps as I rifled through the bills on the counter and checked her spice rack (lots of cumin and dried chiles, but no nightshade). In fact, I was beginning to wonder why I was there. Sure, Maria had had a voodoo doll in her desk, and it was a good bet she was responsible for the yucky powder all over Brewster's office—not to mention her own apartment. But none of that meant she had killed her boss.

As I headed into Maria's bedroom, it occurred to me that I'd been in her apartment an awfully long time for someone who was supposed to be taking measurements for a new love seat. All I could do was hope Kelly had returned to her apartment for a second coat of nail polish.

Maria's bedroom was as neat and tastefully decorated as her living room; she'd even made the bed, which, like the couch, was strewn with quaint and attractive throw pillows. I was beginning to think that Maria had missed her calling; she could have made a fortune selling her services to design-challenged suburbanites. Her taste extended to her wardrobe too. I stepped into her closet and admired the neat stacks of cashmere sweaters, allowing myself to run one envious finger over a Louis Vuitton bag.

But no nightshade.

I took a deep breath—the stench wasn't so bad in here, thanks to the cedar blocks and lavender—and caught a whiff of something else. Something familiar.

I stepped out of the closet, following the scent. Beeswax and a hint of something else.

Whatever it was, it was coming from the bed.

A moment later, I was on my knees, pulling a plastic storage box out from its home deep under the lace-trimmed dust ruffle. Even before I lifted the lid, I knew I wasn't going to find sweaters inside.

A blast of the same earthy smell I'd picked up in the *yerberia* hit me as I eased the plastic top off and surveyed the contents. Candles in a variety of colors—no penis candles, I was glad to see—nestled in the corner of the box. Beside them was a little metal bowl—a cauldron, probably—a roll of charcoal disks, and several plastic bags filled with herbs. And a leather-bound book, the cover adorned with Spanish words in Maria's neat, orderly handwriting.

In other words, all the trappings of your average witch.

I lifted the book out of the box, flipping through it. The pages were filled with Maria's small, controlled hand, but it might as well have been blank. Frustration welled in me as I turned the pages; it looked like a journal of some kind, but since it was in Spanish, I wasn't getting a whole lot out of it. The entries were dated, though. I flipped through the pages to early September and felt my pulse quicken when I hit the entry for September 3. I couldn't read Spanish, but it wasn't too hard to pick out the name *Brewster*. And even a total monoglot knows that *amor* means love.

I peered at the entry, wishing I'd paid a bit more attention in Spanish class. There was a short paragraph at the top—I picked out the words *mañana*, tomorrow, and *esposa*, which I thought meant wife. Beneath it was something that looked like a recipe, but my Spanish wasn't up to the task. As I leafed through the rest of the book, I wondered yet again what had prompted Ted Brewster to drop by Sit A Spell for a love potion. Had Maria suggested it to him?

A thump sounded outside, and I froze, listening for the sound of a key in the lock. It didn't come, thank God—but because I had no idea when it would, I decided I'd better hurry up. As I replaced the book in the box, I got a whiff of a familiar smell, and a chill ran down my back. I quickly opened each of the plastic bags, sniffing the contents. Maria had an impressive array of herbs—I could identify mugwort, chamomile, and a mostly empty bag of that *polvo* stuff—but not what I was looking for.

I had made it through all but two of them when I noticed another series of bags tucked under a hank of silk. My hackles rose as I picked up the one on top; it held a picture of Ted Brewster at his desk, smiling at the camera, along with a few brown hairs. The bag beneath it had no photo—just one long blond hair—and the last one, on the very bottom, contained a blurry snapshot of Brewster's son, Tad, getting out of a car.

I thought of the little wax doll in Maria's office. Did

she use the hairs in the doll somehow? And if so, who exactly was the one in her drawer supposed to represent? I dug through the rest of the box, looking for the source of that elusive smell. As I pushed the silk aside, a little wizened berry rolled out.

Nightshade.

I tucked everything back into the box—including the dried yellow berry, which looked like a golden raisin but wasn't something you wanted to pack in your lunch box. Then I snapped the lid back on and rocked back on my haunches.

For some reason—I still wasn't sure why—Maria had killed Brewster. And if the photos in the box were any indication—not to mention that lone strand of hair— she might not stop with just one body.

But what was I going to do about it?

I had just slid the box back under the bed when I heard the jingle of keys, and then the front door opened.

Thirty-eight

I slid the box under the bed and darted to the closet. As I attempted to bury myself behind a row of dry-cleaned suits, I thought, *If only I'd been five minutes quicker.* Or if only Maria's closet had been a little less organized.

I shrank back into the corner, bonking my head on an Elfa shelf as I tried to disappear behind six pairs of pants. Which would have worked—maybe—if Maria hadn't walked directly into the bedroom and said, "Come out of the closet with your hands up."

So much for plan A.

Because there was no way to actually become one with the line of suit pants and because it was pretty clear that Maria wasn't too keen on playing hide-and-seek, I eased myself out from behind the row of pants and stepped out of the closet. I had no idea what plan B was, but it was something I probably needed to figure out in a hurry.

Maria stood in a Vera Wang suit that was the twin of the one Adele had been wearing. I had to admit she looked a lot better in it than my boss did. The only thing I didn't like about her outfit, in fact, was her taste in accessories. Not the Manolos—they were gorgeous, and I wouldn't have minded having a pair in my own closet. But I could have done without the nasty little gun.

Still, things could be worse, I told myself. I mean, getting caught in somebody's closet was bad, and I'd have to do some pretty quick talking to get out of it. But it wasn't as if she was packing silver bullets.

Then Maria said, "Don't start getting any ideas, werewolf. It's loaded with silver bullets."

Werewolf? I stared at the barrel of the gun—the now potentially lethal gun—and began to sweat. Jeez. Did everyone in Austin know about my little problem? Not that I was going to admit she'd sniffed me out. "Excuse me," I said, drawing myself up and trying to look offended, instead of just petrified. "What did you just say?"

"Don't bother bluffing. My aunt called me when you left the shop. She recognized your eyes. Plus, you picked the wolf amulet."

I stifled a groan.

"Why are you in my apartment?" she asked.

Good question. As she moved the gun a fraction of an inch to the right—just to make sure she got the bullet into the exact middle of my heart—I struggled to come up with a plausible explanation.

But Maria wasn't in the mood to wait. "You broke into my office too. What is your real name? It sure isn't Gertrude."

At least I didn't look like a Gertrude. "Sophie," I said.

"Sophie what?"

"Does it really matter?" I took a step forward, and she raised the gun. Now it was aimed at my head. "Look, I don't know who broke into your office," I said.

Maria narrowed her eyes at me. They were hard and dark, like river stones. "Why are you in my bedroom, then, werewolf?"

I thought about telling another lie, but something in the set of her jaw told me it was pointless. And if you can't be honest with a witch who's holding a gun on you, who can you be honest with? "I want to find out who killed Ted Brewster."

Her voice was sharp. "Why?"

"Because my mother's on the hook for it, and she didn't do it."

Maria's eyebrows rose in surprise. "Your mother? You're related to that two-bit witch who sold Brewster that pathetic little potion?"

"She's not a two-bit witch," I growled, gauging the distance between us. "And she's not a murderer." As I spoke, I stared at the gun—and Maria's finger, which was twitching on the trigger. How was I going to get out of here alive?

"I know," Maria said, her lips twitching into an evil little smile, and I shivered.

With the amount of adrenaline pulsing through my

veins, I could have transformed in an instant. And Maria already knew what I was, so it would hardly compromise my secret. Besides, I was about to be dead anyway.

The question was, could I jump her before she shot me? "You were the one who poisoned it," I said.

She nodded.

"If you don't mind my asking, what on earth possessed Ted Brewster to buy a love potion?" I asked. Not that it was relevant, but I was dying to know—and besides, I wanted to put off the whole being-shot-by-a-silver-bullet thing for as long as possible.

"It was my idea," she said, smoothing her sleek dark hair back with her free hand. The one that wasn't clutching the gun. "But I thought he meant it for me. I didn't want him to know how much I knew about it—for some folks, witches are a turnoff."

Try being a werewolf, I thought.

"So I told him a friend of mine had tried one out of a book," she continued, "and that it worked."

"Why did you tell him to go to Sit A Spell?"

"I didn't. I just thought he'd get a book at the bookstore and mix something up. He came up with Sit A Spell on his own. Which was very convenient, as it turned out."

Yeah, since the cops looked no further than my mom. Maria was starting to look a little impatient, and I hadn't managed to come up with a plan that involved me leaving the apartment alive. *Stall, Sophie. Stall.* "You left some of the nightshade under your bed," I blurted out.

"I did?" A furrow appeared between her tweezed eyebrows. "But I got rid of it!"

"Not all of it." *Keep her going, Sophie.* Maybe if I got her distracted, I could jump her or something. "But what I want to know is how come Brewster died when he drank it but the woman he gave it to didn't?"

"The potion wasn't for him," she said. "I had no idea he was going to drink the stuff. It was supposed to go to that stupid little librarian."

"Jennifer."

"He must have given it to her the day he got it." She shook her head in irritation. "I'd done a charm on him; he was supposed to come to *me*. But something went wrong, and he ended up with a crush on that silly little girl." She shrugged. "The nightshade was supposed to take care of her—I never would have bothered doctoring the potion if I knew he'd already given it to her. Or that he was going to drink it himself."

"So you were in love with Brewster?" I asked, looking at Maria, who, despite her nasty personality, was drop-dead gorgeous. Okay, bad choice of words. Still, the attraction was hard to fathom.

She shivered. "God, no. I just needed his money—and his political influence. Once he died, with the Brewster name—and the Brewster fortune—I could have made a real go of it." She got kind of a dreamy look on her face. "Maria Brewster for Congress." She shrugged. "Who knows? I might have made governor." She shook herself quickly, as if suddenly remembering where she was. And who was with her. "I still might."

"What do you mean?" I asked. Then I remembered the other photos in the box, and it all clicked. "You're going after Tad, aren't you?"

"Of course. What was it Churchill said? 'Nevah, nevah, nevah give up.' "

From what I'd read, I didn't think Winston had been talking about murdering people to attain political office, but I wasn't about to quibble with Maria. After all, she was holding a loaded gun. "Why were you so worried about people getting into your office?" I asked.

"My aunt warned me," she said. "Said to be careful."

Just like my mom had warned me, I thought. Maria and I had a good bit in common, really.

Not enough, however, for her to toss aside the gun and ask me to join her for a latte and some girl talk. She shifted from Manolo to Manolo, weighing her options. "I just have to decide what to do with you now."

I had a lot of suggestions, but I didn't think she'd go for any of them. So I stalled. "What was the doll in your office for?"

"I thought you didn't break into my office?"

I shrugged. "Well, maybe I did just a little."

"It was for Tad," she said. "After what happened with his dad, I wasn't taking any chances."

"It was for a love charm?" I asked. It hadn't felt very loving when I picked it up.

"Command and compel," she said. "I wanted him completely under my dominion."

How romantic.

"But I still have to figure out what to do with you," she said, biting her glossy lower lip. "I'd kill you here, but I hate to ruin my new bedspread. Besides, the neighbors might talk." She nodded me toward the door. "So let's go."

With Maria training her gun on my back, I shuffled through the living room, reviewing my options. Unfortunately, they were so limited that by the time I got to the front door I had gone through all of them, and I still didn't have a clue what to do next. "Where are we going?" I asked, hoping for inspiration.

"None of your business," she said, grabbing her keys from the hall table.

I didn't share her assessment, but I didn't bother voicing it.

Unfortunately, Kelly and the upstairs neighbor were nowhere to be seen as we stepped out into the fading evening light. I glanced back at Maria; she held the gun close to her body, where it couldn't be seen from the cars whizzing by at the end of the walk. Ripples of panic were starting to shudder through me, and I battled the urge to change. I was stronger as a werewolf—and faster—but I was sure Maria would shoot me the moment I started transforming. Besides, if they came to collect a dead wolf, she'd get off scot-free. And I'd be dead, of course.

We were only steps away from Maria's car now, and I knew if I got into her little Audi, I was toast. It was now or never.

As Maria hit the Unlock button of her key chain, I pretended to trip over one of the pavers, falling to the ground with a yelp.

"Get up," Maria hissed, glancing around.

"I can't," I said, forcing a wince. Which wasn't too big of a stretch, really; it had been a tough week. "I hurt my ankle."

"Crawl to the car, then."

"I just need a little help getting up," I said.

Irritation and disgust flashed over her fine-boned face as she stood on the walk. Her options were limited to helping me up or shooting me on the spot, in clear view of all the people whizzing down Enfield Road. She must have come to the same conclusion I had, because a moment later, she took a tentative step forward and extended her left hand.

Which was exactly what I needed her to do.

Everything happened at once. I yanked her arm with my right hand, swinging my left arm toward the gun at the same moment. As I made contact, a flash exploded, and something zinged off the sidewalk next to me. I grabbed for her left hand, smelling Maria's scent— lavender, expensive lotion, gun oil—as I wrenched the cold metal from her fingers. It clattered to the sidewalk; a moment later, something barreled into Maria, sending her sprawling across the pavement.

I staggered to my feet. The gun lay on the sidewalk. Beside it, a giant wolf had Maria pinned to the driveway.

I looked at him—once again, my wolf in shining armor. How had he known to find me here? He had said he was stalking the packette; was he also looking out for me?

So many questions . . . none of which could be answered, at least not at the moment. I grabbed the gun and trained it on Maria, and Tom let her up, gold eyes fixed on mine.

"Thank you," I murmured to him, and he dipped his head. I was about to say something else—I'm still not sure what—but at that moment, the front door of Kelly's apartment opened, and she looked at me with a bright smile. "Oh, you're still here. Did you get the measurements you needed?"

I looked up at her, and at that moment, Tom sprinted away, disappearing into a clump of shrubs. As I gazed after him, wishing I could follow, Kelly said, "Oh my God. Is that a gun?"

Thirty-nine

It took a few minutes to convince Kelly that Maria and I were no longer bosom buddies and that the reason I was holding a gun on her was that she had just tried to kill me. Finally, though, I persuaded her to run back into her apartment and call 911. My arm was hurting by the time the black-and-whites showed up, and it was a relief to hand things over to the professionals.

Tom, of course, was long gone.

As the cops questioned me, I couldn't help glancing at Brewster's campaign manager. Maria was the consummate politician, looking cool and collected even in handcuffs. It was a shame that her potential would be wasted. Despite her repeated claims that I had broken into her apartment and tried to kill her—only partially true, of course—the police got their hands on her journal and decided she needed to take a trip to the station anyway. Evidently she'd been less than circumspect about her political ambitions on paper—including her more murderous inclinations. (All I can say is, thank goodness for bilingual cops.) Which was good news for me, because that meant my mom was off the hook.

The police made me go over the events of the evening about twenty times. Which was a little tiring, considering it was my second tête-à-tête with the police in twenty-four hours. I was a little vague about how I'd gotten into Maria's apartment in the first place, and Kelly wasn't exactly helpful—but I somehow managed to convince them not to book me for breaking and entering. I *did* make a big deal over how a stray "dog" had saved me from being shot. Partly because it gave me a little bit of a warm glow just thinking about it and partly because we "strays" needed all the good press we could get. It was dark by the time I finally walked the half a block to my parked car, and I was more ready than ever for a tall glass of Chardonnay.

I paused at the car, sniffing for a hint of Tom, but the only scents in the air—outside of the reek of polyester uniforms and doughnuts—were exhaust and a hint of yeast from a nearby bakery.

Oh, well.

As I climbed into the M3, the amulet Maria's aunt gave me bumped against my breastbone. I reached down to touch the soft leather. Had the little leather bag somehow helped get me through tonight? I traced the image of the wolf with my finger, wondering briefly what Yolanda had done to it before she wrapped it up. Then I put the car into gear and headed south. As much as I wanted to go home and slip into my bunny slippers, I had one more stop to make.

"I can't believe it," my mother squealed when I walked into Sit A Spell and told her the news a half hour later.

"It was his campaign manager all along," I said as she released me from an aromatic hug and lit some incense to thank her spirit guides. Although honestly, I couldn't say I'd found them particularly helpful. "I figured it out when I went to the *yerberia*," I said. "Did you know her aunt runs the place?"

"Who, Yolanda Jiménez? Her niece was Brewster's campaign manager?"

"How well do you know her?"

"We've met professionally," my mother said. "At a conference a few years back. Nice woman. Practices mainly hoodoo, with a Mexican twist. She knew about the doll, didn't she?"

"I think she was the one who made the darned thing. And evidently she was teaching her niece some tricks of the trade," I said, and gave her the rundown on what I'd discovered.

When I finished my story, my mother heaved a deep sigh. "Such a shame, when things are misused. I'm sure that's not what Yolanda had in mind."

I wasn't so sure I agreed with her, but I didn't share my doubts. "Even Brewster didn't know who did him in," I said, realizing only after I said it that I was admitting he had actually turned up during the séance. "He said the clue to his murder was behind that picture. He probably thought it was Patti Pendergast."

"That's the trouble with poison," my mother said. "If someone stabs you, or shoots you, it's so much easier to identify your killer."

"I'd never thought of it that way," I said with a shudder.

"Well, thank goodness it's all over with, anyway," she said. "And you did such a great job figuring it all out. Terrible about Yolanda's niece, though, of course." She picked up her mug and took a sip. "Mmm. You should try this tea, sweetheart. It's a new blend, with ginseng and gingko. Helps perk you up. Can I get you some?" she asked. "Or is it time for another dose of the regular?"

"I can't stay long," I said, "but I'll have a cup."

"You want to try the ginseng blend?"

"Better make it the usual," I said. It had been hours since I'd had a dose of wolfsbane, and the full moon wasn't too far gone. Besides, even though I had just cleared my mom's name, for some reason I was still jumpy. "I'm just going to head to the bathroom. It *is* safe to go the bathroom these days, right?" I asked. The last thing I needed today was to be attacked by a saucy ghost while I was sitting on the john.

"Oh, yes," she said. "Didn't I tell you? We did an exorcism a few days ago, and it worked like a charm. Haven't had an incident since Tuesday."

"So it's safe to wear thongs again," I said.

"You wear thongs?"

"Never mind," I said, leaving my mom to fuss with the tea things.

On my way back from the little girls' room—during which, thankfully, I remained unmolested by supernatural phenomena—I braved my mother's paper-stuffed office. It was no wonder she lost her spell book, I thought. A herd of wildebeests could have easily found cover behind the drifts of paper. Evidently the missing spell book had poked its head out of the stacks, though; it sat once again on its precarious perch on top of the filing cabinet.

"I see you found your spell book," I said when I returned to the little purple kitchen, which was now redolent of the bitter mint aroma of wolfsbane tea.

"What?" My mother's brown eyes grew round as she slid a mug in front of me.

"It's back on top of the cabinet," I said. "Didn't you put it there?"

She gathered her caftan up around her and hurried past me into the office. "Oh, thank the goddess," she said, running a loving finger over the worn cover. "I'll have to thank my spirit guides for returning it. I wonder where it was?"

"Wait," I said, before she grabbed the heavy tome. "Let me see it first."

"But—"

"I just need to sniff it," I said, and comprehension flashed in her eyes.

"You don't really think someone took it, do you?" she asked as I took a deep breath, smelling old paper, herbs, leather . . . and photocopiers.

And Tania.

"Well?" my mom said, as I took another sniff, just to make sure, and handed it over to her.

"It smells like Tania," I said, conjuring an image of my mother's shifty-eyed assistant. She might look like Mrs. Claus, but I was pretty sure the resemblance ended there.

"Oh, that sweet girl," my mother said, smiling. "She must have found it and put it back." My mother's bangles jingled as she opened the front cover and flipped through the thick, timeworn pages.

A folded piece of paper drifted to the floor, and I bent to pick it up. It was a printout of a Web page. "Yeah, she returned it, all right," I said, scanning the page. "Only after she copied all your spells for her mail-order business."

"Her *what* business?"

I handed her the sheet of paper; it was a list of potions, with prices. "Her online mail-order business," I said. "Featuring your secret formulas."

As she studied the page, my mother sucked in her breath, and her usually warm eyes flashed. "Why, that little witch." Not exactly a cutting insult, considering my mother's profession, but I knew what she meant. "When I get my hands on her . . ."

I laid a hand on her arm. "Easy, Mom. Easy."

"Easy? But she stole my spells! My mother's spells! These have been in the family for generations . . . they're our heirlooms." She shook her head. "And to think I've been *paying* her!"

"Maybe you should talk to your lawyer," I said, squeezing her bangled arm. "See if there's something about trade secrets or copyright law."

My mother brightened. "What a wonderful idea, Sophie. Speaking of lawyers, you never told me how handsome Heath was! And charming!"

"He said the same thing about you, actually."

She bit her lip. "He's not a werewolf, of course, and I still think you need to give that a shot. But he's not a bad alternative, for a man. Speaking of men, I had a wonderful time with Marvin." She reached up to pat her hair, which was shaped with Aqua-Net into a shiny black helmet. Her dangling crystal earrings sparkled in the light. "And now that I'm no longer a client . . ."

I thought of my mother's rotund attorney and suppressed a shudder. "If he represents you for copyright infringement, you'll still be a client," I reminded her.

She sighed. "Maybe I'll ask him to recommend someone." She flipped through the pages of the ancient book. "And if I whip up a little something . . ."

I knew she meant a love potion, and I didn't want to think about it. Speaking of potions, though . . . "By the way, I've been meaning to ask. What exactly did you do to Brewster to make him change his vote on the Barton Springs development?"

"What do you mean?" she asked, but her brown eyes twinkled.

"You know exactly what I mean," I said.

"Oh, I just tossed together a little something. He stayed for tea one day, and we got to talking, and I figured . . . why not?"

I could think of about a million reasons, but decided it wasn't worth bringing up. "Just don't do it again, okay?"

"Do what?"

"The whole potion thing."

"Sophie, dear. It's my livelihood!"

"I mean giving potions to unsuspecting victims," I said, glancing at my watch. If I got out of here now, I could finish up a few things at the office. After what had happened outside of Maria's apartment, I needed some distraction. My mind kept skittering back to dangerous territory. Dangerous, golden-eyed territory. "I've gotta go," I said, banishing Tom from my thoughts. "Thanks for the tea."

My mom enveloped me in a big, patchouli-scented hug, and I struggled to let the tension wash out of me. Maria was in jail, and my mother was out of danger. So why did I still feel like I was on red alert?

"Thanks so much for stopping by, dear," my mother said. "I knew my spirit guides were just testing me. But just think . . . if it weren't for you, I might have ended up in jail!"

I gave my mom one last squeeze and headed for the door, certain that my mother would be on the phone with her attorney setting up a lunch date before I even made it to the car. My hand had barely touched the doorknob when something yanked my bra strap, and I jumped about six feet.

Exorcism or no exorcism, the ghostly groper was still at large.

The office lights were all on when I stepped out of the elevator into Withers and Young a half hour later. I was still too revved up to go home, so I decided to take advantage of it and get some work done. I passed by Sally's desk, wrinkling my nose at the strong smells of Aviance Night Musk, cat . . . and something else.

But what?

As I paused, trying to identify the smell, I couldn't help noticing a stack of mail on Sally's desk. The top envelope, which was addressed to Adele (Sally usually opened it for her), was from Relcore Labs. Was my test result among them? After glancing around to make sure I was alone, I slipped the envelope open and rifled through the contents with sweaty hands. Mine was the third one down. And it was marked invalid.

I blinked at the words on the page. Invalid? Had the wolfsbane somehow thrown them off? I studied the fine print, trying to figure out what the issue was, and spotted it on the second page.

They'd identified the sample as dog urine.

But that wasn't the only interesting feature of the report, I realized. The lab owner was listed as Jerome Zwiercinski. And unless it was a total fluke, that meant the owner was related to Sally Zwiercinski, my spandexed assistant.

I restacked the pile neatly on the corner of Sally's desk. No wonder the testing was so unorthodox—it had been Sally's relative running it. Still, the good news was that the lab hadn't picked up the wolfsbane. The bad news was that they were convinced I'd substituted a fake sample. Which was going to be very hard to explain—especially since Sally had seen me when I provided it. Well, she hadn't exactly *seen* me, but she *had* stood right outside the stall while I tinkled.

I took a deep breath to clear my head and regretted it immediately. What kind of cleaning products were they using these days? Perhaps they should spring for something with a lemon scent instead of *eau de* litter box. But there was something else too. I sniffed again and realized that the weird green smell I had noticed earlier was stronger by Sally's desk. It was leafy somehow.

Leafy?

Whatever it was, it was coming from Sally's bottom drawer.

I looked around to make sure I was alone—I still wasn't sure who had turned the lights on—then slid the drawer open. Nothing but files, nail polish in a startling array of colors, and that smell—a smell I recognized from my college days. I reached in and felt behind the drawer. Sure enough, my fingers soon closed on a plastic bag taped to the side.

When I closed the drawer a moment later, I had a big smile on my face. Now I understood why Sally had hired a family-run lab. I wasn't sure how I was going to deal with the test results, but I was pretty sure Sally wasn't going to rat me out.

Not with the bag of pot taped to the back of her drawer.

Despite the mixed bouquet of cat piss and marijuana, I was still smiling as I strolled to my office, thinking that my days with Sally might soon come to an end. Then I opened the door and just about gagged.

The smell of cat was overwhelming.

And so was the smell of blood.

Forty

I flipped on the lights. A tall cardboard box sat in the middle of my desk, labeled with a familiar curly script. I edged closer and sniffed again; there was blood, all right. In fact, I could see it seeping through the bottom of the cardboard, right onto my blotter. Gross.

As I lifted the lid with a fingernail, the smell got stronger, and I took an involuntary step back.

Inside was a pulpy purple heart. And embedded in it was a wooden stake.

I stared at the bloody package on my desk. It was the same as all the other times: with one exception.

This time, the scent was fresh.

Adrenaline pumped through my veins as I lowered my nose to the desk. A moment later, I followed the trail out my office door and to the left, fighting the urge to transform. As a wolf, I'd be able to track the scent better, but Withers and Young wasn't exactly an ideal place to let my wolfie nature shine through. Particularly when I wasn't sure who else was in the office.

Fortunately, the scent was strong enough to follow even in human form. I followed it into the break room—whoever had left me the package had taken a moment to wash up at the sink—and then farther down the hallway, expecting to follow it to the stairwell.

To my surprise, it led not to the exit but to another office. And I recognized the name on the door.

I pushed it open and stepped inside. Koshka jumped, startled, and looked up at me with reflective green eyes. She might smell like cat, but right now, she looked more like a cornered rat.

"Thanks for the care packages," I said, trying to keep my voice cool.

"I don't know what you're talking about," she said, rearranging a stack of papers on her desk. Cat hair dusted the front of her black dress, just as it had the other day, at the Southeast Airlines meeting.

"Bullshit," I hissed.

And that was when she transformed.

One moment I was staring at a frumpy green-eyed woman in a baggy dress; the next, I was facing an orange tabby cat who was struggling to escape a tangle of black fabric. It looked up at me for a second, and I recognized Koshka's green eyes.

"So that's how you knew," I said, wonderingly. I knew there were werewolves. But werecats? I didn't have much more time to think, though, because a second later, an orange blur escaped from the folds of the dress, and Koshka whizzed by me into the hall.

I caught her halfway to the elevator.

"How come you didn't transform during the moon?" I growled, holding her by the scruff of her neck. She meowed pitifully, and I hauled her back to the office, where I closed the door and waited for her to turn back to human.

A moment later, in human form, she clutched her dress

to her chest and cowered in the corner. "I'm not a wolf," she said.

"I'd noticed that. But that doesn't answer the question. How come you didn't transform?"

"The moon doesn't affect us that way."

I blinked at her. "Us?"

She nodded, and I processed this new piece of information. Evidently there were werecats on the planet. And evidently I worked with one. What other beasties were out there that I didn't know about? And perhaps more important, how had this one figured out what I was?

"How did you know about me?" I asked, staring at her hard.

She gestured toward my face. "The eyes," she said. Then she wrinkled her nose. "Besides, you smell like dog."

Better than reeking of litter box, I thought, resisting the urge to sniff my pits. Did I need to switch deodorants? "There are more of you in Austin?" I asked.

She shrugged. "A few."

"Do you have territories? Packs?"

"We're cats," she sniffed. "Not dogs."

As curious as I was about the world of werecats, I decided to stick with the issues at hand. Specifically, the thoughtful little presents Koshka had been leaving me. Not to mention the awful poems. "Why did you threaten me?"

"What do you think?" she asked, standing a little straighter. She was regaining her confidence, and I wasn't sure that was a good thing.

"If I knew, I wouldn't be asking," I said, baring my teeth just a touch.

Koshka shrugged. "If you can't figure it out, then why should I tell you?"

"Because I'm a whole lot bigger than you," I growled.

Her green eyes darted to the door, and I moved to block it completely. Then she smiled a wicked little smile, and I could see her pointy teeth. "I wanted your job," she said. "I figured if I scared you off, Adele would give it to me."

"Now we're even, though."

"What do you mean?"

"You know about me," I said slowly. "And I know about you. It's a stalemate."

"Perhaps."

"I can be reasonable, though."

Silence. Evidently I'd be doing all the talking here.

"How about this for a proposal?" I said. "You don't send me any more little care packages—in fact, you clean up the one you left me tonight—and you stop trying to get me fired."

"And in return?"

"I don't spill the beans on you. And maybe I don't find a way for you to get every last one of the worst tax accounts. Or talk to Adele about some rumors I've been hearing."

It wasn't ideal, but what else was I going to do? If I managed to get rid of her, there would be nothing to stop her from coming back and messing with me again. This way, we each had a secret to keep . . . and good motivation to keep it.

She blinked her green eyes at me, considering her alternatives. Of which there weren't very many, actually; if she decided to make my life difficult, I would happily return the favor—and because I outweighed her four to one in my transformed state, that was one battle she didn't have much chance of winning. To remind her of that fact, I licked my teeth, feeling like something out of *Grimm's Fairy Tales*. Only Koshka was no Little Red Riding Hood. More like Puss in Boots—without the boots. Or any clothes at all, really. "It's a good offer. I'd take it, if I were you."

She shrank back against the wall, clutching her dress, then nodded almost imperceptibly.

"Good," I said, reaching for the doorknob. "Oh, and one more thing."

"What?" she said, sounding irked.

I gave her another toothy smile. "You can pick up the pig's heart before you leave."

As I strode down the hall, I could hear her swearing as she struggled with her dress.

At 10:30, I stood outside Heath's door. I'd had Koshka go over my desk twice with orange oil, but the smell of pig's blood still hovered in my office, and between that and the faint aroma of Tom that clung to my visitor's chair—not to mention the lingering reek of cat piss—I found it too hard to concentrate on work.

Heath was already at the door when I got to his floor. "Sophie!"

"Can I come in?"

"Sure," he said. "Your mom called; I heard you got her off the hook!" He gave me a little squeeze that made me warm all over. "God, you're an amazing woman. How did you figure it all out?"

"Just luck, I guess."

"I don't think so, sweetheart. You're incredible," he said, brushing the hair from my eyes. "Smart, beautiful, funny . . ."

A girl could get used to this, I thought happily.

Then his voice turned serious. "But why didn't you call me? Your mother told me you were almost shot. I called you a million times, but you didn't answer. I was about to go see if you were in your office."

"I was there; I just had my phones forwarded to voice mail for the night."

"Your cell phone too?"

I bit my lip. "At home on the counter. But enough about me. What have you been up to?"

"Nothing nearly as exciting as you. Actually, I was just doing some work before your mom called. Can you believe they're saying they don't have the budget to keep up the dog patrols?"

"What a shame," I lied, following him into his loft. My butt was still smarting from where the tranquilizer dart had gotten me.

"But enough about me. What can I get you? You look beat."

I collapsed on the leather couch and looked up at him. It was so nice to be taken care of. Heath might not have the same sizzle as Tom, but he was pretty amazing. "Do you have any Chardonnay?" I asked.

"I'll get you a glass," he said, and headed to the kitchen.

He returned a moment later, two glasses in hand, and joined me on the couch, smelling of leather and spice.

"You know," he said, "it's a good thing you figured out it was Brewster's campaign manager who killed him, because otherwise Tad Brewster would have been on the hot seat. Assuming we got Carmen off of it. Did you know he's running for his father's spot on the council?"

"Really?" This was news to me. As of a few days ago, Tad had sworn off politics forever; now, he was running for office. "I thought he was a libertarian."

Heath blinked at me. "Since when are you up on the political scene? I thought it gave you hives."

I shrugged. "After the last week, I know all kinds of things about Tad Brewster. That doesn't mean I'm up on politics."

"At least some things never change," he said.

I mock-punched him, and he laughed. "Well, you're right about him being a libertarian," Heath said, reaching over and rubbing my shoulders in a way that made me want to melt. "But fortunately for him, they don't run on a party ticket. He's a long shot. You never know, though. With the right name and enough funding . . ."

Heath was thinking of his own political future, I knew—I could always tell by the misty look he got in his eyes. I thought of Tad and his unusual political stances. I wasn't sure how well the drug-legalization platform was going to go over. Then again, this *was* Austin.

"If you ever ran for office," I said, "would my mother's . . . well, unusual career path be a problem for you?"

"As long as you're not hiding any deep dark secrets," he said, "I think it'll be fine."

Well, that was less than encouraging. I could just see us on the campaign trail with our little werewolf toddlers . . . yikes. Perhaps we should just cross that bridge when we got to it. "I've been meaning to ask: Since you're so up on what's going on in Austin, have you heard anything about the development at Barton Springs?"

"It got scuttled," he said. "The site work turned out to be really expensive, and between that and the public outcry, I guess the developer got cold feet."

"So all of Patti's blackmail attempts were for nothing." I made a mental note to ask my mom about the development next time I talked with her; I'd be willing to bet she'd done what she could magically to help that along.

"But I don't really want to talk politics tonight," Heath said.

"Oh no?" I asked, moving in closer.

"No," he said huskily, and leaned over to press his mouth to mine. I melted into his urgent kiss, and as he wrapped his strong arms around me, I thought of the tarot spread my mother had done for me. At least in part, I realized, she'd been right; there had been a powerful woman against me—Maria—and Koshka had been after me too. Was she the one who was hiding something?

Or, I thought with a chill, was it me?

I broke away and brushed Heath's hair out of his eyes, feeling a pang of guilt over my feelings for Tom. Was he the second knight in the reading? I ran a fingertip over Heath's cheekbone, his strong jaw. His eyes were so warm, so trusting . . .

My mother had told me I'd have to choose between two men, but maybe she was wrong. Tom was a werewolf, after all, not a man. And Lindsey already had a claim on him.

As Heath scooped me up and carried me into the bedroom, I breathed his familiar, human scent. It didn't have Tom's streak of wildness, but it had a heat all its own, and my body responded as Heath unbuttoned my blouse, his hands fumbling with urgency.

"I love you, Sophie," he said a moment later, as he slid into me.

I hesitated only a moment, thinking of Tom's golden eyes and of all the things that Heath didn't know about me. Then I whispered, "I love you too," and succumbed.

I was burrowed into Heath's white sateen comforter, my head on his warm chest, when something woke me.

I sat up straight, pulling the sheets to my chin. What was it?

Then I heard it—a low cawing sound, from the window. I reached for my blouse and crept to the window, peering through the curtains.

A giant black bird perched on the balcony. When it saw me, it cawed again.

I opened the window to shoo it away, then looked down at the street and swallowed hard.

Next to the curb was a motorcycle. And on the motorcycle sat Tom.

Forty-one

I hastily buttoned my blouse and tugged on my pants. Then I hurried to the door and down to the street, giving the surprised doorman a cursory smile as I pushed through the glass doors into the balmy night.

My breath caught in my throat as I inhaled Tom's foresty, primeval scent, mixed with the musky leather aroma of his black leather jacket. The leather suited him—as did the motorcycle, which was parked a few yards away on the sidewalk. They were both dark and a bit dangerous. Just like their owner.

Tom was leaning against the side of Heath's building. His long blond hair, pulled back in a ponytail, gleamed in the reflected light of a streetlamp, and I could see the strong lines of his Nordic cheekbones. It was probably the stress of the evening, but I had a sudden strong urge to lean my head against his leather-clad chest.

Fortunately, I managed to corral that impulse and crossed my arms over my own chest instead. "Thanks for helping me out earlier."

"My pleasure," he said. "Why was she trying to shoot you?"

"It's a long story," I said. "And again, thanks. But how did you find me?"

He pushed away from the brick wall and shrugged. "A little bird told me you were here," he said.

I pointed at the vulturelike thing that was perched on Heath's balcony. "That thing?"

"That *bird*," he said. "Yes."

"If that's a little bird, I can only imagine what you'd consider big," I said, the wheels in my head starting to turn. I'd wondered how Tom knew where I was all the time, but now it was all coming clear. I knew I'd seen the bird outside Brewster's office, and again, when I was at Maria's apartment. And I was pretty sure I'd heard it on the trail, just before Tom showed up to save me from the packette. Why hadn't I realized it earlier? "That's how you knew where I was this evening, isn't it? When you came to help? The bird told you."

He nodded. "I asked him to keep an eye on you. When it looked like you were in trouble, I decided to intervene."

"Gosh. Thanks," I said.

"Anytime." He grinned, and his gold eyes glowed in the headlights of a passing car. A shiver passed through me involuntarily—partially because he was absolutely gorgeous but partially because there was something about him that scared me a little bit. More than a little bit. "His name is Hugin, by the way."

I glanced up at Tom's feathered friend, which was sitting up there looking down at me. Then Tom extended an arm; like lightning, the black bird launched itself from the balcony railing, plummeted four stories, and landed on his forearm.

I took an involuntary step back. "You have a turkey vulture for a pet?"

Tom laughed. The beam of another set of headlights glanced over the two of them, glinting on Tom's teeth and the bird's sleek black feathers. I could see now that Hugin wasn't a vulture. It looked more like a gigantic crow. One with a great-aunt who was a pterodactyl.

"Okay, so it's a crow, not a vulture," I said. "You can talk to crows?"

"He's a raven," Tom said. "He helps me track my prey."

Prey. I was talking to a werewolf who openly admitted to tracking prey. "Like the packette?" I said, hoping that *prey* wasn't an umbrella word encompassing school-children, slow-moving runners, and nursing-home residents.

"Like the packette—the made ones. Yes."

"Do you ever chase . . . um, humans?" I asked. I thought I remembered him telling me that human prey was against the code, but it didn't hurt to be sure.

"Not unless they want to be chased," he said with a glint in his eye.

"Thank God," I said. "Speaking of the packette, have you seen them?"

"They won't be bothering you again."

I squinted at him. "Did you . . ."

"I unmade them." He leaned his head in toward the giant raven and whispered a word in a language I didn't understand. Hugin launched himself into the air, disappearing into the darkness.

"You unmade them," I said, pulling my arms closer around my chest and wondering exactly what that entailed. "Just like that."

Tom turned back to me. "Well, not just like that, but yes. They are no longer."

I drew in my breath. "They're dead?"

"I didn't say they were dead. Just no longer among *us*."

"So they're not werewolves anymore," I said, just to clarify.

He shook his head. "Nope."

"Still, what's to stop them from dropping by my loft again?"

His eyes glinted. "I told them if they bothered you again, they *would* be dead."

Well, that was certainly a deterrent. "Thanks," I said, swallowing hard. "I think." I looked at him for a long moment, questions welling up inside me. "Does it bother you that I'm not . . . well . . . full-blooded?"

His golden eyes were shadowed. "No," he said. "In fact, I find it intriguing. Besides, sometimes the half-bloods are very strong," he said quietly. "Even stronger than some full-bloods. That's part of the reason some packs don't permit them."

"How can they be stronger?"

"It doesn't always happen. And it's unclear as to why it does. But I think, in your case, it's safe to say that you are an unusually powerful werewolf."

"How can you tell? I mean, I'm almost embarrassed at how poorly I handled the packette the other day. If it weren't for you, I'd be dog meat by now."

"You were weakened by wolfsbane."

"How do you know?"

"I could smell it. You took so much of the herb that it affected your shielding."

"Shielding?" I blinked at Tom. "What shielding?"

He cocked an eyebrow. "You don't know?"

Obviously not, I thought. "If I did, would I be asking?"

"Sophie, you are an excellent shielder—which means you can hide yourself. It's a rare talent, and very useful."

Who knew? "So I'm kind of a natural undercover werewolf?"

"Did you think you managed to stay under the radar for so long just by luck?"

"I just assumed the Austin werewolf population was really, really small."

"Not that small," he said. "Your shielding ability makes you very special, Sophie. Only very powerful werewolves can do it. And yours is very strong."

"Like you?" I asked.

"Like me," he agreed. "And it has protected you for all these years. But now, I'm afraid, you may be in danger."

"What do you mean? I thought the packette was taken care of."

His gold eyes bored into me. "They are. But they may have told others about you."

My mouth turned dry. "And what does that mean?"

"It means that there is a good chance the Houston pack will find out about you. If they haven't already."

Delightful.

"You've done an amazing job of surviving without detection," Tom continued. "But that may soon change."

I looked away from Tom, focusing on the neon lights of the mini supermarket a half a block down. "Shop 24," it blinked, in red and green neon. A dog howled somewhere, and I shivered. "It's that stupid werewolf code again. I don't even know what the code is," I said, turning back to Tom, "and I'm already sick of it."

"I understand your frustration. But if they approach you—I'm afraid you'll have to join the pack." He paused. "That is, if they'll have you."

"And if I don't? Or they won't?"

"You'll be forced to leave," he said shortly. "Packs do not tolerate solitaries."

My stomach clenched. I'd spent my whole life avoiding other werewolves, only to be outed by a bunch of werewolf wannabes. Who evidently weren't even werewolves anymore. "What about you? You're not part of a pack," I said.

"That's different," he said, and something that looked like pain flashed across his face.

I knew he didn't want to talk about it, but if there was some way to avoid being conscripted or evicted, I needed to know about it. So I pressed him anyway. "How is it different?"

"Let's just say it was an unusual situation." His jaw hardened a little bit. "One that will not apply in this case."

Huh. So he left his pack because of an unusual situation that he didn't want to talk about. It seemed to me that Tom was an unusual kind of guy—even among werewolves. He had to be, if the Houston pack was contracting with him to come from Norway, or wherever he lived these days, to deal with extraneous werewolves. Which was another thing I was wondering about. "Why do they hire you?" I asked. "I mean, if they're so big and powerful, why not deal with things themselves?"

"It's safer for them," he said. "I don't have to kill the intruders; I just unmake them, so it's less messy. With forensic science, things have gotten complicated. When they call me in, there are usually no dead bodies. And there's nothing that can be traced back to the pack."

Usually. I decided not to think too hard about that. "So they hire you to help them keep their secret," I said. Evidently the pack was worried about being found out too. Just like me.

He nodded. "Exactly."

"Why can't they unmake them themselves? Why do they have to import you?"

"Only a very few of us can," he said. "It's old knowledge."

I decided to ask the question that had been nagging at me since I first learned that a werewolf can be de-werewolfized. "If you can unmake the made ones," I said, "can you unmake a born one?"

"Why do you ask?"

I took a deep breath. "No reason," I said.

"Sophie," he said, stepping close to me. Even with the heat of the evening, I could feel his warmth; his scent was intoxicating, and my body leaned toward him, as if he were magnetic or something. "It has been a long time since I met someone like you."

I swallowed. "What do you mean?" My voice was hoarse.

"You . . . you are unusual."

He was so close I could feel his heat on my skin. "Unusual," I croaked. "Is that a good thing?"

"Yes," he murmured.

Suddenly his arms were around me, folding me into his chest, and I was engulfed in his spicy, foresty scent. The world retracted around me until there was nothing but me and Tom, and a longing I'd never experienced before. A longing that wasn't just lust, even though I'd be lying if I said that wasn't a hefty component. There was a rightness about being with Tom, like something I had always somehow known was there but had been afraid of. Something deep and true.

Our faces were inches apart, his golden eyes shimmering in the light of the streetlamps. My mother's words echoed in my head. *A girl could get lost in those eyes.* "Tom . . ." I whispered.

"Sshh." He put one calloused finger on my lips, tracing their curve, and I could feel my skin tingle at his touch. My eyes traced his angular cheekbones, the full, sensuous mouth, the gleam of white teeth. I wanted him, wanted him completely, with a driving desire that turned my center to molten liquid.

His body was taut against mine, and I could feel the urgency in him. *You need to stop this,* my brain reminded me, and then his lips were on mine and all thought dissolved.

Liquid heat shot through me as his tongue probed my mouth, and all I could think was *More, more, more.* The world dissolved around us, and a wave of sheer lust crashed over me like a tsunami. Never in my life had a kiss felt like this. Not even close. He pressed against me, and I clung to him, wanting to rip his clothes off, to touch every inch of his warm skin, to devour him right there on the sidewalk.

He's a werewolf. Not yours. Think of Heath.

Heath.

With a tremendous effort, I forced myself to break away.

As I stood on the sidewalk, gasping for breath, Tom reached out to touch my shoulders. "You are very intriguing, Sophie Garou," he murmured, holding me away from him, studying my face.

Intriguing.

He was a hell of a lot more than just intriguing to me. Still, I couldn't believe I was hearing this. From a Norse god, no less.

I glanced up at the balcony above—Heath's balcony— and a knot of guilt tightened in my stomach. Heath and I were almost engaged, and here I was making out with a werewolf not ten feet from his building. A werewolf my best friend had a claim on.

"What about Lindsey?" I asked. *And Heath,* I added silently.

Tom said nothing, and for a second, my guilt was replaced by a searing flash of jealousy.

There was a flutter of wings overhead and a low, rasping call. Tom stepped away, suddenly alert, as if listening to something I couldn't hear. "I have to go now," he said.

My stomach lurched, and I took a deep, shuddery

breath, trying to regain control of my renegade body. Having him leave was like having a limb torn off somehow. As if I would be less of what I was.

But Tom was a werewolf, I reminded myself. An incredibly hot werewolf and the most amazing kisser I had ever encountered. But not exactly ideal mate material. We'd just had an incredibly intimate moment, and he was already out the door.

Never mind the fact that he was dating Lindsey. And I wasn't exactly single either.

"I'll return when I can," he said, and my stomach lurched again. He really was leaving—as in right now. "Be careful, Sophie." He brushed a strand of hair from my eyes. "And if the pack approaches you, be cordial."

"Cordial?"

He grinned at me. "Well, try not to piss them off," he said, and then he leaned in for one last lingering kiss that once again pulled the sidewalk out from beneath me. I clung to him, as if somehow I could keep him there with me.

"Do you have to go?" I gasped when he released me.

"For now," he said. A moment later, as I stood trying to control my emotions, he swung his leg over the Harley in one fluid movement. Golden eyes still on me, he flicked back the kickstand, revved the engine, and gave me one last toothy smile. Then, a moment later, the taillights of his motorcycle vanished into the night, the raven a shadow in the darkness above.

I stood on the sidewalk for a long time, watching the Shop 24 sign flicker in the darkness, trying to get my head sorted out. What was it about Tom that made me lose all reason?

Was it because he was a werewolf?

And if so, were all born werewolves going to have that effect on me?

I took another deep, wrenching breath, trying to reorder my thoughts. Tom could unmake werewolves. He was also a great kisser. But there was no way there could ever be anything between us, so it was best not to dwell on it. Even though I could still smell him on me. And God, did he smell good.

As I pushed back through the revolving doors into the air-conditioned lobby of Heath's building, leaving the dark humid night behind me, Tom's words floated back into my mind. *The pack will find out about you. If they haven't already.* I banished the fear coiling in my stomach and hit the Up button on the elevator. There was no reason to assume that anyone—other than the now-former werewolves and Tom—knew about me. I mean, the Houston pack had hired Tom to downgrade the packette, for God's sake. So I thought it was a pretty safe bet that Fluffy, Stinky, and Scrawny hadn't spent a lot of time with the Houston pack, sharing steaks and swapping gossip.

When I crept back into Heath's bedroom a few minutes later, I was feeling a little more like my normal self. The werewolf thing was a part of me—a part that Tom exacerbated—but it was only a part. And now that Tom was leaving, that part could go dormant again.

I stared at Heath, his strong face, the slow rise and fall of his muscular chest. Then I slipped back under the covers and snuggled into him, breathing in his comforting human scent. My body relaxed into him, and I thought, *This is where I belong.* My future was with my human side—with Heath, with my career at Withers and Young, eventually with the family Heath and I would have together. Of course, I wasn't quite sure how to break the news of my supernatural tendencies, but I knew I'd come up with something. After all, the revelation that my mother was a psychic witch had gone over surprisingly well. And our children would only be one quarter werewolf, so odds were good they'd be fully human—or at least more resistant to the pull of the moon.

I'd still have to find a way to break it to Lindsey that her hot Viking was a werewolf, but if my dad's behavior was anything to go by, Tom probably wouldn't make it back into town anyway. Besides, with Lindsey's dating track record, Tom was already halfway to being yesterday's news.

Heath stirred in his sleep, and I kissed his warm cheek. Whatever happened with the pack in Houston, I was determined not to let it get in my way. And despite Tom's warning, there was always a chance that the Houston pack would never even know about me. Tom. Would I ever see him again? Or was he just passing through? Already his smell was fading, and he seemed less real. As did the whole werewolf world.

I tucked the covers in around me and kissed Heath's cheek one last time, then reached for the little wolf amulet around my neck, finding comfort in the soft leather. Houston pack or no Houston pack, I was sure I'd find a way to continue my normal life in Austin.

At least I hoped so.

Acknowledgments

Thank-yous go first and foremost to my family—Eric, Abby, and Ian—for all their love and support; also to Dave and Carol Swartz and Ed and Dorothy MacInerney, for always being there, no matter what. Thanks also to Bethann and Beau Eccles, who are such dear friends I consider them my adopted family; to my sister, Lisa, and her family; to my fabulous grandmother, Marian Quinton (and Nora Bestwick); and to Hal and Jane Quinton for being my New York cheering section. (I do plan to get up there sometime before 2010, I promise.) And last—but certainly not least—to Merrie MacInerney, who needs to write a book of her own and share her humor with the world.

Many thanks to Jessica Faust, a.k.a. the world's best agent, who provided not just the seed, but her keen editorial eye—and plenty of guidance and support—as the book grew (and changed course). Thanks also to Allison Dickens, Charlotte Herscher, and Signe Pike at Ballantine for all their work to bring Sophie to the printed page; and to Thea Eaton for all her help on the Internet front.

My deepest gratitude, of course, goes to the friends who help keep me sane—particularly Dana Lehman, Lindsey Schram, Susan Wittig Albert, Michele Scott, Debbie Pacitti, Leslie Suez, Njambi Wanguhu, Martha

Winters, Mary Flanagan, Melanie Williams, Jo Virgil, and all my friends at the Westbank Library and my local coffee shop and bookstore. Thanks also to Austin Mystery Writers for their support and keen critical eyes: Mark Bentsen, Janet Christian, Dave Ciambrone, Judy Egner, and Mary Jo Powell—and, of course, to my friends and fabulous fellow authors at the Cozy Chicks (www.cozychicks.com).

If you enjoyed this hair-raising novel
of werewolf fun . . .
read on to catch a sneak peek
at the next novel starring
the fabulous Sophie Garou

On the Prowl

by

Karen MacInerney

It's always those days when you think to yourself, "Life is just perfect" that life comes up and bites you in the ass.

It was a sunny Tuesday morning, and I was sauntering into the office—my new partner office, with a big window, tall ceilings, and a mahogany desk I sometimes just liked to stare at. In one freshly manicured hand was my traditional skinny latte, extra foam. In the other was a little bag with a blueberry muffin in it. (I used Splenda in the latte, which kind of cancelled the calories out.) Tucked under my arm was today's paper, and in my purse—not as yummy as the muffin, but definitely necessary—was a fresh box of wolfsbane tea.

"Good morning, Sally," I trilled to my perpetually spandexed assistant. If she hadn't been hired by my boss, I would have fired her a year ago, but we all have our crosses to bear, I guess. She smiled tightly and adjusted her cleavage, then turned her back on me. We weren't exactly bosom buddies, but ever since I'd discovered a little bag of pot in her desk, at least she was no longer actively trying to get me fired and/or hauled off to jail. Which was progress.

I walked past her to my office, admiring the gold sign next to my door: SOPHIE GAROU, PARTNER. Although it had been there for a week now—which was when

Southeast Airlines, the big account I had pitched a few months ago, decided to hire Withers and Young as their accounting firm—it still felt like Christmas morning every time I saw it. I was probably the only werewolf in the country who was a partner at a Big Four firm, I reflected. Not that anyone at Withers and Young knew I was a werewolf, of course. That's where the wolfsbane tea came in; it helped me keep my animal impulses in check. Slobbering all over the clients and dashing out of meetings to howl at the moon isn't great for career advancement—not to mention client retention.

With the exception of my hairy little secret, I reflected as I tossed the newspaper on the desk and opened my muffin bag, life was pretty sweet. Withers and Young was on the fifteenth floor of one of Austin's plushest buildings, and my new office had a great view of Lady Bird Lake. Sinking into my cushy leather chair, I took a bite of muffin and watched a couple of ducks swimming aimlessly on the glassy surface. The only downside of the view, really, was that I kept getting distracted by ducks and squirrels—that whole predator thing. And now that I was in charge of the humongous Southeast Airlines account, that could be a problem.

Still, it was a minor concern, all things considered. Valentine's Day was next week, and since I'd seen my boyfriend, Heath, leaving a jewelry store recently—with a small, ring-sized bag in his hand—I was, to put it mildly, looking forward to it. My mother, the semi-psychotic psychic witch, hadn't been indicted for killing off a right-wing politician in months. And the equinox was more than a month away, which meant there were no obligatory full-moon transformations in my immediate future.

As I finished my muffin and ran my tongue over my teeth—I always got crumbs stuck in my canines—the phone rang.

"Sophie!"

"Hey, Lindsey. What's up?" Lindsey, who was also an auditor at Withers and Young, was my best friend—and a dead ringer for Angelina Jolie, which could have been a problem if she wasn't such a fabulous friend.

"Have you seen the paper?" she asked.

"No. Why?"

"They quoted Heath in one of the big articles. It's on the front page."

"Really? Good for him." I glanced at the front page of the *Austin American-Statesman*. "Three men found dead in Greenbelt: dog pack suspected."

My hand froze halfway to my skinny latte. Heath's pet cause, so to speak, had been eliminating Austin's stray dogs, which he viewed as a menace. I wasn't too keen on his crusade—needless to say, I wasn't a big fan of dogcatchers—but this would just be fuel on the fire.

"Which article?" I asked Lindsey, even though I already knew.

"The one about the three guys who got murdered by dogs. The quote's on page six. Can you believe it? I always thought Heath was blowing smoke about the dangers of stray dogs, but maybe he was right after all. It gives me the heebie-jeebies. I went hiking there just last week!"

"I haven't read it yet," I said, scanning the text.

"Three guys turned up dead," she said. "Mauled by dogs. And it looks like Heath was one of the first people the reporter called."

I scanned the article. Three unidentified men, two Caucasian, one Hispanic, had been found in the Barton Creek greenbelt, which was a mere mile from my loft, dead of massive bite wounds. I hoped the reporter was right, and that it was in fact a rogue dog pack attack. But what little hope I had flickered out when I discovered that the victims had been found (a) naked and (b) with fur stuck between their teeth.

"Isn't that great?" Lindsey said.

"That three guys got killed in the greenbelt?" I asked.

"No, dummy. That Heath got a quote in the *Statesman*."

"Oh. Right. Yeah." I stared at the photo of a black body bag being pulled out of the undergrowth. Unless there was some new group in town whose idea of a good time was stripping down, rubbing ground beef all over themselves and taunting packs of feral dogs, I had a sinking feeling I was looking at the fallout from a werewolf squabble. Which was more than a little bit disconcerting. I hadn't seen a single werewolf in Austin since last September, and before that, I'd run into a grand total of two in twenty years. The whole dead-in-a-public-park thing was an unpleasant new development, to say the least.

"Sophie? Why are you so quiet?" she asked.

"Sorry," I said, reaching for my latte. "Not enough coffee, I guess. Can I call you later?"

"Sure," she said. "Tell Heath congrats from me when you see him."

After we hung up, I read the article again, feeling a growing sense of dread—and not just because of the extra dogcatchers I was sure Heath was already out recruiting. Ever since I'd moved to Austin at the age of eight, I'd kept my identity secret from the werewolf community at large. So far I'd been successful, but that was largely because there were almost never any werewolves in Austin. If this article was anything to go on, though, that was no longer the case.

My eyes kept returning to the picture on the front page, and I couldn't help imagining what was under the black plastic. Finally I forced myself to turn the paper over and push it away. My eyes drifted to the picture of Heath, which was framed and placed in a prominent position on my desk. White teeth, dark silky hair, biceps to die for . . . and major political aspirations. Which was unfortunate, really, particularly given his penchant for going after the feral dog population. I still had a scar on my butt from my last dogcatcher run-in.

My thoughts flashed to that jewelry bag again. Could it be that there was an engagement ring in it?

And if there was, how was I going to break the whole "I'm a werewolf" thing to him?

I sighed and sipped my latte, trying not to think about werewolves. After all, none of them had come knocking at *my* door, so why worry? I'd just stay away from the greenbelt for a while. Right now, I told myself, my first priority was to get cracking on my new account. I shoved the paper into a desk drawer and forced myself to focus on my computer, clicking on e-mail to check for missives from Southeast Airlines. As I scrolled through the spam, my mouse stopped at a weird message titled "Audience required." It was from the Lupine Society. *Maybe it's some kind of society for bluebonnet lovers,* I told myself. Hope springs eternal, I guess.

My latte forgotten, I clicked on the message.

It wasn't about bluebonnets.

In fact, unless I was very much mistaken, it was from the Houston pack.

Crap.

I sucked in my breath and bit my lip, almost puncturing myself with a canine. I had broken twenty years of anonymity a few months before when I tangled with a few made werewolves (made werewolves aren't born werewolves; they've just gotten their paws on enough werewolf blood to join the pack, so to speak). When I found the three of them harassing a sorority girl in the Sixth Street alley, some deluded hero instinct had made me decide to be Wonder Woman and step in to save her. Even though she *had* been wearing awful shoes. I mean, bad taste isn't enough to die for, is it?

Anyway, the sorority girl got away, but not before the packette (my pet name for the trio) got a good whiff of me. And although they had since been unmade (sort of de-werewolfized), evidently the cat—or in this case, the wolf—was still out of the bag. Either that, I realized with a shiver, or someone connected with the incident on the greenbelt had sniffed me out.

"Your presence is required by the Houston Lupine Society," read the e-mail. "An audience has been scheduled for Saturday, February 7, at one o'clock p.m. Failure to appear will result in forfeiture of any and all rights."

An *audience*? Forfeiture of any and all rights? Who did these people think they were? *They aren't people*, I reminded myself. *They're werewolves.*

I cursed whatever werewolf rule it was that made Austin an official part of the Houston pack's territory. I'd recently discovered that my living in Austin made me an intruder.

To make things worse, the date was this coming Saturday—the same day, naturally, as the office retreat my boss had been planning for months. And, of course, the full moon, but with enough wolfsbane, that wouldn't be too much of a problem—thanks to the tea my mom made for me, I'd limited my compulsory transformations to the full moons closest to equinoxes and solstices. Unfortunately, I doubted Adele would be up for rescheduling the retreat—she'd been selecting table centerpieces for a month now. And somehow I doubted the Lupine Society would be willing to compromise.

As if on cue, my phone rang again. It was Adele.

"Sophie, so glad I caught you. I need your help picking tablecloths."

"Tablecloths?"

"For the retreat. I'm thinking suede or gingham. What do you think?"

"Um, about the retreat . . ." I began.

"It's going to be incredible, isn't it? You can't miss a minute of it. So, I'm leaning toward suede. With gingham napkins."

"Sounds fine," I said faintly.

"Great. I'll see you soon; don't forget to pack your boots! There'll be horseback riding—and maybe even a cow patty toss!"

After I hung up, I wiped my sweaty palms on my skirt and tried to focus on work.

But all I could think was, *Crap*.

I was closing up my office for the day and about to head home for a restorative tumbler of wine when my mother called.

"Sophie, darling! How's my favorite girl?"

"Fine, Mom." Which wasn't strictly true, but I wasn't up for talking about my e-mail from the Lupine Society right now. Or the little issue that had taken place in the greenbelt. I just hoped my mother's psychic abilities were on the fritz today. "What's up?"

"I was making plans for Valentine's Day, and I wanted your opinion. Do you think I should make reservations at Romeo's, or Chez Nous?" Chez Nous was an intimate little French Bistro in downtown; Heath had taken me there many times.

"Who are you going with?" I asked, cringing.

"Why, Marvin, of course." Marvin Blechknapp was the pool-ball shaped attorney who had defended Mom on a murder case recently. I couldn't understand the attraction—he was more Dom Deluise than Brad Pitt—but my mother was gaga over him. As he evidently was for her, even though she was a bit left of center. Okay, so maybe running a magic shop called Sit A Spell and having a werewolf for a daughter was more than a bit left of center. But you get the idea.

"I think either one would be good," I said. "Mom, can I call you back? I'm on my way out the door."

"Sure, honey. But I just had a quick question."

"What?"

"Have you noticed anything unusual lately?"

I sat down. "What do you mean, unusual?" Had she read about the incident in the greenbelt? I wondered.

"Oh, I don't know. Maybe a chicken head or something."

The hairs on the back of my neck prickled. "A chicken head? Um, no. I'm pretty sure I would have noticed a chicken head."

"No dirt, or anything?"

"Dirt?"

"Oh, you know. Graveyard dirt."

"No, no graveyard dirt that I know of. Although I'm not sure how I'd distinguish graveyard dirt from regular dirt."

She breathed a sigh of relief. "Thank goodness."

"Mom . . ."

"Just keep an eye out, okay?" I heard a bell tinkle in the background. "Whoops, customers. Got to go. Catch you soon. Love you, sweetie!"

She hung up before I could respond.

Chicken heads and graveyard dirt? As I powered the computer down and headed for the door, I found myself—not for the first time—wishing for a mom who did something normal. Like waiting tables, or knitting afghans, or running a corporation or something.

Then again, if I had everything I wanted in life, I wouldn't be addicted to wolfsbane tea and have a Bic razor habit, either. Sometimes I guess you just have to play the hand that's dealt you. Even if they do turn out to be tarot cards.

I drove the five blocks home to my building, said hi to

Frank the doorman, and headed up the elevator to my loft.

As my mother requested, I did a quick survey of the hallway. No chicken heads. No graveyard dirt, either, although I did spot a dust bunny in the corner by the stairway.

As I fished for my keys, I took a deep breath and froze.

Werewolf.